MATISSE'S WAR

Peter Everett was born in Hull, East Yorkshire, in 1931 and began writing at the age of nineteen. He is the author of seven novels: *A Day of Dwarfs*, *The Instrument*, *Negatives* (which won the 1964 Somerset Maugham Award), *A Death in Ireland*, *The Fetch*, *Visions of Heydrich* and *Matisse's War*. He has also written for both television and radio. He lives in Sheffield.

BY PETER EVERETT

Peter Everett

MATISSE'S WAR

VINTAGE

FOR CARI,
MAX AND FREDDIE

Published by Vintage 1997

2 4 6 8 10 9 7 5 3

Copyright © Peter Everett 1996

The right of Peter Everett to be identified as the author of
this work has been asserted by him in accordance with
the Copyright, Designs and Patents Act, 1988

First published in Great Britain by
Jonathan Cape Ltd, 1996

Vintage
Random House, 20 Vauxhall Bridge Road, London SW1V 2SA

Random House Australia (Pty) Limited
20 Alfred Street, Milsons Point, Sydney
New South Wales 2061, Australia

Random House New Zealand Limited
18 Poland Road, Glenfield
Auckland 10, New Zealand

Random House South Africa (Pty) Limited
Endulini, 5a Jubilee Road, Parktown 2193, South Africa

Random House UK Limited Reg. No. 954009

A CIP catalogue record for this book
is available from the British Library

ISBN 0 09 973531 8

Papers used by Random House UK Limited are natural,
recy-clable products made from wood grown in sustainable
forests. The manufacturing processes conform to the
environmental regulations of the country of origin

Printed and bound in Great Britain by
Cox & Wyman Ltd, Reading, Berkshire

1939

Blue Nude (Souvenir of Biskra)

'NONE of us knew the Biskra oasis before André Gide put it on the map; but we all lusted after that roasted corn and barley bread – those cactus fruits, figs and melons. I boarded the train at Algiers to cross the Sahara. The oasis was a military outpost, a paradise where the women of the Uled Nayls tribe came to earn their dowries by selling their bodies. My wife Amélie used to say that they were shameless for money; but they were for sale in the same way as pots, brass trays and carpets, and everything else made in darkest Africa.

'The women's foreheads and cheeks blazed with henna and bright orange tribal marks; they had a bad smell under every flap, in every cranny. In Africa, you put up with those odours, the good and the bad. I was a Christian dog, who knew they called him that. Had I not spent money in a liberal way, I felt sometimes that I risked having my throat slit in the Rif mountains. Most of the Arabs, however, were poor cowed specimens.

'As soon as the S.S. *Radjani* reached Tangier, there was a biblical flood; it rained for forty days and nights. There were flowers – first the irises, then the violet morning glories twining on the blue trellis. I had gone there to seek an authentic experience; to find objects crafted in the back of beyond, outside European culture. I met tourists from all parts, and missionaries who broke bread with the army. I made nothing of them. I was as narcissistic then at thirty-nine as I am now at seventy. It was only later that I understood that my task was to harmonise the primal with modern art as I was making it. Everything I saw in Africa, I tried to tame for French consumption. I brought home bric-à-brac; a litter of colourful beachcombings that I picked up on the edge of the dark continent. Like Jules Verne with a sweet tooth, or Rider Haggard on a donkey craving the illicit, I felt I was panning for gold in the backward abyss.

'One of my trophies was *Nu bleu*, but I did not paint the picture until some months later at Collioure. I called it a souvenir, but it was the outcome rather of an accident. I was making a clay figurine, *Nu couché*, and thinking about catching the ten o'clock train to Banyuls to visit Maillol. I could see the church tower clock, and I was sure that I had time enough to do this and to mould that. In the end, of course, I missed the train. My unease did not leave me for days. As I worked, I dropped the figure. Amélie heard me swear and ran up from the kitchen. Her answer to anything of that nature was to take me for a walk. I did calm down, but my agitation grew as soon as I got back. I had to fix the pose. So, when I had finished thumbing her clay body back into shape, I set about painting the canvas.

'I worked quickly, using blue-violet pigment to define the angularity of her pelvis and jutting hip. I forgot Maillol as the subject woman took shape on the canvas; I felt the colonising principle very strongly. She was in paradise, and was of paradise, with those full, ripe orbs of breasts. Can you hear the sound of water? It was there, everywhere in Biskra; quite amazingly so after the desert. I loved to see the rhythms of the over-arching feathered palm fronds and the blue grass.

'Many critics did not like the painting – what had happened to my delicate and knowing drawing? They thought her head and shoulders were too masculine. The students at the Art Institute of Chicago burned her in effigy, but the five-year-old son of Gertrude Stein's concierge said, "The blue woman has wonderful breasts." '

Matisse catches the flicker as Lydia Delectorskaya turns a page of her book.

'What are you reading now?'
'A novel by Louis Aragon – *Les Cloches de Bâle*.'
'Ah yes, the Surrealist poet.'
'You know him?'
'We never met, although I put my name to a petition that Breton circulated to save him from prison. I read part of his *Passage de l'Opéra* in Philippe Soupault's *Revue Européenne* on a train once. It was obviously a fine piece of writing. I don't know why I didn't read the book when it came out. We had many mutual friends, of course; Apollinaire when he was alive. Is that a recent book of his?'
'He wrote it some time ago. It is about three women. One of the characters, Catherine Simonidzé, a Georgian girl, leans towards the exploited, but her father's monthly cheques bind her to the bourgeoisie. He owns oil wells in Baku. She tries to resolve her personal problems by helping the Paris taxi drivers during the strike in 1912. Klara Zetkine plays a part. Yes, it's a blend of fact and fiction. She helped to establish the German Communist Party, which for Aragon means that she is the ideal woman for modern times.'
'Not Rosa Luxemburg?'
'You mean that Rosa Luxemburg was a superior model?'

4

'I think her life was more crucial, certainly more dramatic; an unemployed worker murdered her.'

'Meaning what?'

Matisse is silent, then says, 'Don't you think that André Malraux's novels deal better with social ideas?'

Lydia sighs. 'Have you ever read his books, apart from a paragraph or two quoted in a review?'

'All of them – Drieu la Rochelle, Aragon and Malraux – are writers whose experiences of the Great War left them questioning the meaning of life.'

Picasso has a show of recent paintings at Paul Rosenberg's gallery. He has been a victim of sciatica until the art dealer Pierre Loeb's uncle, Dr Klotz, helped him with an electrical cure. It is Paul Rosenberg on the telephone as Matisse and Lydia dress for an outing. He asks Matisse whether he has read the critics on Pablo's new paintings.

'People tell me he is busy painting flowers, for which you are asking a hundred and fifty thousand francs apiece,' Matisse replies. 'Is this some novel way now to vent the anxiety he must feel about the situation in Spain? I can live without another Guernica.'

'Did you know his mother died? He says the fall of Barcelona killed her. His being ill during these past months has made him feel very low. Since the great cure, Pablo swears by Dr Klotz; he is as lyrical about electricity as any Soviet poet. Sabartès tells me this; enthusing the while over the portrait Pablo has done of him as a sixteenth-century nobleman.'

'The hidalgo, you say; are you sure you don't mean the king's flunky?'

Rosenberg laughs. 'You know Picasso's jokes. Are you planning to show any work soon?'

'You seem to imagine that I finish paintings, these days.'

Matisse hears Lydia in the hallway. She comes into the room, and taps her wrist-watch to show the time. Matisse nods.

* * *

Although the writer Elsa Triolet's divorce from Pierre André-Marie Triolet was not yet final, she married the poet Louis Aragon using her maiden name of Elsa Kagan. 'Just think, I am a bigamist now,' she said. She wrote to her sister, Lili, that she had become a Frenchwoman again so that she could stay with Louis in army quarters when the war came. She went on writing under the name of Triolet.

Unhappy with her fiction, she had tried to keep a diary since the previous autumn, and decided now that she would not go on with it. One of her last entries, which she had torn out and thrown away in the Tuileries gardens, spoke of her sudden urge to go to some hotel and open her legs for the banal stranger who sat down next to her, urging and taunting.

There was the hope that such a stranger would start by ordering her to unlace his shoes. She knew how her fingers would tremble when she obeyed. Shoes had aroused her sexually since childhood, though she could not recall when it had first come about. The first thing she looked at when she met a man was his shoes.

Elsa could not see Diego Rivera's wife's shoes under the table at which she sat with Jacqueline and André Breton. Elsa had heard that Frida Kahlo was having trouble finding a gallery that would show all her latest paintings, and how she hated the squalor of the rue Fontaine apartment. Breton now found her presence irksome; his Mexican fling was over; he was no longer half-way up the pyramid at Xochicalco arguing with Trotsky about the unconscious.

There was a barber-shop across from the café; the windows fogged over with clouds of steam. Beyond the gilt letters, shadows went to and fro between tropical plants. In front of ornate mirrors, the barbers were grooming men for the war between the sexes, their razors glinting in an air laced with the smell of cigar smoke and pungent oils. Elsa had seen Agence Havas men lighting their cigars on the doorstep – pimps waiting to work for Dr Goebbels. Drieu la Rochelle had his morning shave there, too. Now the barbers and the orphan boy with bony ankles who swept the floor all awaited Hitler's Panzers for their army crop. All Paris waited: barmen, brothel owners, lawyers, river officials, butchers, scene-shifters, priests, *flics* – they were all keen to see fresh faces, eager for new clients.

Kahlo raised her glass of red wine to the winter light to call a toast; there was a blast of music from Radio-Paris. Her vivid peasant skirt flared as she limped by with Jacqueline. Elsa saw how ill she looked; her black-knit eyebrows gave her blunt sensual face a mannish quality. Her cheeks were the sallow olive-green of those grieving women Elsa saw in Madrid. She felt suddenly bereft of that centre of gravity of such women, water bearers, heavy with child. Suddenly, she could not fathom the crazy joy of the poor, their resignation and despair. With Barcelona fallen, the war was over; she felt that she was wasting time in the wrong place; but of what use could she be to border refugees in the dead of winter?

At the next table an American couple and their French woman friend,

Anna, talked about Zanuck's bio-pic *Suez*. They had arrived in a chauffeur-driven Daimler and, ordering coffee, had read out telegrams praising some musical they had put on in New York. The man was older than Fitzgerald, of course; but an itch of impatience with the world at large marred the woman's beauty, which reminded Elsa of Zelda.

'Tyrone Power is not to blame for the script,' the Zelda woman said.

'Whoever wrote it is an idiot; de Lesseps was sixty-four when the Empress opened his canal,' said Anna.

'Yes, true enough,' agreed the man.

The Zelda woman was one of those pathetic dolls who did nothing except lie around naked ready to serve men's appetites.

The Zelda woman cried shrilly, 'I was so jealous I had cramp in my stomach!'

'That's exactly what's wrong: you need food,' the man said. 'Isn't that right, Anna?'

Elsa shook her head; with such empty characters controlling events, was fiction worthwhile?

Darkness was falling; arm in arm now with Jacqueline, Frida came to a halt by Elsa's table and smiled. Jacqueline must have told her who Elsa was. Breton was waiting by the door. Time had treated him less well than his wife, who swam nude underwater at the Coliseum when they met. His mermaid, his Ondine, would still look good naked, whereas Breton was not the man who thrust aside the manager of the Bar Maldoror, with an imperious 'We are guests of Count Lautréamont' that February night the Surrealists burst in on the party for the Rumanian princess.

Lemons and Fluted Pewter Jug

In March, a pewter jug Matisse painted during the Great War with fruit and a glass of water appears again. Today the jug is larger, although it is to scale with the goblet and some lemons on the table.

Lydia is patient, listening to his woes. 'I do not trust the Bank of England. I do not trust any French or German bank. There is a war in the offing, so why is Doctor Schacht conspiring with that charlatan Montagu Norman! They are both master criminals, confidence tricksters! For the past eight years the Royal Mint has been printing paper without the backing of gold. The Anglo-Saxons are no longer shopkeepers; they are book keepers. Quite the nastiest part is that our masters of finance are as blithe as Mickey Mouse about the mess.'

It is noon in Nice; Matisse turns into the rue Verdi. He is on his way to visit Simon Bussy, a friend of his from Moreau's studio. He had known, then, where to find all their easels – Bussy, Bréal, Rouveyre, Camoin, and Marquet. Bussy had given up large canvases in favour of miniatures: birds, animals, fishes, butterflies. He had gone to work in London, and there met and married Lytton Strachey's sister Dorothy.

Despite being seventy, Dorothy is hopelessly in love with André Gide, whose books she translates.

'We don't have many visitors these days,' she says, taking Matisse's hat.

Sipping a glass of mint tea, Matisse tells Bussy that he learnt nothing from dreams, nor did Baudelaire; dreams were not keys to anything; they clarified nothing, no matter what Freud or Jung said.

'I cannot see Amélie without thinking of my *Femme au chapeau*,' Matisse says, 'I feel the joy of every brush stroke that went to make her hat that pyramid of festal colours.'

Bussy recollects how women gloried in their hats at the turn of the century. 'The feather trade killed myriad poor birds to adorn their bonnets.'

'Yes, there were milliners everywhere: the rue de la Paix, the rue Royale, the Opéra,' Matisse says. 'Camille Marchais, Charlotte Enard, Georgette, Suzanne Talbot all built storks' nests. I hated the laughter that greeted the portrait. All I could do as I stood there was console myself with Amélie's gloved arm glowing like a green snake.'

Matisse says he could not sleep when painting *La conversation*, and could not explain why there was an air of sleep-walking about the canvas. It had been an end rather than a beginning, despite the fact that his life as family man had many years to run.

'I still feel every nuance of emotion that I had when painting Amélie's portraits; but the bad dreams have become real at last; those feelings that existed long before I found a shape for them,' Matisse says.

'When I saw Amélie, she told me that our marriage was over. If I could forget my other women, she could not: Olga Merson at Collioure; Lisette, Henriette – she had to put up with them all. She would take no more. She didn't deserve it. We had to part. Afterwards, I would be able to find a new word to cover my liaison with Lydia. It was the only sensible course for us both, otherwise the charade would be the death of her.

'She is convinced that I made her ill; I am responsible for everything that has happened to her,' Matisse continues. 'She wants a new life, having lain in bed for twenty years. She will stand alone at last, resolute and firm.'

Dorothy has no time for Matisse and his ego-centric woes. She knows how Amélie feels. Amélie had given her life to the creation of the Matisse myth. She had worked for him selflessly, posing as a model as well as bearing two sons. She had identified with his studio *mise en scène*. She had helped bring about those anecdotes that are a boon to biographers, such as their tiff the day she posed in the blue toreador outfit and Matisse broke his easel in a fit of rage. She had made the myths snug; had become as crucial to his genius as Shakespeare's second-best bed. She had been Gertrude Stein's Amélie, the woman who nursed Matisse's love-child because some heroine in a novelette she admired had done so; who made her own hats and opened a millinery shop so that he could afford to buy oils and canvases. She had been the cook-housekeeper who kept him in domestic bliss. The role had now turned sour; and she had found the energy and malice to use some very sharp weapons.

Lydia asks what happened when he met Amélie again.
  'I had more abuse and recriminations,' says Matisse. 'You have heard it all before.'
  'She is going through with the divorce?'
  'Indeed. I don't know what to think any more. I have lost all my peace of mind. I kept seeing her as the Sainte Amélie Derain painted, the martyr of the century, with that shawl over her shoulders. The past conspires against me. I fear losing my identity. I have to tell myself that it was Derain who would brag that he drove the fastest car in the country; that I was slower, more sedate, and could never live like him. When he married Alice Princet, it came as a shock, you know; she had been in Picasso's bed. However, it was a smooth transition, amicable even; my divorce from Amélie is not going to be like that.'

Music

At seventy, Matisse says, he thinks of himself in the second person. He is *un monstre sacré* who depicts with passion and delight only what he takes pleasure in, only what he chooses to see. He is art personified. If there were no Matisse, there would be no art as such. He is ripe and serene; his desires, his wishes, have carried the day; the world has said yes to his vision. He has purged all thought from his painting except anxieties relating to structure and colour; his struggle is with these alone. His enriched insight has informed his canvases since the turn of the century.

All his life he has treasured objects with great tenacity. It is rare for them to get broken or lost; he has charms and magical gestures to conjure their appearance, which change their colours when needful. What does not change is his sense that objects have an inner meaning around which he can construct his metaphysics, his infinite play with surfaces.

He is a prim, clean old gentleman with a passion for naked women. His models do not heed his presence, they are passive; with some rare exceptions, they do not look at him as he appraises them; they do as he bids, these chosen ones who surrender their biography. They seem sure of their immortality in his world, fixed in his refinement of reality.

Hélène Galitzine sat alone with her guitar in *La musique* until Matisse began to paint in the girl on the black cushion in her mustard-yellow dress. This tawny yellow is the same yellow as the guitar.

Hélène's large naked foot curves out from under a grey-green dress; a pivot of which Picasso would be proud, that anchors, yet lets her float on her red perch above the sheet music on which an orange reposes. Her hand curves limply as though to strum a chord, echoing the roundness of her breast. Above and behind the women's heads are the cool turquoise rhythms of four big tropical leaves. Everything fuses now with the zest of a fashion plate.

He calls the painting *La musique*, a title he used in 1910, and a subject to which he often returns. In the first version, the piper's fingers were so dainty that you could almost hear the notes he played.

After his labours, Lydia brings her camera to record the work in progress.

'The photographs you took on Friday were invaluable. I have to paint the girl's legs again.' Matisse watches as Lydia wipes them away with benzene. 'Tomorrow I will shift her knees over to the other side.' He waves his hand to show the new position. 'You can see how that will change the structure.' He nods. 'I recall Picasso asking whether an artist would kill off his mystique if he allowed a motion-picture camera into his studio. I pointed out how your snapshots can change everything. Dora's photographs must surely be a help to him? I could not see how our painting habits would be of any interest to cinema audiences. The old masters got by without help from the camera, of course, but then their friends were all great painters who could advise when the need arose.'

Lydia sits at the writing desk. 'They want to know the date of your marriage.'

Matisse is doing a self-portrait and stares fixedly at his reflection in the mirror. 'I married Amélie-Noémie-Alexandrine Parayre in 1898. She was from Bouzelle, near Toulouse.' He pauses to nip a shred of tobacco from his lip. 'Ingres's great advice was that one must never leave the ear out when drawing the head. As I observe reality, I am striving for the truth. Not the truth of my cigarette smoke, although it has to be there; my glasses, too; even these last wisps of hair on my skull. Amélie was no stranger to that blind spirit of locality, which so often refuses to accept the reality of a situation. I could teach Amélie nothing; the discipline that had formed her character was in place long before any I could impose.'

Although Matisse had not known it when Lydia Delectorskaya came along, Amélie stood no chance, even after years of staunch service. The exotic blonde from Siberia charmed Matisse with her beauty and her ability to deal with things. She had the strength of the survivor. He endured the uneasy truce between the two sides of his nature for some time before he decided. Picasso told his friends that Matisse chose Lydia because she was clever at making out his income tax returns; but did that constitute grounds for divorce in French law? As a caretaker, Lydia has no sense of herself as separate from Matisse; what would she be, what could she do? She knows her place. Since 1934, when he first drew her, she has become her role; now there is no doubt that she has ousted Amélie. She has always known that there was no future in being the consort of a famous artist. However, her role has allowed her enough scope to convert her submission into devotion; her chief task as she sees it is to make sure that he keeps signing his masterpieces. The only threat to this day-to-day pleasure, this routine, is Hitler's war aims in Western Europe.

*　　*　　*

Sadoul, a friend of Aragon's since their Surrealist days, brought the news that Madrid had fallen, and that people were fleeing from the city. 'None of them made any effort at street fighting; the Republicans caved in. The Falangists had no need to fire a shot. All they had to do was honour the white flags. Give us the radio, they said. Madrid is ours, *Viva Franco.*'

Elsa shook her head. 'Then it is over.'

Aragon shut his eyes, trying to see the stricken *madrileños*. He heard the city's tram cars clang by, painted half-red, half-black by bandit anarchists. At night, in the sweat of making love to Elsa, searchlights lit the walls of their hotel room, illuminating the two balloons anchored above the War Ministry. After each bomb blast, the militias roared defiance in the streets, with *¡Arriba España!* They would see these men next day, in their dark-blue boiler suits, unable to afford a drink or a haircut, heading for the Prado because it was free. Fighting tanks with shotguns and flaming bottles of gasoline, they knew their luck would run out; Goya's *Tres de Mayo, 1808* was the picture they wanted to see.

'It has been a farce; the Moors were the spine of Franco's Army of Africa,' said Elsa angrily. Mohammedans fighting to save the Catholic church in Spain! A farce! After blessings by bishops and cardinals, they put on their first and last pair of hob-nailed boots, then died to defend some bull-ring, river bank or hole in the ground. Those who came through with their lives must have learned a thing or two about their white masters.'

'Any man or woman who served in the International Brigade, or aided Republican Spain in any way, is now on the blacklist that Franco has sent to the French security police,' growled Sadoul.

Sadoul saw the Civil War through Picasso's eyes. He had interviewed Pablo when he was dealing with the bombing of Guernica by Hitler's Condor Squadron. Signs, prophecies of an apocalypse that became a triptych of stills from a black and white newsreel fused into a present tense as Pablo built his act of condemnation of the ongoing horror of the world. There was a woman with her dead child on her lap, a bull with the face of a man, a corpse with a broken sword, a naked light bulb. Truth, holding her oil lamp high, had the face of a Grecian goddess, yet was a ghost who had lost her children.

Aragon was unsure about the mural. 'I don't know why Picasso painted a clenched fist, only to wipe it out a few hours later – that is one reason why *Guernica* fails for me. Yes, I agree, Pablo has Goya's technique, but he fails to grasp his method. You have to read too much into what is an oblique cartoon. *Guernica* is a symbolic painting, whereas Goya's *Los Desastres de la guerra* has lost none of its power to move us; Goya was a visionary as well as a realist.'

Sadoul shakes head. 'What do you think, Elsa?'

Elsa said she did not know why Sadoul had found the domestic bout of fisticuffs between Marie-Thérèse and Dora Maar so funny. It had been a sordid combat to decide who would sleep with Picasso, while he, perched above, painted the teeth of a terrified horse that was losing its guts.

'Pablo's private life debars me from seeing it as a public work,' she said. 'I cannot deny its power, but I don't understand why Marie-Thérèse had to appear twice in the picture. She is not the class of woman they were digging out of Guernica's ruins.'

'Isn't that a quibble?' Sadoul said.

'Then Picasso is idealising, and taking the first step towards creating a lie.'

A million or more people were dead already in Spain; despite this, the U.S.A. recognised Franco's regime, and England concurred. Chamberlain had also accepted Mussolini's conquest of Ethiopia. 'He will also write China off to Japan,' said Aragon; 'he has already told the world that the United Kingdom has warm feelings for Emperor Hirohito the same week as Japanese planes raided Chungking.'

'When the storm breaks in Europe, people's illusions will shatter fast enough,' Elsa said.

Sadoul laughs angrily. 'The Anglo-Saxon upper class can never honour its craven promises; England will not stop Hitler; he is far too wily. Nobody wants to die for Danzig!'

'Do you expect me to?' Aragon laughed.

* * *

In Morocco, Matisse tells his models, marriage was a more occult and noisy affair; the women were the keepers of the tribe's history, hiding their faces behind gold masks. It was that role that gave them power to choose the brides. The marriage ceremony went on for days. There were pipes, drums, dancing and singing; then they fired off rifles and Browning pistols, as the butchers hacked the throats of camels and sheep to feed the multitudes of guests.

'All the Arab word *hareem* means is: women,' Matisse says. 'Nothing is more crass than the idea of the harem as a sexual paradise. Europeans do not realise that the harem is a place of worship; there are prayers at first light, at noon before they eat, and at nightfall before they sleep.'

'You can see what use I made of the Moroccan jugs in *Les oignons roses.* I think it was my children who taught me how to paint the picture.'

Matisse owes his way of working to the nineteenth century, although he has no time for nineteenth-century speculations. He focuses on the singular moment, the particular. Any semblance of narrative has gone, and how can he re-create those conditions in which it thrived? His memory will not serve him in this respect. He gave up seeking to extract the meaningful at the same time as he gave up any interest in the audience's anticipation of narrative.

'It was Camille Pissarro who urged me to spend my honeymoon in London. I could make it an excuse to see Turner's paintings.'

In his reverie, as his room darkens, he hears the half-crown tinkling down the steps of the National Gallery in the yellow gloom of a London evening, the creak of his boots in the gallery and the whispering echo of his voice as he speaks to Amélie. *'Turner's father was a barber. His son was down-to-earth, too, despite the unearthly light that suffuses his landscapes. He would often spend days in a cellar in order to see nature with a fresh eye. I suppose he owed his persona to his mother, who went insane. In old age, he lived in Chelsea with a woman called Booth; his neighbours thought he was her husband, a retired seafarer.*

'He would have had to be leaning out of the carriage window at an impossible angle to see the engine steaming towards him through the rain.'

'What is a hare doing on the track?' Amélie had asked.

'Since the picture is about Speed and Time, I can only guess the hare is a symbol for threatened nature as it tries to outrun the train across Brunel's bridge, a poetic allegory.'

'There were postcards on sale, and I bought one to send to Pissarro: *Snowstorm – Steam-boat off a Harbour's mouth Making Signals in Shallow Water, and going by the Lead. The Author was in this storm on the night the Ariel left Harwich.*

'I took off my top-hat to touch a handkerchief to my forehead. Turner had begged the crew to tie him to the mast, so that he might see everything. He was over sixty years old and froze there for four hours, feeling that his time was up, but it was something he felt he had to do. He could never understand, when he came to exhibit the painting, what people found to like in it.'

* * *

Aragon had sold the manuscript of his novel *Les Cloches de Bâle* to pay for a honeymoon cruise to attend a congress in New York.

It was clear that many passengers were escaping to America, but none of them would admit to that. Elsa was blithely cocooned aboard the luxury liner. Nothing pleased her more, knowing what would happen soon in Europe, than to sun-bathe to the fizz of Schweppes and dance every night. She felt an odd pleasure whenever a purser asked her if she wanted Indian or China tea, or whether he should bring her Gold Flake or Players. The only dramas centred on which couple came together, which would drift apart; the result of a deck quoits game or who won at backgammon or bridge. She would line up at noon outside the radio room to send a telegram or read news of the world; but it was more thrilling at night, listening to the crackle of messages as the stars turned in their courses. A truly jarring moment came when a drunken German woman gripped her arm in the bar, warning, 'Stay in America! Do not return to France. First they pass a law that requires you to register as a Jew at the police station. Do not do it. They keep your name in their files and, when the time comes, they will knock on your door. You are a Jew, I can tell. That is why I must testify to you. You must know, as a Lithuanian, what happened when the Tsar ruled. It is the same again in Germany, and will soon spread everywhere in Europe. The Reichstag, books, synagogues – what do those butchers care? They are killing us. Believe me, we count for nothing; we are so much garbage to them.'

The bartender called the purser, and together they helped her to her cabin. When Elsa saw her again, the woman did not mention their meeting.

The moonlight was bright on the chalk-white lifeboat lashed above. Aragon turned away from the sea's shining mirror to kiss her lips. 'One day,' he vowed, 'I'll write a black mass for you: introit, orison, credo and offertory.'

'There was a German woman at the bar who was drunk—'

Aragon smiled. 'That shouldn't come as a surprise, these days, surely?'

'I could smell the blood of Jews being murdered in Austria. Not just some furrier falling foul of stormtroopers who kicked him to death. Things are going beyond street beatings. They are worse now than they ever were in Russia or Poland.'

* * *

Matisse journeys to Paris and takes a suite at the Hôtel Lutétia to work on his designs for a revival of Massine's ballet *L'étrange farandol*. He goes every day to a Mary Calley's studio in the Villa d'Alésia. 'It's perfect with its large, white, light-filled rooms; and so hidden away in that warren of streets, I never see anybody,' he tells Lydia.

It was not a commission he wanted when Diaghilev first came to him, but a visit from Léonide Massine had persuaded him to try. Already the music has changed: from a Liszt concerto to Shostakovich's First Symphony. It does not augur well.

Georges Brassaï sat outside the Flore. The sunshine was making his glass of chilled white wine tepid. He opened his wallet and took out the message the model had brought him the day before. It said that Matisse would like Brassaï to photograph him at his studio in the Villa d'Alésia, near Saint-Pierre-de-Montrouge. It was a district familiar to Brassaï; it was around the corner from that steep flight of wooden stairs under the ailing sapling that led to Giacometti's studio, between Hippolyte-Maindron and the Moulin-Vert.

Matisse, photogenic as ever, wears a long white doctor's coat. Having shown Brassaï into the studio, the Hungarian girl, Wilma Javor, slips off her robe and resumes her pose. She sits on the edge of the table, with her hands clasped over her head, beside flowers in a white enamel jug. Her body is lithe and sallow, with small breasts; Brassaï sets up his tripod and lines up his camera so that Matisse is behind her. In the corner, there is the set-up for the unfinished painting on the easel. Later, Brassaï will record Matisse painting the model reading as she leans against the white table. 'I am never happier than when a naked woman poses for my delectation,' Matisse says.

Matisse tells Brassaï about the designs for the ballet. 'I felt the same unease at Merion, as I shaped up to the challenge of *La danse*. To get down to basics, I hunted up this wooden crate and fitted a light bulb in the top; then I cut out these bits of coloured paper to serve as the dancers, which I shift about inside my little mock-up. I have left nothing to chance. I have created this white Gothic arcade, with yellow arch supports. The rural dancers' costumes echo these colours. Under this middle arch, there is a blue triangle; to the left of it, behind the column, a red setting; to the right, a black. When the ballet opened in Monte Carlo in May, it was as *Rouge et Noir*, a more apt title, I think.

'The ballet is in four movements; each shows Man, the poetic spirit, danced by Youskevitch, facing various setbacks, which include Destiny. Alicia Markova dances the Woman. In the third movement, an evil spirit plagues her after she loses the Man. I don't know whether Massine is responding to the October Revolution or not. Lydia thinks that there is a feeling of this in the second movement, when the city dwellers come to blows with the rural dancers, and end by carrying them off. No matter, the fourth act brings about the joyful reunion of Man and Woman.

'Sadly, their joy is short-lived. Destiny appears in the guise of dancer Marc Platov, who puts the lid on things. Léonide told me his focus was the eternal war between the spiritual and material forces in Man. These two figures in white are the hero and heroine; the others here, in black and red, represent evil and destiny – while yellow signifies the rustics. Blue stands for the spiritual. I chose these flame-like strips for their costumes; I think that they make things seem less schematic.'

Matisse is nervous, going to and fro in the final stages of donning evening dress. His cufflinks have been missing, so has his wallet; public occasions are more trouble than they are worth. By the time Lydia manages to get him to the Théâtre de Chaillot he has made up his mind that the ballet is going to be a failure. In the bar at the interval, a woman complains that she finds the costumes so abstract that they impair any feeling she has about the dancing itself. Her companion, who wears a Légion d'honneur, points out that to him they seem right for the dancers and suit the spirit of Massine's choreography very well.

Lydia fans herself with her programme. 'You see, I told you so; all the men are wearing their medals; but I suspect that you would find some Nazi Party buttons if you looked behind their lapels. They mingle well, and seem to be enjoying themselves.'

'Are they?'

'You will see in the morning papers that *L'étrange farandol* is a great success, another triumph for Matisse. You need have no anxiety on that score.'

It is the divorce he finds upsetting. There are all the legal pitfalls; those questions he does not want to answer, and the sudden guilt that overcomes him every so often when the ghost of Caroline Joblaud returns to haunt him. He has not felt this way since painting *La desserte rouge*, another version of the picture in which Caroline posed as the maid ten years before. She had been his mistress and the mother of Marguerite Émilienne, whose birth in 1894 had upset his father. Caroline was also in *La serveuse bretonne*, *La desserte* and *La liseuse*, whch Madame Fauré, the old President's wife, bought. It pains him to recall how bright the light was on Caroline's nape, how tenderly he placed her in front of the objects he set on the corner cupboard to create that sense of depth, which hurts now. They had lived out their four years together in such gaslit rooms, amid the colour tones of the Dutch masters, in a twilight that inhibited his impulses.

Sometimes, when he relives his escape, he feels shallow and callous, but never for long; his sense of sobriety comes to his rescue and allows him to dismiss such feelings.

The sound of a vacuum cleaner woke Elsa. She had overslept. She wondered where Aragon had gone; then, turning away from the glare of the burnished porthole, she thrust her arm into the coolness between the bunk and the wall panelling, and pulled out the magazines she found there.

On the cover of the January issue of *Time*, under the caption Man of 1938, a dwarf Hitler sat at a grand organ that turned a huge wheel on which dangled his murdered victims. The other was a copy of *Life* magazine. It showed a photograph of Senator Henry Cabot Lodge with mail from American Catholics imploring him to end the Neutrality Act so that the U.S.A. could arm Franco and ensure a fascist victory in Spain. On the same page, there was a picture of Dorothy Parker sitting in tears on a grand piano. She was at a party in Washington D.C. to raise money for Spanish refugee children.

When she went on deck, Elsa showed Aragon the photograph.

'I thought she was brave picketing in support of the Waldorf waiters' strike,' he said. 'She was in Spain, too, of course. I found her *Soldiers of the Republic* moving. A photograph like this – well, her literary reputation can only be a burden these days, feeling as she does.'

'Whenever you praise women like Nancy Cunard and Dorothy Parker you make me feel dull and dowdy,' Elsa said, brooding. 'I think your Pasionaria version of her is a bad joke. Her socialism is born of her need to revenge herself on the rich. She is a Jew who suffers from the same personality disorder that I do. What I do envy her for, are those barbed witticisms that sparkle right up to the time she starts to spill the alcohol.'

Headed for 48th Street pier, they passed the Statue of Liberty, the Hudson and East River waterfronts, staring towards Manhattan Island and the Empire State building.

An ironic smile crossed Elsa's face as she said:

> *'Keep, ancient lands, your storied pomp!' cries she*
> *With silent lips. 'Give me your tired, your poor,*
> *Your huddled masses yearning to breathe freer,*
> *The wretched refuse of your teeming shore,*
> *Send these, the homeless, tempest-tossed, to me.*
> *I lift my lamp beside the golden door!'*

Smiling, Aragon took her chin and made her face him.

'America's ruling class showed a sense of humour when it chose Emma Lazarus's poem,' she said. 'As soon as the emigration officials had finished looking for lice, the immigrants fled Ellis Island's cattle pens, and the illusion of a golden door came to an end. They thronged to Hester and Ludlow Streets, the East Side, the slums and sweatshops, eager to invest their backwardness in new forms, to prosper, to sicken and die. Poor Jews will find it impossible to get into America now.'

'In Emma Lazarus's day, America was the future; for European Jews, given the life they had left, it promised hope.'

When Matisse landed, he said, the weather was cold and Roosevelt had only just begun his New Deal policy. Art and artists were headlines because Diego Rivera's mural had riled the Rockefellers so much they had it wiped from the walls of their Center. It was not art, it was propaganda; the Mexican was nothing more than a crude tool of the people. Such were the times, that you were looking for trouble if you spurred on the workers by portraying them as heroes. So the newspaper reporters, out for anything they could use to smear Rivera, wanted Matisse's opinion of him as an artist. He told them that he did not see the necessity for an artist to join the class struggle or for him to interpret it. His own message for society was of another order. His mural would be the outcome of a physical encounter between him and several square metres of surface of which his spirit had to take possession, he said. He would not use tracings to blow up a painting in a dead fashion. A man using a searchlight to track an aeroplane, he said, did not traverse space in the same way as the pilot.

'Too many American poets are still dazzled by Surrealism, which lost its punch years ago,' Aragon said. 'Robert Frost has succumbed to pastoral egoism, while E.E. Cummings can only juggle with typographic tricks instead of lyrics. Neither of them wrote anything about Spain. What, if anything, will either of them do to prevent the coming war in Europe?'

'You say this because E.E. Cummings attacks Russia, Mr Aragon,' the reporter accused.

'No, I am saying it because his poems have become empty formulas that replace all thought, all true feeling.'

'Can you name an American poet whose work you do like?'

'There is Zukovsky, of course; and Muriel Rukeyser, whose *Theory of Flight* was very fine; so was her *Book of the Dead*, about the Gauley Bridge disaster.'

'Do you intend to stay in the U.S.A.?'

'Not at all.'

Around 5th and 7th Avenue, Elsa began to notice that everybody owned a radio and played it loudly. Aragon bought some Oriole label and RCA Victor records of 'Blind Lemon' Jefferson and Tampa Red. The singer Paul Robeson was showing them the sights. They were to visit the Harlem public library; but they never got around to it. He lived in Harlem, and introduced Aragon and Elsa to his neighbours there: William Patterson, Thurgood Marshall, and Robeson's brother, Ben, who was a pastor at the AME Zion Church, where they heard Robeson sing songs by Joe Hill. A union organiser murdered by copper mine owners in Utah in 1919, Aragon told Elsa.

Robeson had been giving concerts in Spain for the International Brigade, and he spoke of that. He said that he had just left England, where he had seen Chamberlain wave that futile paper and mouth the line, 'Out of this nettle, danger, we pluck this flower, safety'. You'd think the fool would know what Shakespeare said next: 'The purpose you undertake is dangerous, the friends you have named uncertain, the time itself unsorted, and your whole plot too light for the counterpoise of so great an opposition.'

A happier memory for Robeson was his London appearance as Toussaint L'Ouverture in a play about the rising in Haiti. He and the playwright had swapped the roles of Toussaint and Dessalines on alternate nights. Sergei Eisenstein had expressed interest.

He would have been a magnificent Toussaint L'Ouverture if Eisenstein could have raised the money to make the film, Elsa mused. He told her how much he had hated *Sanders of the River*; only the wisdom of Jomo Kenyatta had kept him going. Along with two hundred unemployed Negroes, Kenyatta had been in the cast. With the way events were shaping in Europe, they would soon find work enough in war factories. In America, too, it would be shifts around the clock at U.S. Steel; public works would be a thing of the past.

Elsa took off her hat, sat on the bed and kicked off her shoes. She had been to see Alfred Hitchcock's *The Lady Vanishes*: a thriller that had Margaret Lockwood convincing Michael Redgrave that a passenger on the train had vanished. A spy, of course, the missing lady was the bearer of a coded message: a tune she whistled during the final shoot-out at the frontier, begging Lockwood and Redgrave to get it to London. Conrad Veidt was the haughty villain; as comic relief, two droll Englishmen's chief concern was the latest score in the Test Match.

Starting a letter to Ehrenburg, now Paris correspondent of *Izvestia*, Elsa thought again of *The Lady Vanishes*. Should she mention it? The plot was up to the minute, touching on the nightmare threat to Europe. The film had made her feel lonely: fatherless, motherless, her only sister in Moscow. Jews were at sea everywhere, penned aboard cargo and cattle boats; the news was of quota lists and suicides. There was no refuge in Egypt, in Palestine, in Cuba. Of course the woman at the bar was right. She and Aragon would be foolish to return to Paris.

The hotel room was drab, dim except for the early hours when a shaft of sunlight reflected down from a rear building. The strip of carpet had worn threadbare. The bedside lamp lit scars left by brimming whisky glasses, and the chill gold cross on the Gideon Bible. When the knock came at the door, Elsa did not move; it could only be the man from next door, a retired fire-fighter who had told her he deserted his wife in Pittsburgh.

What was hideous about New York was that there was a glut of everything, and everything was too much, yet America was going to decide the fate of Europe. From the sweatshops in the Bronx to grand opera, progress was the driving force. It took no heed of human needs; they served merely as goads to the good life. It promised a plenty that never satisfied. Instead, there was the all-day theology of radio, serials with suspense built in; while every newsreel showed Hitler ranting, chalk-faced, in the same limelight as fashion parades. Jackhammers pounded everywhere, set in motion by federal money. The New Deal was trying hard to hold capitalism together.

Matisse disliked Harlem, Aragon said. He felt it was a black hell where Americans went in search of their paradise. 'Somebody hoodooed the hoodoo man' was a line from a slick number in the Harlem club to which Paul Robeson brought Aragon and Elsa.

'Negroes can have talent, but not electricity,' Aragon said. 'They have to be content with Roosevelt's fireside chats.'

The President was all for the Triborough Bridge; those jobs for Negroes Mayor LaGuardia promised, which never came true. Only white folks build bridges. Instead, there were food handouts and fresh pie in the sky: a road-building programme.

The moment Elsa left the tinkling of the white baby-grand piano behind her, she knew she had opened the wrong door. The tall Black turned his head into the light, one elegant finger propping the toilet seat, his horse cock hanging out of his beige trousers. 'Pardon,' Elsa said retreating.

The Negro smiled as he gushed piss into the bowl. His grasp of French was poor, but the nuance was there. Madame need have no fear; he was at her service.

Someone had fed her some drug; sudden images came at her cranked at furious speed, a low comedy of her father's sex life that starred him in a sequence of dirty postcards. Her mother was part of the nightmare, too, holding aloft her Moscow Philharmonic diploma to signal each fresh sexual bout while her beloved portraits of Scriabin, Debussy, Wagner and Schumann came to life, nodding approval of the Jew's sexual prowess as they ate wild strawberries.

Yuri Alexandrovich Kagan had been a radical Lithuanian lawyer who handled musicians' contracts. Any notion that a woman would take his circumcised cock into her mouth was madness, crazy jazz. Back at the table, as she sat down, Elsa realised that she had been holding her breath since the encounter. When she exhaled, she felt shabby and genteel.

* * *

'Satie wrote the music for Renoir's *Entr'acte*, and he acted in the film, seemingly very happy to hop and monkey about on the gargoyles of Notre-Dame. Maybe it was because he was with Erik that Man Ray came to see the flat-iron as a gift. He said that the row of tin tacks glued to the iron made a useful object useless therefore a work of art, and his first Dada piece since he left New York. Everything we did not know about Erik remained as queer as that hammock in his attic, where we found a hundred umbrellas after his death; yet we should have anticipated them.'

Lydia only half listens to Matisse ramble. She is reading about two naval disasters: the American submarine *Squalus*, near the Isle of Shoals, and a British submarine, the *Thetis*, off Great Ormes Head. Four men had got out so far by using Davis escape apparatus: two officers, a stoker, and an observer from the shipyard that built the *Thetis*.

'A calamity, madame,' the waiter says. 'All they could do was sit and wait for the air to run out. Why did the rescuers fail to burn a hole through the hull in time?'

The newspaper shows a photograph of the stern of the *Thetis* before the salvage cable broke and the submarine rolled over and sank.

'You are not from Paris,' Matisse says.

'No, the Auvergne, Monsieur Matisse.'

'You know my name?'

'You are the famous painter, monsieur.'

Flattered, Matisse fills the plate with loose change. 'Time to go, Lydia, I think.'

*   *   *

'When I first met you, I thought you worked for the police,' Aragon told Elsa.

'That's untrue. It was Breton who said I was a spy. You merely repeated it along with so much else.'

They had returned to France in time to read and argue over Camus's articles on Kabylia in the *Alger Républicain*. The editor, Pascal Pia, had worked for Aragon at *Ce Soir*. As an anarchist, Pia could never join any group; Aragon used to feel that he was a great loss to the party. However, that Pia doted on German mystics, medieval scholars and pornography, did not mean his heart was not in the right place; two of his heroes were Alfred Jarry and Rimbaud.

Camus was reporting the trial of a group of Arab workers charged with arson when striking for higher wages. He went on to depict the poverty and hunger in Kabylia.

'Yes, I can feel the rectitude of his fury,' Elsa said; 'but I don't know where he stands. I share his disgust, and yes he gets all the facts, as any good journalist should: the facts, the statistics – but the way he deals with these lacks a specific analysis of the colonial question.'

'The problem of hunger in Kabylia will not be solved by setting up mills to crush the olives that grow locally,' Aragon argued. 'Such solutions will not purge capitalism of its crises. Camus knows that figs and olives fetch nothing on the market. He must also see that, even if the farmers were to diversify their crops, nothing would change: France will remain there as a colonial power.'

'The photographs say it all,' Elsa sighed. 'The lack of food robs them of their sight. It's awful what famine does to mothers and children. Why do Camus's reports fail to move me? I'm afraid that, all too often, I distrust his sensibility.'

'After startling Algiers as Synge's Playboy of the Western World, he is writing a play about Caligula,' Aragon said.

'You knew this was here; you wanted to see it.' Elsa was angry. It was a reproduction of Alvaro Guevara's portrait of Nancy Cunard, Aragon's old flame, hoping as usual to be taken seriously. There was no show of emotion in Guevara's painting, yet he was mad about her at the time. It had the refined quality of a fashion plate. Nancy, svelte, yet little-girl-lost, wore a scarlet hat and stood in front of a red screen with her fists thrust deep into the pockets of a long black velvet coat. She was clearly moping as the war dragged on. It stood in the way of her departure for France.

Elsa said the portrait had enough charm perhaps to adorn the lid of a chocolate box. 'Beautiful? I used to see her as Buster Keaton's double.'

'As your rival—'

'She was never my rival.'

Aragon frowned, asking her why she hated Nancy so much. 'When did she ever let me alone?' Elsa demanded. 'She had you traipsing around Moscow to get her an Intourist visa when we were there. She never misses a trick to come between us. She does it under the guise of the struggle now, of being a comrade.'

'She atoned for some of her past follies with her efforts in Spain. She was always loyal, brave and generous.'

'Anybody who went to Spain was loyal and brave. So was I, touring around in our awful van to show *We are from Kronstadt* three times a day! I don't think I would have relished being rescued by Nancy Cunard if I had been a Spanish refugee.'

'What you say is nasty – false, too. You'd be grateful no matter who got you out of Spain.'

Chastened, Elsa realised that she had gone too far. 'You are right. I shouldn't have said that.'

'I brought you here for this,' Aragon said. He pointed to a copy of Matisse's *Poissons rouges et palette*. 'He painted it during the war. All you can see of him is this thumb on the palette. I think it's quite beautiful the way the red fish float in their glass cylinder.'

'It must have been before she went crazy for African bangles,' Elsa said, reverting to Nancy Cunard. 'They killed herds of elephants to load her arms with those ivories. They were such glorious weapons when she was brawling with her Negro subjects.'

'We are here to see a painting, not to fight over Nancy.'

'I admit that it's a better picture than Guevara's *Vogue* illustration,' Elsa said; 'but it is too decorative for these dark times.'

What she could never forgive was that Nancy Cunard had inspired Aragon to write *Irene's Cunt*.

As they crossed the bridge Aragon stopped and looked down at the river. 'Baudelaire knew that the camera would transform French painting. It was changing art already; and the decline, as he saw it, could only get worse. He said that the photographer would best serve in the role of secretary or clerk to art. It was a vain hope.'

'I don't see how you can blame Baudelaire for history.'

'I admire him now for his lapses, his spleen; I prefer his newspaper articles to his verse. I blame him for the life he lived in dreams and surfaces, and because he hated the idea of progress. It threatened him; it threatened his species, and his view of the world and of art. His dreamy longing undid him. It led him to the dead-end prospect of art-for-art's-sake. The angst of Baudelaire's Janus view about the new drove Matisse and other painters into their studios, where they made modern art to refute the photograph. That was Baudelaire's legacy.'

* * *

Matisse and Lydia are going to visit Amélie's sister, Berthe, in Toulouse, who has written to say that she is to undergo surgery. On the train, he recalls the letter he sent Jean Renoir praising *La Règle du Jeu* and Renoir's use of montage. He told Renoir not to heed the howls and whistles at the première. The film's chief delight, he said, was that it worked on so many levels: as farce, as the theatre of human relationships, besides being so keenly alive with a sense of the times.

Matisse reads that his old dealer Ambroise Vollard is dead. 'He was on his way to Paris from Tremblay when the steering-wheel of his car broke near Pontchartain,' Matisse tells Lydia. 'His chauffeur lost control; a Maillol bronze fell off the rear shelf and hit Vollard's neck. He lay in agony through the night before they found him. Imagine what his first words were! He wanted a lawyer; he hadn't changed his will since the turn of the century. If he had seen a doctor sooner he could have survived. As it was, he died in a hospital at Versailles. His head-scarf gave him the air of a bloodthirsty Creole pirate; he lived on sea biscuits to feed his passion for buying paintings. Mother Weill hated him. She could never conceive what his mistress Madame de Galéa saw in him. It was obvious; they were both Creoles. It doesn't say who will inherit his four thousand paintings. Maybe his papers will reveal more about his dealings with Gauguin, though I doubt it. Vollard was not the sort to let much slip. I dare say that somebody is writing a flattering obituary. Whoever does it will not say he ate like a hog, nor will there be a word about his hatred of Jews, Dreyfus in particular. Yet, without Vollard, modern art might not exist. Cézanne said he was a slave trader; Gauguin called him a crocodile. He had all the instincts of a rag and bone merchant; he was less an art dealer than a speculator. He buried painters prematurely by hoarding their paintings until they fetched his price; then he would dole their treasures from his tomb. When I knew the man, almost every room in his house was full of paintings. Luckily I met the Steins and Shchukin; they were rich enough to know what they liked, so I never had to entrust myself to Vollard's tender care.'

'Will you go to his funeral?'

'I feel no urge to do that.'

'Who is running the gallery?'

'Martin Fabiani is taking over.'

* * *

Picasso was sitting gloomily in the Café Flore. He told Aragon and Elsa how he and Sabartès had buried Vollard, and joked about how adroit the dealer was when it came to selling paintings; the artful way he had of pretending to sleep, his ears pricked for what his customers were saying about his pictures. 'Vollard taught me everything I know about selling paintings. Kahnweiler uses the same tricks. He is not as good at it as Vollard was.' Picasso sighed. 'I am alive, and he is dead; I feel a chill in my bones. I find it very sinister that Maillol killed Vollard.'

'Who else attended the funeral?' Aragon asked.

'Let's not talk about it. I was at Antibes when I heard. The things that flash into your mind! My mother dead, Vollard dead, and now another war is coming; it is one evil after another. He was not the best-looking man alive, yet artists fell over themselves to paint him. Renoir would order him not to move, to be as still as an apple. I painted him, of course.'

'Are you planning to go back to Antibes?' Elsa asked.

'No. Sabartès wants me to go to Fréjus for the bullfights. I hope we arrive in one piece.'

* * *

At the corner in the rue de Vaugirard, turning into the narrow canyon of the rue Férou, Matisse looks at his watch before entering the office where Tériade publishes *Verve*. The Greek leads in book production, keeping up with all the latest changes in illustration. He is a fat gourmand with plump hands and delicate fingers, dark blue-glazed chin, who jokes about being born on the island of Lesbos. It delights Matisse to make cut-outs using printer's ink albums, while Tériade shows him his antique typefaces. They talk about Albert Skira's hope that Matisse will write and illustrate his memoirs.

'I am a painter; and there, you have said it all. There is no reason why I should write about my life. Unless an artist is as mad as Van Gogh, I can't see why anybody should take an interest in his memoirs. Is there anybody you know who did not, as a child, half-strangle a cat to see what would happen next?' Matisse sighs. 'You ask me what I can remember of the Great War. I met Renoir in Cagnes in 1917, still painting his roses. I went to Satie's *Parade*, and had a hard time getting to Bohain. My mother was ill when the Kaiser parted us. She told all her friends she would wait for me; and she did. When I attended the first night of *Parade*, Diaghilev waved the red flag and the audience screamed, "Dirty Germans!" It was Apollinaire, in that army uniform he loved, head bandaged, who stood up to try to calm them.'

Matisse's mimicry is clever enough to make Tériade smile.

'I'm afraid that outer events are shaping up to decide my life again,' Matisse goes on. 'I had to wait a long time before I could go to Morocco. The political situation was so uncertain. As soon as Caillaux signed the treaty in 1911, I packed my bags. Of what possible interest could this be to a reader? Yet it's how I came to paint *La porte de la casbah* and discovered that blue of the sky, blue of the archway. Ah, that was a strange passageway!'

'Memories are useless except to old people. I can see Amélie with her cane, with a handbag stuffed with remedies for anything that might befall us. I can see her sallying forth to look for Zorah in Tangier's brothels. As for me, I seem a Tussaud waxwork in our hotel room, but booted and spurred for action. If I am not Livingstone about to set out to discover the heart of Africa, I am some European mountebank, my ironbound chest full of dubious magical props.'

'I've stirred up dust in shuttered rooms, chasing a pale girl until her cheeks flushed: when I caught her, the girl tickled my nose with a plume from the hat I made her. Her name was Antoinette. Sometimes the tears would fall from her eyelashes.'

Tériade nods. 'I remember her glum pout.'

Matisse sighs, saying that he would prefer to discuss yoghurt and forest mushrooms, nuts and *pahklava*, and that is what they end up doing.

Tériade hands a Turkish coffee to Matisse. Glancing towards Velázquez's portrait of Philip of Spain's wife, a poster for the Prado exhibition, he asks, 'Will you go to Geneva?'

'I have to dismiss my fear of war.' Matisse sighs. 'No European country is ready, or can afford to fight Hitler. How long will our foreign secretaries play their games of bluff? Peace is going on for so long; it is so frail that I feel I must take its pulse every morning. Still, I don't like the idea that I might be away from France when the worst happens.'

'How will you deal with the Master Race?' Tériade tries to make light of the threat. 'You do understand that everything will change?'

'I cannot let this barbarism affect my work; I'd fret more perhaps if I were a Caspar David Friedrich, whose paintings appeal to Herr Hitler's taste. I have lived too long with my spots. I have never understood war painters as such. Manet had no interest in the war. So, why did he paint in the grand historical manner? He hated the genre. It was the Salon, of course; a big canvas to impress the Hanging Committee. A naval action took place off Cherbourg; the U.S. Navy corvette *Kearsage* sank the *Alabama*, a Confederate raider. Manet's depiction of the event was one of the last attempts by a modern artist to treat a historical subject, until Picasso's *Guernica*.'

Tériade nods. 'That's very true. I never thought of it in that way before.'

'War.' Matisse grimaces. 'The action took place off one of Manet's old haunts, but he was not there. His life in the navy stood him in good stead; the French pilot boat sailing towards the stricken *Alabama* flies the right flag.'

* * *

Louis Aragon joined the Communist Party in 1927. He soon found notoriety with *Front rouge*: four hundred lines of abuse that urged outright revolution, the dynamiting of the Arc de Triomphe, and the death of Léon Blum by firing squad:

> ... *Kill the* flics
> *Comrades*
> *Kill the* flics
> *Farther, farther west where the rich*
> *Infants sleep and the high-class whores*
> *past the Madeleine*
> *Proletariat your rage sweeps the Élysée*

You have a right to the Bois de Boulogne weekdays
Someday you'll blow up the Arc de Triomphe . . .

The poem brought Aragon the charge of demoralising the Army and the Nation. It was the outcry after Breton's petition that kept him out of prison. Brecht, Thomas Mann, Le Corbusier and Picasso were among those who signed. As a result, he evaded a five-year term; but now, in 1939, it was time for him and others to pay for their criminal insults. The French police began to arrest hundreds of Communist councillors, trade unionists, and other agitators. After freeing Cagoulard assassins and terrorists, the outlawed Reds took their place in the prisons. The police smashed working-class organisations, broke six hundred trade unions, and closed down the PCF's paper *L'Humanité*.

'I can't endanger any of our friends,' Aragon said. 'There is only one place to hide, if Neruda will take us in.'
  'The Chilean Embassy?'
  Their friend the poet Pablo Neruda was glad to give them asylum.

It was the *chargé d'affaires* Arellano Marín who charmed Elsa into feeling at ease with her situation. He took off his pince-nez and polished it in a vain attempt to look business-like. 'You know you are ten times more glamorous than any gangster moll on the run.' Elsa laughed. Arellano's idea of diplomacy was caviar and champagne, with as many orchids as he could afford for his various girl-friends.

Neruda leaned forward to see himself in the mirror, brushing his hair back from his brow. 'Paul Reynaud is besotted with Hélène de Portes, a trashy Medusa who hauls her domestic tiffs into affairs of state! She uses cabinet ministers in the same high-handed way she treats her hairdresser. She is now a key player in a cheap second-rate theatre company, the mistresses all eager to be leading ladies, the men fighting and intriguing to win plum roles. Hélène de Portes was no friend to France in peacetime, but God only knows what catastrophe she will bring down on the nation in war.'
  'It is quite usual to find such women in French politics. She is simply the latest sensation.'
  Delia del Carril, Neruda's wife, smiled. She was the beautiful daughter of penniless landed gentry, with whom Elsa was biding her time before questioning her about Pablo's relationship with Nancy Cunard.
  'There is one man who rubs his hands over these arrests and Cagoulard murders: William Bullit of the U.S. Embassy,' Neruda went on. 'The idea of a Red take-over unnerves him more than Hitler invading

– if that's what lies behind the vile Soviet–German pact. Action Française doesn't like it, any more than you Communists. So, what do I tell my barber when he asks about von Ribbentrop being greeted in Moscow by swastikas flying from every flag-pole and a brass band blaring the 'Horst Wessel'? Hitler can do what he likes with Poland now.'

Aragon touches Neruda's shoulder. 'When you join the Party, Pablo, you will learn more. After all, you did more than many comrades in Spain.'

'I was Chilean consul in charge of the emigration of Spanish refugees, and I still am. It is not a title that will cut much ice when the Germans occupy Paris.'

'The idea that Chile will declare war on Germany is too comic to hope for,' Aragon said.

Neruda shook his head dejectedly. 'You are right.'

'Santiago has no interest in European events?'

'Chile recognises only natural disasters. One day, I shall write a long poem about my homeland. It will have plenty of wildlife in it, snakes, birds, the heights of Macchu Picchu, but you can't expect much more than that.'

'What is going to happen when Germany defeats France?'

'I don't know. Maybe I will go to Mexico.'

* * *

Matisse watches Lydia tug at her beads as they wait for a taxi. She is *La dame en bleu* again, a mirror image of Ingres's Madame Inès Moitessier. In his painting, the Venetian chair seemed to float above the black tiles, as red and as ample as a sofa under the large blue bell of her dress, with its lacy edging and frothy bodice. Her elbow rested on the sinuous yellow arm of the chair, so that the solid pink finger aimed at her temple propped her doll-queen head against the mimosa-yellow explosion of flowers behind her. Her other hand lay in her lap, twisting a loop of black and white beads; a rosary told with royal boredom.

He finds it calms him to call up old paintings, especially those in which he has solved the problems they posed.

The Prado exhibition at the Musée Nationale in Geneva is to close at the end of August, so they have little time left to see the masterpieces. The rescue from Madrid of works by Velázquez, El Greco, Goya, Van der Weyden makes Matisse think of his own canvases. 'I suppose it would be

30

fruitless to try to trace where they are. Those paintings in Basle, New York, Beverly Hills, Chicago – they'll be safe.'

'It's not like you to forget that the art trade has invoices,' Lydia says.

Lake Geneva glitters in the noonday sun; sweat itches as it runs down inside Matisse's shirt collar. He sits in the shade on a green, iron seat that rings the bole of a tree. There are children feeding swans.

'I can see now why Proust thought this lake was like the sea at Beg Meil.' He sighs, then goes on, 'It isn't the first time that barbarism has sent paintings shuttling around the world, nor will it be the last.'

Lydia yawns. 'Picasso can take credit, being an honorary director of the Prado; and José Bergamín deserves a medal for his part in saving these treasures.'

Taking off his spectacles, Matisse pinches the bridge of his nose. 'El Greco and Goya were survivors; they came through the disaster of their own times in one piece. They will see out this storm.' He sniffs. 'A lemon, an apple, a jug in any studio remains the same yet it changes in the changing light. The Dutch had their way of painting a still life, Cézanne had his; now it is my turn to gaze at things for hours.'

Lydia undoes the top of her blouse, and fans her neck with a catalogue. 'Everybody must be here.'

'Of course; this is a wake to mark the end of civilisation.'

A young woman, who had seemed lost to everything except the lake, confronts Matisse suddenly. 'Yes, certainly we must praise Picasso for his help in saving our treasures from the fascists. He is a true Spaniard, yet there was no room in the trucks for any of the footsore half million refugees fleeing on the same mountain roads. They had no shelter, fed their babies in the snow and washed their rags in icy streams. What is Picasso doing now to help his countrymen, rotting in the camps by the sea at Argelès?'

Matisse watches her hurry away. 'So passionate, so angry – how very strange! An odd girl – would you say she was French?'

'You have nothing to do with the plight of the Spanish refugees.'

'Did she know me?'

'To imagine that you are a master these days is an illusion,' Matisse says. 'I have taught myself everything I know, but I could never attain the genius of Giotto. Anyway, what is an artist? In Morocco, even the baker's bill is a masterpiece, with its symbols for kilo and corn. The butchers were artists, too, sticking bouquets of scarlet peppers in the nostrils of their dead bulls.'

The next day, France declares war. Lydia calls the station to book seats on the Paris train. She puts down the telephone receiver, and Matisse sits numbly watching as she packs a suitcase. 'As soon as the country voted for the Popular Front, things changed; maids were going to turn to murder.'

'Yes, you said so when Blum took over. You told me then that he was not alone in the comfort and shame he took from Munich. You always need a scapegoat. Of course the Papin sisters were going to lose their temper when the electric iron gave them trouble; and, being maids, who more natural to kill than their master and mistress.'

'Why now? Why that domestic drama? It must be six years since it happened!' Matisse feels stupefaction.

*   *   *

Aragon finished his novel *Les Voyageurs de l'impériale*, writing night and day while France mobilised. He could see men in greatcoats of all shapes and sizes arriving every day at the Invalides, across the road from Neruda's window. Then, through some clerical error, his own call-up papers arrived, and Elsa laid out his uniform.

Nothing had happened, yet people were already behaving badly; worse-than-usual scenes erupted out of nowhere. Conscripts boarding trains to join their regiments spat on the ticket collectors' uniforms. For some people, what they had pined for was going to happen, and it was a relief. The ones who thought they knew what to expect were bitter. They hadn't done enough to stop what was coming. Others were getting out before the roof fell in.

The army sent Aragon to Crouy-sur-Ourcq, where he began to serve as an auxiliary doctor to a labour regiment of refugees. There, he listened to hearts, tested urine samples, gave shots for typhus, malaria and dysentery. The men dug trenches, while he idled away the 'phoney war' listening to Czechs curse Gamelin for not arming them to fight Hitler, while Republicans sang laments for Spain. Since the War Office pay was seventy-five centimes a day, the men did as little work as possible. The worst part was having to inspect the suicides; some of them had become his friends.

Aragon's most pressing problem was to avoid the homosexual advances of a lonely Greek, who fixed on him because he resembled his lover who had died recently.

Left alone, Elsa felt that her Parisian life, as she used to think of it, was now an out-of-date newspaper blowing in the wind. She passed under the entwined classical nudes that loomed above the entrance to the courtyard. There was always a solitary child playing with a ball, or an old man sweeping with a broom. It was the kind of courtyard that Atget loved to photograph. It was somewhere to nurse old memories and feelings. 'Jewish girls are all alike,' she told Aragon as she saw him off at the station. 'Our parents keep us warm, and spoil us in their greenhouse; yet there is a dark abyss in us, in which we yearn for our own destruction.'

After the mobilisation, with its sudden changes, the tempo abated across France. Nothing happened; there was no invasion; no bombs fell on Paris. People began to feel that the politicians would be able to talk peace in Europe again. Several towns held mayoral meetings to choose a street to rename Neville Chamberlain that would not slight some local son or French hero.

Aragon wrote to tell Elsa that he ached to be with her already, but he saw no chance that the lull would last for long. It would surprise him if it lasted long enough to train raw conscripts.

Elsa wrote about the mood in Paris: who had stayed, who had taken flight. She bought a pair of red shoes. She knew such things would soon vanish from the shops. She saw Adrienne Monnier riding a store escalator. It was in her bookshop that Aragon had met Breton all those years ago. Adrienne failed to see her wave of greeting.

Elsa went to galleries whenever she could, though several of the owners had already left Paris. She had time to read, of course, and she would buy a set of matching suitcases, to be ready when Aragon sent for her.

Young Woman in a Blue Blouse

There are posters on every wall that tell Matisse what he must do in case of German bombs or gas attack; no car may use its lights, and the blackout means no streetlights. Such conditions have closed the Louvre. At noon each Thursday, the siren tests annoy him. He hates the subtle ease with which democracy wilts and dies, overcome by new orders and strictures. Paris, he tells Lydia, is now a refugee camp. Telephone operators enrage him when they ask whether he is German or Spanish when he wants to send a telegram.

There is a letter from Picasso:

Well, another war again, old friend. There will be no place for us to hide except in the white light of the Riviera. I see corruption all along the coast, to which its denizens turn a blind eye. It can only get worse when Hitler's stormtroopers arrive.

I have just finished a painting. Two men crouch waiting in the dark; one with blue canvas trousers rolled up to his knees is about to spear a fish with his trident, while the other is leaning over the gunwale intently. Both men inhabit, and help form, an egg-shaped unity in the cradle of the boat. Dora is with Breton's wife watching from the quay. Dora wears a pale green head-dress and green skirt; I have given Jacqueline her bicycle and a plum-coloured dress. She was there because she had just had a fight with Breton. She licks an ice-cream cone, while telling Dora malicious stories about him.

My moon is yellow, with a red spiral. You can see Antibes in the upper left of the painting; gas lamps light the sea to lure the fish, and a crab hangs on the rocks. I feel as precarious as that crab: how long do I have left before it will be impossible to paint such subjects?

Matisse sees a poster advertising the woodland beauties of Rochefort-en-Yvelines as he leaves the Geneva–Paris train. On a sudden whim that shows how ruffled he is by the political situation, he decides to escape for a while near Rambouillet.

The Hôtel Saint-Pierre is not far from a cross-roads. Every morning, car horns wake Matisse early, as refugees head south for Chartres. Dressing quickly, he strides out into the forest to sketch as much as he can before lunchtime.

After a short burst of thudding hoofbeats, a woman rides a white stallion out of the mist into the glade. She starts to put her mount through a dressage routine, advancing, weaving in a diagonal across the clearing. It is quite certain that she is the daughter of some local aristocrat, reining her horse tightly, a dark veil hiding her pale unsmiling face. She is certain that control and mastery are all that matter in life. When she finishes her routine, she slaps the horse's neck with a tender, loving cry and rides away as abruptly as she came, hoofbeats in the mist, to leave Matisse with a smile, humming Mozart.

He does not tell Lydia about the rider when she brings her camp-stool and thermos flask to join him. It is as though the performance had been for him alone. By now, the sun is lifting the mist out of the trees, to leave

34

a delicate mass of spider webs glistening amongst the orange and yellow foliage.

Matisse tacks the canvas on the board as Lydia touches a powder puff to her cheeks, staring at herself through the bluish gloom of the old mirror. He is ready when she turns and sits in front of him. As he roughs in the shape of her face, the baker's van arrives. The boy who plays the mouth-organ hefts two baskets over his arms and, glancing up at Matisse's window, nods his head blithely, as he has done since the first morning.

Lydia stares straight ahead. 'That was the bread van arriving?'

Matisse glances into the yard and nods. 'Exactitude is not truth,' he informs her.

A quicker flicker of a frown crosses her calm brow.

'I thought of that line at dawn. I want this portrait to illustrate what I mean. I am painting your character and personality with verisimilitude; I want to bring the two sides of your face together, to organise an expressive distortion.'

Matisse stares at the blouse that Lydia wears, idly speculating what colour it will turn out in the finished painting. For the moment, he is shaping the collar around her long white neck. Her blonde hair shingles back in waves from a middle parting; her nose is long, aquiline. He is trying to make everything simple to the point where it is direct and straightforward.

It is not long before he achieves a sense of calm by placing her face off-centre, to the left of the canvas. The work is shaping up to become the *Jeune femme à la blouse bleue*.

The boy leaves the hotel kitchen playing a burst of 'Sonny Boy'.

Matisse smiles, delighted with the progress he is making, then says, 'It would be quite easy to prove you wrong, you know; I don't have to be a detective to know that there is a sunset over a mawkish woodland path hanging somewhere – all these hotels have them.'

Through the window behind Matisse, Lydia waits for the red sea of leaves to rise and fall under the breeze. She remembers those scarfed peasant women at work in the fields she used to see from the train who, when night fell, went home to their cabins to sit around smoky oil-lamps, singing while they stitched and told old tales.

'Russia's storks will be flying off to India soon,' she says sadly.

Matisse does not like to hear this note of nostalgia in her voice; it seems to bring home his dependency on her.

The film is *Entente Cordiale*, in which Gaby Morlaix plays Queen Victoria. It is a throw-back to 1938, when England's King and Queen made a state visit. They inspected a parade of bearded soldiers of the Foreign Legion; then a mounted squadron of *spahis* in their white cloaks, trotting by in close formation.

Matisse is dour. 'Such events are ringing down the curtain on the Third Republic; they reveal the idiocy of General Weygand's promise that France will win if Germany invades. The cost of it all must be enormous. First we pay to entertain their King; now we are to show Winston Churchill the Maginot Line. Will anybody be fool enough to ask him what he thinks of that fortified *métro* system, I wonder? How can they pretend they are soldiers? The ones I've seen look like mechanics, lift operators, kitchen and canteen workers.'

'Don't you think that we are all living charmed lives?' Lydia says, powdering her nose.

They visit Paris every week or so, although it saddens him to see the haunted people scuttling about with gas masks. Lydia wonders whether she qualifies for one. The woman who did her hair has told her that foreigners could not have them.

Matisse frowns in disbelief. 'Do you mean to tell me that you would wear one of those awful things?'

'Most certainly. If the Germans attacked with gas, so would you.'

Every window in public buildings has lozenge patterns of brown paper to stop glass flying when the air raids start. Cinema newsreels show Poland preparing to defend Warsaw. Matisse shakes his head over a wild charge of cavalry officers brandishing sabres. They wear the same light opera costumes in which their fathers died during the Great War.

* * *

Elsa's birthday was in September. When Warsaw fell to the Germans, the Soviet Union invaded Poland. Earlier in the month, Uniprix told its customers that it was French, lock, stock and barrel. Elsa caught a glimpse of Breton in uniform, about to enter the Dôme. As she turned away to avoid him, a limp barrage balloon spun round in the late sun.

She met Dominique Desanti, who asked why she looked so down. Elsa did not mention Breton. 'Maybe because I don't dance any more,' she said wistfully. 'Artaud knew what was coming when he told us that he had met the horsemen of the apocalypse over coffee at the Deux-Magots.'

Dominique lit a cigarette. 'Maxim Litvinov tried hard to forge a common front against fascism; the Stalin–Ribbentrop pact was the result of his failure,' she said. 'The Soviet Union's only hope now is that the Western powers will drag each other down.' She laughs. 'We live in ghastly times! With Marais in the army, God alone knows how Cocteau will find his opium.'

It was raining, and Elsa ran to shelter under the striped awning. It was that time in the early evening when sad shop girls turn into domestics and start to mop the floor. To her right, a man crouched by the window making a study of a bronze horseman waving a plumed hat. Elsa would have thought him drab and a nonentity had it not been for his open sketch-pad: a notary, perhaps, or schoolmaster. When she realised that it was Bonnard, his blazing interiors and flower gardens burst into her mind: a world under threat, where girls lazed in bathtubs and colours shone out of, and seeped back into, the blaze of noon or quiet moonlight. He painted the old world Renoir had mastered, his gardens were those that Monet had already done; a private world at ease with itself, a condemned world.

When Bonnard stood up, a rain drop ran to the tip of his nose and down into his moustache. He took off his glasses and wiped them, smiling to greet the woman who came out of the shop. Elsa was sure that she was Madame Bonnard.

She wore a blue dress under her pink raincoat, a twenties hat fitted snugly tight over her ears. Elsa watched as she put several gift-boxes into a bag, aware of the gossip that surrounded the suicide of Renée Monchaty, Bonnard's other cherished lover. The idea that this dry stick of a man might attract more than one woman seemed laughable.

Madame Bonnard had aged but her body was still girlish. She opened an umbrella, taking his arm as he bowed his neck to find headroom, then led him off towards the *métro*.

Two labourers were digging turnips into a clamp. They waited for a third man to lead another cart-load out of the field. It was raining; sacks covered their heads against the rain that was falling across France, which had brought floods to the valleys of the Marne, Meuse and Moselle. As Aragon drove by, one of the diggers noticed his uniform and saluted. The salute seemed ominous. The next thing he saw was a band of soaked Moroccan *spahis* with turbans tied on their helmets. Some sat huddled around a war memorial, with their faces hidden inside the hoods of their djellabas. Nearby, a tricolour hung over the rusted wall of a *pissotière*, and

37

the man who came out from behind the iron screen had paused to stare at the flag with his mouth open as he buttoned his flies.

Thorez had fled to Moscow. The Party deputies were under arrest. Paul Nizan had resigned as Aragon's co-editor at *Ce Soir*. In Paris, barbed wire barricades blocked the boulevards, and the censor banned *Quai des Brumes* and *La Bête Humaine* from cinemas. The Germans had invaded Poland, the Luftwaffe razing Warsaw as a warning to other European capitals.

Tourists in Nice are uncertain what to do, so they linger beside the sea in the last of the fine weather. The news that Britain has sent a large force of men and equipment to France does not seem to alarm them. There are the usual jokes in the cafés about the Maginot Line, but nobody imagines that it can fail. In September, the London Stock Exchange had closed its doors for a week to decide what course of action it should take when the air raids started. It chose the perfect moment to protect its shares from the wave of panic selling that hit Wall Street. Gangs of top-hatted dealers had to stand in Throgmorton Street to transact their deals. These new street traders could not believe that the police would move them on. Was such a thing possible on the Bourse?

Simon Bussy and Dorothy are passing the frame-maker's shop on the other side of the street. As Matisse steps out to hail them, a fight breaks out three floors above between two Italian women. Insults fly back and forth as a line of washing jerks between the two windows. A yellow scarf flutters down, which Dorothy picks up. Holding her pince-nez, she tilts her head and lifts the scarf to gesture to the women. Bussy turns and sees Matisse.

'Anybody wearing this could join a tribe of nubile Gold Coast virgins,' Dorothy says.

'That's the problem with a Bloomsbury girl; she cannot come to terms with reality,' Bussy says.

'I'm well aware that my hair is falling out; my teeth too,' she replies, with asperity. 'I know my hearing is bad, and my eyes are failing me.'

'Have we time for a coffee?' Matisse asks.

Bussy glances at Dorothy, who says 'No' firmly.

'We have Gide staying with us now,' Bussy says, as though by way of explanation.

'Another of my critics who thinks that he can see through me,' Matisse says.

'King Lear's self-inflicted wound was the result of being a patriarchal egotist,' Dorothy says pointedly. 'I cannot see that the storm that will soon pelt about our heads will make any of us more human.'

'I shall miss going to the Regent's Park zoo,' Bussy says.

'That was the time when I almost gave up painting to join the *préfecture de la Seine*, and care for the bridge *clochards*,' says Matisse.

'Bréal will not discuss it when I remind him how hard he tried to get you the post,' Bussy says laughing.

'There were a hundred men chasing three jobs,' Matisse says. 'Michel was a good friend. Without him, I don't think I would have got far with my school; he brought me a great many pupils.'

'I allow my first efforts to shine through the paint,' Matisse says. 'Ghosts. I'm thinking of my Collioure balcony; of Manet's too.' He speaks of the grisly display of Communard corpses, which Couture's class found on a cold afternoon in Montmartre's cemetery, as he and Bussy conduct yet another autopsy on Manet. Matisse says he never saw Manet as an Impressionist. 'He was not of their persuasion; he held on to the classical; his world was solid, four-square.'

Bussy speaks of photography and Impressionism as being two sides of the same coin. He reminds Matisse that Nadar showed the Impressionists' early works in his studio. 'Those were the days, you remember, when the smell of flour still haunted the Moulin de la Galette; it was there under the stink of stale tobacco and booze.'

They have reached the sea. 'I find it easy to imagine Crusoe's dismay when he saw the footprint: his surge of hope and fear, his wild surmise,' Bussy says. 'Sometimes I see life as a chaotic Mother Goose yarn, which only a fairy-tale truth can unravel; that fairy-tale truth we could accept when we were children.'

Smiling, Matisse shakes hands with Bussy and raises his hat to Dorothy; they part.

Dorothy shakes her head. 'Is Matisse the King, or the Fool? Lear can only blame his folly for his situation. Yes, I agree that there were criminals around him, too; and the gods in heaven are not kind – but, when order collapses, can values remain intact? I think not. Shakespeare, never mind what we think about his private life, was always a public man trying to make sense of his times. The very private Matisse sees the world as his oyster still. The fate of the crew of the *Graf Spee* means nothing to him; nor does he have time for the Nazis, who will soon kick down our doors. Our naval losses at Scapa Flow mean nothing to him. Life has given him one lesson in authority and family, like Lear, but it does not seem to have impinged a great deal. There's no chance that we'll see him raving in his nightshirt, cursing the heavens on the heights above Cimiez.'

Reader against a Black Background

Matisse cleans off his brush. 'I suppose some critic will try to analyse this painting in the context of the year in which I painted it. The title means only what it says. It has nothing to do with Spain, the German attack on Poland.'

'Nevertheless, people are going to think you painted it in your luxury air-raid shelter,' Lydia says. 'Why did you dismiss the airy light of Mary's studio?'

Matisse stares at the rectangle of the table, which he painted face-powder pink, the salmon-pink of satin underwear. The background is now an overall ebony black that gives every colour an edge; it heightens the fragility of the vase of flowers, despite the matter-of-fact way he renders them. Every aspect creates problems, none more so than the reader, leaning with her elbow on the table, reflected in the mirror behind her. The yellow-framed mirror itself offers the reason for the painting, echoing the pink slab of the table as it projects into deep space. His own cursory self-portrait is to the right; the size of a postage stamp, it fills a corner and gives an illusion of depth to the structure.

France

Matisse paints the seated girl he calls *La France*. Given the dire state of affairs, he chooses red, white and blue to depict threatened 'French' values; they are the colours Coco Chanel chose for her collection of gypsy dresses in the spring. The girl poses with aplomb, plumb centre of the canvas, the curve of her arms echoing the curves of the chair; her tiny waist lends emphasis to her ample breasts and the bell shape of her skirt. There is no hint of that antique Roman imagery which David used to dignify the Revolution; no Phrygian helmet, no hint of martial *patrie*. Why? Does he intend the picture as a veiled criticism of his country? If he had not called it *La France*, she would be merely a pert nonentity, a girl with a perfect hour-glass figure.

'Yes,' Matisse agrees with Lydia, 'I'm glad that we have a new law to reduce divorce time from three years to one.' He thinks, however, of the family at Issy, the banquettes and divans playing off their patterns against each other, stippled or criss-crossed, on either side of the pale blue-grey monument of the fireplace. It is so calm against the rich decorations and fabrics, the wallpaper pattern of flower sprigs. Pierre and Jean are sitting at their draught-board, whose distorted perspective underlines the perverse viewpoint of the painting. He seems to be looking down, yet his eye line stays level at the same time. He can see Amélie, Marguerite and his sons, even though their faces are as cursory as those in *La musique*. The boys are otherworldly twins in their one-piece red costumes. Marguerite wears a black ankle-length dress, with a white lacy bib and ruffs, as of some austere religious order, except for the fairy-tale green of her shoes.

'You seem to be elsewhere,' Lydia says.

'You're right. I was in another country, far from the threat of war.'

The Rumanian Blouse

Matisse's title for the new painting is *La blouse roumaine*, but he feels a slight yet entirely enjoyable spasm of protest, as with *La France*, when the red, white and blue of the flag emerge as the inevitable, most harmonic combination. His canvas has gone through fifteen stages in all. He examines Lydia's photographs showing how, at first, she sat on a sofa, against a flowered background hanging. 'The discovery of a flaw is always a way back, the point at which to begin a re-creation of the whole,' Matisse said as he painted out the sofa, using carmine red. In two of the versions the blouse's stitching had become too fussy; now, his musings done, he dashes in the motif on the pneumatic sleeves carelessly, as though with ease. It is Lydia's clasped hands that did not change during these many wipe-outs and adjustments.

*　　*　　*

Aragon was home on leave for Christmas. Elsa had bought a tree that touched the ceiling. It was thick with baubles and loops of tinsel, and lit up the apartment with a joyful festive air. Both of them knew that they might be apart for a long time, perhaps forever. 'I want to feel gay,' Aragon said. 'Whatever happens, I want to remember us being gay together.'

He gave her a Japanese bowl painted with an exquisite cherry tree blossoming in the snow. 'It's so fragile,' Elsa said. 'Will I be able to bring it through my life in one piece?'

'Time and turbulence have always threatened its beauty.'

Later, they discussed the letter Nizan had sent to Duclos in October resigning from the Party.

'One has to ask why he elects to betray the world's best hope at this moment in time,' said Elsa.

Outside in the blackout, the *flic* patrols wore tin hats, and were stopping men to check their papers.

1940

Striped Blouse and Anemones

THE Russians are fighting the Finns in Karelia. Lydia does not know why they feature Siberians in the newsreels except to imply that winter is no obstacle to these sub-human scarecrows with rags around their feet. On the other hand, the Finns are uniformly heroic, magnificent skiers and natural victors. They appear naked, thrashing their flesh with birch twigs as they brave enemy fire in saunas built within yards of the front line trenches.

Pineapple and Anemones

It is hectic during February; as soon as Matisse finishes a canvas he starts another: an interior with Spanish vases, another with a Persian robe; he ends the month working on *Ananas et anémones*, which Lydia takes to with relish. 'It's quite wonderful, Henri, how you fuse hot colours and cooler tones in the same space.'

Against a background of saturated alizarin crimson, his favourite philodendra hang above the hot orange of the table top, on which he has arranged his objects. There are the blues, reds and whites of the anemones in a green vase, and a pineapple that lies in its blue-grey nest under the opened yellow lid of the presentation box.

Lydia continues to read eye-witness accounts in the papers of the raids on Helsinki; atrocity stories about Stalin bombing civilian targets in Finland. Some editors give space to comparisons between the Mannerheim Line and France's Maginot Line. Trade union delegates throng there, too, hoping to discover a reason for the war that will satisfy their members; one that will excuse a workers' state being at war with a neighbouring country. They all report on the intense cold: thermometers registering 36 degrees of frost.

The Woman in a Yellow Armchair

Matisse begins work on an interior with a woman in a yellow armchair. She wears a green skirt and a smocked and embroidered blouse; the chair has bright fabric, the flowers are mauve against black, and the sideboard is pale green; these colours vibrate at different wavelengths above the blue

45

of the floor. 'I tried three times before I found the right blue for that,' he says.

*　　*　　*

In Paris, the snow was ankle-deep, in places it had drifted against walls and the boles of trees; there were no able-bodied men left to clear it. Elsa spent long hours in cafés: it was a cheap way to stay warm and feel less lonely.

It was a cold grey afternoon, and the *zouave* had fallen asleep with his head resting on a table. Aragon watched the officer run towards the man, lashing out with his boot. The *zouave* rolled away in a cloud of dust as the officer booted him again; he scrambled up and ran, half-limping, trying to escape the demented attack. Aragon had to stand and watch, or risk an enquiry into his army status; he gave a half-hearted shout that went unheard. The officer was merciless, forcing his victim to scuttle on hands and knees into the cookhouse, which echoed with his cries and the crash of pots and pans. Aragon strode off, ashamed that such attacks were a form of discipline in the French Army.

Aragon's post-mortems and fortification days were over, and he had spent some time with Elsa before joining the Third Light Motorised Division in training near Laôn. He would shave outside his tent, while the city on the whale-back hill glinted in his mirror as the morning mists faded. He had little to do except study the use of sabre and lance in the Cavalry Training manual, whose updated appendix dealt with armoured cars in the field. The same phrase 'mounted drill' applied to armoured cars as well as horses. He felt alone and lost; bored by the monotony of army fiddles and rumours. Life itself was in abeyance. It was not a feeling he could live with, and he had to resist it. He was unhappy, and longed for Elsa so much that poems came to him easily again:

> *The rising mists of Flanders*
> *Insist that spring is late*
> *— The skies are easy to read*
> *　When we are apart . . .*
> *. . . Unhappy passion drove Verona's lovers*
> *To drink black veronal*
> *Yours this vivid cup of blue*
> *This rising trill, my brief song,*
> *Among these armoured cars*
> *Ascending clear and pure*

> *Above these walls*
> *Over the friends we knew*
> *My sole love, my wound . . .*

He left this poem hanging when orders came for the Division to move to Belgium.

*   *   *

Only the roof and a patch or two of the pink walls of the Villa du Bosquet are visible beyond the jungle of the garden that hangs above the street. The house is one of those suburban villas built in their hundreds to attract retired people; small, modest, yet homely and welcoming. Matisse pauses on the steep path. He can hear Bonnard's dogs yapping as he begins to climb again.

'Come up, come up, my dear Henri!' Bonnard calls, coming out of the house. Marthe stands smiling in the doorway behind him. It is a good omen that she wears a red blouse, the colour in which Bonnard loves to paint her.

Bonnard is sceptical, lean, informal, dry. The small linen hat he wears pulled down over his ears gives him a nautical air, as if he had just stepped off Signac's yacht. His toothbrush moustache, rather than evoking Hitler, suggests that he could be an eccentric country pharmacist.

He met Maria Boursin in 1894, when she was working in a shop in the rue Pasquier making funeral wreaths. To distance herself from the cheese, she said she was Italian. She had adopted the melodious name of Marthe de Méligny, innocent of the fact that the real Marthe de Méligny was a courtesan. She told Bonnard nothing about her past, her family, or where she was born. They lived together for thirty years. Then, when they moved to Le Cannet, he married her as an afterthought. Bonnard dwells on her unfocused, day-dreamy look in his portraits of her, despite her darkening persecution complex that leads her to distrust his friends and obliges Bonnard to live as though in retirement.

Often he would ask Matisse, 'What life is there, other than sharing Marthe's fantasies? My isolation is a small price to pay, if it means I can see and paint her as the girl I met. Everything else has gone. We create our own happiness. When we were young there were families, large families with children who had dogs and other pets. One room led to another, with ever more voices echoing in rooms beyond. They are silent now.'

Bonnard painted many nudes of Marthe, to celebrate his domestic adoration. In many of them she floats in her bath; her body made up of blooms of colours amid pearl and lilac tones. They live the poetry of daily life in the dusty white interiors of Le Bosquet, with worn carpets and run-down furniture, a canvas tacked here, a drawing tacked there; no easel, just the bamboo table with the usual chipped plate for his colours.

He has been adding a few touches to his painting of the mimosa that grows outside the studio window, *L'Atelier au mimosa*, which he started work on the year before. The mimosa's glory fills the studio window, while to the left, distant, there are the red tile roofs of Cannes: its green trees, struck out in bars and lozenges of lilac, and a pearly sea. As usual, he is working on a number of unstretched canvases, going from one to another in a quick, bird-like way, a dab of colour here, another there. These endless touches are obsessive. He has sought out paintings sold years before to some museum and, as soon as the guards left the gallery, slipped out his paint box to make a change or two.

After blowing his nose, Bonnard rubs his hands together matter-of-factly. 'I used to enjoy the Bouglione Circus more than the Médrano, but that was where Gide, Cocteau, Larbaud all wanted to go to see Rastelli, the acrobat,' he says. 'I liked the bar where the clowns drank, and the stables, of course, where I used to talk to the horses and other animals.'

'We both follow the special logic of our pictures,' he tells Matisse. 'Yours may be different from mine, yet it is just as inevitable – colour is everything for us.'

Marthe feeds the dogs in the kitchen, and they nose the dishes around the tiled floor. There is an acid smell, either of a leaking accumulator or of hot valves as the old radio on the mantelpiece in the dining room crackles and buzzes with reports of the British Navy sinking seven German destroyers in Narvik fjord. Bonnard looks across at Matisse, then shakes his head and switches it off.

'Sadly, we can't turn reality off so easily,' Matisse says. 'Another war is on our doorstep again. The last time, we sent the children to Amélie's parents in Toulouse. We left in the autumn for Collioure, arriving there in time to read the casualty lists on the Marne. As Max Jacob said, a week in Paris had become a drab succession of Sundays. I fretted about my family in Bohain. Then the farm went up in flames during that first offensive. My brother was a prisoner in Heidelberg. I did not know what was happening to my mother. Critics said that the colours I used were symbolic of my anxiety. That was the red; yes, red ruled at times.' He sighs, and it echoes in the room. 'I did landscapes because I could dash them off, working with nature I felt tranquil.'

Bonnard nods. 'You came to see me at Antibes on the day they signed the Armistice.' He smiles as Marthe starts singing in the kitchen.

'Although we did not know it at the time, Apollinaire would join the Glorious Dead.' Matisse sighs again.

They return from their customary stroll beside the Saigne Canal, which borders the garden. Matisse is standing with the sun behind him, one hand on his lapel. 'A memory can never match the original experience,' he says, 'so it has to become a new version. That's why Proust was so desperate in his pursuit of time.'

'Yes, I plan to visit Paris. No doubt we shall have to languish in some ghastly wartime hotel.' Matisse shakes his head. 'You know nothing of the fear that hotels can inspire! You have never had any use for an easel. Chambermaids are creatures who live their entire lives around the axiom that cleanliness is next to godliness; they turn everything upside down in their mania. I mark the carpet, so that I can set up my easel in the same place where I had it the day before.'

After a short stay at his apartment in the boulevard Montparnasse, Matisse joins Lydia at the Hôtel Vendôme.

Matisse winces. 'There they go again, the sirens!'

'Well, come on then.' Lydia picks up her shelter bag.

'My stomach hurts. I don't want to go down to that bolt-hole. I feel fine here; and that's how I'd like to die, in comfort. You go, if you wish.'

'No doubt it will be another false alarm.'

Matisse opens the book she puts down. Outside, doors begin to slam along the corridor as guests quit their rooms; wardens are blowing their whistles in the street below.

'Flaubert? Not *Madame Bovary* again!'

'Anything to avoid this threat that hangs over us.'

A postcard marks her place. It is a reproduction of his *Les Maroccains*. Matisse studies it. 'I spent nine months on this. I must have been mad. It was ten feet long. I had delusions of being Hercules. I told Camoin that I was not in the front line, but that I was digging a trench of my own. It was a terrace whose shadow and heat he knew well, of course.'

Everything shifts in a Matisse canvas before it assumes its final form. He says his Moroccans are lying on the terrace among watermelons and gourds. It is hard to say whether these are watermelons among leaves or men at prayer; or perhaps shapes only, placed to echo other architectural forms in the painting. In the end, these circles might be nothing more than the turbans of kneeling Arabs. Above their huddle, near the grey-white dome of the mosque, there is a pot of large blue flowers on the balcony, each orb criss-crossed with diagonal blue bars. It is more probable that they are freak blue cacti; for they are unlike any flower in the floral canon.

To the right, a seated imam dominates, legs crossed, sitting in front of a pink wall. He seems to be lifting an outsize crab-claw arm aloft.

Matisse taps the figure. 'Can I hear this imam calling me again? Maybe we could escape the war in Morocco.'

'Do you think you could live there?'

Matisse winces again. 'If I felt better. Medical science may owe its existence to Cordoba, when the city was part of the Islamic empire, but I can't entrust my aches and pains to an Arab doctor now. That's a horse of another colour.'

Matisse is going to see his tailor when he runs into Picasso. He tells him he has just booked a ticket for Genoa, and that he will need a light suit in Rio de Janeiro. 'Bolting before the *boches* get here?' Picasso accuses.

'Is this a court-martial?'

Picasso shakes his head with a wave of the hand, and asks, 'Why are you going, then?'

'I don't think returning to Nice would be wise. Pierre cabled me that New York is rife with rumours that the Italians intend to invade any day now. My health and well-being must be my chief concern. If I stay in Paris there will be more air raids or false alarms. I shall have to squat in a dank shelter where I shall catch my death of cold.'

'How do you feel, these days?'

'Some stomach pains, from time to time.'

'Not bad, I trust. I've told you: see Dr Klotz if you're sick. He could well burn your house down; he will certainly blow all your fuses before he cures you, but he works miracles.'

'I will seek medical advice if my pain gets any worse.'

'At your age, you must not neglect such a thing. I won't let you die on me; I could not bear that. I write your name every morning; to guard you from death, you know.'

'What are you doing?' Matisse asks. 'Somebody told me that you were in Royan.'

'I am. I'm here to fix a permit to stay in France. I want to catch the train today. Painting is impossible, of course. I spend my time staring at the lighthouse and the ferry going to and fro. If I were not Picasso, people would say I was mad. People visit from time to time. We had Breton and Jacqueline in January. He's serving at Poitiers.' He grunts. 'He prophesied that art materials are going to vanish shortly. So, you and I will have to make sure that we have enough canvases to work on until they chase the swine back to Berlin.'

'You think so.'

'Everything; they are going to eat everything. They will land on us like locusts. We shall have to start painting over old canvases. Sculpture will be a thing of the past when the scrap merchant gang arrives. They will take your teeth. Everybody I talk to is hoarding whatever they can lay their hands on. Paris is hopeless already. The capitalists have sent all their money to New York; the dealers have their berths booked, too, all except those cute enough to realise that the art market is going to erupt when the fascists get here. As for me, I can't walk the streets without some *flic* demanding proof that I've not just parachuted out of the sky.'

Matisse mentions the Banque Nationale de Commerce et d'Industrie, which they both use, saying:

'Your strong-room is bigger than mine. Do you have enough space to store some of my canvases until things settle?'

'Settle!' Picasso laughs.

Picasso grins: 'Is Amélie happy? What's she doing?'

Matisse tells him she is in Toulouse.

'She is going through with the divorce?'

'Yes, nothing has changed, if that's what you mean.'

'Sensible. I told you that you must deal firmly with women. You must also be careful concerning any Russian. You have never had a bitch use the law to seal up your studio. Of course, you know that I have not resolved my divorce from Olga. You can thank your stars that your sons did not turn out like my Paulo. You would not believe what the clinic charges me to keep him locked away. I feel for you. You don't need this sort of drama in your life. There is quite enough of a débâcle already in France. The situation is hopeless everywhere. Now that Churchill is boss, he is going to order his soldiers to scoot back to defend the home of Empire.'

Matisse smiles. 'When did you study the art of war?'

'Art? There is no art to war. What generals do is argue about strategy, the same as they did last time.'

Those flatlands, with their fields of flax, hemp and beetroot, were where Matisse had been born. The only glory was the sky; some days it was a sheen of bright silver light. At other times, the church steeples were as baleful as the pillars of smoke rising above them. There were belfries that had summoned worshippers since the Maid of Orléans's voices told her to save France. They dominated tight-fisted weaving villages whose people lived between the loom and the land.

A thunderstorm inked in the dusk in the field. The only light came from burning haystacks, which lightning had set on fire. Somewhere wounded men cried out every so often, as they lay in the rain. There were four half-tracks hidden at the edge of the wood. A captain stepped out into the path and waved Aragon's convoy down. He wanted to know where he thought he was going. Aragon pointed to the field and said he had orders to save the wounded.

The captain was curt. 'I cannot allow you to risk your life; the Germans have us in their sights.'

Aragon's temper flared. 'I have my orders!'

He might have said more if mortar grenades had not landed, destroying more haystacks and the wounded sheltering near them. The captain turned to face him, and said with a bow that he was Guy de Rothschild and was at Aragon's service.

Aragon and de Rothschild derided André Maginot's fortress as a costly concrete trench for bored conscripts to play cards and dominoes in until the order came to hoist the white flag. Aragon shook his head. 'Poor Maginot did not live to see his task completed; was it a dish of bad oysters or diabetes that did for him? It was a dud, even as they tried to sell the idea; a memorial to his terror in the Great War; the colossal blunder of an idealist, with nightmares of No Man's Land, and a blessing for the building contractors. However, we cannot blame him for everything; the guilt of Painlevé and Pétain was greater. As War Minister, Pétain was in charge of the budget.'

'Well, the Marshal is back from Spain now, eager to serve the country in any capacity,' de Rothschild said. 'He has no strategy to halt Guderian's blitzkrieg. Most of my fellow officers are of the same ilk; they are all guilty of instilling fear into the men by reminiscing about their exploits at Verdun. Yet they remain sanguine, dreaming that they'll survive our present disaster.'

'Only one course remains: to drape her naked corpse with the tricolour before burying her with full honours,' Aragon said. 'Then Laval can make another fortune printing brothel passes for the Germans. Meanwhile, Gamelin is letting us rot in this death trap.'

'You heard the rumour that he shot himself?' De Rothschild smiled. 'Sadly, it is untrue. However, I can't see why he should kill a fine poet too. I want you and your men to fall back from this sector of the front, if we can call it that. Remember, too, that you will always find a welcome in the avenue Foch.'

They did retreat. After they had done what they could in each town, they waited until dark then crept off with the taste of disgrace in their mouths. Often they had to fight their way through the German lines, avoiding Arras and Vimy in the night. There, drifting flares lit up a village war memorial against which sprawled a headless French sergeant with a shattered rifle. At daybreak, there were the same corpses of civilians and soldiers near burnt-out trucks beside the road. They passed a bony old woman curled up in a wheelbarrow being trundled along by her husband. Their daughter perched on bicycle handlebars, with some poor chattels. A fire brigade was on the move; the men's families hung on to the polished tender with their canaries and sewing-machines, while their gramophone played an aria from an operetta as though they were on their way to a picnic. A fireman's wife smiled as she pointed to an old man playing *boulle* as he argued with his son. A girl, his daughter perhaps, was kneeling to change the tyre of their old Fiat.

Then there were more people with wagons and prams, blocking the way for tanks, guns, motorcycles and trucks. Some women limped along in high heels, hauling suitcases with sore hands. They no longer cared how they looked, though their clothes were chic enough to remind Aragon of Elsa. His heart was heavy as he tried to imagine what was happening in Paris. There were signs of defeat everywhere; every village had its white flags, sheets or table-cloths. Sometimes there was a scent of laburnum, but more often a stench of rotting horseflesh.

* * *

Matisse is gloomy. 'How will we sail from Genoa? The tickets will have to go back.'

'What then?'

'I have no idea. Nice is out of the question, if the Italians do invade. I don't want to stay here.'

Crowds of refugees mingle with troops at the Gare d'Austerlitz.

'Gauguin worked here when he used to paste bills around the railway stations.' Matisse points up at the glass roof. 'If a Zeppelin released its bombs now, the death toll would be awful; far greater than it was in 1918.'

'Never mind your Zeppelin bombs; Hitler sends Stukas, and they flatten everything.'

'Before Princep shot Franz Josef in Bosnia-Herzegovina, women idled on piers, showing off their finery; they wore white lawn dresses and twirled parasols. A thunder clap, and every shopkeeper barred his doors; civilians marched, drilling on the esplanades. Our newspapers became no more than a page of lies – the official communiqué. It took me a year to start any work. I had a visit from Derain, whose excitement and war fever left me feeling that I was missing something by not being part of the carnage. I played the violin to soothe my nerves and calm my uncertainty; as though music, or rather endlessly repeated scales, could stave off the war. What changes?'

Lydia returns from her audience with the station master. 'We can take eighty pounds of luggage. We shall have to leave two of the suitcases here.'

Matisse looks at the morning paper she hands him and finds that it has only four pages. The editor's apology says that these will shrink to two the next day. People are talking about the bombing of Le Havre and other ports.

The plan, if it is a plan, is to visit Castel Foirac, in the Gironde, where Matisse's dealer Paul Rosenberg is staying.

* * *

The anti-aircraft gun on top of the Arc de Triomphe poked up from a rampart of sandbags, as absurd as a pipe stem guarding the pile that took thirty years to build. It was Napoleon's victory arch; defeat loomed now, and the city's defenders loafed up there, sun-bathing, smoking, watching the people outside the cafés and shops. Elsa had often promised herself that she would climb the monument one day for a tourist view of Haussmann's *grands boulevards*; but the war had closed it to the public.

Alone in the city, she began to notice how many women were weeping and might start again at any time. One of them sat at her café table and began to talk about astrology and the fall of France, of Nostradamus and his prophecies. Her insight did not stop her tears; her eyes were just as red as those of any concierge whose son had left to join the army. She was a character who belonged to these new times; one of those victims whose name ought to be on the Rendezvous for Lost People lists seen now in Paris. Too depressed to send her packing, Elsa listened, nodding while she thought of a story she was writing: 'La Belle Épicière', named after Modigliani's painting. It started with a suicide pact, a couple jumping from the window of the Hôtel Providence.

As soon as the woman left, Elsa headed for the cinema again, where she spent most afternoons. Life was a dream, and nothing was more pleasing than to listen to Yvonne Printemps affirm it in song.

As she packed her suitcase she unearthed an old, faraway smell of Russia fading on an old dress. Where could she go, though, when she had finished? The weather was hot. Moths invaded the room to beat against the brown paper she had pinned around the lampshade. Each time the light bulb ebbed she thought of the power stations, then of the factories. Were they still working? It seemed suddenly essential to know that. There was still water, but she filled the bath daily in case they cut it off. The gas was so low it was useless to try to cook. The banks were closing, evacuating their clerks; angry, abusive, drunken troops looted the shops, crying, 'Down with the war!' All she could sense and share was the fear of French Jews.

* * *

At Carvin, near the La Bassée Canal, a tearful teacher showed Aragon the corpses of sixty schoolgirls lying on the pavement in the moonlight. The next day, the sultry heat brought a storm, its thunder echoed the barrage and intensified the darkness created by a burning slag-heap south-west of the town. As the British Expeditionary Force coaches passed the abandoned petrol station, a rumour spread that Franco had sent troops from Morocco to aid the Germans. This frightened the *zouaves* so much they almost mutinied, and might have done had they not joined the exodus. Carvin looked deserted except for dead cycle messengers; then Aragon glimpsed a boy and girl, gilded briefly by the day's one shaft of sunlight, before a wall fell on them. The light stayed with him; he was to use it in his *Défense de luxe* to describe Matisse's art.

* * *

'Why am I traipsing around the country in a dither what to do?' Matisse shakes his head. 'I must be mad. Of course I am not going to leave France.'

Several cars with Paris number-plates stop at the restaurant where he and Lydia sit eating on the terrace; yet more families arrive to try to find a table.

'I think it's atrocious that they expect the service to be what it was pre-war!' Matisse shakes his head in disgust. 'They want their steaks cooked to a turn, and served up with every trimming by a smiling waiter.'

When this does not happen promptly, the men grow hot and peeved. They are talking about shares falling on the Bourse. It is more worrying than the refugees on the roads or where they will sleep. They complain loudly again about not being served, curse the waiters, then damn them with a shrug. Their money is good; it should pay for anything, even an illusion that there is order. They want to forget their panic; they are not actors in a low comedy; it was their servants who tied the mattresses on top of their cars.

'They seem to think those mattresses will protect them against an air attack.' Matisse gazes with scorn. 'I see myself in these people; and I do not like it.' The thought that the fate of France will affect his work is both hateful and distressing: and that he is in flight mortifies him.

'I hate not knowing what will come next. Is this any way to live? I am a gypsy without a horse or a basket of pegs.'

'The country will fall; that is what will happen next,' Lydia says.

It is as though the whole of France has chosen Bordeaux as a refuge. Matisse feels reassured to see that the tram cars are still running through traffic-crowded streets, and that there are ships along the quai Maréchal Lyautey. The city is so full that refugees claim every chair and sofa in the hall of the Hôtel Splendide before the ten o'clock curfew. The porter tells him that the refugees sleep in their cars, using the toilets every morning to wash and shave before ordering breakfast on the terrace. If he looks across the square he will see His Majesty's subjects besieging their Consulate, in the same plight. There is no room, even for Henri Matisse.

The wife of Rosenberg's friend, with whom Matisse and Lydia have found a bed for the night, says, 'There are guards on the suspension bridge checking all identity cards.'

'Yes, the Gironde is under threat; they say that the Germans have seeded the river mouth with magnetic mines.' Her husband hides a grimace of distaste behind his napkin. 'Everything is chaotic. Roubier told me that the staff of Auxerre's asylum had fled, leaving their patients wandering in the fields. Because some swine saw fit to plunder the funds of the orphanage, there is no money to feed the children. Morgues across the country are full of corpses because the undertakers and gravediggers have run off to save their skins.'

'I cannot see how Rosenberg will reach New York,' says Lydia.

The wife hands the plate to Lydia. 'He has left it too late to get his art treasures abroad. He told me he has twenty-one of your paintings, seven by Bonnard, and thirty-three Picassos in the bank at Libourne, plus others in the villa he rented at Floriac.'

Matisse nods. 'Octave Duchez has agreed to run the gallery for the duration.'

In the silence that follows, children shout, playing hide and seek in the garden. When one of them runs into the dining room to hide, the wife scolds her husband for losing his temper by asking what sort of behaviour he expects with the world falling to pieces. Matisse sips his wine. 'The bookshops in Bordeaux seem to be busy, business was brisk; I saw heaps of Mauriac novels on display.'

'Well, he was born here, of course.'

If Matisse hears the porter's wife right, Bacharach is the name of the owner of the hotel. An aroma of onion soup stays with them as they climb the stairwell, until they pass a newly painted door. At the end of the landing, a fat man argues with a girl in a dressing-gown. Matisse catches the murmur of their conversation, but fails to hear what they are saying. He tries hard, because he feels that there is something amiss with the place.

'Madame says he's a painter.'

'He doesn't look like a painter; a diplomat, perhaps. I don't know why he's here.'

'The Germans are coming up the road.'

'He has money.'

'He didn't buy that suit in Prisunic.' The redhead, Marie, paints her nails.

'Is she his wife, or a mistress?'

It is not until pain forces Matisse to use the lavatory that he learns the truth. There are notices that show the porter at the Splendide has sent them to a brothel.

Lydia remains calm. 'A brothel is fine by me. At least this bed is comfortable. Some people don't have one.'

Matisse waves at the red shades of the wall-lamps with their drum-majorette gilt fringes. 'You can see what the place is, and that awful perfume everywhere ought to have given the game away the moment I set foot in the room.'

'Pleasures from the past?' Lydia smiles. 'What do they say?'

'Say?'

'The notices.'

'What they always say.'

A saxophone begins to wail across the alley. It will be a long time before the player is of any use to jazz.

Matisse sighs. 'My destiny is that of France; so it is hardly surprising to find myself, tired and melancholy, cast up in a brothel. I don't see myself as a coward. I am a Frenchman, what else could I be?' He groans. 'I am going to be ill. What I want is a pain killer. I need an aspirin. Have we any?'

Ciboure – my window opening onto Masson's garden, Mme Masson on the ladder

At seven in the morning they push through a mob of refugees and board the train to Saint-Jean-de-Luz. In Ciboure by noon, Matisse refuses to walk another step, and they sit debating how long it will be before Madame Masson gets home. They face the windows of the house on the Quai Maurice Ravel that command a view of the harbour and Saint-Jean-de-Luz across the Nivelle delta.

Matisse dislikes all the rooms that Madame Masson shows them. Lydia sighs wearily as they follow her through the house again. It has been a long day; she wants a bed before night falls.

'That?' Madame Masson turns on the staircase. 'Yes, there is another room; but you won't like it.'

One of the walls is yellow, with a dark engraving whose subject is hard to make out. The red Louis XV armchair seems to have been waiting for him, as he will tell Louis Aragon when they meet. Its living presence makes Balzac's Eugénie Grandet so palpable that he can smell her perfume. Yet he will not remember anything of this seance when he comes to paint the chair. Between the two windows, there is a mirror in which he can already see himself at work. Outside, there are steps to a garden path that leads up steeply until hidden by fruit trees. Nothing of the sky is visible. He feels that the place has been waiting for him. What Mallarmé said about Gauguin comes to mind: that it was uncanny how he put so much mystery into such brightness.

Matisse decides that the room will suit him very well.

Madame Masson says that it is not for rent.

Lydia folds her arms by the window, unmoving. 'Surely in our case you could make an exception. We will take the other rooms too, of course.' Her pale skin and hair seem to glow in the room, enhanced by contrast with their sallow landlady. Matisse seats himself with a sigh of contentment. He is in his studio, and there is no doubt. He picks up a magazine to learn that Max Factor, who sold cheap Hollywood glamour to the masses, coined the term 'make-up'.

Lydia is terse when, later, he passes her the magazine. 'Hollywood has always sold cosmetics; isn't that why the studios make films?'

Madame Masson's opinion is that the Basque coast is ideal for painters, the sky, the elements, the ultramarine fishing boats with their red smokestacks hunting for anchovies and sardines. Always uneasy with sea weather, Matisse prefers to draw the path that leads up through the garden, with his landlady on a ladder amid the branches. He feels at home. It is as though he can reach out and touch her dress. There is the red armchair, too, which he sets at various angles and spends long hours sketching. He would like to paint again, but has no idea when he will be able to.

The house where Ravel was born is only a short walk away. Each time Matisse hears the church bells, he tries to imagine the composer hearing them. A futile task, he decides. His other conclusion is that Ravel must have left as soon as he could, since sea weather had no place in his music. Style was everything to Ravel, just as it was in his pictures; a discerning elegance, a love of animals and children. Matisse hums a snatch from *L'Enfant et les sortilèges* as he strolls with Lydia, then says:

'Satie joked that Ravel refused the Légion d'honneur, but his music accepted it.'

* * *

Aragon came into polder country, which meant the sea was not far away. The sun shone on artillery pieces sunk in the canals, with their sights and elevation gear broken. Nearby, a British soldier neatly lined up several wireless sets, then hit them with a pickaxe while his grinning comrades sabotaged their truck with sledgehammers.

59

On the night of 28 May, Aragon reached the grey dunes at Mâlo-les-Bains. There, he lay in his sleeping bag reading the proofs of *Les Voyageurs de l'impériale*, reliving the news of the failure of the Panama Canal, which hit Paris in 1880.

Ferdinand de Lesseps, fresh from his success at Suez, was the obvious choice to build the canal. Mercadier, Aragon's hero, had shared this illusion when he bought shares in the Lesseps Company, along with thousands of French investors, all wanting to make their fortunes. Sarah Bernhardt gambled too, singing de Lesseps's praises in Panama at a gala performance to celebrate the first excavations. While de Lesseps basked in his Suez glory in Paris, his company cut through the jungles of the isthmus. How could he know that mosquito-infested tracts were selling for a hundred times more than their true value? The bankruptcy came swiftly, and Paul Mercadier and the other investors found themselves paupers. Later, in court, de Lesseps denied any part in stealing a third of the capital. The Jews were to blame, with their bribes to senators. He said he did not know how the rest of the money had leeched away in waste. Another 'hidden cost' had been the lives of the 50,000 coolies who died of yellow fever and malaria, more than in some European wars.

Aragon ate a biscuit as the light faded. It made each Very light burst brighter over the phosphor-glowing sea, as it washed ashore more corpses. He stuffed the proofs into his knapsack and closed his eyes.

Waking at first light, he remembered that his dream had been about Lewis Carroll's *The Hunting of the Snark*, with its insistent rhymes:

> *They sought it with thimbles, they sought it with care:*
> *They pursued it with forks and hope;*
> *They threatened its life with a railway share;*
> *They charmed it with smiles and soap.*

He had struggled to translate this agony in eight fits between the wars.

*   *   *

'In *La fenêtre bleue* there are spheres, rectangles and ellipses, one of which is a bright cloud floating beside a blue tree's tinted circles. Its thin trunk seems to sprout from the white chimney of a lamp with a green shade. It is not so much a trunk as a window mullion whose black holds different blues apart. I can see the roof of my studio in the distance. I place my ochre cast beside a vase of flowers, two of which are bright red. The vase balances on a floating dark blue mat. A mystery of a brooch lies on a yellow orange; above, is a mirror with a red frame. On the blue-green vertical to the left, I set a green Chinese vase.

'It is the view from my bedroom at Issy, yet how many shades of blue and green, tempered with white, go to make it such a nowhere place in this world, a place of meditation and calm.'

* * *

Elsa went to the cemetery of Père Lachaise to visit the graves of Proust and Honoré de Balzac. She wanted to feel a sense of continuity, a togetherness with a threatened culture.

After standing beside them awhile, she lay her flowers on Gerda Taro's grave, near the Communards' memorial wall.

Alberto Giacometti had made the monument: a horizontal block, with a split granite cube incised with Gerda's name and a line or two about her death. He carved a bird for her, and a bowl to catch water to sustain her during her journey through the underworld.

Gerda and Ted Allan were north of Brunete when they hitched a lift to Madrid. Three wounded men filled the rear seat, so they had to cling to ride on the running board of the General's touring car. Everything was fine; they had survived in one piece; they were happy, looking forward to a bath and fresh clothes in Madrid. Then, as the driver turned a corner, the car hit a Loyalist tank that was out of control, which crushed Gerda and Allan's legs. They took them to an American field hospital at El Escorial, where surgeons operated on Gerda during the night. She was deep in shock. At six o'clock on the following morning, she died.

Robert Capa learned of her death from a newspaper in a dentist's waiting room. He went to the offices of *Ce Soir* to have Aragon, who had heard the news from George Soria over the telephone, confirm the report.

Capa and Paul Nizan left with Ruth Cerf for Toulouse to bring Gerda's remains to Paris. They learned there that international law did not permit the transport of the dead across frontiers by air. Gerda's body arrived at Perpignan, where the Paris train awaited. The coffin still had piles of flowers from Valencia when it reached the Gare d'Austerlitz. Gerda's father began to moan in Hebrew. Capa's grief was such that Elsa led him away to his studio, where he wept all day until the funeral, refusing any food or drink.

Gerda's funeral was worthy of an anti-fascist martyr. After she lay in state at the Maison de la Culture, thousands of mourners with banners, flowers and music, marched the coffin to the Père Lachaise cemetery at 10.30 on Sunday morning, 1 August. It would have been her twenty-sixth birthday.

Aragon had stood at the graveside beside Capa, who hung weeping on his shoulder.

When Georges Sadoul came to call, Cartier-Bresson was photographing Elsa. Bresson had turned up out of the chaos of the defeat, a corporal in the army now. He still liked to think of himself as invisible, rolling film on as he took up his positions in the room.

Sadoul and Aragon had shared the apartment in which Elsa wrestled Louis into an armchair, breathless, pulling her skirt up to her breasts as she forced his hands between her legs. Nothing had mattered that night except the joy they gave each other. The party was to please Mayakovsky's new girl-friend, Tatiana. Elsa never knew why she chose that particular setting to make love to Aragon for the first time.

Elsa had soon led Aragon away from Surrealism, from Breton. Sadoul had gone with them to the Kharkov Congress. On the train there were writers, novelists and poets from every nation. She would awaken, a faint moon shining over the misty woods, worn out from casting spells over men and drinking too much vodka. Before they left Moscow, she and Aragon slept at Osip's apartment in the room where Mayakovsky shot himself, leaving his letter addressed to Everybody. Above their bed, Lili stared with glaring eyes, fiercely hypnotic on the cover of *It*. All Vladimir's books were there, just as he left them. Even now, she kept a handful of tokens he had won for her on café roulette machines in Paris.

'Any news?' Sadoul asked.

Elsa shook her head. 'The *flics* were here, asking questions. They said his papers had gone missing. I was not sure if they were doing the Gestapo's job or not. They took away my copies of Mayakovsky.'

Sadoul said she should try not to worry; the police would have enough problems soon keeping Paris intact for the Germans. One of his friends had been with the Citroën workers, demanding arms, when the police set about them, arresting ten men for being Communists.

There would be no defence of Paris by the people, as there had been of Madrid. There, they burned the churches; those that still had a roof became a garage, an arsenal, or a storehouse for bourgeois loot. Paris was in the pawnshop, waiting for its rightful owner to redeem it. To defend the city the people needed arms, but the spectre of the Commune was too real for that.

'What do you intend to do?'
'Go on sending telegrams in the hope that one of them catches up with his unit.'
'I mean, when the Germans arrive.'
'I don't want to think about that.'
'We will both be in the shit. You must leave Paris; it's not the place for you.'

All this time Cartier-Bresson hovered in the background. For as long as Elsa could remember he had been present to fix them at various stages in their lives. When he was not there he was in Andalusia, in Madrid or Mexico, seeking to snatch the living moment. In 1937, after helping Kline to make *Victoire de la vie*, a film on medical relief during the Spanish Civil War, he had worked for Aragon at *Ce Soir*. She watched his footwork, advancing, retreating, pausing after a quick skip. This ballet revealed how time was of the essence when Henri took his photograph. He was always chasing that exact moment when everything fell into place; the light, the architecture, the gestures of the actors: the man in the act of leaping a rain-pool behind the Gare Saint-Lazare.

It was amazing how his vigils brought forth such clarity and surgical precision. He had haunted Trafalgar Square during King George's coronation, capturing a sleeping drunk under Nelson's Column; above, His Majesty's loyal subjects stood on tip toe – none of them curious about the man's condition, except a child. The boy's expression was Cartier-Bresson's own; the curate blushing at the girl in Jean Renoir's *Une Partie de Campagne*.

Cartier-Bresson laughed. 'André Derain never thought he would be a bistro owner, until Jean offered him the part.'

There was no escape from time, from being an artist observed by other artists; any more than she could avoid being a Jew and a Communist, a member of a rare and threatened species to be captured on film. Cartier-Bresson's philosophy bore witness, caught her in the act; even at that moment when, missing Aragon, she felt lost and trapped.

Cartier-Bresson nestled his camera in the crook of his arm, and said that it was time for him to go. 'If you should hear from Louis; tell him I was thinking about him.'

Aragon's telegram arrived the next day. It urged Elsa to leave Paris: to go where?

*　*　*

Dunkirk was ablaze; a fine rain of grey ash falling on the oily sea. In the harbour, ships were sinking; others, already sunk, sent up a mess of flotsam and jetsam. There were rats, dead gulls, and putrid bodies floating amongst the debris. More corpses were lying on the sea front, legs sticking out from the gas capes and groundsheets draped over them. There were dead horses and dead men everywhere. Some bodies were naked; white faces stared up at the darkness made by a blazing oil storage tank. Stukas were strafing the beaches. They drowned out the firing of the Bofors and Hotchkiss guns, and left rising water spouts as they banked away.

On the mole, Aragon's men found maps, courtesy of the Luftwaffe. They showed the enemy ring around Dunkirk. The English version of the text called for the B.E.F. to lay down its arms; the other, in French, told them how their leaders had betrayed them.

Aragon found the bar in a narrow street that amplified the screech of broken glass underfoot. He paused at the entrance, feeling like the porter in *Macbeth*; a man who does not know his place, who does not know what is happening. There were racks of fading postcards on each side of the door: views of the Pyrénées Orientales and other sights that had the air of dreams now; a France in microcosm for which men were dying that afternoon. It was lunacy that any bar was open. The Germans had breached the mains, and there was no water in Dunkirk. Everybody was crazy with thirst.

Someone played an upright piano in the corner. Hard to see in the dimness, he wore a pilot officer's uniform and had a cigarette hanging from his lips. Aragon had stepped onto a sound stage lacking a script. He had no way of guessing what could happen next until an English soldier groaned. A kneeling woman rested his foot in her lap and was tearing strips from her underskirt to make a bandage. 'The bastards here already, are they?' He groaned again.

Aragon was right. There was no drink, but an old man gave him a glass of tepid Vichy water. The light came through an open, shuttered window in the rear of the bar, a sudden radiance that filled him with a sense of *déjà vu* until he remembered Matisse's *L'intérieur au violon*.

Having failed to board the steamer that sailed at dawn, laden with Moroccan troops who shrieked as it cleared the sunken hulks, Aragon's men sang 'Les filles de Camaret' to keep up their spirits. He could hear Kiki's version at the old Jockey cabaret, the girls in the bed with red curtains, as the mole rang with the blue lyrics. Camaret was a village in Brittany where Saint-Pol Roux lived, a poet Aragon praised at a banquet in his honour at the Closerie des Lilas, staring at the corner where they executed Marshal Ney, whose bronze statue with sword unsheathed seemed to be striding towards the park. He had too many such memories to fall prey to the futility and despair around him, made worse by a rumour that the wounded would not find a berth. This news had scared the Moroccans into shedding their bandages to leave a trail of bloody rags fluttering along the mole.

In the final hours, the deserters crawled out of their hiding-places. They joined those troops who had fought for nine days as a rearguard. They hoped to find ships waiting to take them home, and were dismayed by what they saw. The *Royal Sovereign* had come and gone with men. Aragon had seen a cross-Channel steamer ram the *Medway Queen*. The vessel stayed afloat, listing to port, with four hundred scared Frenchman aboard. At three o'clock, a French general and his staff acknowledged a slapstick salute as they sailed off in a motor launch leaving men standing to attention on the mole. Aragon smiled, and told them they must not feel too alone.

> *He dreamed that he stood in a shadowy Court*
> *Where the Snark, with a glass in its eye,*
> *Dressed in gown, bands, and wig was defending a pig*
> *On the charge of deserting its sty.*

The youngest of his men had tears in his eyes, but was manfully trying to hide them. Each man hoarded his own memories, which they did not intrude on others. This boy, however, missed his mother, and wanted to talk about her whenever he could find someone to listen.

'You will see her again,' Aragon promised.

On 3 June a torpedo boat came alongside the mole to take them off.

*   *   *

Matisse is drawing Madame Masson's garden again. 'I sketched nothing in Tahiti except a beached outrigger canoe and a rocking-chair. Chairs are a weakness of mine. Your baroque chair is quite exquisite. Anything to preserve the illusion that I am still a painter. I feel secure only when I am working.'

Thadée Natanson has heard that Matisse is staying in Ciboure, and has come to visit him. In the old days, Thadée and his brother published the *Revue Blanche*, a magazine that dabbled in anarchism and defended Dreyfus, with contributors such as Verlaine, Proust, Léon Blum, Gide and Mallarmé. Bonnard designed an edition, and Thadée wrote a shrewd study of Pierre's work. Even Thadée's suit seems to smell faintly of those lost days as he talks about Vuillard's arteriosclerosis being so bad that he could not leave Paris.

The master stares at him while he draws, trying to recall the name of the perfume that clings to Thadée Natanson's linen. He was Apollinaire's first publisher, who had dedicated a book of short stories to him. He talks of Bonnard and of Le Cannet, where he says things are still normal.

'This place is sure to stir memories. Ravel dedicated *La Valse* to Misia.'

Matisse says that the concierge at the Régina sent him a letter to assure him that Nice was normal too. He hopes now to get home as soon as he can; he is sick of paying food prices that are beyond a joke.

Later, a soft rain falls as they walk along the quay. 'I don't think that sea air does anything to promote that feeling of well-being the quacks promise it will.' Natanson laughs.

Matisse smiles. 'This weather could put me on my back for months!'

Fishermen are hefting their catch ashore; three grim women in stiff white aprons and canvas hoods hold up a herring to peer at its glazed eyeballs. One of them shakes her head and stares down at her shoe. None of this interests Natanson, intoxicated by grief. He sighs. 'I was fool enough to think that things could go back to being the same; yes, some days I did think so. I started the *Revue Blanche* for Misia. We chose the name because white was the sum of all the colours.'

Matisse nods, feeling that he knows all this.

Natanson is proud. 'Lautrec's poster of Misia was on every wall in the city, so vivid, so alive, as she skated toward the spectator in her grey fur cape and muff.'

'Her hat had spirals of dark green feathers,' Matisse recalls. 'Like those divine plumes Gilberte sported on the day that Proust saw her slip on the ice in the Champs-Élysées.'

This image gratifies and moves Natanson.

Matisse could see Misia next to Apollinaire at Picasso's wedding to Olga Khoklova. Cocteau was there too. It was a ceremony whereby Olga hoped to make a silk purse out of a sow's ear. She was the daughter of a Russian general, and a dancer in Diaghilev's Ballet Russe, where Picasso met her when he was working on the décor and costumes for Cocteau's *Parade*. That was how the general's daughter saw Picasso: as an up and coming designer of ballet scenery. Cocteau introduced everybody who was anybody to her tea parties in the rue La Boétie. Max Jacob dubbed the marriage Picasso's 'Duchess period'. 'Poor Olga, nor was she a great dancer.'

'Mallarmé saw Misia as the blind girl in the Andersen fairy tale who held in her hand the dust of the Wise Men's touchstone,' Natanson says. 'She stood before the book that held all the great secrets of the world; she opened her hand and a bright light fell on the page, illuminating everything. In the evening, she ran to him, laughing, a fairy with the cap of knowledge. When we buried our friend at Samoreau, that autumn day should have said more than it did about the awful passing of time. Sometimes my heart is as heavy as a stone as I speak those lines he wrote on Misia's fan.

'Others tired of the fashion, but Misia's craze for fans never waned. She bought them in Madrid on days when Edwards let her out of the room where he held her prisoner. No wonder Proust found two of his characters in her.'

It was Natanson's friend Octave Mirbeau who began the scandal when he brought Alfred Edwards to Misia's theatre box. Edwards was an actor out of melodrama, a crooked financier and owner of *Le Matin*. His father had been a dentist to a Turkish sultan and made his fortune selling false teeth. If you did not believe this story, then you had to accept that his wealth came from the opium trade. His son was already world famous as a scoundrel, a lecher, and a coprophiliac.

Natanson admits that Misia was never happy until she lay squirming at the feet of some brute.

'Of course the man was a fiend; she told me so. What possible charm could a man have who needed women to shit on his face?'

The rumour was that Edwards got Thadée out of the way by making him the manager of coal mines he owned in Hungary. However, a man Renoir respected could not have been as black as Natanson is painting him. Every week, Edwards used to bring a new doctor to see what he could do for Renoir. Matisse can remember him at a party bending coins with his fingers, and ripping decks of cards in half.

'The swine held off until I left for Koloschvar; then he began his attack, making telephone calls, leaving flowers.' Natanson touches a handkerchief to the corner of his eyes.

Matisse sighed. The war situation was grave enough without having to listen to this man dig up his private cemetery. How could he stop him?

Natanson blew his nose. 'I left her alone; I was to blame. Of course Edwards's tenacity would flatter her. She used to tease him until he had asthma attacks. The affair became more serious when Edwards used his wife and brother-in-law, Charcot, to pimp for him. His pursuit had become a persecution; Misia fleeing to Vienna on the Orient Express, when there was a sudden knock.'

Edwards had taken the next door compartment. Later, he did the same with every room in the hotel where she was staying. There was no one to whom she could turn. She sent telegrams to Vuillard and Thadée. Vuillard arrived first.

'I ought to have killed the swine; why didn't I shoot him?' Natanson lamented.

Vuillard was a poor bodyguard; he wept a great deal. He had been in love with Misia for years. He wept even more when Misia told him of the mess that Thadée had made of running the Koloschvar mines. He owed thousands, and only Misia could save him. If she would divorce Thadée, Edwards would pay off all their debts.

When Thadée arrived he confessed that he had lost everything and, worse still, that her brothers, Fred and Cipa, stood to lose the cash they had invested in the mines. There was no way that Thadée could protect her. Unless Misia gave in to Edwards, Thadée faced prison; already the idea of being one of the wealthiest women in France had done for Misia. She used Thadée's abject appeal to exorcise any feelings she had left for him. She surrendered to Edwards. He appropriated her.

'She came to the station to see me off. She broke her emerald pendant in half, and handed one of the larger stones to me. I went back to Koloschvar in tears.'

In the spring of the year that the Fauves burst upon the world, Misia married Edwards at the town hall in Batignolles.

All her friends remained faithful. Ravel dedicated his Introduction and Allegro for Harp, String Quartet, Flute, and Clarinet to Madame Edwards, née Godebska.

Thadée sighs. 'Bonnard came to visit me at Oulins. The war was almost over. Urged on by some idiotic patriotic spasm, I had gone there to manage a factory that made munitions. I used to sit and watch Pierre paint Reine. He had his dog Ubu with him, of course. It was all very cosy, until Marthe fell ill.'

'A friend wrote that he had heard the bombardment in the Bois de Boulogne,' says Matisse. 'Then, at the end of August, the frightened refugees began to arrive, flocking into Paris in rags. Renoir kept on painting his bunch of roses.'

Natanson nods. 'They were taking wounded soldiers to the Grand Palais, which had become a hospital. I have a clear vision of Misia staggering up the steps with a poor fellow clinging to her back.'

'At the outbreak of war,' Matisse says, 'Sembat was Minister for Public Works. I asked him what I should do; he told me my duty was clear, I had to paint fine pictures. I suppose that *La leçon de musique* was an anti-war painting. My sons were going to the front. I painted it in the hope that we were going to go on being a family, to convince myself that my boys would survive. I wanted the war over. I wanted us together, as usual. Pierre served in the tank corps, and Jean serviced aeroplanes for flight. Jean had already received his papers, and he left a day or so after I finished the canvas. Yes, he is reading in the bottom left hand corner, while Marguerite sits with Pierre at the piano. Amélie is in the garden, sewing. Everything is there, even a version of my *Nu couché* watching the goldfish in the pond.'

'It does not matter if we lose our possessions, we have to stay alive,' Natanson says. 'I have only memories; I can see no future. There is nothing to look forward to; there are only these awful upheavals.'

'You know you must get away, Thadée.'

'Yes, I know. I dreamt of Oslo last night. It was such a sterile town; if anybody typified the place it was Ibsen, peeking at himself in a mirror hidden inside his hat. I was joyful when I took Misia to Elsinore, so that she could scatter her violets where Ophelia strewed hers. She fell asleep on my shoulder as I steered our boat back to Norway.' Natanson shakes his head. 'Any private life now consists only of hideous partings – Europe is a Kafka nightmare.'

Matisse stands as a gust shakes the blue fishing nets and brings a quick downpour. He stares at his reflection in a rain pool shivered every so often by the wind.

'Go, Thadée,' he insists.

When Matisse tells Lydia about Natanson's visit, he is angry with himself both for listening to the old man's recital, and his willingness to fill holes in the narrative. Natanson wanted a squalid episode from his past to have the three-act majesty of Ibsen, rather than the tears and bathos of a farce. 'They were both without scruples,' Matisse says; 'having listened to his version of the affair, I know now why the country is in the state it is.'

What really troubled Matisse was that Natanson had stirred his guilt over Caroline Joblaud.

'Misia! He forgets that two million Mad-Hatter refugees picnic by the roadside in France!'

Lydia was playing Patience. 'I saw her once with Chanel. She had lost her looks. She was thin as a rake, yet moved like a jaded old movie queen. They say she sticks the hypo through her skirt whenever she needs morphine.'

An American, Varian Fry, arrives. He offers Matisse asylum at the Villa Air-Bel, near Marseilles; a point of departure for America. It is an offer that Matisse declines. Not long after this talk with Fry, there is a rumour that the Germans are hours away on the road from Bordeaux.

* * *

Aragon sat in the Mount Wise dockside NAAFI store at Plymouth. Around the walls of the ill-lit shed, the tired and wounded remnants of the B.E.F. had come to rest, waiting for labels to be tied to their filthy tunics, smoking cigarettes. Some were on stretchers; others shambled around with blankets on their shoulders, cadging matches, asking after their mates. Many were asleep, their hands between their knees, dead to the noise of ambulances that came and went along the quay in the afterglow of sunset. Aragon shared the general sense of relief and disbelief, amid a stench of sweat, oil, dirt, with a whiff of chloroform and carbolic each time the nurses wafted by. Other women came and went swiftly with their sudden scents, cups of tea, tears and telegram forms.

Aragon had tried to wipe away the greasy black spots Dunkirk's blazing oil had rained on his face and uniform. He felt tired, but could not sleep.

'Louis Aragon, isn't it?' The lieutenant jerked his mangy dog to a halt as he leaned down to seize Aragon's hand. 'Aragon, the Surrealist poet?'

There was no escape from the Snark.

> 'For England expects — I forbear to proceed:
> 'Tis a maxim tremendous, but trite.
> And you'd best be unpacking the things that you need
> To rig yourselves out for the fight.'

Aragon got to his feet and saluted.

The lieutenant waved the gesture away. 'We don't need any of that crap. The honour is all mine to meet you. I bring news. You and your men are to embark for Brest in the morning.'

A bell-tower in the town rang the hour as a sentry came to a halt with a clatter of hobnailed boots. Nearby, vessels groaned at their moorings. Aragon could smell the dog, Percy, which the lieutenant had told him he rescued from France. The man said he was something of a poet himself. Have you come across any poetry by David Gascoyne? You must know his book about you Surrealists. He writes some fine stuff now. We have Dylan Thomas, too, of course; I love his lines:

> *I see the boys of summer in their ruin*
> *Lay the gold tithing's barren,*
> *Setting no store by harvest, freeze the soils;*
> *There in their heat the winter floods*
> *Of frozen loves they fetch their girls,*
> *And drown the cargoed apples in their tides.*

'Correct me if I'm wrong, but isn't that syntax awry?' Aragon caught his breath. He was croaking badly, the result of shouting hard to make himself heard over the bombardment at Dunkirk.

The Englishman smiled. 'Poetic licence.'

Aragon grimaced. 'It would be good to get out of this uniform. What I need is a bath.'

'Yes. We all stink.'

'Impossible, I suppose?'

'Plymouth's baths are an arcane mystery to me.'

Aragon nods a mute acceptance.

'What time do we go tomorrow?'

'I don't know. That's the Navy's business.'

Leaving England at first light, Aragon had time to mull over how he and his men had been under fire for weeks. It was futile that they should go back for more. If the Germans did not kill him, their prison camps awaited. As he stared at the blue and green bow wave, his tiredness made him dizzy. He could see the circus the Stukas hit, the bleeding elephant screaming as it ran, and the dead body of a girl in spangles hurtle by, dragged by two white horses. Had it happened, or was it a bad dream? He could have lived it through someone else's eyes. He spread his groundsheet on the cold deck, and huddled next to his kit bag.

71

They hunted til darkness came on, but they found
  Not a button, or feather, or mark,
By which they could tell that they stood on the ground
  Where the Baker had met with the Snark.

In the midst of the word he was trying to say,
  In the midst of his laughter and glee,
He had softly and suddenly vanished away –
  For the Snark was a Boojum, you see –

A drunken, bleary-eyed corporal jabbed Aragon's chest, asserting loudly that he used to sell him a newspaper in Montmartre. 'You remember me, sir!'

Aragon felt shamed by the man's dogged familiarity. His blithe boast that France would win the war was also unnerving. It was too much to listen to him tell how he intended to set up a real business, a shop where he would sell coffee and cakes as well as newspapers.

Coming into Brest, there were oxy-acetylene torches showering sudden bursts of blue sparks in the hazy light of the dockyards. When they berthed, new weapons and trucks were waiting. It came as a shock to learn that the front was now at Vernon. La Chapelle-Réanville was near Vernon. It was there that Aragon translated *The Hunting of the Snark* with Nancy Cunard, learning how to print it on their nineteenth-century Belgian press at Le Puits Carré. It had not worried him then what crashes on Wall Street were doing to those Austrian banks that were as solid as rocks when Marx and Engels were alive. He did not fret about German industrialists financing Hitler's lumpenprole Brownshirts. His problem was Henry Crowder, a black pianist in 'Jelly Roll' Morton's Hot Peppers, who played better jazz piano than he did, and could make Nancy Cunard's cunt throb. His memory of those times and places was sharp and poignant; but his present happiness was greater, knowing that Vernon was only sixty miles from Paris, from Elsa.

The corn was ready to cut, but no farmer was reaping. There was a combine harvester on fire, burning a black scar on a tawny hillside of barley. Pigs and hens rooted for food in the deserted farmyards. It was as though some plague had killed the villagers. On the roads, where vehicles drove at different speeds, there were long delays. Several cars had crashed; German fighters had strafed others. The bourgeoisie had taken to the roads again; they were not fleeing from Belgium this time, but from Paris. His Surrealist dreams had come true wherever he looked; the artdéco Egypt of a Singer sewing-machine left beside a wrought iron gate with shield-bearing stone lions, a typewriter in a ditch buried under old files. There were love letters blowing across the fields, toys and dolls, dead animals, and all the human debris of retreat.

An old man sat honing his scythe. He did not look up the long time it took Aragon to drive past, then he went on mowing the roadside meadow, slicing down buttercups and poppies with the same slow, graceful stroke; Aragon knew the sound it made, even if he could not hear it for distant shell bursts.

* * *

Elsa's first encounter with the Germans was at Arcachon; they were at ease, their braces dangling like those of ordinary men as they washed and shaved. The tango 'Jealousy' was playing on a looted gramophone. Some of them whistled and waved as she drove by, urging her to fraternise. There was a scent of resin from the pines, laced with sea salt, a piercing invitation to swim, which she had not done for years.

* * *

There was all the usual chaos when Aragon and his men arrived at the front: dead telephones, rumours, nerves and fury. To reach the rundown hotel, which had the only restaurant, he passed a field kitchen for other ranks. A grimy cook leaned over a cauldron, empty cans strewn around his boots, ladling out stew. The men sat in groups, their mess-tins glinting in the sunset. They pointed out the hotel the colonel was using as his headquarters.

The colonel was too old for his command and had clearly lost his grip. His officers gave him scant respect as they came and went; his hand had shaken too much during his evening shave and the numerous cuts still bled. He was sitting at a table covered with red-and-white oil-cloth aimlessly brushing the crumbs away. Somewhere in the kitchen, a jar of pickles had broken and a girl was sweeping up the glass. The colonel waved away Aragon's salute, tossed his orders aside, and said he hoped that he had eaten because there was so much bloody fighting in the kitchen that nobody would get a meal.

At first light, German guns took off the roof of the battered garage next door. The colonel already had his bags packed; he tossed them into the boot of a Citroën as he told his batman to get a move on. The next shell hit the hotel and blew gas masks, boots and military overcoats into the street. The field kitchen had gone. A dog, which was nosing around the tins, went on to sniff an abandoned stretcher case. To have come so near Paris and failed to reach it, made Aragon feel forlorn; the colonel did not know whether it had fallen to the enemy.

It was five o'clock in the morning when the orderly woke Aragon and told him that a new batch of casualties had arrived. There had been an accident in the forest. Captain Guy de Rothschild's truck had overturned, killing one man and wounding the other passengers.

By six o'clock Aragon and his assistant finished jabbing morphine into the wounded and helping the medical orderlies set broken shoulders. They took de Rothschild to the room they shared and gave him a glass of whisky.

'This is an odd turn of events, don't you think?' de Rothschild said. 'We come through Dunkirk unscathed, return to Brest, but miss each other by a day or so.'

'You heard Pétain's broadcast yesterday?' Aragon asked.

De Rothschild nodded, filling his pipe. 'You were right about the Marshal's role. Another armistice, eh!'

'You should have stayed over there,' Aragon's assistant said.

'I take it that you mean I am a Jew.'

'What will you do?' Aragon asked.

'I intend to fall asleep now. When I wake up, I might feel more like addressing the problem. I think I shall go to La Bourboule. I can only visit Ferrières in my dreams.'

After more days of hit-and-run fighting, Aragon's division retreated until the fuel ran out. There was nothing more they could do; they had to surrender.

The enemy troops were the first he had seen alive; some of them had faded poppies in their helmets; all of them were younger than he, even the officer in charge. These specimens of Hitler's Master Race were soon handing out the stolen apples that bulged their tunics. The surrender took place in an orchard, whose owner, attended by a German medical orderly, was trying to die of shrapnel wounds.

Driving to Angoulême, Aragon urged his men to take his lead if any chance came up to shake off the armoured car and motorbike riders escorting them. Their tanks were full of petrol again, and anything could happen before they got there.

When he did decide to drive abruptly off the road onto a track that ran through an olive grove, he feared that his age would tell against him. Maybe he was crazy, too, imagining they could outrun the motorcyclists. His hope was that the gunner aboard the armoured car would miss. The olive trees took most of the bursts from the Spandau; both the cyclists crashed; one of them came out of it dancing like a dervish, beating at his blazing uniform. Aragon's men were fine, apart from a wounded corporal, who died when his head hit a stanchion.

There were more refugees with their carts and bundles, trudging with tired children into limbo. South of the Loire, a crowd of women surrounded his vehicle, pointing to the West, and shouting:

'Is this the way to Brest? We are looking for Camaret.'

Aragon shook his head; they were heading for the Aube, and all the country thereabouts was in German hands. Again the name of Camaret evoked Saint-Pol Roux's images: god-children as white as moonlight, and grandsires the colour of the stones of Calvary. He could hear those tinkling bells at Ronscavel hung round the neck of a great stone goat.

* * *

After teaching Elsa how to handle the gears on the steering-wheel of the Pontiac, her friend Arellano Marín drove her to eat at the Chapon Fin.

'Bordeaux is rife with Borgia plots, full of dark twists and turns. It is a foretaste of what is to come; it has sucked in swindlers, prostitutes and hopefuls. It is the terminus. The refugees have nowhere left to go. There is a rumour that the government is off to Vichy, where there are plenty of hotels. The city stood in for Paris in 1871, and in 1914 when the Germans were threatening to take the capital.'

Elsa had found Marín at the temporary Chilean Embassy.

'Who knows anything any more?' he said, handing her the keys to Neruda's car. 'I used the Pontiac more than Pablo ever did. We both know that I am doing what he would want. I don't care if it ends up in a ditch. I have no more use for it now. You must be careful, though; you know what conditions are like out there.'

She was crazy, of course, to search for Aragon at such a time. She would be wiser to wait until the death throes ended. 'Nobody is going to know where anybody is until after the war.'

'Suppose I do have an accident?' Elsa said.

'That would be the least of your problems. You should go; leave for America and find a place to wait until Louis can join you. Not many people know this, but the embassy of the Republic of Haiti will stamp your passport for 150 francs. Don't worry about money; I have plenty of money.'

Pétain spoke on the radio to say that the President of the Republic had asked him to assume control of the government, and that he would give his person to France to assuage its misfortune. The people had to remain calm and have confidence in the men who had taken charge of the nation's destiny at that fateful hour. 'It is with a broken heart that I tell you today it is necessary to stop fighting,' he said. He had spoken to the Germans the night before to seek an honourable end to hostilities.

*　　*　　*

Nothing is holding the country together except voices on the wireless. It is as though the armistice negotiators have vanished from the earth. Matisse listens to Pétain's voice float from Madame Masson's wireless, urging calm and fortitude, as he exhorts the people not to panic. Lydia, by the window, looks at her watch and wonders if the taxi is going to arrive on time. Had Pétain taken lessons from Sarah Bernhardt in public-speaking? 'The Dominicans are not famous for rhetoric, nor are military schools, yet he has every cheap stage trick at his command to stir one's emotions.'

The radio hammers Pétain's speech home with blasts of the 'Marseillaise'. Later, Matisse and Lydia will hear it again outside cafés over loudspeakers, along with other fools urging resistance until the Marshal can conclude an armistice.

Matisse shakes his head. 'These are the politics of Jarry's Ubu! All we need is a signboard saying that the action takes place in Poland – nowhere, that is. There is a fireplace, through which the actors enter and exit. Snow falls on the curtained bed. I see the boa constrictor coiled round the palm tree, the skeleton on the scaffold, the owls on the window ledge. The world waits for Ubu's resounding: "shit". It is the word Jarry chose to welcome us into his world; it very aptly describes our present fiasco.'

*　　*　　*

On the day France signed the armistice, Elsa's telegram, which she had sent twelve days before the Germans took Bordeaux, reached Aragon. A friend had seen it on the wire outside the post hut. How it had got there was a mystery, considering the state of communications in France. However, if her telegram could reach him, then it could be worth trying to contact her by the same means. He had reached Ribérac, where he waited in limbo to learn what was going to happen to the French Army.

Aragon won a Croix de Guerre in the Great War. He squinted against the sun as they pinned another to his tunic. It came with a divisional citation for his courage in Belgium when rescuing wounded men from behind enemy lines. Along with these, he won the Médaille Militaire for leading the escape from Angoulême. He bought the ribbon for the Croix de Guerre at Brest. It was nearly identical to one from 1915, green – but with five thin black stripes and narrow black edges. Holding it to his lapel, he looked like an old veteran; his past was dead; he was white-haired and respectable now.

In one of those Surrealist visions to which he was still prone, Aragon felt breathless, buried among worms crawling in the death's head of France. There were sailors drinking outside the bar, whose out-of-date tattoos of Empire showed faded serpents entwining Pétain's emblems of family and country. They were arguing about the terms of the armistice and what they might mean. One man was irate that France had to foot the cost of the occupation army. His friend was sure that Hitler was a man of honour who would not overstep the mark. One player was absent from the table when they were making the deal, a sailor said, that was Mussolini. Mussolini? They told him that it had not been an Italian blitzkrieg. Another sailor's advice was that Laval should shoot Pétain at once, and run the country himself. Laval was a man who knew how to talk to dictators.

More ratings joined them, along with the barber who had done their tattoos. Only the degree of their stupidity varied. There were cooks enough, the barber said, but only God knew what dish they were going to serve up. The cheer they gave him had more to do with the tray of drinks he carried. One sailor was sure it was going to get worse ashore; he couldn't wait to get back to sea.

None of it was going to be easy.

* * *

As soon as she received Aragon's reply to her telegram, Elsa bought a nurse's uniform. Her idea was that it might help in obtaining petrol, and that it would probably make it easier to stay at a military camp. It was

77

eight months since she had seen him. She was afraid. She was a stateless Jew without a country, who would have to live with Aragon as an outlaw. There was now a decree in force that made the dissemination of Communist literature punishable by death. It seemed certain now that the Gestapo would enforce this law.

* * *

The old widow Elsa picked up told her stories about the looting she had seen during the flight from Belgium. She said she was going to her daughter's farm. She was old enough to remember the last war, but the present business was far worse. 'People have gone mad. If you are old and weak, you are the first they fall upon. Women are being raped, knifed and drowned in rivers. Never take chances with strangers. Be wary of nuns; many of them are German soldiers in disguise. You should not pity anyone, even me.'

As soon as she was alone again, Elsa took off her uniform, afraid to come upon anybody in need of treatment. She did not want to dash any hopes the uniform might raise.

She got lost using local roads; they lacked signposts; and the widow was right when she said that people would not help. Somebody else was on the wireless pleading with refugees to clear the roads, to stay where they were.

Aragon was not at Ribérac. It was a market town full of German-speaking refugees from Alsace. Later, Aragon would tell her that the poet Arnaut Daniel had lived there. After driving all night, she found a camp that was more of a dump for war surplus, full of ruined tanks, trucks and heaps of steel helmets. There were soldiers idling to blasts from loudspeakers, being ordered out of one row of wooden huts into another. Elsa did not know why there were so many dogs; they led them around with all the same fuss that women used to walk poodles at the seaside. The Germans could have already taken over. A pair of glossy cart-horses went by, hauling an artillery caisson in a cloud of ochre dust, as she stood talking to the captain, who flipped a glove to boost the shine on his belt as he told her she might find Aragon at Javerlhac. She could try Nontron, if she didn't find him at Javerlhac.

* * *

Matisse waves his hand emphatically. ' "Art is a circle, you're either inside or outside, by accident of birth," as Manet used to say. I feel a great kinship with him. Above all, he was a painter; he dealt in colours, slabs and slashes of colour, not moral pieties; and he was a genius at pictorial invention. Think of the blonde behind the bar of the Folies Bergère. There is such a loud emptiness in the bright electric light of the mirrored audience under the trapeze artist's green pumps. Do you doubt Manet's technique? Study the faces of Berthe Morisot and Fanny Claus in his balcony group; ask yourself how they could be the work of the same artist.

'What can I say about *Olympia*? There were nudes galore at the time – why, then, did Victorine's nakedness create such a scandal? Manet gave her a sallow belly and dirty flesh tones. Her feet were not very good, which is probably why he painted her wearing mules. The colours would be more vivid then; age clouds all our colours. It was an unwelcome anatomy lesson that gave great offence; the black maid proffers the client's bouquet, and it all speaks of the coming mechanical ritual of the bidet.'

'Do you know that you often speak as though I'm not here?' Lydia says, loosening her veil and folding it back over the brim of her turban hat.

* * *

Aragon had often ridiculed the line: 'He drank her in with his eyes'. It was a line from a novelette; yet it had an exquisite ring of truth now as he drew Elsa to the table, forcing her down on his knee to kiss her mouth, thrusting with his lips and tongue. Her mucus tasted thick and salty; he had to stifle his cry of joy when she found his prick; her teeth hurt his nipples and made his throat tight. Her presence was healing, that night. He had been edgy since dawn, a victim of a black fit; now he felt calm, taken into a sanctuary of precious relics that augured visions and miracles.

The croaking frogs woke them early, nature going about its business as usual.

* * *

Matisse and Lydia stay overnight at Pau. The hotel is full of refugees hoping to reach Spain or Portugal. Matisse shakes his head; the food is cold; he is in another ridiculous situation. 'I want to go home. Our next port of call could be some awful asylum, with a bed among cretins.' It has upset him to learn from an old newspaper that Vuillard had died of a heart attack at La Baule. 'Poor Bonnard, Vuillard's death will come as an awful shock.'

Jézureau arrives early and waits outside the hotel for the great painter. He has been awake since the early light, cleaning his taxi, sprucing up the dingy interior with carnations. He has had the honour of seeing Matisse's paintings in Paris, and is elated that Madame Delectorskaya has hired him to drive them to Saint-Gaudens, never mind that the day is going to be hot.

Jézureau helps them to load their luggage, lashing some of their suitcases on the roof. The car starts after some trouble cranking the engine, and they set off. The road to Saint-Gaudens is clear except for a fiacre they overtake, a dusty horse-drawn relic that has not been out since the eighteen hundreds. Matisse remembers dozens of sketches he made of them when they filled the streets of Paris. He sighs. 'Manet drew them too, standing at his studio window in the rue Mosnier. Their customers paid the cabmen quickly, then sauntered off to ogle each Nana who sat waiting. Everything has gone. A whole world vanished when the carriage passed away: the sound of rain on canvas, that charming jingle of harness. We have lost all the craft: the artistry of the coach builder, the skill needed to train horses and men – to say nothing of those wonderful horse farts that brought nature home to us in the heart of the metropolis. I can remember when the critics said that the Impressionists had declared war on beauty; when they reviled Cézanne as a madman with delirium tremens.'

Jézureau has to shout over the roar of the engine as he urges the taxi along the mountain road. 'My father died at Verdun. I was eight years old. I am lucky; they decided I wasn't fit for the army. They left me to marriage with Félice and caring for our goats – yes, we make our own cheese, madame. Soon a man will be glad of his goats. I think we should find some shade, so that I can give the engine a rest. If we don't stop, we'll be in trouble before we reach Saint-Gaudens.' He laughs. 'My wife went off to Mass when I told her I was driving you. She hears more voices than Joan of Arc, maybe that's why she never pays any attention to me.'

Matisse sighs. 'Our "Tour de France" has become too much for me. I don't want any more.'

Matisse sits with the car door open sketching the olive trees. The sky is cloudless, a clear blue. In the distance, women with scarves tied around their straw hats stir up a cloud of dust as they work across a field.

'When I was learning to care, I was young; since then, I have found that caring is never easy. To care, you must not be afraid of what could happen to you,' says Lydia. 'Do please tell your wife how much we enjoyed her cheese.'

Jézureau smiles in agreement.

They find a room at the Hôtel Ferrière. Sometime in the early hours, the British Navy attacks the French fleet at Mers-el-Kébir. When the full picture emerges, Matisse learns that the Anglo-Saxons have sunk or put out of action the French fleet, with the exception of the *Commandant Teste*, four submarines and some destroyers that reached Toulon on the following day. France buries its dead sailors, while three hundred and fifty others lie wounded in hospital.

Matisse is angry. 'It is how the Anglo-Saxons behave. They are the same butchers who burned Joan at the stake.'

'Did you expect the Royal Navy to hold fire while Pétain and Laval debated which side they're on? Anybody could see that this might happen; even you, if you had thought about it.'

'I won't ask you to explain what you mean by that.'

'The English intend to fight; of that you can be sure.'

'You are saying that Pétain had a choice; that he did not have to agree to an armistice?'

'You don't read the papers properly. Some headline catches your eye, and your pity for dead sailors makes you see red; you revile everything Anglo-Saxon.'

'England is as guilty of war-mongering as Hitler. He has been cashing cheques on the Bank of England since his Brownshirt days. The Anglo-Saxons have used him from the start, ever since the German industrialists made him their creature.'

'Do you believe that?'

'Do you think it is the politicians who decide such matters? The powers of which they dream come with strings attached. They are dancing consorts; the monkeys rather than the organ grinders.'

'You slept badly, otherwise you would not get so heated.'

'Can you tell me what war is, other than an endless calamity that piles up corpses of soldiers and civilians? It is a monstrous event, always unthinkable yet always the same. Yes, we can be sure of the dead bodies; there will be plenty of graveyards and ruins when it's over.'

There are views of the Pyrenees, sunset's cloud chasms; but mountains have never said much to Matisse. The other guests are losing their fear and panic. They are the usual holidaymakers until they speak of their escapes and tell their sob stories. They drink cheap wine in the mountain villages, then return, tipsy, laden with melons and pumpkins. Some of them say that they will head for Paris just as soon as Laval can enrol France in Europe's New Order.

One of them, an old woman, grabs Matisse's arm to quote Paul Claudel to him:

'After sixty years, France is free from the yoke of the radical and anti-Catholic party; from schoolmasters, lawyers, Jews and Freemasons. The new government invokes God and restores the Grande-Chartreuse to the religious orders. There is hope that we may escape from universal suffrage and parliamentarianism; and also from the evil and imbecile domination of the schoolteachers who covered themselves with shame in the last war.'

Then Lydia arrives and gently ushers her away.

'You're right, what has Mers-el-Kébir to do with me?' Matisse decides he can do nothing about this disaster. 'What can I do about anything, except work to make my paintings as beautiful as possible? I am the way I am, and I must live with it.'

*   *   *

Demobilised in July, Aragon and Elsa joined their old friends the Pozners at Varetz, near Limoges. There, Aragon's friend, Renard de Jouvenel, had his château, Castel Nouvel. Colette had been the wife of the Baron de Jouvenel's father: her heart-shaped face seemed to haunt the mirrors in the smoky candlelight, coming and going behind Elsa's shoulder as de Jouvenel turned the pages of the photograph album. His stepmother wears tights at the Moulin Rouge; she makes a balloon ascent – and here she is, down again, grateful to smell the flowers of the earth.

Beyond the mossy urns on the parapet, the garden was heady with Colette's scarlet roses, scenting the night where her nightingales sang.

At present, de Jouvenel told them, Colette and Goudeket were unwilling guests at Curemonte, staying with his half sister, Bel Gazou. 'Colette is desperate to get back to Paris, but there is no telephone, newspapers, or gasoline.'

Finding Schwob's translation of Defoe's 'Moll Flanders' in the library, Elsa decided that she would read it.

At first, Aragon was happy to escape the world of army duties and strictures, and Elsa shed her feeling of wayward loneliness. Soon, though, growing ill at ease with a sense of loss, he spoke of his feelings in a poem he called 'Le Zone Libre':

> Cross-fade of grief to nothingness
> The crushed heart beat falters,
> The coals turn white and lose their fire;
> I drink the wine of summer's hazes
> Sheltered by a rose castle in Corrèze,
> Dream forging in this golden August.
>
> What is it that swiftly brings
> A sound of sobbing in the garden,
> Reproachful murmurs in the air?
> It is too soon, ah do not wake me;
> Let this laden burst of song free
> Me from the barracks of despair.

They lazed the afternoon away eating the ice-cream Ida made, while squadrons of Heinkels and Junkers left Villacoublay, Chartres, Tours, Laon, Combrai. High over the Pas-de-Calais, the bombers met their Messerschmitt escorts from Dieppe, Abbeville and Saint-Omer for the onslaught on British airfields.

When the sun went down, they gathered in the library and tuned in to the B.B.C. to listen to the result. It amazed Pozner how the British would report these deadly aerial battles over Kent and Sussex; as though each wave of enemy bombers was some boorish visiting cricket team.

Elsa studied her face in the long mirror: a burnished spectre at the heart of the glare of red-gold light flooding the room. Aragon and Pozner were still rejoicing in those unnatural scores, while the swallows swooped to feed above the crumbling stables.

'It took Hitler a month to smash Europe, so there has to be a reason other than military why he does not invade Britain,' Pozner said, after brooding in silence. 'The reason is that the same class runs the country as here. Drieu's novels were full of them before the war. They will be waiting to welcome the Nazis, just as they did here.'

They spent hours in a long post-mortem over the corpse, the betrayal of France. Then they argued over which pre-war cultural event said most about what was to come. Pozner opted for René Piachaud's Comédie Française staging of Shakespeare's *Coriolanus*, sponsored by Action Française, which led to riots in the streets of Paris. 'Coriolanus must rise again, with an authoritarian policy to get the country back on the rails,' he said. 'I don't wonder that they let an ex-*flic* take over the theatre. It was only days later that Brownshirts began to burn books at the Berlin Opera House.'

'Stalin's attack on Finland and Poland had a strategic reason,' Aragon said. 'The Soviet Union has influenced events in Europe ever since the Revolution, because of capitalism's fear and hatred of Bolshevism. In that sense, the Soviet Union was Hitler's midwife. His swift rise to power was the result of the growth of Communism in Germany.'

'So you say, but that fails to explain why Stalin feeds the butcher,' Ida said. 'Nor can I see why *L'Humanité* should take comfort from workers fraternising merrily with German soldiers. Bravo, comrades, they say, keep it up; it will enrage the stupid bourgeois.'

It was a cloudless morning. They sat around on the terrace watching de Jouvenel speaking to the postman, who leant on his bicycle. Pozner said that he had begged Nizan not to resign from the Party when Stalin signed the Nazi–Soviet pact. 'I was harsh. I regret my hard line, now that he's dead. Has it ever occurred to you, Louis, that you have a contemptibly short memory?'

'Because I can shed no tears for Comrade Nizan?'

'He died at Dunkirk. Why do you still call him an enemy of the people?'

Aragon shrugged. 'A lot of good men died there. His fear of death finally caught up with him.'

'You are very callous,' said Ida. 'He was your friend.'

'Nizan was a traitor.'

'Can you be sure of that?' Pozner shakes his head. Perplexed, he reminded Aragon of his friendship with Nizan; their joint editorship of *Ce Soir*. They had joked together at the Writers' Congress in Kharkov.

In the same wistful mood, Pozner spoke of Malraux's passage to Moscow, sailing from Southampton aboard the S.S. *Dzershinsky*, with his wife Clara and Ilya Ehrenburg. 'As they went through the Kiel canal, the German workers lined up to give the red flag a clenched fist salute,' he said. 'They will be dead by now.'

'Louis had Rimbaud and Zola high on his agenda, of course,' Elsa said. 'Whereas Malraux was linking art with conquest, as usual.'

'Only Radek had the guts to attack him over his speech,' Pozner said.

'Your friend was drunk. I always wanted to pull that silly wisp of his red beard.' Ida laughed, then went on, 'He could speak seven languages, yet they stood him in front of a firing squad!'

'The armistice means that Laval and his cronies can get on with their pre-war pursuit of wealth and power,' Pozner said. 'Renault will find it easier to deal with his workers' wage demands. He will ship them to Germany if they ask for too much.'

'France will be undone by its business-as-usual attitude,' Ida said.

'What will happen to Indo-China, West Africa, Madagascar, Martinique?' Elsa asked.

'No colony can muster an army to liberate France,' Aragon said. 'Besides, the *colons* will choose Pétain. The French Army fears the unknown. De Gaulle is the unknown.'

De Jouvenel came onto the terrace waving a letter. Elsa shaded her eyes from the sun as he handed it to her. It was from her sister Lili.

Aragon lay with Elsa, listening to the owls. 'Malraux heard a storyteller sing of Sheba's beauty, in Isfahan,' he said. 'The mad poet brought the queen to life again every day in the market-place. Malraux wanted to fly off at once to find her city. He started in Cairo, with a visit to the Valley of the Kings and a quick look at the Pharaohs' funeral masks.'

'A crash course in archaeology to whet his appetite,' Elsa said.

'Max Jacob foresaw a fiasco when I told him why the Malrauxs were going to Indochina. I don't know what he said when André and his new partner in crime flew north from Djibouti. They were sure that some ruins and tombs they saw from the air were the remains of Sheba's kingdom. The telegram about their near crash went out to the world. It was another brush-with-death experience for Malraux to boast about.'

'He had to listen to it all again at the Writers' Union Congress, when he wasn't head to head with Eisenstein, plotting to film *La Condition Humaine*, or dragging up Sergei Kirov's death in Leningrad.'

A car arriving set the dogs barking. 'Who is that, at this hour?' Aragon went to the window.

'Stalin again?' Elsa ventured, with a laugh.

She could see Maxim Gorki wince as Josef Vissarion arrived at the *dacha* late at night. How Malraux, when Stalin asked what was the latest thing in the West, talked about a Laurel and Hardy movie.

'Somebody can't find his way home after too much to drink,' Aragon said, turning away from the window.

'Clara lost control over her knees whenever she came near Stalin. If he had given her a wink – who knows? I can't think that such a fling would change history, but it might have threatened André's romance with the Party. We have all lost our way,' Elsa laments, reverting to the death of Radek and the cheering Red workers of the Kiel canal.

* * *

On his slow road to Nice, Matisse reaches Carcassonne, where he tries to paint some peaches. He never tastes any food he paints; but, relaxing his rule, he ate a couple of peaches before starting work, and is convinced they have caused the attack of enteritis from which he is suffering. The belladonna Lydia bought for him has been useless so far, and the lavatory where he groans without relief is not roomy enough to turn around in. There is nothing in the newspaper to offer an escape from misery. The state of the country is unbelievable. He lapses again into the old fear that his illness is something more than gripes and runs caused by peaches.

When he stands, he notices that the cistern has a delicate floral pattern, which charms him enough to sketch it; the window is open and he can see a woman beating a carpet. Through the dust haze she creates there are glimpses of the citadel's walls and defences. It pleases him to redeem the cistern's pattern from the limbo of its lowly station, to elevate it, to affirm its creator.

Lydia finds Air-France's offices built into the city wall. A plane to Nice is out of the question; there is a military order in force banning all internal flights until further notice.

When Lydia arrives at the café in the square, Matisse tells her that Carcassonne owed its existence to war. He wipes his neck with a handkerchief. 'Cloth merchants built the citadel to defend the road from Spain. I find the citadel very imposing. I suppose we owe it to the fact that things were not too good in those days either. There was no real freedom. Why is it that we think we are more deserving of freedom? They accused the Jews here of poisoning the wells, then slaughtered them. If they did not poison the wells, then it was a fact, people said, that they had spread the plague by trading in the clothes of the dead.'

'Quite as many Christians as Jews must have died,' Lydia points out. 'If the Jews poisoned the wells, why did they go on drinking from them?'

Matisse tells her of the plot hatched in Toledo, whose Rabbi Jacob sent poison hidden in an egg. 'They tortured a Jew to get this confession, then used it to destroy other Jews in Carcassonne and Narbonne.'

* * *

'If Zola had been a painter he would surely have chosen *The Ball at Suresnes* as a subject,' Aragon said, handing the book to Pozner. 'Derain copied a photograph.'

In the painting, a short-arsed officer with a bristling moustache danced with a tall spinster as though on a stage. His small stature obliged him to hold her below the waist, so that his white clown glove plastered her hip, while his genteel little finger seemed to point the way to later sexual advances.

'Quite how he will manage that, I've no idea,' Elsa murmured. 'She looks so sober and joyless.'

'Derain always had more insight into theatre and character than Matisse,' Aragon said.

'How cleverly Derain makes his gloves echo his white spats, and how that serves to accentuate the mincing way he dances,' Ida said.

'His fellow savages are primed for anything,' Elsa observed; 'ready to gallop off and put workers to the sword.'

There was another glorious sunset. Elsa walked in the grounds with Ida. Workers talked together on ladders among the fruit trees; women smoked as they stood around the laden baskets, they laughed as if the war could never touch them. Elsa turned to Ida. 'I can't bear to listen to them. You'd think there is nothing amiss. When are they going to wake up?'

'We plan to go to America,' Ida said. 'Where are you making for?'

'Here, there; somewhere in the Free Zone, where we can organise some sort of resistance,' Elsa said.

Arriving in Carcassonne from Varetz, Aragon and Elsa joined its jobless citizens. They were penniless except for what Aragon had of his army pay; they mingled with throngs of men who owned only their uniforms, from which they had stripped all insignia. These men wore armlets that said '*démobilisé*'. There was no work in the vineyards, whose owners came with their cartloads of casks to sit in the shade of the place aux Herbes offering samples of their wine.

Their landlady had spent her life selling groceries before her retirement. She had an oil painting of Pétain over the fireplace, and she often spoke fondly of the Marshal as though he were her son. He would bring France through those dark days if anybody could; though of course the country was in error; it had sinned, as the Marshal said on the wireless. She knew that her faith in Pétain meant nothing to Aragon and Elsa, and that the police suspected them of being enemies of Vichy. However, Aragon's lovely poems sang of Elsa's beauty; they were poor, and their plight touched her.

'There is an obvious solution,' she said. 'I shall have to set you up in a grocery shop. It will give you an income until you sell your work, and if things get really bad you can eat the food. I think it's a perfect idea. If the police come pestering you, as they did yesterday, you must show them your medals again.'

At night they joked about Pétain haunting the house, his boots creaking as he searched the rooms for *la France éternelle*. Elsa said it was more likely that he was looking for the landlady's bedroom; while his hard-on itched and ached in the dark, ready for trench warfare. No, Aragon opined; he was going about like an old soldier, greeting the ghosts of old soldiers, with the observation that they could only be loyal to their country in one way. Nothing would ever come between him and his image of France: slumps, strikes and lock-outs, scandals and racketeers could not wreck his vision, nor was defeat going to disturb his narcissism.

Aragon's publisher Gaston Gallimard was in Carcassonne with his wife and old mother. He was so unsure of the times that he refused to advance Aragon any cash. Jean Paulhan and Germaine were there, too, with his mother; as was Julien Benda, whose insight into medieval doctrines chimed oddly with his need for the latest B.B.C. news. His work found no publisher now, nor did that of Romain Rolland and others. It had been the Dreyfus Affair that revealed the true face of France to Benda; but, despite all his penetrating pre-war insight into the treason of the clerks, the war had washed him up in Carcassonne.

Aragon had made a start on his new novel, *Aurélien*. In the evenings he and Elsa joined other exiles at the court of the poet Joë Bousquet, who had been blind and bedridden since the First War.

At night in Bousquet's shuttered room, the perfume of the women vied with the sour odour of Joë's bedridden body. The audience sat, eager to hear Aragon's poems that spoke of love for Elsa and France, despite warning him against such readings.

Aragon stood up to read his poem 'Printemps'.

> *Long halloos from barges on the Scheldt*
> *Shook the night, like a warm girl, from sleep:*

The radio warbled a cheap love song
So love-imbued it hurt the heart.

Sprawled on deck, a man lies beside his
Dreaming girl. Did I dream, too? Hearing a voice
Call out a promise − 'Be seeing you' − another
Mutters, 'Men die in Norway now.'

People of the border, whose longing drifts along
Slow as old canals, to countries with a foreign name:
Here Belgium ends, here France begins; and here,
Though flags may change, the sky remains the same. . . .

'I'm Pierre Seghers; your poems moved me deeply. I am the editor of *Poésie*.'

Aragon saluted Seghers with a warm handshake, and said how much he admired the magazine and knew his name.

'The version of 'Les Lilas et les Roses' you read was not the one *Le Figaro* printed,' Seghers said.

'I had nothing to do with that; it has given me nothing but trouble since its publication. Pétain's gendarmes are after me now in Carcassonne.'

'Bousquet told me how upset you were by Roux's death. What I am asking is whether you would write something about it for *Poésie*. I know Joë lent you Pol Roux's manuscripts.'

'Give me an hour to do it,' Aragon said, sitting at the table by the window.

Saint-Pol Roux's murder had merited only two lines in a Vichy newspaper. There were no details until Aragon learned the truth in a letter from Morocco. Some drunken German soldiers shot the poet as he tried to stop them raping his daughter, Divine.

Aragon found Nadar's photograph of Pol Roux among Bousquet's collection of manuscripts. The face was a living link with Baudelaire. It reminded him of the banquet the Surrealists gave in honour of Pol Roux, when they attacked Paul Claudel, saying that his skin was not elastic enough to contain a French ambassador and a poet at the same time.

* * *

As they leave the Gare Saint-Charles in Marseilles, Matisse pauses on the steps leading to the boulevard Gomier, staring at the mountains beyond the town and the glittering steeple of Notre-Dame de Garde. 'I can see

Marius with his back to us in the café again as he stares at the ships in the harbour,' Matisse says. 'Marcel Pagnol is everywhere. It's good to smell the sea.'

A woman greets them shrilly outside a café as they walk in the Canebière. Lydia mutters that it is Maria Jolas, leaving him to greet her.

'This is amazing! How wonderful to see you!' Maria Jolas pecks twice at Matisse's cheek.

He has never known quite what he feels about this woman, nor how to deal with her. Maria McDonald Jolas is a Kentucky woman, of Scottish descent. She and her husband, Eugene, published *transition* before the war, an international review for creative writing. Matisse met Jolas when he was illustrating *Ulysses*.

Madame Jolas grasps suddenly that he is in the dark. 'Marguerite hasn't told you?'

'You are saying that my daughter's here?'

'You didn't know?'

'I have heard nothing from her since I left Paris. Why is she here? Is she with Amélie?'

'No, she is fixing up a passport so that I can take your grandson to America with me.'

'America? I don't understand you.'

'Georges wants Claude with him in New York. Margot has agreed; though parting with the boy will not be easy.'

Maria had to transfer her pupils from her Neuilly school to Saint-Gérard-le-Puy, near Vichy. Then Eugene cabled her to come home as soon as she could arrange a passage. She is in Marseilles to arrange passports. Joyce? He is almost blind now, and with his family in Gérard-le-Puy. She has been trying to persuade him and Nora to come with her, but they could never decide about anything. James spent his time correcting misprints in the manuscript of *Finnegans Wake*, which he wanted her to take to America.

In the hotel restaurant there is a large mirror all the way to the top of the stairs, where an aquarium shines on the gloomy landing. On the wall of the dining room, some local dauber has left a mural instead of paying his bill: a Last Supper of French sailors done so woodenly that it depresses Matisse. Over the years, cigarette smoke has aged the crude colours, dimming the red pom-poms on their hats. He sits so long with a cigarette dangling from his lips that the waiter steps over and offers to light it.

'Could I beg one of those, monsieur?'

Matisse proffers the packet, and the waiter takes one, saying, 'Maybe not yet, but tobacco will soon be scarce.'

'You may be right.'

'We have to import it; ships will carry other cargoes, of strategic importance.'

Matisse nods.

'May I bring you another coffee, monsieur?'

'I suppose so, since coffee is going to vanish, too.' Matisse hooks his stick over his arm, and enquires whether Madame Duthuit has returned yet.

The waiter will ask at the reception desk. When he returns with the coffee, he says that she does not seem to be in her room. Matisse watches as he strips each table, and bundles the cloths into a laundry skip.

'An afternoon at Issy,' Matisse murmurs aloud. He glances across at the waiter, who gives no sign that he has heard him. He sighs again, in the garden, in the shade under the trees. Margot's shoe dangles from her left foot as she sits with Antoinette Arnoux at the rose marble table. It is the same table he painted two years ago under the dark linden tree, with ivy around its base. The tea urn is almost plumb centre. Both chairs are green, each a subtly distinct shade. The dog, Lily, scratches her ear, panting before dropping her jaw onto her paws. It is too hot for the birds to sing; the sun stipples the path leading to the gate. The title is obvious; he calls it *Le thé*; simple, yet as symbolic and complex as any motif in Proust.

Matisse sketches Claude, talking while Marguerite paces to and fro in the hotel room. 'Do not send him to Georges, Margot. I see no reason why he cannot stay here.'

'Everything will change here, especially our schools; do you think I want him to grow up a fascist, Father?' Marguerite demands. 'Germany has defeated us. I do not want him here. Please try to accept my decision. It's too late to argue. I have made up my mind. He will go with Maria Jolas.'

'I should think she has her work cut out looking after James Joyce and his brood.'

'You can be very cruel, Father. Joyce is almost blind now, and he is ill, too.'

'I am sorry to hear that his eyesight is worse; but he's an Irishman, the Germans will not intern him. All this has nothing to do with Claude crossing an ocean where shoals of U-boats are operating by now.'

'I don't want to hear such a thing. I don't want to lose him either, but it will be for the best in the end. If he misses this chance, it will be too late.'

At night while Lydia sleeps, Matisse is wakeful with his memories. The night is turning over the day's odours and Marseilles is still active; its three white lighthouses are flashing, olives being pressed, traffic moving. Women are busy marketing their bodies in the Old Port. It is easy to feel that it is all going on without him; that he might never see his grandson again. He counts the drawings; surprisingly, he has done eighteen. He tries to think of his childhood in Bohain, its many odours – the smell of the granary lofts where, as a boy, he used to work; licking his fingertips to dab up every last grain of corn to earn a sou. He can smell the paint mixed by his mother, the dead air of winter and the dust of summer. There is the licorice breath of a hypnotist, too, who once set out to mesmerise him. He wanted all the children to believe that it was a July day, and that they were standing by a river. When the man asked whether Henri could see and smell the flowers, he said that he saw nothing except the floor-boards.

As the train pulls into Nice, Matisse remembers Apollinaire – anything is better than brooding on France under the jackboot, trampled like that old asparagus bed he had seen once at Argenteuil. Nice used to be an artificial paradise for Apollinaire: fliers, cocaine, revolver practice in the morning, sabre in the afternoon. There had been those classic cooking smells, too, coming from the Italian houses in the old quarter, where he idled in his pale blue uniform under the washing lines.

Turning to Lydia, he says, 'We've all suffered from scalp wounds in our time.'

'What are you trying to say?'

Matisse shakes his head, and lifts his arm so that she can help him from his seat.

The model Lydia ushers in looks promising. She has a chic dress sense and wears red high-heeled shoes that click as she crosses the studio floor. Her hands are small and her neck is good. Her body gives off an aura of expensive perfume. 'I must say, your home is beautiful, Monsieur Matisse,' she says. Her name is Muriel Avalon, and she has taken some culture aboard since she left New York in the hope of finding romance in Paris. 'Do you know *The Tempest*?' Matisse has an air of Prospero about him, an English quality.

He smiles. 'I look like Prospero, Duke of Milan, an Italian despot?'

'Prospero, a despot?'

'You seem surprised. Surely it's the act of a tyrant to compel Ariel to police his island from end to end?'

'They said that talking to you was better than paying a psychoanalyst. It is true.'

'My appearance often deceives people. I'm really quite light-hearted most of the time. It must be my beard. You are confusing me with Dr Freud. I'm not sure that is flattering.'

'I cannot see you ever needing psychoanalysis.'

'Is that a good or a bad thing?'

'I am a prostitute.'

Matisse nods.

'Well, I'm glad that's over. I wasn't going to tell you; then I thought, what the hell; these things do come out. I don't like lies. People lie about everything, these days.'

She has charmed Matisse enough by now for him to set aside his charcoal. He dips his pen into the ink and begins to draw her body.

'You must have lived a very sheltered life before launching on your present career,' he says.

'You think so? Why?'

'To assume that artists and their models do not live in the real world.' Matisse laughs. 'A lot of Renoir's girls were prostitutes, and I forgot how many of mine were. When I went back to Tangier, I rented my old room, worked in the same garden. When my wife and I looked for the girl who had sat for me, Amélie found her at work in a brothel. Manet's Victorine Meurent and the girl in the bar of the Folies Bergère sold their bodies. Zorah of my *Sur la terrasse*, if you know the painting, was a child prostitute.'

Muriel shakes her head.

She has taken off her wrap and sprawls near his feet, staring at his shoes, as she turns away from her reflection in the mirror. Her pose reminds him of a girl he drew in 1935; her hand lying languidly near her left breast, where a bead necklace set off her nakedness.

'Look at it like this, Monsieur Matisse: this chore is an easier way to earn money than under some sweaty German pig. As soon as I heard that the Studios Victorine sent you models, I knew it would be something less bone grinding than my usual routine, a bit of immortality. Do you mind that I lied to you?'

'No,' he says. 'I don't think of it as a lie. Besides, I hired you to pose for me.'

'I don't know much about painting, but surely you're going to be in trouble when the *boches* take over.'

'You think that's what they are going to do?'

'Some of them are here already. I thought I'd shaken them off; but no. I see them everywhere: businessmen, spies and crooks, all ready for a quick service. They have the money, the silk stockings that they imagine you'll do anything for.' She looks up at him. 'I'm serious. Don't the Germans worry you?'

No, Matisse does not see why he should worry. His work does not threaten Pétain, Adolf Hitler, or their system. His high culture is privileged and private. His paintings are now 'priceless', despite their price tags; a price that even Goering will pay to own them. 'Varian Fry, one of your countrymen, came all the way to Ciboure to tell me the same thing. He's an unlikely Scarlet Pimpernel who is helping artists to escape from France. There was a wonderful light in New York, and I found America dazzling. The difficulty would be to live and work there.'

'I've been ordinary all my life. I don't know any other way to live. Work, my dear; that's the secret of happiness.'

'Our work is not the same,' she says. 'You've never had a police surgeon poke you with his instruments every month. You don't have to worry about syphilis and gonorrhoea.'

Matisse shakes his head, musing. 'In Manet's time, there were forty thousand prostitutes in Paris; five thousand of them were on a police register.'

It was the Belgian cars she noticed first, going fast on their way south; the wan families lost under the burden of their luggage. A couple of days later she knew how bad it was. The farm carts rolled in, with kids perched on mattresses. They were too weary to cry. Nobody in Paris knew what to do with these refugees. They camped in parks with their pots and pans, on street corners; anywhere they could find space. They had nothing except what they carried, and some of them had died on the road. They were something out of dust-bowl newsreels back home. 'My French may be poor, but you must be able to follow my drift.' Of course, the laugh was when the Germans arrived with their horses and carts; some with mules, even, when the Parisians were expecting tanks and guns. She saw Messerschmitts landing in the place de la Concorde. It was not long before Hitler arrived at Le Bourget and got into a Mercedes for a triumphal drive around his city. They said he had a sculptor with him. Did Matisse know the name Arno Breker? Goering had showed up later.

He was with that phoney blue-blood von Ribbentrop. They were lolling in a looted Rolls Royce. She had noticed that it had a Dutch number-plate. By then, the Arabs had come out of hiding and were busy on every street corner and boulevard hawking nuts and choc bars to the Master Race. It was the military band she couldn't stand. Every day in the Champs-Élysées, fifes, drums and cymbals beating out the 'Horst Wessel' march. A clockwork piece for clockwork soldiers who thought they had a right to anything, including her.

She troubles him now; her body hinders now rather than invites lucidity, and his hand begins to falter. She reminds him of pornographic photographs; those he used in Collioure when he could not afford a model. He tears the sheet from the pad.

'No good?'

Matisse is testy. 'I don't want to hear about the fall of France again, madame. I am striving to find a rhythm so that I can translate what I feel about your body into a line. An act that is akin to walking a tightrope. Each time I try, you set the rope vibrating. I can find no peace. Your reminiscences prevent me from achieving any sense of voluptuous repose, and it is that repose I hired you to provide.'

She cannot understand what he means by 'voluptuous repose'. She never lets herself get mixed up with stuff like that; men get what they pay for, and no more.

'I want to be the slave of your flesh. I want to encompass you lying there; but you deny me access, symbiosis.'

'You must think I come pretty cheap,' she says, dressing. 'Usually I fake it, but with you I was being straight.'

'See Lydia as you go. She will pay you.'

'Is that right?' She turns. 'I don't think it had anything to do with the fall of France. It's because I am a whore. That's right, isn't it?'

Lydia stands waiting with the envelope. 'You don't want to count it?'

'No.'

After the door slams, Matisse stands by the window, toying with a fancy of her poking the money down the top of her stocking. Every chance or arranged harmony that charms his eye, allures in any way, seems fraught with the problems he would find if he felt the urge to paint it. He has always remade his studios. What greater joy was there in life than changing the colour or shape of objects whenever he chose? He can visualise again the silver edge of a storm, gleaming with unearthly

95

brightness on the girl's bare legs. Only Bonnard could render that exquisite light. He sighs again. He is a prisoner; his only comfort is that age makes it less of a hardship now.

In his dream, masked figures torture and abuse him. When they stop, they pin a sign on him, a stigma that is visible to others of their brotherhood. This sign shows that he has been their victim, and that he can expect more pain and abuse each time he falls into their hands.

* * *

There was a portrait of a moon-faced peasant woman wearing a neat lace cape in the concierge's lodge. Her husband had gone to church. During the rest of the day Aragon could see her in the garden, tearful over a photograph of her son, who was a prisoner of war in Stettin.

Seghers shook the dice and rolled a three and a five onto the backgammon board. They sat in the shade of the dusty vine on the trellis overhead. Radio-Paris was playing the German anthem.

'I have decided that the title of the volume will be *Le Crève-Cœur*,' Aragon told Seghers as they drank more wine. 'I have finished most of the poems now.'

'The quarters of Paris shaped me; in them, I rubbed shoulders with Jacobin postmen and onion-sellers. After that, even before the war ended, the maelstrom of Surrealism sucked me in: a heady experience that led us all to defer growing up. Even now, I can't accept that I am ageing.'

Later that night Aragon kept his promise to Seghers. He wrote to Henri Matisse to introduce himself, and ask whether he had any drawings they could publish in *Poésie*.

Carmelina

Matisse featured as the industrious artist for the first time in his painting of Carmelina. There, he lent the onlooker the use of his eyes, but left no clue to what the observer ought to feel. How did Carmelina come to make her presence felt in the history of art? She was a low-class model, hired and paid for, whose swarthy nudity was as earthy as the *bistre* pigment with which he rendered her flesh tones and her navel's black cleft. Her dumb condition did not address the artist, or impart the taste of bread in her mouth; she was there for him to delineate her body.

It was a frame from a film with no plot. Matisse's image in the mirror was a fleeting Hitchcock appearance; a trick they had both learned from Velázquez. Clearly he was using the girl; there was also an intimation that she sat upright only after being spread-eagled under the man who lurks in the mirror.

It could have happened yesterday.

'When a man becomes Mother Nature, Monsieur Matisse,' the bird-seller says, 'he does not realise what he is taking on. It is only when a plague hits the aviary that he is humbled. You don't know what it means to have an outbreak of aspergillosis in the cages. It is fatal to any breed. The birds catch it from breathing *Aspergillus fumigatus* spores, which thrive in rotting vegetation. Impossible to cure, you can only try to prevent it by lacing their drinking water with a dash of potassium. You live in fear of everything when you owe your livelihood to birds. Even if you diagnose tuberculosis you cannot treat it. Your birds grow thin and listless; they just die in front of you. The only thing you can do is to sterilise the cages. The nights are long, endless. It is painful, I know, as a bird lover, to have to do my own post-mortems, but sometimes it is the only way to discover how they died. An autopsy can reveal things you never suspected, which may have caused the fatality. It would amaze you what you can learn from analysing a bird's droppings. Sometimes I feel like Vidocq, Monsieur Matisse.'

'Madame Delectorskaya hung up bits of meat under a deck chair in the garden to try to breed maggots. She thought that the flies would soon plaster them with eggs. The idea was to catch them in a tray when they fell off to pupate. That was all very well during the summer, but with the winter coming. . .' Matisse shrugs his shoulders. 'There was also a plan to breed crickets and locusts, which fell through. It's the war. I don't want to have to worry about birdseed, on top of everything else.'

'You should be wary with any maggots you give to birds,' the bird-seller warns. 'You can pass on botulism. It is always wise to feed any maggots with corn-meal at least twice before you use them. The meal cleans the maggots' gut.'

'Highly edifying,' Matisse says.

'It's always in times of trouble that people turn to the exotic, Monsieur Matisse. You must know how true that is, painting as you do. Is there any sight more wonderful than a Hunting Cissa in the sun, its green plumage fading to blue in the light? Paris? There are not many changes yet. Every Sunday, I go to the market on the quai aux Fleurs; but those exotic breeds from Indonesia, the West Indies or Africa – well, you can't buy them now. I manage to get a few birds from Ethiopia, through Italy. It's the same with stamps; the war has made a difference, but my son says that it's still possible to find a rarity or two at the Rond-Point.'

Sleeping Woman

Again, the Rumanian blouse in another manifestation. Lydia rests on her arm, her hand limply curving near her face. Her head lies horizontal; the face is as hieratic and idealised as any Byzantine icon.

Lydia does not care for the painting. She has to stop herself from asking whether he has Christmas in mind, and when will the Shepherds and Wise Men make their appearance.

Still Life with Seashell on a Black Table

The old man is busy on a canvas again; yet after many sketches, nothing is as simple as it seems. His present subject is a large pink seashell that rests on a black marble table with three apples. Two bands of dark lemon-yellow accent the black table top and bottom. The top band is twice as wide as the lower strip. There is a whitish jug with a blue pattern, and a cup and saucer, adorned with a red, white and blue peasant motif. Next to them stands a pot-bellied copper coffee pot with a black knobbly handle. Its colour has undergone so many changes that it is no longer recognisable. It has become a reddish purple, traces of which he touches inside the lustrous pink of the shell, whose curves and spines charm him more each day. After thirty sittings, it is shaping up to be a painting he will find it hard to part with.

During the night, Matisse wakens with a groan. He had been in Papeete, drawing the Tahitian girl who lolled on the divan so that her cunt gaped pink in the dark flesh, as though it were the most natural thing, as indeed it was. It had the same lustrous glint as that inside the seashell on his black marble table, and it was hard to stay aloof as one greyish pearl followed another, which soon became a visible flow. How did Gauguin get any painting done there?

*   *   *

As America voted, Aragon tried to believe that what the people were deciding would affect the course of history. Radio-Vichy was busy dismissing Compiègne as an act of revenge by the Germans by presenting it as the righting of an old wrong. CBS and German cameramen covered the event, filming the place cards in the rail-car where Marshal Foch and his party sat in 1918.

German troops were behaving well at the Tomb of the Unknown Soldier. The curfew was in force one hour before dark. The Eiffel Tower had a swastika. Gabriel Péri had served a month of his life sentence of hard labour. Yet, when Pétain visited Marseilles, despite the cheering there were red flags flying on the churches and the suspension bridge.

*   *   *

Late in December, Varian Fry comes again to offer a visa and passage to America. 'Think what might happen,' he urges; 'even if you escape being a degenerate artist, you will soon face food shortages. Your health will suffer.'

'Has Soutine managed to get to Villa Air-Bel?'

'No. He is not listed as an artist the U.S. Emergency Rescue Committee wants to save. I talked to him. He seemed to think that there were no trees to paint in America. He is a Jew, but he has no identity papers. God knows what will happen to him. I can only fear the worst.'

'Very few artists have an eye like Soutine's. He is able to see red gladioli as writhing in a blend of blood and flame. I was closest to understanding Soutine when I did *L'Idole*; but that was long before Soutine painted his *Woman in Red*, with her vivid flesh tones, those arthritic hands.'

'I find it difficult to imagine Soutine influencing your work.'

'That is not what I meant. Let us say this: we could be talking of the Rembrandt of our time. When Barnes bought Soutine's paintings from Soutine's poet friend, Zborowski, for three thousand dollars, he regarded him as more important than Picasso.'

'You can't be serious?'

'I suppose I do exaggerate. Is Picasso with you at Air-Bel? They tell me he plans to go to Mexico.'

'He says he intends to stay on in Paris.'

'Good. He is keeping his promise to look after my paintings.'

'You are not taking your plight seriously,' Fry says. 'You don't seem to realise what life will be like under the Nazis. Picasso will have trouble looking after his own paintings, never mind protecting yours. The Germans will not behave like officers and gentlemen. How can I make you understand? Chagall did not make the same error; he listened to me. You will find a safe haven with us until I can secure your passage; Breton and many of the Surrealists are there. You must know Marseilles, of course. This summer, the garden flowers invaded all the rooms with their perfume.'

'You had official intruders, too, I'm told,' Lydia says, carrying a vase of flowers into the room. 'I hear that the *flics* arrested your guests and held them aboard a prison ship in the harbour.'

'A security measure while Pétain was visiting the city,' Fry explains, pleading with her to persuade Matisse to listen to what he is saying.

'Don't waste your time, Mr Fry,' she says. 'Our days of being vagabonds are over. Monsieur Matisse is painting now; we have no intention of running off to Marseilles again.'

Matisse smiles. 'I am grateful, though, for your kind offer. I know you mean well. Convey my regards to Breton and the others, and my hope that they'll be able to work in America.'

* * *

When Aragon and Elsa left Carcassonne, they went to stay with Seghers in the hillside village of Les Angles, near Avignon. They said that they would go on to Nice after a few days, but changed their minds and stayed on in Villeneuve-lès-Avignon until December.

Looking down from the bridge, Aragon said, 'I find it easy to see Petrarch standing here, at peace with this river.'

Elsa smiled. 'He always seems to notice Laura's robes. He celebrates the violets embroidered on her green dress. Is it true that she was only thirteen when he met her?'

'During early Mass on Good Friday, in the church of Santa Clara.'

'She was a real person, not a figment of his imagination?'

'She was the wife of Hugues de Sade, a remote ancestor of the Marquis de Sade. She had eleven children by him, nine of which survived. Only someone who was very real could manage that, I'd say. Documents prove that when she died of the plague in 1348, Petrarch was in Italy.'

The bridge at Avignon was so newfangled that the townspeople said it was the Devil's work. Bénezet, the architect, was a twelve-year-old shepherd boy when he heard God's voices ordering him to build it.

'Bénezet's corpse lay here, in the chapel on the bridge, for five centuries, until the winter floods of 1669 brought fears for the structure's stability, and the city fathers had the body moved into the chapel ashore,' said Aragon.

They had come to the city of the Popes to admire the palace-fortress. 'In medieval times, every road in Europe led to Avignon,' Aragon said; 'it was the centre of world power, patronage and diplomacy. It seems peaceful enough now. We don't know, of course, what goes on after dark. In those days, the place was notorious for its corruption, and Petrarch stresses that in his poems.'

'It was Petrarch's other mistress who gave birth; is that why he ran off in search of the simple life?' Elsa opens her compact and powders her cheek.

'According to the guidebook, he wrote poems to Laura in England and the Orkneys. When he returned to Avignon he climbed Mont Ventoux with his brother, a climb that was less a mountaineering feat to see the Alps and the valley of the Rhône than a spiritual ascent. What book did he have on the summit for the wind to blow open? Augustine's *Confessions*: "Men go to the heights of mountains and the mighty flood of seas and the broad swell of rivers and the compass of ocean and the wheeling of the stars, yet to themselves they pay no heed" . . . He had begun a journey that took him in 1337 to the spring at Vaucluse. He lived there for sixteen years before going to Arqua, near Padua, where he died with Homer in his hand.'

In the porch of Notre-Dame des Dômes there was a fresco of the Virgin encircled by angels. Laura de Sade served as the model for Saint Marguerite. She knelt beside the dragon that Saint George was slaying; the saint's face was Petrarch's. 'They must have been friends of the artist,' Elsa said.

The sun was setting on the hill, gilding the fleeces of the sheep, which a man was driving to a farm gate. Distant, there came the sound of thunder.

Aragon told Seghers how fond Elsa was of Avignon. It had become her town. It was an ideal place to spend Christmas with Pierre and his wife; somewhere to forget the plight of France as they sat discussing Picasso's *Demoiselles d'Avignon*.

'I think it is a copy of this group that you can see in the background of El Greco's *Vision of Saint John*.' Seghers passed the volume of El Greco's paintings across to Aragon.

Aragon had not known this. He tells him how Picasso had bullied his mistress Fernande Olivier to pose for the nudes. She loathed the way he distorted her face. He was echoing the Louvre's Iberian antiquities and the Negro art of the Trocadéro. She would get used to herself in time. In his first sketches, a sailor and a medical student were customers in the brothel. 'He used to speak of it as an act of exorcism. The bodies of the three white women evoke Greek statues. He chose these masks from the Ivory Coast as an afterthought when he painted the other two women. El Greco is present, of course, but I think it is Cézanne's architecture that holds them all together above the watermelon, grapes and fruit on the plate.'

'Why *Les demoiselles d'Avignon*?' Seghers asked.

'It was not Picasso's idea. André Salmon said that Barcelona's Calle d'Avinyo was full of whorehouses, and that amused Pablo.'

Aragon says it took a Spaniard to import such ideas into France. Their origins ought to have been veiled, as Delacroix and Moreau had veiled them, in a mythological or harem setting. Pablo had subverted the Western eye; he had torn away atmosphere and spatial depth at the same time, and had dealt perspective such a blow that it was impossible to use again. There was nothing left except distortion, and the large-scale appropriation of the fetish. He elevated a clever idea to the condition of a new art form.

The light from the snow-covered rooftops glimmered a brightness across the shiny page as he held up the book.

* * *

Glomaud says he fought in the Great War, too. He has cut all insignia from his officer's tunic, and fires with resentful ennui in the shooting gallery, hitting shot-bitten ducks and clay pipes with ease. 'I soon learned that I was too old to be in another war,' he says. 'Maybe that's why I made such a mess of it.'

'You don't believe what you say,' Matisse says, accepting the airgun and snapping it open.

Glomaud takes a pellet from the tin lid nailed to the counter and loads Matisse's rifle. 'No. We had too few tanks, and not enough bombers to give Hitler second thoughts. I heard Paul Reynaud telling lies on the wireless about conducting the war from North Africa. He was whistling in the dark when he appealed to Roosevelt to bring America into the war. Did you serve in 1914, Monsieur Matisse?'

'I was robust; there were men of my age serving in the army, yet all the War Office could find for me to do was guard railway bridges, a period that did not last for very long,' Matisse says.

Glomaud says, 'The Jew may live in fear, but that doesn't stop him from being a greedy parasite on the host. Léon Blum would have done better to keep his job as legal adviser to Hispano-Suiza.' He taps open a snuffbox to proffer a pinch, which Matisse declines.

'My wife's mother told me she was a refugee when I let her move in. I have no choice than to come here, unless I want to row all day. That's how cowardly Frenchmen are now.'

When Glomaud's wife arrives with two bottles of wine in her basket, he uncaps one and, after taking a swig, offers Matisse a drink. Matisse refuses, patting the head of the dog that came with Madame Glomaud. 'You like dogs, I can see that,' she says.

'I used to have one, years ago.'

'My husband had sent his friend on ahead to the house,' Glomaud's wife says. 'I looked out of the window, and there was Glomaud, ghostly with dust, struggling to get his kit bag out of the bullet-holed car. At first, I thought he had deserted, but I should have known better. Men like my husband stay at their posts. Why had he left the army, I asked him. What army, he said. Where was the army? Where was anybody?'

'She didn't give a damn!' Glomaud complains. 'Nothing would keep her from her dancing lessons. She would have gone on with those, even if I had walked home on crutches.'

'You were called the Fauves,' Madame Glomaud says.

'I was a painter long before I became a Fauve. It was Berthe Weill who found us all. For some, she was a second mother (not that it did her much good). She was sharp and outspoken, but treated us all with great fairness. She'd sell you a Picasso for two hundred and fifty francs. Pablo and I met regularly in 1912, to saunter and talk about our paintings. He used to say that we should have a joint show; that there was nobody who had looked at my work as intently as he did. We swapped paintings in 1907; I got his *Cruche, écuelle et limon* for a portrait of my daughter Margot.'

Glomaud says the chief thing is that the Germans will cleanse the filth from France's abysmal stable.

'You think so?'

'Hitler has sworn that the new Germany will live for a thousand years. France must not refuse to take part in his vision. We must become crafty; we must look beyond this defeat.'

'You men are all the same; you dictate what you want and the way you want it.'

Glomaud asks abruptly whether Casagemas's death led Picasso to his Blue Period.

'You know of Casagemas?'

'I read the newspapers.'

Matisse affects to ponder the question. 'Opium was a more likely cause,' he says. 'What I do know is that smoking was not the same at the Bateau-Lavoir after Pablo found Wiegel's corpse hanging in his studio. Opium was cheap enough: thirty centimes, as I recall, and sold at every pharmacy. Whether Casagemas was under its influence, I don't know, but he set out for the Hippodrome intent on killing his mistress. Germaine realised this as soon as he came through the door. Slithering to her knees, she scuttled under the table to take shelter behind Pallarès, who began to fight with Casagemas. The gun went off, Germaine fell. Casagemas, sure that he had killed her, then turned the pistol on himself; he died later that night.'

'Gypsy riff-raff, of course,' Glomaud says.

'You are sweating, and you look sick,' Lydia says, by way of greeting.

'Perhaps I overdid it,' Matisse admits.

'Are you in pain? I think I had better call the doctor.'

Matisse nods a rueful assent. 'Some people believe that life is born of chance, but I know that fate determines events. Did Manet know that the music in the Tuileries was the accompaniment to the first truly modern painting? Nowadays, like Robinson Crusoe, we do the best we can with the washed-up jetsam and flotsam of art history. Picasso feels envy, even as he insists that his art is a purgative, an act of exorcism. I try to fool myself that I have done away with the need for perspective, and meanings with which I can no longer live. You know, I think the fall of France hurt me more than I realised.'

* * *

Nice was Jean Vigo's city in *À Propos de Nice*. Aragon could see Vigo's opening aerial shot, a clear assertion that the camera would be shooting from every angle, going into every corner. The film would be a voyeur's portrait of a city of voyeurs; that would splice together road sweepers and waiters, *pétanque* players, ostriches and crocodiles. Vigo merged zoo animals with rich idle women; he made the parade of carnival dolls on the promenade echo a grinning Negro by the sea, as well as probing the poor quarter of Nice, where nobody swam or owned a pleasure boat. Here was the base on which the city rested, with its pimps, garbage collectors and nameless ill-paid workers.

Above all, Nice was the city where Matisse lived.

It was New Year's Eve. Elsa lit the candles, and savoured the moment before she opened the parcel Lili had sent.

'At least there is no damned snow,' she said.

'You never know; it could happen here,' Aragon told her.

'Not in Nice.'

Elbows on the table, she cupped her face in her hands. 'The years have gone. What have I done with them?'

Aragon poured a glass of wine for her. 'Open the parcel. We should be happy; we should be making our new year resolutions. England has beaten Germany in the air, and there is no talk yet of a separate peace. Things can only get better.'

Lili had sent them a tin of caviar.

Aragon held the tin up to the light to study the label. 'What we need now is a slab of black Ukrainian bread.'

'Do not say such things. You make me feel even more homesick; my eyes fill with tears; I remember Pathé cameras filming Tolstoy dying in the station-master's house at Astapovo. It has all gone.' Elsa shivers. 'I stand shivering in the shadow Mayakovsky cast; even then he is a greater comforter than Boris Pasternak. Do you remember how *Pravda* said that his funeral was the most solemn since Lenin's? We should have been there. We should have gone to Moscow.'

Aragon tried to lift the conversation. 'This is a very Proustian tin of caviar! You know my doubts about Pasternak; you have damned him, too, for the provincial fashion in which he fell in love with world literature.'

Elsa frowns. 'Every Russian comes out of the womb with the same sense of inferiority.'

'Shakespeare had to live with the burden of a Greek and Roman past. He was a provincial. The great difference was that he never ceased to tinker with the machinery he found, whereas Boris remained on his knees.'

Elsa shakes her head. 'Shakespeare was not a Sephardi Jew, and a Russian to boot.'

Aragon nods. 'Nothing that you say can redeem Pasternak's *1905*. He stole his images from *Battleship Potemkin*. He had no insight at all into that glorious quarter-deck, and added nothing to the film's version of the mutiny.'

'Is there any work of literature that does not show traces of what went before? We hide our sources like jackdaws. We are Draculas; we quit our coffins after midnight to go in search of human blood.'

Elsa went to the window as though to fly off into the night; there she mimed Bela Lugosi, spread her arms wide, staring out to sea to utter Pasternak's lines:

> Scarfed against the cutting air,
> I shield my face at the window
> To halloo the children, Hey!
> What century is it out there?

1941

Still Life with Oysters

MATISSE is sure he has no qualms about painting oysters. Those on the plate have dried out and are starting to smell. He is in pain; he has to grin and bear it; so have many others in France, who suffer also from cold and hunger. He feels that his oysters will not be a patch on last year's *Nature morte au coquillage*, which took him thirty sessions to paint. Problems arise; they are inevitable; it is the angle of the table now that lacks authority against the frame. He has placed himself to look down on the plate of oysters, which, according to his canvas, now lies on a dark-blue cloth near an ultramarine napkin with scarlet bands. There is a yellow-handled knife, two lemons and a jug, which has become pale lilac as the red angularity of the background deepened around the pink border.

Matisse has no time to languish in the Saint-Antoine clinic. Yet here are his daughter Marguerite, Lydia and Camoin fussing around the room, making him fear that he lies on his deathbed.

'Feel?' he replies to his friend Camoin, who has come from St-Tropez to show his concern. 'I feel as if I am pissing blood. To amuse myself, I tried five times to draw the coffin I shall lie in shortly. Finally, Lydia had to draw it.'

'You know what Dr Angier is saying?'

'That I have duodenal cancer, and that I must go to Lyons for an operation. How did I come to this, Charles? Where are our flesh-coloured tights, plumped out with fake muscles, our masquerades?'

Camoin laughs. He had been one of those three wrestlers at the fancy dress party.

Marguerite and Lydia arrive after talking to Dr Angier. 'We have agreed what you must do. We are leaving for Lyons.'

Camoin touches his hand. 'When will you go?'

Matisse shakes his head. 'With the railway under a foot of snow?'

Lydia's retort is sharp. 'That doesn't matter. The snow is not going to stop us.'

Matisse studies the old man who slams the carriage door and sits beside him. He has dusted off the rosette of his Légion d'honneur, which he says it is his duty to wear in these black days. In his opinion France deserves her defeat. The quicker Pétain took firm action against the Israelites and Freemasons the better, since they had caused the disaster with their greedy plots. They were the guilty parties who had handed victory to Hitler.

The countryside darkens, hiding peasant farms buried in snowdrifts, whitewash flaking from their walls. They remind him of those farms to which his father would take him which gave off the same sour stench of sodden thatch as they had in the Hundred Years' War. He knows this world, its sudden deaths, its mysterious cures, from which he escaped by means of his art. Yet it still runs as close as blood in his veins, a fearful prospect that he cannot allow to threaten his practices.

As night falls across France, the wives light oil-lamps, stand quietly in the rutted passages that link their kitchens to their bedrooms, listening to their husbands sharpen knives for the kill. Matisse knows that token wave of a handkerchief that brought them there: a ring, a proposal, a dowry. They hoard locks of hair and the fingernails of the dead to ensure good fortune. Their rooms reek of that dark atavism that he has fought all his life.

He is under the threat of the knife, too; afraid, recalling that Ravel did not survive the operation on his brain tumour. Matisse feels he has too much left to do to resign himself.

When Lydia enters from the corridor, taking off her hat and coat, she adds to his sense of anxiety by seeming a stranger for a moment. Her hairstyle and dress loom large suddenly, and make her a different woman from the one he knows. He felt the same loss when Amélie no longer wore those dresses she bought before 1900. He had a future in those days, the urge to destroy persistence of vision. He has only a sense of his age now; the certainty that Lydia will live on, and wear other fashions aboard trains hurtling to other destinations.

'Do you want anything?' She looks down at him, holding onto the luggage rack.

In Lyons, in the gloom of the Gare Perrache, he waits for the taxi Lydia has gone to find. The two children who sit near him on the bench are using sign language to express themselves, their hands fluttering like birds in a cage. His pain is intense again; he hopes that they will not have to take a tram to the clinic. If he had his pad, he could sketch the children's hands to pass the time. He thinks of the implicit calm of the palmed hands the Renaissance masters drew next to a didactic skull or text, a monkey, or some other emblematic device.

Things take so long to achieve in the Marshal's France. Blowing his nose, he finds a smear of soot-fall on his handkerchief.

There is a chill blast as Lydia leads him towards the taxi in the cours de Verdun.

The clinic is on the boulevard des Belges; he can hear the muffled clang and screech of trams as he thinks about Camoin. If he closes his eyes he can see Moreau's studio, where they were students together with Marquet, Bussy and the others. He sighs. He has seen so much; he has known so many artists and would-be artists, charlatans and clowns. He used to crack jokes with Rodin, a sure guarantee of a death certificate.

'Give me two or three years,' he begs the surgeons when they come to prod him. 'I have so much left to do.'

After the operation and the taste of chloroform, Matisse relives the flight from London to Paris. The plane cruises above the clouds over the Channel, clouds that seem motionless; the sky is azure, the sun blazes. It is an event that stays with him until they begin to instruct him in his decay. Instead of simply having a 'turn for the worse' the surgeons give him words like 'infarction' to chew over. Later, he will tell Marguerite how naked he felt in their presence, felt himself to be opaque to those men.

Their views, their definitions, prevail. For days, babied by the nuns, he loses any sense of his worth, his *gravitas*, while he pecks over his disabilities like a hen.

The past, however, is now a garden of delight in which he feels serene as his pain abates. The nuns whisper as they come and go, sudden black and white shadows as he returns to his senses. They nickname Matisse 'the resurrected'.

Santy and his assistants, Professors Wertheimer and Leriche, tell him that his progress is highly satisfactory, and they are confident he will make a full recovery.

Leriche, who looks like a village butcher, is the author of a book on the philosophy of surgery, a tome remote from the meat trade. Matisse sees them as three Zola characters, without knowing why, except that it makes them seem familiar.

Matisse has to laugh. 'Why do you look at me as though I have taken leave of my senses? All surgical incisions imply an autopsy to me. Yet, what lessons did Lombroso learn from his study of Zola's cranium except that he was the pig-in-a-sty who offended French taste? Such is the power of science! Lombroso's verdict was that Zola was prone to epilepsy and hysteria, and that this was manifest in the novels. You are saying that

I will live awhile longer; that I must try to blot out that recurring nightmare of the two peasants hauling Monet's coffin on their handcart.'

*   *   *

After Aragon had wined and dined Paulhan, they talked about his poems. 'I intend to call the volume *Le Crève-Cœur*. I tried to speak of my experiences using simple words: what I felt on the sands of Dunkirk, how it was to be lonely and afraid with my comrades. The poems were about listening to Mozart on Hilversum and feeling part of history. In them I drew my daily breath quite as heavily as Richard II. A sorrowing monarch, I felt desperate to redeem those hours I had wasted solving crossword puzzles.'

'There is nothing I can tell you about Drieu that you don't already know.' Paulhan clicked open his cigarette case. 'When the Germans sacked me as the editor of the review, he took over. Now only fascists submit stuff – yet he spoke up and got me out of prison. We use Drieu as a cover; if we don't have him, they will close Gallimard down. I collaborate on the review, because it helps me to cope with my clandestine tasks.'
    'Watch out for his fatal need for the absolute,' warned Aragon.
    'He never asked for any sort of assurance when he got me out of prison. He must suspect that I use the office for Resistance business, yet we meet on the stairs and gossip.'

*   *   *

The nun arranging the flowers that Marguerite left asks him about his work. Matisse watches her hands as she smoothes the bed sheet. 'I am sure that we both yearn to see a medieval fruit tree growing, Sister, a green orb, solid with glowing apples, as holy as any in our nursery rhymes. We all leave footprints. Monet taught Signac, and it was Signac who led me to Collioure.' He realises from her look that he has lost her, and talks about the curtains instead. 'The art school I went to taught textile designers; fabrics were always close to my heart. I keep in touch with the way women dress; materials still delight me. Amélie ran a millinery shop to pay for my painting. Rembrandt bought his Turkish stuffs in the bazaar to deck his biblical subjects. It was Salmon, I seem to recall, who said that I had a dressmaker's taste.'

*   *   *

Elsa languished, feeling blue after rewriting the same page since she woke at dawn to find Aragon had already gone. She sat for a long time at the window waiting for the woman in white to pass below. She had written about her in *Mille Regrets* as a waif adrift in time, a character whose dresses, mostly white, were the outward sign of some loss; of innocence, perhaps.

Elsa was herself prone to aimless beachcombing in search of the unattainable. If she did not get a grip, she would find herself drifting to the château park again to mourn her sense of lost identity. There, she would try to flesh out the chimera, hoping for any chance liaison to forget her pain.

Her other escape route was to spoil herself; that she did by filling a bath as hot as she could, then lowering herself into the scented water. She leaned back, sliding under until her pubic bush slicked into waving fronds. When she lifted her pelvis, her red pubic hair sprang hoops of spangled gems, her nipples stood in tingling gooseflesh as she thumbed and teased them. It was safer to re-live old trysts than suffer the temptation of new ones. Slowly, dreamily, she began to spoil herself.

Getting out of the bath after her orgasm, her cunt unwashed (she whispered the word aloud that best defined its state), she dried her breasts and mopped the sweat on her shoulders and nape. Her sighs were heavy as she brushed her hair at the mirror. At such times her childhood loomed in images and sounds, but she could never grasp why that was so, or face those feelings she stifled. She spread her legs wide, so that her cunt gaped, and slid her forefingers teasingly inside the lips; then, slowly, she took the black silk stockings and began to put them on.

With Falla's *Noches en los jardines de España*, perfumed, languorous, on Célimène's gramophone, Elsa made love to Aragon as of old, the light fading and the candlelight blazing in the mirror. Between her bouts of lust, she had pampered herself, shaping her lips scarlet, painting vamp-dark caves in which her eyes glittered; but cosmetics could no longer disguise the truth that she was fifty. She was happier masturbating than feeling her breasts for signs of cancer. She could smell her feral odour of rut and satisfaction; she knew that it would be the first thing that Aragon would smell too, when he came home.

Aragon came in to find her asleep, lying on her side, one leg drawn up to show her white haunches in the mirror. He crouched beside her, fondling her breasts. When she woke, she smiled and kissed him; lightly at first, then opened his lips with her tongue and unbuttoned his fly.

She felt like a tart of the *belle époque* whose client's lust was to have his prick handled at the opera; a man who, later, would force her to take it into her mouth, under a table in some lively bar.

*   *   *

After leaving the hospital, Matisse recuperates at the Grand Nouvel Hotel. He soon feels well enough for short walks in the Parc de la Tête d'Or, named after a Gallo-Roman gold head found there. He throws seeds to the swans on the path beside the river. Once a marsh, there are greenhouses now; warm oases in a chill air. Their odour reminds him of Tahiti, and he finds camellias growing, a flower he has not looked at for years; ever since deciding that it had no form. After his rebirth, however, even the waxy reds of camellias charm him. Their pinks delight him as much as the yellow eyes of a lioness lazing in the sudden sunshine that floods her cage; her lofty gaze fixes the llamas, bolting every so often around their enclosure.

Recognising Matisse, the *patron* sends his assistant away, and tells him what a great honour it is to have him visit his shop. He has heard that he was having treatment in Lyons, but he had never dreamt of meeting him. How can he be of use?

After the homely twang of the doorbell, the place is old-fashioned; the hiss of the gaslight reminds Matisse of the flaring mantles in Gertrude Stein's apartment. He expects to hear Picasso's voice at any moment.

It is the shopkeeper who speaks again: 'Your painting of *Le dessert* has given me great pleasure over the years.'

Matisse nods. 'You mean my decanters that Moreau said were so real that he could hang his hat on them. The typhus germ was so prevalent in those days that people were afraid of any glass container, no matter how they sparkled. I painted a table I could not afford to eat at except as a guest. One of my relations lent me the crockery; I paid a fortune for the guelder roses and the apples, since it was winter in Paris. When my model couldn't afford to pose any longer, I used a mannequin. My painting was a homage to David de Heem. Of all the paintings in the Louvre, his *Dessert* of 1640 was probably the work that taught me most. I copied it in 1893.'

'Fine, it is very fine.' Matisse takes a pinch of ultramarine blue. 'What a

114

pity it is to spoil the purity. There is no joy to equal that of buying a kilo of blue pigment, or of yellow ochre; even of black.'

Matisse pauses to reflect; then, although he knows it means nothing to the man, goes on:

'My mother gave me my first box of paints. I was ill in bed for a year. I spent days copying the chromolithographs that came with the box. In the post office in Picardy, I drew her face on a telegraph form; it was a good likeness and taught me how to let my pen run freely. There is a sense in which, regardless of their father, all sons fulfil their mother's wishes.'

Matisse is happy to relate this memory; it does not matter what the shopkeeper thinks, who shakes his head as he opens a catalogue to prove the quality of goods he stocked before the war. 'I am no Hennequin, but even here art needs raw materials, and they are no longer a priority. I don't know how I will survive. I had hundreds of Chinese hog bristles. Asiatic mink, and squirrel brushes from Kazan. It is a joke to order them now. With Belgium in enemy hands, I don't know what the canvas manufacturers will do. Every Van Gogh in Lyons, every local barber, grocer and dentist, has been here; they are hoarding materials that will soon be as rare as gold dust.'

'Do you have anything left?' Matisse asks.

'Baltic linseed, perhaps, and some South American La Plata. Since the German mills gave up making good, cheap oil seed, Lyons' Sunday painters use Indian Bombay. They don't buy Baltic oil; they don't like the price.'

'Hitler shocked us all with his art lesson in 1937,' Matisse says. 'I was one of the first painters the Nazis purged from Germany's galleries. Kaiser Wilhelm didn't care for my work either. My value on the market is doubtful these days; but that is no great matter. I have known worse times. One has to work; that is the hard part. To do that, I need these.' He thumbs the brush. 'You can reach me at the Hôtel Régina, in Nice, should you unearth anything useful. My friend Bonnard will need materials, too; he lives in Cannes.'

*   *   *

Roger Stéphane had come from Perpignan, where he had been visiting Jean Cocteau, who had shown him his photograph albums: Picasso with Fernande; Gide aged fifteen; a nude Radiguet rising from a bed of reeds. 'We hooted over Carpentier's first pair of communion boxing shorts, and a photograph of Misia Sert and Coco sporting ju-jitsu outfits.'

'Is he keeping his opium supplier busy?'

'Under Pétain, all sinners find sinning harder. You know, of course, that Chanel's perfume company is at war, too. Coco sees a way to rid herself of the Jew who runs her company. Although, as Jean said, she will find that the Israelites have effective friends in France.'

It was an odd remark coming from Stéphane, who was the son of a Jewish banker, Roger Worms. Elsa had no wish to hear any of it, of course. 'Chanel has always liked playing with fire,' she said. 'She should stick to making clothes.'

Stéphane's arrival had upset Elsa, who was working, but he was easy to talk to, and she soon regained her good humour. 'I should have had a camera to hand when you used the word ju-jitsu. My dear Roger, you should know by now how scarce are the ways in which women can rival men!'

Stéphane laughed. 'You can guess how galling exile in Perpignan is for Jean,' he said. 'How is life in Nice treating you both?'

Elsa's grimace was accusing. 'You mean here, one room and kitchenette in the rue de France? Given Vichy's status in the new Europe, I'm lucky, I suppose. Besides, as the wife of a poet, what more could I want? What does any woman want? I longed to go to bed with the prince who drove the blue Bugatti I used to see outside the Coupole; I wanted to be as single-minded as Suzanne Lenglen, world champion at fifteen, flawless mover, winner at Wimbledon five times.'

'Lenglen was so ugly; there was nothing for her to do but practise hard.'

Just turned twenty, Stéphane did not know how seriously to take her flights of fancy. It was easier to nod as she picked and teased the thread of her thought. What he could not understand was what Aragon saw in this dumpy, ageing woman that inspired him to write such beautiful poems.

'Breton had no time for Nancy Cunard. I shared his taste in that, of course. He used to say that she tried to buy herself into their circle. Just as it cost her a hundred thousand francs for the hysterectomy that would liberate her sexually – or was it an abortion that went wrong?'

When Aragon arrived, Stéphane hesitated before mentioning Cocteau. 'Why do you write about Matisse? It isn't as though he is going to give us *Los Desastres de la guerra* when he returns from Lyons. Being a poet, I understand how difficult the novel form must be for you. Nobody can think of Matisse as a character; he must offer very little from that point of view; he is a known entity, who lacks Picasso's gusto and panache.'

'I can't think of a better artist to honour. We live our lives in black and white, whereas Matisse is heroic enough to live his life in dazzling colour. He is inventing and giving birth to the future in his studio.'

'You are squandering your talent. How can you adopt such a humble Doctor Watson role? Think of the time it will take.'

Elsa laughed. 'Doctor Watson! You are mad, Roger.'

Aragon threw up his chin in a Nigel Bruce pose, stoking his pipe and huffily clearing his throat to growl:

'I am trying for the same truth that I find in his work when I write about Matisse. He is the true author of the book. I seek my understanding in this text.'

'Yes, you are being pompous, Louis,' Elsa warned.

They began to argue about the Nazi–Soviet pact. It was what all left-wing people did. Aragon was forthright in his views.

'After the Spanish Civil War, any attempt by the U.S.S.R. to bring about a united front against fascism ended in vain; the appeasers tore up existing treaties to hand over the Sudetenland. They let Hitler rape Czechoslovakia. The final straw came when Pilsudski refused to allow the Red Army into Poland, which would have deterred any invasion threat. Stalin could not let Germany eat Poland whole, and that is why a "Communist" country signed the Nazi–Soviet pact. It gave back to the U.S.S.R. tracts ceded to Russia by the Versailles Treaty. What howls greeted this purely defensive move! Explain why Stalin should want a slice of Poland other than as a buffer zone. It won't be long before Germany attacks the U.S.S.R. Stalin needs every day he can get to prepare.'

'Do you think he is doing that?' Stéphane shakes his head. 'He is selling Hitler war materials. Some way to prepare for the invasion! That is not the act of a true socialist.'

After Stéphane left, Elsa felt melancholy and wrote Cocteau into *Le Cheval Blanc* between the Infanta of Spain eating a lobster sandwich and Michel Vigaud's solo with a black jazz band. It all came back: those early warning signs, bright flashes that lit the sewer flowing under their mayfly lives; the perfumes, the music of glittering pre-war Paris, where Stavisky had begun his career as a café singer.

*   *   *

Matisse has known Jean Puy since they met at Carrière's in the boulevard de Clichy. They shared the same beliefs, and felt at ease with the sacramental quality of the studio; a temple dedicated to hard labour. It taught artists who were serious in their pursuit of art, laconic loners amongst girls from rich families who had no time to behave badly, either.

Puy has taken refuge in Roanne, where he was born, near enough to Lyons to visit his friend; now that Matisse feels better, he totters around on *père* Puy's arm.

'Marquet and I lived with that Belle-Île canvas of yours for years.' Puy pauses. 'You say Georges Besson came?'

'Yes, he came and sat on my bed the other day. He boasted that his doctor had recently given him a clean bill of health and told him he could go on smoking his pipe. I asked whether what I had said about the portrait I did of him had come true.'

'Oh, what was that?'

'That I tried to make it a mirror in which he could see both his ancestors and descendants.'

Puy held him at arm's length. 'The nuns seem to have got to you, Henri. Has your joust with death and monotheism dimmed the light of day? When you get home to Cimiez, you must grab the bum of the first model who bares it for you!'

'I may be old, but yes flesh is flesh when it comes to hand. As the years go by, I want to be near my models. Perhaps I don't see them so well, these days. Speaking of age – I've doubtless told you a dozen times that Renoir was the one artist I went out of my way to meet.'

'Perhaps you did. I am too old to remember. I forget now.'

'On the last day of 1917; it was my forty-eighth birthday. Besson took me to Cagnes. Renoir taught me what to do after arranging flowers in a vase. I have always heeded his advice; when I paint them, I always take up a position on the other side. I remember him whenever I do so. Ah, his thin glazes, his "juices", all poppy seed oil and turpentine; they had not dried twenty years later.'

'What did mystify me,' Puy says, 'and I don't think you are about to clarify it now, was why you told me your postman painted *Oignons roses*.'

Puy looks about him. 'Where are we going?'

'Shall we take another look at your Lycée du Parc decoration?'

Puy shrugs. 'If you feel up to it.'

The Hôtel Terminus is a late nineteenth-century building near the Gare Perrache. Thousands of hotels have the name in France, but Matisse has never liked its finality. Gustave Eiffel built the one in Lyons. It has six floors and one hundred and forty beds. In two years' time, the Gestapo chief Klaus Barbie will make it his headquarters, torturing his victims in baths of scalding and icy water. Now, Matisse warms to its solid comfort, its pastoral prints, sipping English tea as he waits for the Nice train. He can see again the light on the other side of the Equator, no more unearthly than the light in Tangier after sunset.

With the train running along the Rhône valley, each new station – Vienne, Valence, Montélimar – teases with prospects of the future, of hope. Then, near Cassis and La Ciotat, the landscape starts to change, to delight him with the fretted silence and beauty of the umbrella pines at Fréjus.

It is not far now to the Golfe-Juan.

At home in the Régina, Matisse goes through his mail. One of the letters is from Picasso, who writes:

This letter stems from my involvement with poetry again; that I finished my new play, yet feel the need to go on filling pages with words. I drew a portrait of myself writing it: a bald sixty-year-old; a djinn, who had spent ten thousand years stuck in his bottle.

Often I wake up in the night and find I am calling Apollinaire's name. Then I am cold, and hate everything, especially the Germans. I've had a firm sense of personal identity ever since I was a boy. So it was very nasty to find myself being treated as nothing more than shit on the heel of the Master Race. What was scary was that the two of them, Gestapo men, were hard to see as human. I don't know if they were trying to embody the machinery of the state for my benefit, but they were deaf to any appeal or emotion. I have to thank my Ministry friend, Dubois, who arrived on the scene like one of Cocteau's guardian angels. He had a special power of his own to send them packing.

Matisse quotes the letter to Lydia. 'He says, "Can anything be crazier than the way I wrestle with rubbish I find in the streets." He says that trying to make art in wartime is madness; but he goes on doing it, and knows I will understand. He knows nobody who understands this better than I do.'

'Who sleeps with him now?' Lydia says. 'I lose track.'

'Dora Maar, I should think.'

'Not Marie-Thérèse?'

'I know nothing of Marie-Thérèse's love life. I do know that Picasso has always behaved like a shit towards his women.'

'He is no better or worse than your friend Maillol, who has sex with a child. He is five times her age, old enough to have played the fool with

Gauguin. Dora Maar had not been born when Picasso began to paint *Les demoiselles d'Avignon*. Does that make you jealous?'

'I don't know what you mean by jealous.'

Ronsard's Amours

Matisse wakes after a bad night and opens the scrapbook in which he has pasted Ronsard's love lyrics. He wants Lydia to be awake so that she can comfort him, but it is still too early. He works, waiting for her to bring the apartment to life, wondering what he would do if she were to leave.

The shutters stay closed against the bright May sunshine during the day. He wears an iron support he calls his chastity girdle, which allows him to lie propped up in bed for brief periods. He has to wear it to strengthen his stomach muscles.

* * *

Often when Elsa walked the streets of old Nice, it was easy to see or imagine gangsters in the cafés. The city was more labyrinthine than any district she had known in Paris: a casbah, a citadel with the tang of olives, the aroma of cheese in dank cells and of pizzas baking. There were many old women living dried-out lives in the dark burrow; the odour of leather tomes mingled with incense from the churches, between which high dignitaries shuttled, clearing a path through the crowds the width of their hats.

She watched as old men greeted each other at the street corner. They crouched down over their shopping bags, waving their hands as they bartered local produce. It was best not to go too close, since the police could be watching any possible black-market deal.

Moving on, she stood to listen to a fiddler in an old Italian costume. A horned red devil jigged in front of him, fixed to his waist by an elastic-jointed armature. The fiddler controlled his manic dance by the use of his playing arm and thrusting knee. Every so often, this devil threw back his head with a cackle of Grand Guignol laughter.

What disquieted Elsa was the feeling that she had known these events before; that she was simply catching up with them again. Then she sensed that the boy was following her.

Leaving the narrow streets, Elsa came to the *préfecture*. There were two sombre heads either side of the iron gates, dated 1826; the woman on the pillar to the left looked downcast; the one on the right, implored the heavens. Elsa did not scrutinise these baleful sisters long. She crossed the square to the archway, went under to the sea front and turned left towards the Château Park.

After a slow climb, she halted between the stone sphinxes guarding the donjon cascade. The boy was still there, and dogged her footsteps as she went up to the terrace where Friedrich Nietzsche scribbled notes for *Also Sprach Zarathustra*. A rabbi had a leather-bound tome on his knee. Elsa used to see him outside the Hôtel Roosevelt, which the Jews used as a synagogue. Afraid of her tail, she snubbed his nod and crossed to the parapet to stare down at the ochre rooftops of the old city. The boy was loitering at the foot of the steps below.

An old horse-drawn orphanage bus passed by. She watched the nurses lift the children out to play; one of them, a Moroccan boy, stood apart, head on one side, making zoo noises and bird cries every so often. Most of the children had some defect, were clumsy, unable to co-ordinate their limbs as they tried to run.

The boy still followed; would stop when she did, would feign an interest in the harbour or pretend to read a newspaper. Did he know her? Did he know where she lived?

It was the same ungainly boy who turned and faced Elsa when she opened the door. He smiled. His name was Georges Dudach and he had come from Paris. If that were true, where was his half of the torn postcard that would match hers? He blushed; he did not have it, he said. He must have lost it.

'You expect me to believe you?'

'It's true. I tailed you because I didn't know what to do.'

It was the bluster of his pained schoolboy protest that led her to feel he was telling the truth.

Elsa gave him some food. He ate fast, pausing only to boast how his group had pasted up the first anti-Nazi pamphlets when the Germans marched into Paris. He told her how proud he was that the comrades had chosen him to guide the Aragons across the demarcation line.

'Only a national movement can destroy the people's faith in Pétain. Our turn is coming. Now that Germany is at war with the U.S.S.R., Hitler has made a grave error.'

They made the crossing on foot, south of Tours. Not given much time to prepare for the journey, Aragon and Elsa risked using papers in their own names. Aragon laughed. 'I doubt whether many Germans know what I did before the war.'

It was a clear moonlit night. Other travellers were crossing too; passing shadows to avoid. Elsa knew that she could expect internment, death even, if a patrol caught them and the Germans realised that she was a Jew. Dudach, however, was as good as his word; he knew every sentry post. What he could not foresee was that the Germans would raid all hotels within eight miles of the border.

After their arrest, the German officer sent Elsa, Louis and Dudach to Tours, which had served briefly as a provisional seat of government in 1940. Elsa knew it only as Dora Maar's birthplace. The fleeting glimpses she had of the city proved what Dora once told her, and what the railway posters boasted: it was old and beautiful, noisy, with blue trams, whose staid passengers seemed absurd in the early light. When she learned that the *préfecture* had been a convent, it did not surprise her to find that the prison once quartered a cavalry regiment.

Left alone in her cell, Elsa tried to dismiss her suspicions. The woman they were to have met on the bridge in Paris could have been a traitor. Were they torturing Dudach and Aragon? When would they come for her? Could she face an interrogation? How was she to hide that she was a Russian Jew? She shook her head. She was not alone. Where could those millions of Jews in Russia hide? To shake off her fears, she re-created the map of the Tsar's empire on her old classroom wall. All she could see there now were the black arrows of Hitler's Panzers driving deep into the heart of Russia, an awful event that could change the course of history.

There were women arrested in a brothel raid in the other cells along the landing, awaiting transfer to the Eastern Front. There were collaborators, too; a peroxide blonde Elsa met in the blaze of noon in the courtyard, who said she would let anybody fuck her so long as he could get her out of there. She had lived in Tours all her life. They had caught her in the place Jean Jaurès, on a Friday, shopping for her no-good stepsons and their father. Her sloven slouch made her back ache. It was because she had worn high heels all her life, which had done for her stomach muscles. She said she bleached her hair but that it never did her any good. So thick was her stifling mask of make-up, that Elsa began to fret about her own ageing skin. It was easy to let one's personal habits loom large. She began plucking her eyebrows with the tweezers she found in the lining of her skirt pocket, then spent hours pulling every hair from her legs.

Her greatest trial was that she had nothing to read except for the tattered romances the blonde lent her. The blonde had stacks in her cardboard box where she kept her things: a mess of make-up, hair curlers, documents, letters, along with newspaper cuttings about Jews. The Jews were to blame. They buzzed around like flies. It was a Jew who had turned her in for her dealings in the black market. They were all envious, vicious; and competitors, of course. If she were in charge, she'd make every yid hand over more than his lousy radio and bicycle.

Elsa's skirt had been tight before her arrest, but she lost so much weight so quickly that she had to pin it. She would stand with the whores in the yard, talking over their fears whenever the black Citroën arrived. None of them knew when her turn might come. The cars were worse at night, coming and going, when every door slam and footstep evoked outrage and crime. What she envied the girls was their ability to see off their fears with good-natured abuse and jokes. 'One thing is sure, our problems are just starting,' said the madame. 'We are going to become victims of Death's Head and Panzer regiments, ready and eager to poke us to death. If we can cope with those, hordes of Bolsheviks lie in wait, desperate to give us a dose of the clap.'

Nasturtiums and 'The Dance'

After Dudach went off to another cell, Aragon found himself with the Hamel brothers, Georges and Christian, from Angers. Somebody had told him that these men were saboteurs. He would have liked to know more about their crime, but since they suspected that he was a police stooge, they had nothing to say. He gave up trying to talk, hating the accusing silence until he found he could project Matisse's *Capucines à 'La danse'* on the prison wall. Matisse had left out anything dark or morbid by his suspenseful framing; there was no past, no future. There were nasturtiums coiling out of a pink flask on a three-legged table. It stood in front of a cobalt-blue depth in which the dancers leapt in a ring. The actions of these Corybantes were so vital that those other dancers, outside the frame, might whirl into the picture at any moment, even into his cell. Of all Matisse's paintings it was the most fitting because it had such an enclosed interior, yet the pagan vitality of the dancers sucked Aragon into the depths, into freedom.

What marred these illusions of freedom were the sudden intrusions of Georges Hamel, pacing up and down as he held up his trousers with one hand. With his torn shirt collar, he seemed a candidate for the guillotine. The brothers had come a great distance from their peasant farm, from those old beliefs that families confirmed by kneeling at shrines before visiting their dead with flowers. Their clothes still smelt sourly of earth and potatoes, as was usual; their sole hope was that they would survive to go on living in their usual fashion, year after year.

Aragon would look down into a small courtyard where the inmates exercised. It was twenty feet or so wide, and prisoners would cross a narrow gap at the far end, so that they were often partially visible in the same way as Matisse's dancers, but Aragon never saw Elsa or Dudach. Above, there were sudden flurries of pigeons on the far slates.

Every night, the warder went by whistling 'Flying down to Rio' or some other tune that left the heart heavy in Aragon's body.

The nights were worst. Elsa's anxiety grew with her fear that someone had betrayed them. It was hard to bear, but it was even harder not to know what was happening to Aragon and Dudach. There was a rumour throughout the prison that the Germans made use of torture during interrogations. There was poison everywhere.

On Bastille Day there was talk that the French Revolution had been a Jewish conspiracy; the inmates demanded that the Germans ban the celebrations. Yet some prisoners roared the 'Marseillaise' as though they had been drinking, and Elsa heard herself join in the chorus.

Their luck held for ten days; then, after many rumours, the yard rang with cheers as a loudspeaker spoke of the release of a hundred prisoners. Aragon, Elsa and Dudach were among them. Even then she felt that the enemy was playing cat and mouse with them in the hope that they might lead them to other comrades when they reached Paris.

* * *

Radio-Vichy is commenting on the speech in which Goebbels called for a crusade against Bolshevism. The Germans have crossed the Soviet border and struck deep into the U.S.S.R. Grodno is in their hands; Vilnius and Slonim have fallen. The newsreels show French volunteers giving the Nazi salute as they march out of the Vélodrome d'Hiver to join Goebbels' crusade. The New German Order will extend from the coast of Europe to the China Sea.

Another item deals with the secrets of the Russian Embassy in Paris, where the Germans had found gas-fired ovens and sinister inquisitional peep-holes. What use did the Slavs have for such apparatus?

The programme ends with a film about the Jewish peril: a scampering huddle of rats, as the commentator condemns the hygiene in ghettos.

* * *

Jean Paulhan and Germaine were waiting at the station. When Elsa remarked on the *vélo-taxis* on the concourse, Paulhan told her that Paris had few buses now, and how, since the Germans banned taxis in the city, there were even more *vélo-taxi* drivers. They would pay two hundred francs to ride to Jacques Lipchitz's house. After dark the price would double. However, it was a safe way to travel since the Germans rarely stopped these vehicles.

Aragon and Elsa felt foolish sitting in the rickshaw, with a straining white coolie hauling them. The vehicle was a throwback to colonialism, and led Aragon back to Pierre Mercadier, the hero of *Les Voyageurs de l'impériale*, based on his grandfather. Both men had lived for the view from the *impériale*, the upper deck of Paris buses, which Aragon made a moving stage on which they rode without a thought for the world below.

Elsa bought some cheap *ersatz* platform shoes and wore her scarf turban-fashion like the other women she saw in the district where they were staying.

The Lithuanian sculptor Lipchitz's house was full of twenties and thirties bric-à-brac: ornaments, knick-knacks, some photographs of his work, including one of his reclining nude with a guitar. His clothes still hung in the wardrobes. Everything was clearly the same as it was when he fled to America, leaving Édouard Pignon in charge.

Pignon saw himself as a Communist, even though he had no Party card; he had painted *L'Ouvrier mort* in the thirties, and was busy now with what he called Fauve-tricolours as a protest against the drab misery of the times. He said that they would have to sleep rough; he had Georges Politzer, his wife Maïe and Danièle Casanova staying there already. Elsa was a friend of Danièle's, who had trained as a dental surgeon, and had led the Young Communists since 1935.

'What happened to Lipchitz's sculptures?' Aragon asked.

'They're here,' Pignon said.

'Where?'

Smiling, Pignon led him to the window and pointed to the garden. 'I buried every piece he left behind.'

Aragon could hear Elsa and Politzer in the living room damning de Gaulle as an imperialist and a tool of the English. Then Elsa called to him through the open door, 'You should never have let that martial pontiff hitch his worm-eaten wagon to your star by reading your poems over the air waves.'

'If he had said that was his intention, I might have done something,' Aragon called back.

The Germans were victors in Europe. They had fixed a huge V on the Eiffel Tower to show it, as crude as a prop from some Surrealist stunt, and hung ceremonial swastikas on the façades of the Meurice, the Crillon and the Hôtel Continental, which served as their headquarters.

The streets Elsa walked had been the hub of her universe. It was the city Brassaï photographed by night: the solitude of the *quais*, rotting graveyards and frenetic parties. Lulled into the past by familiar places, German posters hit her with the force of a blow, or sudden bells as a patrol in field-grey uniforms swept by on bicycles. Voltera no longer owned Luna Park; after the fire, it was now the haunt of cheap, low-life girls who seemed to revel in that ambience of greasy distorting mirrors to sell their bodies. Conquest had turned out to be a boring business; the *boches* pined for letters from home. Nothing in them could explain why they were there; the girls had no meaning in their pre-war dresses and faded scarves. Even their pimps were out-of-date Staviskys, aloof as their girls haggled with the master race.

'One of the first things the Germans did when they occupied Paris was to confiscate every copy of *Mein Kampf* they could find,' Paulhan said the next day.

Aragon was quick with the reason. 'Hardly surprising. It's a political agitator's primer; it could put ideas into people's heads.'

'Perhaps. There are few ideas elsewhere. The only real spark of resistance in Paris now is the Free University, and *La Pensée Libre*. Our friend Georges is behind both. You must know the review, I think. Germaine and I have fixed a meeting at its offices so that you can present your plan for a National Writers' Committee to its contributors.'

Elsa turned to face Germaine. 'Who will be there, apart from Georges and Maïe?'

'Mauriac, Guéhenno and Blazat promised to come,' Germaine replied.

Left alone while Aragon and Paulhan went to talk to the writer Georges Duhamel to ask for his support at the meeting, Elsa spent the day walking the streets again, piecing together a photomontage of past and present images. She relived some of Aragon's walks with Breton; how their one-time bravura had seemed to set them apart, yet confirm that they were part of the same rat pack. They all sought, but never found, those occult powers they craved. They saw themselves as the heirs of Gérard de Nerval, but to

Elsa they were mice scuttering around in a treadmill. Often it seemed to her that all Aragon and the Surrealists ever did was to idle away their days writing chain letters – boasting triumphal sneers against religion, usually. Then she was sad; she could see the light in the Opéra arcade as she entered the Café Certâ, long defunct. Quite what the Basque had in mind when he opened the place, nobody knew. The names he gave his cocktails were exotic, but the place was seedy and working-class, customers sat on greasy chairs hunched over oak barrel tables, the lighting so poor you could never see who was there. Then Tzara and Breton took the place over, adding Manhattans and other lethal Dada cocktails. Elsa felt her eyes smart again in smoky dance halls and Zelli's night-club.

Why were the Surrealists so mad for Anglo-Saxon things? Was it, as Breton said, because the British Empire was so much greater than the French? That was not it; they envied the English for Lewis Carroll, for the detective stories. They were like children; captivated by bizarre conjunctions: dolls with sex organs, eyeballs and insects, elephants, maps and clocks.

A pale German soldier with black-rimmed spectacles had set up his easel at the gate of Montparnasse cemetery as Elsa waited for the Politzers and Danièle Casanova. 'Not much of a recruiting poster for the master race,' Danièle said by way of greeting, with a nod towards the artist. Politzer's smile reminded Elsa that he had been the inspiration for Sartre's Antoine Roquentin.

It was one o'clock; the plan was to dine with Aragon. He was not in the Dôme and did not arrive before the mandatory ten minutes elapsed.

Politzer looked at his watch. 'We can hang on a while longer.'

Elsa puts on her gloves. 'No, Louis is very strict. I must always act as though things have fallen out badly.'

'Five minutes can do no harm,' Danièle said.

Elsa hated having to pass the two German women in grey uniforms. She gagged in the swift ambush of their perfume as she left. They were police women known as grey mice, who were about to enter the doorway. She loathed the fear they inspired in her. She hesitated a moment, concerned for the Politzers and Danièle; but they joined her as soon as she began to walk.

'Where are you going, then?' Politzer caught her arm.

'I don't know. Back to the apartment, if I feel it's safe.'

They had reached the Saint-Cloud *métro* when Danièle cried out that she saw Aragon. He was standing on the steps and waved to them as he came across.

Elsa's voice was shrill. 'Why are you here?'

She took his arm and they quickened their pace.

Aragon glanced back, smiling at the Politzers. 'I went to the wrong restaurant. As soon as I sat down, I knew I'd made a mistake. I was trying to leave as soon as I could, when I saw Robert Desnos. He realised, as I did, that to speak would draw attention to us both. He had the same dazed look as when he found Breton's postcard from the Île-de-Seine. We just smiled at each other, and I ran out of the place.'

Politzer, who walked abreast now, shook his head. 'His features are so Jewish. It is suicidal of him to go on using cafés.'

Desnos had written the script of *Starfish* with Man Ray, the libretto of Darius Milhaud's cantata *The Four Elements*. For Aragon, Robert had been the shaman, more a seer than a poet. He had admired his piece about Atget and his film criticisms for *Ce Soir*.

Danièle smiled. 'That trance: did he chase Éluard around a garden and try to knife him?'

Aragon did not seem to hear her question. He shook his head. 'I saw him, then I didn't know what to do. I knew I had made a mistake. When I got to the *métro*, I was trying to form a plan of action. I knew I was late. I suppose I hoped that Elsa might turn up soon to catch a train, since I don't have a key to the house.'

Elsa now felt calm enough to kiss his cheek. 'How did your meeting with Duhamel go?'

Aragon shrugged. 'He pushed his spectacles up on his forehead, you know his habit, and said that he knew we were fighting fascism. However, I was still Stalin's stooge. Bolshevism was Bolshevism, no matter what the guise. After that, he showed us the door, with another salvo of anti-Soviet bile. I told him he should have done with it; he ought to join the Legion of French Volunteers and help bring down the Soviet Union.'

Duhamel's refusal left Aragon still gloomy during dinner with the Paulhans the following evening. Elsa said he had been too sanguine in imagining that Duhamel was going to risk his livelihood with any show of solidarity; it was never a theme he dealt with in his novels, those she had read. She recalled that Doctor Georges Duhamel had abused Apollinaire as a junk shop poet when he reviewed *Alcools*. There were other writers, and they would join. Aragon did not have much patience.

They touched on Elsa's photomontage. Her labyrinthine itinerary moved Aragon to ask Paulhan how Picasso and other friends were coping.

'Last winter he wrote a play called *Le désir attrapé par la queue*. He did it in three days; with himself as the star, naturally.' Germaine laughed.

'He wrote Tzara into the character of Onion, and himself into Bigfoot, whose final cry is, "1800! Good-bye misery, eggs, milk and milkmaid! I am the master of the jackpot!" The second act takes place on the landing of Sordid's Hotel, which is full of naked feet complaining of chilblains. There is a Punch and Judy crocodile that eats a policeman. It reminded me of Apollinaire's *Mamelles de Tirésias*. His paintings? Zette Leiris is looking after Kahnweiler's gallery, of course. She is at risk every time she stages a private showing of Pablo's work.'

'Where is Breton now?'

'In Marseilles, I heard last, where the U.S. Consulate runs an Emergency Rescue Committee for escape artists. Max Ernst and Victor Serge have gone there.'

'It sounds like a bolt-hole for Trotskyists,' Elsa said coldly.

'Carrots appear in every dish, because everything else has been looted for Germany,' Germaine told Elsa.

'Artists play doggo,' Paulhan said, 'but art is not dead. We have a glut of fakes. Prices at the Jeu de Paume auctions are ridiculous. Some Fritzes are stupid enough to buy anything; but, since the exchange rate is in their favour, any junk they take to Berlin makes a profit. Haberstock snaps up the choice titbits for Hitler to gloat over. He paid almost a hundred thousand francs for Courbet's *Rivoli*, and made off with Veronese's *Leda and the Swan*.'

Germaine sighed. 'Damning painters is bread and butter to vultures like Lucien Rebatet and his filthy gang. They spend their days spitting on Chagall; sneering at his women who walk upside down, and abusing his Jewish morbidity – what they call his "palavers of rabbis".'

Just before they left, Germaine took Elsa to one side and said, 'Do you mind if I ask you whether you have any food tickets to cover the meal, otherwise we'll starve the rest of the week.'

'The Germans destroy hospitality, too.' Aragon was sad. 'They sully friendship and make everything sordid.'

Outside, a late sunset tinted the city with a harsh glare. The sirens began to warn of an air raid. The wail rose and fell as people ran for shelter. None of it meant anything to the couple in a doorway they passed. They were intent on kissing, wrestling with furtive, illicit urgency, the woman on tip-toe to reach the man's mouth as his hands groped inside her blouse.

Elsa turned to look back. 'There's the Paris I love; neither the R.A.F. nor the Germans can stop that.'

The street lights came on; masked with the same blue paint as the railway stations, the light they shed was dismal.

On the way home to Nice, they went to Varetz to see Rénard de Jouvenel. They had not been there long when the poet Léon Moussinac arrived with his wife Jeanne. He was a friend, and an old comrade who had joined the Party before Aragon, in 1924. He was there to recuperate from his sojourn in prison.

'"La Belle Épicière" is a piece about life as repetition,' Elsa told Moussinac. 'It is about everything I loathed in the street where it takes place. Things happen without people knowing why; they meet, only to lose each other again in the habitual, living out what is unknowable in each other. In my story, Madame Bovary has trouble with her ovaries as well as her banal dreams.'

When Aragon went to see his mother, he found the Communist painter Boris Tazlitsky in Cahors. They talked about Aubusson in the Renaissance period, and how Lurçat, Dufy and others were creating vibrant new tapestries again. Why had it taken a defeat to bring this about? Aragon suggested that they should incorporate poems as border legends, as weavers had done in the fifteenth century. 'You must use these tapestries to rescue those themes from being exploited in Pétain's vile studios.'

In Toulouse, Sadoul brought Jean Cassou to meet Aragon. The Germans had fired Cassou from his post at the Musée d'Art Moderne. He had a decided view of things; his firm, strong face was more like a judge's than an art critic's. He was a Spanish-born Catholic idealist, and had been one of the first to take up arms against Vichy. He was now teaching railway workers how to sabotage their trains.

It seemed almost a pre-war afternoon as they rode their bicycles into the meadow, a slick of green seeds building around the men's turn-ups before the grass tangled in the wheel spokes and brought them down. Elsa undid the straps of the picnic basket, her blue dress dark against the fretted lacework of meadow herbs.

'I read your book about Matisse,' Aragon told Cassou.

'I can't think of it as a book; a brochure, perhaps. The last time I spoke of Matisse was with Maillol, shortly after France fell apart.' Cassou laughs. 'It all seemed so awful that day. The only time I laughed was when Aristide told me that he would do a war memorial, but only if he could use his naked girls.'

The picnic had the tranquillity of idyll, but they were only a metaphor away from yellow buttercups to the yellow pig-skin of Jean-Hérold Paquis's pistol holster; Paquis, mouthpiece for fascism on Paris radio, who loved to strut the boulevards with the enemy.

'Their uniforms and weapons are the outward proof of the *collabos'* desire for a new civil war,' Aragon said.

'The only people they could want to shoot would be us,' said Sadoul.

Walking along the river bank, they passed a man eating sandwiches under a willow tree. He was wearing rimless spectacles, and his heavy leather coat seemed too heavy in that heat not to be suspicious.

Cassou craned his head round to look. 'That's not how the locals dress.'

Sadoul laid his arm across Cassou's shoulder. 'What do you think he's doing, then?'

'Communing with nature, I hope.' Aragon flicked at the grass with his stick.

'And if he isn't?' Cassou's calmness impressed Elsa.

'You want us to kill him?' Sadoul demanded.

'None of you is armed,' Elsa pointed out, struck by the surreal comedy of the idea. 'Are you going to use your bare hands?'

'If it comes to it, we will have to,' Aragon said.

'One step at a time,' Cassou ordered. 'We'll head quickly for the bikes, as soon as we pass him; then, separate if he follows us.'

They agreed to the plan, and the incident was over, but by the time Aragon and Elsa went to stay at Seghers's house in Les Angles, Cassou was in solitary confinement at Toulouse prison.

Seghers and Aragon came with news of an assassination attempt. A youth had shot Laval, Marcel Déat and three others at a parade at the Borgnier-Desbordes barracks. Laval was reviewing the Légion des Volontaires contre le Bolchevisme when Paul Collette, an ex-sailor from Caen, fired at him. Two of the bullets hit Laval in the shoulder and chest. He was coughing up blood on his way to hospital. The X-ray showed that the 6.33 mm bullet had narrowly missed his heart.

'I take it that this Collette has nothing to do with us,' Elsa said.

Aragon shook his head. 'No. He signed up for the L.V.B. in the hope that he might come close to, and be able to kill, some of our leading *collabos*. The Germans wanted to shoot him immediately, but Laval interceded on his behalf. Ever the politician, Laval knew what effect the execution of young Collette would have. Of course, there will be a trial and a sentence, before Pétain signs the reprieve.'

'We need young men as brave as him.'

'I think we have to ask why he joined the L.V.B.,' Seghers said. 'It attracts more criminals than the Foreign Legion.'

'I say: bravo, Collette!' Aragon gave a clenched fist salute.

* * *

Matisse's letter to Aragon tells how gall-bladder attacks hamper progress on the Ronsard plates. Then Varian Fry arrives. To make it hard for him to urge flight to Air-Bel again, Matisse climbs a step ladder to examine *La verdure*, a large woodland scene in which a faun charms a sleeping nymph with pan-pipes.

'This painting has worried me ever since I started it in 1936.'

'What's the problem?'

'How much to paint, I think. If I leave out too much, it will look unfinished. So I seek an empty radiance of colour, which is hard to find; also the right balance is difficult to achieve. Objects should never look as though they are falling into non-existence. You have come to repeat your offer of a refuge at Air-Bel again.' Matisse sighs. 'There are many insecure abodes in France these days. How safe is your safe house?'

'No, this time I'm asking for your help. I would like you to be a patron of our Emergency Rescue Committee. Your friend Maillol has agreed, and André Gide has come aboard.'

Fry polishes his spectacles, and asks whether Matisse would object to him taking some photographs.

'Not at all, unless you expect me to take up a pose or assume an expression of some sort.'

'As you are will be fine.'

The faun leans over a nymph. She is lying on her back, one arm above her featureless face; her body is candy-floss pink amid white tree trunks. Between this palisade are the various shades of green that give the picture its title. The border has two grey strips inside an outer maroon frame.

Albert Skira arrives from Switzerland, with gossip from Shangri-La, a world remote from Vichy. He is critical of the banks in Geneva and Lausanne for transacting dubious deals between the combatants. He damns the banks for using the old words: absolute secrecy, confidential and discretion as they have always done. 'Nothing changes except the number of those people they murder; the Reichsbank's gold is bloodier. Now I have said enough about my life, Henri. I did not come for that. I came to plead with you to write your autobiography.'

'Writing one's memoirs must give such a dubious pleasure that one ought to resist the temptation,' Matisse says. 'I would prefer to illustrate an anthology I have taken from Ronsard's *Amours*.'

Skira applauds the idea. 'That is wonderful! Such a book would be the best antidote to the poison of war.'

Matisse nods agreement, and smiles. 'Poisons have always been part of my life. Copper arsenate is a dreadful pigment, yet they call it Emerald Green, a name that hides any threat to the user. It is as old as painting itself, and doesn't mix with other sulphur-based colours. In Romanesque murals, this green is fresh and deadly as the day it came off the brush.' He pauses. 'Yes, I aim to do some thirty or so lithographs for the Ronsard. If my health continues to improve, I could visit Zurich for the printing.'

'No,' Skira says, 'Malraux has written nothing since the war started; until then, his books were of a piece with the plight of France. It seems centuries since I published *Royaume farfelu*. As he said, God died first, then Man. I see Giacometti now and then at the Café du Commerce. We discussed Brecht's *Mother Courage and Her Children*, which had its première in Zurich. Brecht has to keep a foothold in Europe, Alberto said. He misses his Paris studio, of course. He is paying sixty francs a month to live without heat or running water in a drab hotel. He has to beg the rent from his mother.'

'I thought his father left him money.'

'Did he? Well, it is his mother who controls the purse strings.'

* * *

In the early hours, there were six bomb blasts in Paris that wrecked the city's synagogues; the seventh came as an official 'safety measure'. As Elsa mulled over the explosions, she knew what was missing from her books. Unlike Aragon, she had no way to speak of the Paris blasts, such was the nature of her writing. Aragon dealt with actual events; his narratives were not fictions, and she envied him that. She determined to come to grips with reality in future works.

When Aragon met Elsa on the beach, he stripped to his bathing trunks. It was autumn; the weather was still warm enough to bring the Italian ice cream sellers out. Italians were everywhere now: bar owners, shopkeepers and tradesmen. Nearby, the old Englishwoman in her faded red straw hat had plumped for her usual place. Firm in her testy tenacity, she seemed to deny that Dunkirk had happened. She was one of those fictive beach characters of the period, all living out their mutual illusions, letting life drift by until the breeze grew chillier.

'Here's Célimène,' Elsa said.

Célimène kept her body in shape, despite being well into her prime. She still felt entitled to those fresh leases of life that bronzed young men gave her. Why her current spineless Adonis had put up with her vagaries for so long, Elsa had no idea.

Célimène sat on the orange leather mock pumpkin that she took to the beach every day, smoothing lotion on her face. Her lover was about to hand over her sun-glasses, when he saw them and waved. He told Célimène, and she came over and knelt beside Elsa to kiss her on the cheek. It was a gesture she had never made before.

'You must go,' she said.

'I don't understand, Célimène.'

'The police came round again to ask more questions. They want me to spy on you, to listen in to your telephone calls. I'm no stool pigeon, and I don't want to be one. You can't stay any longer in my apartment.'

* * *

Lydia brings the news that the Vichy authorities are to expel Varian Fry from France.

'Yes, it was only a question of time,' Matisse says.

'He did well to save as many refugees as he has,' Lydia says, opening the window. 'You need some air. I will take you for a walk.'

'Perhaps, but not too far. Where would we go?'

'Anywhere you want.'

Lydia stares at her reflection, then fastens the buttons of his overcoat as he sits in his wheel-chair.

'I don't need a coat.'

Soon, they are among the tombs and gravestones of the cemetery.

'I can see my coffin being buried here.' Matisse gestures towards the tombs.

'You're making a mistake if you think I brought you here to discuss that.'

'Here, or below the château.' Matisse is silent for a moment. 'My father could never understand why Australians were dying at Gallipoli, just as I find it impossible to grasp the horrors of Hitler's war. Varian Fry deserves some sort of award.'

'Vermeer often used camera obscura to view his subjects; it lent an arcane quality to his paintings. If I hung a Mallarmé mirror in my interiors, my aim was not to echo his quest for mystery; for me, as for Vermeer, the mirror translated reality through reflection. I was thinking of my Collioure pictures this morning, especially the one where Margot sits at the table reading. I was there in sepia, and the mirror was brightly steady at the heart of things reflecting sky, sea, and the palm tree.'

Matisse knows what is about to happen as soon the wind rises and whirls in chill spirals, blowing grit into his face. He pulls his hat brim over his eyes as Lydia heads for the shelter of a wall. Above, a woman runs into a room, then out onto the balcony; her voice is a sudden bird-like twitter as she closes the shutters. Lightning flashes in the mountains above the city; the loud cloudburst brings the rain. Quick rivers turn swiftly into floods that swirl sudden rafts of leaves.

Glomaud and his wife are sheltering under the trees near the Régina. He wears a Légion Française des Combattants uniform, and tells Matisse that the storm caught them leaving a rally. After a botched attempt at a Masonic handshake, Glomaud laughs to bridge the awkward silence.

'You must stay with us until this storm is over,' Matisse says, lacking enthusiasm.

Lydia sniffs critically as the lift ascends; Glomaud reeks of spirits. Matisse racks his brain for the original Madame Glomaud, until he calls to mind Degas's absinthe-drinking woman in the bar.

Madame Glomaud's basket is as heavy with bottles as it was the first time they met Matisse, and she insists that they must all have a brandy to warm them up.

'Monsieur Matisse, I have to tell you that I did not hold with the treatment the Légion meted out to André Gide when he came to lecture in Nice,' Glomaud says. 'No, he is a man of culture; whatever else he gets up to in private.'

'I don't care for Légion rallies; but he can't get anywhere unless he belongs,' Madame Glomaud says quietly as she fills the glasses Lydia has brought.

Lydia has dried her hair, so she can think of no reason to leave the room. She stands by the window to watch the lightning. Madame Glomaud hates the bright bolts that still flicker around the walls every now and then, and the thunder rolling in the mountains.

'I have gone back to being a barber.' Glomaud strops an invisible razor. 'It's not a trade I like – far from it – but, at my age, I have no choice. In me, you see a peasant, Monsieur Matisse; a sad man who cannot return to his rightful place in the scheme of things.' He takes off his beret and sits with his legs apart, hands resting on his knees, looking at the paintings. 'You have a beautiful apartment, Monsieur Matisse, with every comfort.'

'Courbet, Manet, Degas, Lautrec and Cézanne were lucky enough to have independent incomes,' Matisse says. 'I had a hard time making ends meet. The price was high. Now I find it costly being a painter; there is the material aspect; the quality of the canvas, of the oils, the frames, and other things we artists use to obtain our effects.'

Glomaud's chuckle is sly. 'Now, I'm not some nosy tax inspector, Monsieur Matisse, but I know that you must be worth more than a few francs.'

Two Friends

The two women share the same chair; the brunette in the green dress leaning back with her head resting against her friend's wine-coloured blouse. Glomaud does not care for the painting, which Matisse says he is working on. 'What are you going to do about their arms?'

Matisse wheels his chair across the room. 'Do? I don't know what you mean.'

'They seem a trifle too long; not quite right, to my way of thinking.'

'An artist should not worry too much about anatomy.'

'Are they actresses or models?' Glomaud asks.

'They are friends; that's why I call the painting Les deux amis. However, you would do better to see it as a fusion of surfaces and patterns.'

Glomaud inspects another painting. 'Are these the same women? Is the dark one a Jew?'

'Yes, they are the same women; it is a variation on a theme.' Matisse is testy now. Glomaud's wife offers another brandy.

Her husband raises his glass in a toast to Xavier Vallat, the lawyer now in charge of the Légion Française des Combattants. As he does so, he sees that Lydia has put her glass down in a pointed refusal.

'I can understand your refusal to salute my chief, madame; the actions of great men are often hard to fathom. In France, there were five thousand Jews pre-war; now we have sixty times that number; this is a blight that Xavier Vallat will put right. As a Russian, madame, you will know that the Soviet Union has more Jews than fleas. The Germans will correct that, I hope. Being a White Russian, of course, you must hate the Bolsheviks quite as much as we do.'

'I think we have all had enough to drink, Monsieur Glomaud,' Lydia says.

Glomaud turns to Matisse. 'Believe me, we know how to take care of people; those who are our friends, whom we respect; and those who are our enemies and have no right to be in our country. We are analysing the problem of the Jews on a scientific basis. Things have changed since we met last, Monsieur Matisse. I am confident now that our future lies in the new united Europe.'

By now, the storm is almost over, and the room dims as evening falls. Somewhere, children shriek at play before the light goes. Glomaud opens the lid of his fob watch. 'Marianne, we are late again,' he says. 'I can hear your mother now.' He puts on his beret and clicks his heels as he salutes Matisse.

'I know the Marshal married Eugénie Hérain when he was sixty-four, but I do think that we have only ourselves to blame for our troubles when we grab an older man for security,' Madame Glomaud says.

Lydia blushes hotly at the thought of sinking into familiarity with the woman. It is also becoming clear by now that Matisse has had too much to drink.

Lydia rounds on Matisse when they have gone. 'What a gruesome pair! How do you come to know them?'

'Didn't I tell you? I met them in the shooting gallery I used to go to.'

'You were mad to ask them here. Was it because you were afraid?'

'What do you mean?'

'Anybody could see that he was threatening us.'

'Glomaud is an old soldier, a patriotic Frenchman who fought for his country in two wars.'

Lydia's laugh is derisive. 'These days it is a patriot's duty to find traitors wherever he goes; to brand them for ideas he does not share.'

'You think I'm a marked man now.'

'Glomaud and his friends are the ones who knock on doors at night. Don't imagine you will be exempt.'

* * *

Napoleon Bonaparte once stayed at the hotel next to the Opéra where Aragon and Elsa rented a cold, drab room. They lived there until November; then they found a small apartment above a restaurant on the

Ponchettes, between the quai des États-Unis and the Cité du Parc. Nearby, through the arch, was the place Gautier where the Niçois came to buy fish and flowers in the outdoor market. The *préfecture* was on the far side of the square; but Aragon was sure that the police would never look for them there.

'Like Edgar Allan Poe's letter – in full view, yet unseen,' Elsa told Célimène when she met her in the market some months later. Their landlady expressed surprise to find them still in Nice; the police chief had informed her that they had left the city.

Elsa was writing *Le Cheval Blanc*. Aragon chafed at not being able to visit Matisse. He could compromise the old man if he went to Cimiez while the police were tailing him.

* * *

The assassins who shot the German officer have become enemies of the state, guilty of the crime of murder. The killers are Jews or Communists in every paper that Matisse reads; as though Vichy wanted to play down the fact that they were Frenchmen. Now that Vichy is living with Germany, it is essential to maintain law and order. Pétain, our saintly Father, has offered his life to save one of the 'terrorists', but has been talked out of his gesture because of fears that the Germans might take him hostage, and force him to sign any law they wanted. The stability of France is at stake, of course; so the Marshal does not say a word about Chateaubriant in his radio broadcast. He attacks the murderers of Lieutenant-Colonel Holtz, *Feld kommandant* of Nantes.

Matisse has a reply to a letter he wrote to Bonnard suggesting that he could solve his winter heating problems by booking into a Cannes hotel. Bonnard points out that even luxury hotels have no heating before the middle of December. No, he is better off in his own crib. He has wasted some time flattering the mayor, trying to coax a scuttle or two of coal out of him. There is no coal anywhere. He has enough wood and coal for two months, and he is going to wrap up like an Eskimo. In any case, the hotels were lousy with German spies and people he disliked. He feels more at ease with his grocer and tobacconist. He agrees that he has to keep his old bones on the move, and he does that well enough. His eyesight worries him, of course, but he uses the drops the doctor gave him. In the last two months, there has been a great improvement.

Ivy, Flowers and Fruit

While Matisse works every morning on *Lierre en fleurs*, which features ivy trailing from a white vase decorated with a red flower, Panzer tanks roll into the suburbs of Moscow to fight the last battle of the year. For Hitler, it will decide the fate of his crusade. He says he will raze the Kremlin to signal the death of Communism.

A great evacuation is taking place. Eleven million people are moving to Siberia; state farm workers, thousands of factory workers, the teachers of schools, museum staff, doctors and nurses, artists. Machinery, herds of cattle, art works and libraries travel with these refugees. Everything at risk is being shipped to Kazakhstan by road and rail. The epic scale of the enterprise is unbelievable.

Lydia listens to the B.B.C., hating the Germans and hoping that the city's defences will hold. She leaves the radio and deals the cards for a game of Patience. Sometimes it would seem as though she will never escape from her artificial paradise; that she has hurt herself by her renunciation, has sacrificed her life to live with Matisse's mediation of it.

* * *

It was one of those mornings when a fog hid the sea, so that people were no more than shadows, watercolour tints. Soft and subtle, its pastels smoothed away all trace of the war; yet, somewhere, a military band boomed from a wireless set.

Aragon could hear the regular splash of waves to his left. It was a calming way to reach the bookshop run by Pierre Abraham and Gabrielle Gras, one of the few places in Nice where he felt that change was feasible, and that revolt was stirring in France.

As he went up the steps, a sudden shower fell from the palm fronds above. A boy on a bicycle whistled past as he crossed the promenade. Already the fog was lifting out to sea, leaving a bright haze of pink and blue, burnished with gold.

Gabrielle met him in the doorway. From her look he knew that the news was bad: a comrade arrested, another German execution. This time it was worse.

'They have shot Gabriel Péri,' she said, taking his arm to lead him inside the bookshop.

Péri was a Communist and Aragon's friend who wrote on foreign affairs in *L'Humanité*. He had been active in the pre-war period against

France's anti-appeasement policy. The Germans told him he could save himself if he renounced the Party, which he refused to do.

Pierre came over with a glass of brandy. Aragon shook his head numbly. 'Where did Gabriel die?'

'In the moat at Mont-Saint-Valérien, I suppose, as usual; there were others,' Gabrielle said.

'Jacques Decour?'

Gabrielle nodded.

Aragon was scathing of himself. 'I feel bad because I can't do anything. I can't retaliate. I'm impotent, a creature of words, a writer. Facing an enemy firing squad, our people must feel that they are dying alone in an indifferent France. The best that we can hope for them is that they remember the warmth and solidarity they felt with us.'

'We can only go on fostering our belief until it is an irresistible force,' said Abraham. 'France needs your words, Louis; we need words of hope.'

He gave Aragon the facsimile of Gabriel's final letter, which Aragon used when he wrote his 'Ballade de celui qui chanta dans les supplices' – fifteen stanzas in praise of Péri:

> *'If I had it to do again*
> *I would tread this path.'*
> *His voice sang of the dawn*
> *Rising lightly from his shackles.*

'I must write to Mathilde,' Elsa said. 'Not only is Gabriel dead, but she is alone among the swine who killed him.'

Aragon handed her the poem to deliver to the bookshop. 'I feel I have to go to Cimiez now,' he said.

Aragon went alone to see Matisse. 'I told him that all I knew about Cimiez was that the English writer D.H. Lawrence died there. I mentioned the phoenix carved by a local peasant on his gravestone, which he had never seen.' He describes Lydia Delectorskaya for Elsa, then goes on to describe his visit.

The master of Cimiez's beard was no longer red, of course; but he was the same stern, upright figure who used to sit alone with a glass of mineral water in the Dôme café, hand on the gold knob of his cane. Unlike other artists – Braque, Picasso, Derain and Kees Van Dongen – Matisse kept aloof. No one dared to disturb his reverie. It would have been unthinkable, an act of sacrilege. Aragon said he found his presence daunting when he saw Matisse, the artisan – sleeves rolled up, facing his easel, out of focus and intent as he studied his model, Henriette. Aragon showed Elsa the photograph that Man Ray took through his spectacles because he had forgotten his camera lens.

It was a dismal Christmas Day as they boarded the bus outside the Galéries Lafayette. Soon, with four other huddled passengers, they were shivering as the bus climbed through a dank mist that hid Nice below.

'Surely, you could have met him sooner, in Paris?'

'I don't know. I thought I would in 1914, but I went to war instead, with his portrait of Madame Matisse in my suitcase. I was sharing a room with Breton, who loathed the painting when I pinned it up. We had rows about it. I tried to fix a meeting to take your mind off Vladimir's death. I am glad that it has come about.'

They rode uphill for fifteen minutes until they reached a fork in the road where dark cypresses hid the Roman ruins of the Arena. There, a white statue of a woman with a broken nose loomed briefly out of the mist. Adoring girls knelt around her, offering a chaplet. 'Queen Victoria,' Aragon said, as they turned towards the Régina.

Elsa craned her head over her shoulder, lifting one leg to check her stockings. 'Are my seams straight?'

*   *   *

Matisse studies the catalogue of his exhibition at the Louis Carré Gallery in Paris. 'It is gratifying that the government has bought *Nature morte au magnolia*,' he says. 'I see it as an act of affirmation. It cut me more than I want to admit when Paris turned down the first version of *La danse* in favour of Dufy's *Électricité*.'

'I find it odd that you let such a thing get under your skin. The grateful nation is never short of cash when it comes to war memorials.'

'I fail to see what that has to do with buying my painting.'

Lydia glances at her watch. 'They should be here any minute.'

Matisse nods. 'Did you know that Apollinaire invented the word "Surrealism"? He used it in his programme notes to *Parade*; Breton was still an army psychiatrist, dealing with cases of shell shock. When he wrote off the politics of Dada, he replaced them with the poetics of Surrealism – an umbrella he was sure would shelter everybody. He donned the robes of a high priest, with an instinct for publicity that Tzara lacked. He tried to talk me into his church the day I took Margot to Man Ray's studio for her wedding photographs.' Matisse smiles. 'I think Breton distrusted humour. I heard a rare bark of a laugh now and again, if laughter is what it was. Aragon knew Apollinaire, of course, who asked him to write a piece about him. I read Aragon's early poems in *Nord-Sud*, the magazine that Apollinaire, Reverdy and Max Jacob founded. Is that the elevator I can hear now?'

* * *

'You didn't tell me that he lived in a palace.'

Aragon and Elsa leave the lift and ring the door-bell. Lydia ushers them past the six-foot plaster cast of the *Delphic Charioteer*, telling Elsa that it will give her an idea of the size of the apartment.

Matisse leans back in his chair to call out as Lydia shows their guests round the rooms, 'They built it for Madame d'Angleterre and her relations.'

Elsa's high heels click on the tiled and parquet floors as they move into each of the five high rooms off the hallway. The doors are solid wood and close with a heavy finality. She can hear the birds in their cages: Cardinals, Bengalis, Japanese warblers clamouring and singing to the African masks on the walls. For Elsa, these Negro carvings seem nothing more than curios in their lush setting, devoid now of witchcraft. They are in a room beside the conservatory, where a huge Tahitian philodendron overhangs a small tropical garden. Dried pumpkins and gourds lie on a black marble table next to some Chinese statuettes. Lydia speaks in Russian as she charms the weather away to point out the view of the Bay of Angels.

Matisse interrupts their tour when they come into earshot again, informing Lydia that he is ready for his tea, which he is sure everybody must be looking forward to.

In the kitchen, Lydia tells Elsa that she was the daughter of a Russian doctor, born in Tomsk, orphaned after her parents died in a cholera epidemic in 1922. 'A year later, my aunt took me to Manchuria, where I attended the Harbin High School. I went to Paris when I was nineteen and fell for a Russian refugee. He tried to fool himself that he was an adventurer. Our marriage was over by the time I was twenty. I had no ability, no skill, nothing Diaghilev could make something of; so I left for Nice. It was the time of the Depression, and I ran up against the French law that forbade me to work for wages. If things were awful for the French, they were worse for refugees. The only jobs I could find were casual: movie extra, fashion model, baby-sitter. I did some studio posing, but it was drudgery. I was lucky. I began to model for Monsieur Matisse in 1933; then, later, I nursed Madame Matisse, who was suffering with spinal trouble.'

'If he had not sold a Braque he owned, Aragon said he would have tried to commit suicide again; the cash financed his escape from Venice and Nancy Cunard. In Paris he moved in with Thirion and Georges Sadoul, where I joined him,' Elsa said.

'Oh yes, it led to all sorts of problems.

' "Don't think I enjoy being accused by a sewerage-worker's wife of taking part in orgies!" I can hear myself screaming. The woman had everybody in the building believing her nonsense; it gave them something to gossip about. She had worries of her own. Her husband messed around with other women. He drank, too, unless he was pumping ordure out of some cesspit.'

Lydia shudders. 'Yes, we both understand how difficult it is to live with creative people. It is probably easier for me because I am not much in myself; I have no special talent, I mean. Being a writer, your trials must be harder to bear.' She laughs. 'You are very Russian. Your accent is no credit to Mademoiselle Dâche.'

'Being the daughter of French parents born in Moscow, she wanted to turn me into a Frenchwoman too. I'm afraid I was a failure. I feel even more Russian, now that the Soviet Union is at war.'

'The Germans' behaviour is cruel and vile. I cry when I think of the savagery they are using against women and children. As soon as Monsieur Matisse falls asleep, I turn on the wireless to hear the news.'

'In those days, Aragon was a weaker man. I used to storm at him to get that bitch out of his life. She was poison for him, and he was just poor white trash for her. Instead of "*le Canard sauvage*" the joke was that he was "*le Cunard sauvage*". However, it was Aragon or some other fate; the other attractions were lesbians, or men I could not control, washouts; everybody was eating everybody; there were gulfs, pitfalls everywhere. I did not want to become a casualty, so I allowed Aragon to save me from myself, from going under. We are such perverse creatures. I play games now to fool myself that he can make me suffer. Do you have other men?'

'Do you expect me to tell you? Would you believe me if I denied it? No, there are these flowers; I bring them home; I arrange them, then sit still, hands folded, behaving while he makes the final touches. Is that sufficient?' Lydia says with a sigh. 'You have no idea.'

They speak in Russian; it is the language of their childhood, of intimate confession.

Aragon comes into the room where Matisse is sketching, saying, 'It occurs to me that I never thanked you for signing the petition Breton circulated for me.'

'We cannot lock up poets for writing poetry. You would not have been happy in the Santé; Apollinaire wasn't.'

Aragon stared down at the statue. 'For me, Victoria will always be Lewis Carroll's Queen.'

'Cézanne used to say that he painted for his coachman; not some meat baron in Chicago,' muses Matisse.

Elsa laughs. 'How many of his master's masterpieces did the coachman own?'

As a feint to Elsa's sarcasm, Aragon asks, 'Do you regret not meeting Cézanne when he was alive?'

'I could think of nothing to say after I bought his *Trois baigneuses*. Camoin, who used to write to him, did his military service at Aix and went to visit him. When he found the house, Cézanne came to the door in his night-shirt and cap – stolid, prickly. He held a lamp, with a yellow glass that shone against the blue wall, seemingly more fascinated by that optic marvel than Camoin. A fortunate distraction, I'd say. Camoin would do things like that. When he was in Arles, he knew no peace until he found Van Gogh's Doctor Gachet. Why? What did Gachet know about Van Gogh's art?'

Lydia offers them more tea. 'You say you are living in the Ponchettes?'

Matisse had lived near the church of Saint-Suaire; anybody could ring his door-bell; the card read 'Matisse: ring twice'. The sea front meant the promenade and the Hôtel Méditerranée, where he had found so much to delight him. The only thing he disliked was the festival, when everybody took part in the flower bombardment. 'The jazz bands made my models so skittish that they refused to sit still. One year, the thing was so distracting I had to paint it. Then Raoul Dufy came like some Riviera jewel thief, and he has been painting it ever since. He missed his calling as a shorthand typist or a fabric salesman. After he took Fauvism into the fashion houses, the department stores stole it, and now sell it by the yard.'

* * *

They left Matisse and walked to the Arena to wait for the bus. The statue was no longer visible in the fog. Aragon told her how Madame d'Angleterre chafed at her man-servant Tom Brown's fear of halting her carriage at the cross-roads in case of Fenian assassins.

'In those days, there was a one-legged comedian from Marseilles who begged around Nice in a go-cart pulled by two dogs. One morning he saw her carriage on the Villefranche road and opted to race his contraption against hers. It was the year of her Diamond Jubilee; she found his insolence amusing. She handed him a few francs. The trouble was that he began to meet her coach everywhere, with a sign boasting 'By special appointment to the Queen'.

Elsa laughed. 'You've just made it all up!'

'It happened. It's true.'

Numbed by the dimly lit bus, Elsa likened Matisse's models to Disney's Snow White, with her small breasts, her face devoid of any emotion. She said how much he seemed a prisoner of his situation, of his versions of reality; that birth and death had no place in his studio dream. None of his women menstruated or, if she did, it was unthinkable that she would admit it. At least Picasso's women had wombs that could give birth, even if the idea terrified him.

* * *

'A very attractive woman,' Matisse says.

'Yes, I could see you thought that.'

'She did not like it when I called her Madame Aragon.'

'Not at all.'

'She didn't impress you?'

'I thought both of them were charming. It quite moved me to speak Russian again.'

'I must write to Madame Triolet; I shall send her a small gift or a drawing. She must sit for me. Do you think she will?'

'Does she care for modern art? I'd imagine that naturalism would attract her more. Your work would strike her as decadent and formalist.'

'Decadent?'

'Come, come; don't pretend you haven't heard the word before. She supports the Communist Party. Repin would probably say more to her, or one of those heroic Soviet mechanics who paint Lenin inspiring the workers.'

Matisse shakes his head. 'I don't think so. Nobody married to a Surrealist could like Ilya Repin. Repin's sole talent was for making facile sketches. Madame Aragon is too chic and elegant, with too much good taste, to like a man who pictured Tolstoy as a soulful dolt.' He intends to find out.

It is Lydia knocking at the door. Matisse sits in the Victoria he has hired. As Elsa glances from the window, he raises his hat in a *droit de seigneur* manner that annoys her.

It is a sunny afternoon. At first, Matisse complains of being too hot under the rug Lydia insisted on for the trip, but the wind soon turns chill, swirling sand grit as the sun begins to set. As the coachman takes them at a brisk clip along the sea front, Elsa feels the pomposity of such an old-fashioned gesture at such a time of year. The weather, the hour of day, makes her recall the visit she and Aragon made to Coney Island. Why? There is no dwarf in a clown's costume, smoking a cigar. Nobody is on the beach, the streets are empty; there are no neon lights or booths, nor any hint that the masses would fill the beach and boardwalk in the morning, no candy floss, no truck with ice-wrapped, fish-smelling sacking.

Matisse frowns, looking at his watch; his face is pale. Lydia fusses another rug around his shoulders, asking if he is in pain.

Matisse rubs his brow. He asks whether either of them knows how the Promenade des Anglais got its name.

Elsa looks across at Aragon. He shakes his head.

Matisse closes his eyes to think. 'It was in the winter of 1821, if I have the date right, that a frost killed most of the orange trees around Nice. An English clergyman, the Reverend Louis Way, went among the British residents and persuaded them to fund relief work for the starving workers and their families. They built the coast road, which soon became known as the Promenade des Anglais. It was here that James Joyce began his dream of *Finnegans Wake*; and we are not far from where Isadora Duncan was strangled when her scarf caught in the wheel of her car.'

Abruptly, Matisse speaks of Ronsard. 'What I have in common with him is a love of stringed instruments: he played the viola.'

'Cassandra was the daughter of Jean Salviati, a Florentine banker,' Lydia replies to Elsa's question.

Elsa nods. 'I cannot excuse Ronsard for his anti-Semitism.'

Their drive along the promenade ends as Matisse orders the coachman to go to the rue Masséna.

The food served in the restaurant is better than that they ate at Coney Island, and far more expensive.

Matisse shivers, staring up at the moon. 'In the end, we find ourselves prisoners, just as Goya was.'

*

La Grande Illusion was showing at the cinema. Aragon fell asleep after his exertions; Elsa crammed bread into her mouth, moaning softly and trembling as she sat through Renoir's film again.

When she had first seen it she had thought that it was softening up France for a second German occupation. After a war of such slaughters, here was the 'good' German again; not a Grosz portrait of some atavistic butcher but a sympathetic von Stroheim with his monocle, his Utopian code of conduct. Here, the French natural aristocrat met his class counterpart in a closed society where honour ruled, felt in the bones, the blood. How could the Left fool itself that it was an anti-war film? It had served as a prelude to appeasement, and now as an ongoing parable for Vichy France, with its statutes against the Jews.

She wanted to share her anger with Louis, but he looked so pale in the flickering light. Leaving him to sleep, Elsa went out for air, tripping over the threadbare carpet as she met the old woman coming down the aisle. She was pumping a mist of disinfectant, nervous of the grunts of 'shit' greeting her.

The man in shirtsleeves, smoking by the kiosk, was surely her husband, for the cinema had a forlorn air of a family business that was failing: his wife to sell tickets, the skinny daughter to light patrons to their seats, the husband to work the projector.

The door to his booth was open, and the soundtrack was loud as von Rauffenstein ordered Boeldieu to come down or his guards would shoot him.

In the grim light of the foyer, the projectionist's face had the sunken cheeks of a dead man, as he asked whether Elsa felt all right.

Elsa told him she was fine as he opened the door for her, beaming his torch down onto the three steps. She said she did not intend to leave; cramp had made her leave the auditorium. She asked his opinion of the film. As a projectionist he had none, but he enjoyed Jean Gabin in gangster movies. A smell of almonds rose from his waistcoat. The Jew, Rosenthal, was whining now. He and Maréchal were in the mountains near the border. Rosenthal would never be other than a Jew. The loud soundtrack made sure there was no escape, so Elsa returned to Aragon to wait for Gabin to fall in love with the German farmer's wife.

Outside, the first snow of winter had begun to fall. On the other side of the world, Japan bombed Pearl Harbor.

1942

Woman with Veil

MATISSE folds his newspaper with a snort. 'There is nothing that war does not poison or kill; as Renoir said, it destroys the wrong people. The Shanghai art market sank without trace since the Japanese bombed Pearl Harbor.'

Lydia nods. 'To say nothing of America's fleet.'

Matisse twitches with disgust. 'The white race has lost face in the Pacific. There is now the Greater East Asia Co-Prosperity Sphere, whatever that is in practice. Even if America defeats the Japanese, things will never be the same again.'

* * *

Aragon heard that Nancy Cunard was putting in six-hour shifts in London translating or monitoring Ezra Pound's ravings on the evils of usury and the cleansing force of fascism. The same source spoke of having dull weekends at Berkhamsted with de Gaulle and Yvonne; how the General would drive to the Connaught Hotel early on Monday, with a fresh tirade against Churchill for his refusal to promise him the title deeds of France.

'Whenever I imagine England, I see the fat creamy throats of the red-haired women Burne-Jones and Rossetti loved to paint,' Elsa said.

Aragon smiled. 'A medical condition due to enlarged thyroid glands. All I see are those five hideous villas, circa 1890, which we had to admire when I suspected that Scotland Yard men might be tailing us. We were about to meet your mother to walk on Hampstead Heath.'

'Oh yes, our war had already broken out,' Elsa said, smiling.

'We were equating the Special Branch with the Gestapo.'

'I cannot conceive why our comrades in Marseilles are dealing with collaborators and criminals. The struggle is now a game; there are players and rules. Men and women trapped in this web of deceit die for nothing. I fear that we shall have more of this; it is the shape of things to come. I'm sure that Scotland Yard's men could fit very nicely into such a scenario.'

* * *

When the sound recordist finds a voice level that allows for the twittering of the birds, the interviewer asks Matisse why he paints. His reply is that he does so to translate his feelings into colour and design. 'No film camera can do that, even though the quality of Technicolor is better, these days. The cinema, however, has certain advantages over my canvases.'

If this is so, why do we need painters?

'The artist uses rhythm and colour to give form to his innermost feelings. One must talk about purity of procedure. Unmixed colours are the key to expression, and expression has little to do with anything intellectual. I consider a work finished when I can add nothing more; when it reflects my emotions. I have been a painter fifty years now; I can remember all my canvases.'

The artist must always paint well; eternal vigilance is the price he has to pay.

Could Henri Matisse say why his open-window paintings are so charming?

'Their charm for me lies in the illusion that the space from the horizon to the interior is continuous. The window frame does not divide two worlds; one could perhaps reach out and touch a passing boat as easily as any object in the room.'

* * *

Elsa was busy making *foie gras* to repay the master of Cimiez for taking them to dine at the Coquille. Jeanne Moussinac had made her a present of some goose liver. The problem was how to prepare it. Their landlord offered to help. He used to cook at Larue's, and now owned La Pergola on the quayside. He scribbled a recipe and said he would bring the port in the morning, when he would have time to oversee her efforts.

That night, the sudden arrival of cars woke Aragon and Elsa. Afraid that the police had come to arrest them, they dressed quickly; but when Aragon ran to the window, he saw the landlord and his wife leaving on stretchers. They were unconscious, overcome by fumes from their stove.

Elsa recounted this incident to Matisse and Lydia over lunch.

'They're all right, I hope,' Lydia said.

'They should be back tonight or early tomorrow.' Aragon opened the wine.

Matisse sank into the chair with a sigh, and looked round. 'I like this room; everything is to hand, neat and tidy.'

Elsa set the plates out on the table. 'You mean we live like sardines in a

152

tin. Louis likes the bustle of the Ponchettes. The noise of the flower vans gives me headaches.'

Matisse sniffed the aroma deeply. 'Vollard's girl, Odette Mathieu, always served curried chicken when I dined with him. I came to see it as Réunion Island's national dish.'

'I began to see how to paint Nice when the American Army took over the Hôtel Beau-Rivage, and I had to move to the Méditerranée. There, I found inspiration in the room's wallpaper and decorations. A low sun cast shadows of the stone balustrade on the carpet. The sea was slate-blue under a brightening storm sky. On the sea front, the pedestrians resembled flakes of soot between the balustrades of the balcony. Some were Yankee soldiers, as I recall, but I did not see them as such. They were moving black marks in a brightness that fused with the light in the room, until the luminosity of the air was palpable. The painting was *L'intérieur à la boîte de violon*. Each soft colour chased into its patterned neighbour to achieve an overall calm under the Italian ceiling. I created a homely feel by using subdued and neutral tones, which set off the green-blue plush lining of the violin case lying across the dull gold of the armchair.'

Aragon told Matisse about the café at Dunkirk.

Elsa and Lydia tried to steer the conversation into other channels. 'Those were the days when a woman had no need to talk. She could make love by playing with her fan.'

When Lydia's remark failed, Elsa reverted to Picasso; as though nothing was more natural. 'Any woman who says she doesn't know what she is doing when making eyes at him deserves everything she gets.'

Matisse laughed. 'Pablo takes an unholy delight in creating gossip. Dali is the only painter I know who outdoes him in this respect. What a ghastly responsibility it must be to be born a Spaniard, eh?'

'Yes, Dali squanders his talent,' Elsa agreed. 'He is one of those artists who, avid to become legends, fall into the pit of being a celebrity.'

'I suppose I tried to flee Cubism by going to Morocco, but there was no escape.' Matisse half turned in his chair and stared out to sea. 'I shudder now to think what will happen to our colonies after the war.'

Lydia shook her head. She did not see how a Frenchman could show his face in Dahomey now, with the Germans strutting the boulevards of Paris.

'To whom we make a gift of four hundred million francs a day for the pleasure,' Matisse said with distaste.

'Nobody who looks down on Collioure can fail to see a Matisse,' argued Aragon.

Matisse shrugged. 'I always felt the place was Spanish; it had only been French for a hundred years or so.'

When Elsa offered more *foie gras*, Matisse protested. 'I have already stuffed myself. You'll have me lumbering out of here like a bear who has had his paw in a honey-pot.'

Aragon raised his glass to announce that his marriage to Elsa was three years old, and that Matisse and Lydia's visit had made him doubly happy.

Later that day, Aragon and Elsa finished the rest of the goose liver with Francis Carco and his wife, Germaine. Carco had aged into a thick-set, worldly prelate with a big hooked nose, the flesh sagging now around his jaw. He spoke of the life of Verlaine he was writing, then of his meeting Matisse in the arcade of the place Masséna the previous year. 'He was so benign; he had the air of a saint. He asked me up to Cimiez to see his paintings. How hard he works, I felt ashamed! I recalled Colette saying to me once that discipline cures everything. It was a maxim that Matisse embodied; that masterful old man was hauling France out of the shit single-handed.'

'You did listen to the interview?' Elsa asked.

'From the tone of your voice, I gather I missed something.'

'Matisse must not give the regime his public support.'

'You can't think he's doing such a thing,' Germaine said.

'If we are at war with Vichy, how else can I see it?'

Carco cannot agree. Living as Matisse did, how could anything seem changed in France? Rouault was around the corner painting in Juan-les-Pins. There was Puy; there were Camoin and Rouveyre, and there was Bonnard. Some shortages, yes, but no hardship that could come between him and his life's work.

Carco spoke of boarding the Trans-Siberian express at the Exhibition in 1900, enjoying the comfort of the salon, dazzled by the glitter of crystal and mirrors as the painted scroll of steppes and great rivers unrolled in the window. Surely Marquet's brushwork? As he sped past vast gold mines and Mongol tombs, a moujik poured vodka; then, in the same way as a bag of gold became a spear in a Méliès film, that hairy actor vanished; a Chinese lad in blue silk pyjamas served jasmine-scented tea; Carco stood at the gates of the Forbidden City.

'Ah, to be young again,' he said.

Aragon accused him of nostalgia for the empty way of life they used to have; those long afternoon parties on the lawn, kept up until the end of 1939. 'The war has shrunk the world forever, where now can you hope to locate your earthly paradise?'

'When I met you on election day, you were afraid that the rain would make people stay at home,' Carco reminded Aragon.

'Eighty-five per cent of those who did turn out voted for the Front Populaire, Blum and his "Judaeo-Masonic riff-raff"',' Elsa said.

Carco smiled. 'Rich people were quick to bolt their shutters when they heard the result. That there were no riots must have been a bit of a let-down; but I did see a subtle change: servants began to answer back. The Stock Market fell; the nabobs began to buy gold and export their assets abroad. In May, as we know, the Renault workers at Boulogne-Billancourt shut down the assembly lines and workers came out everywhere: rail-men, taxi-drivers, waiters. I met Robert Capa who had just been drinking wine with the strikers on the rooftop garden of the Galeries Lafayette. After the first wild excitement of the strike, the occupation of the store, they found life boring, he said. They were playing cards, reading about themselves in the newspapers, or falling asleep.'

Germaine goes to the mirror to touch her hair. 'Had he been to Copenhagen to photograph Trotsky and Laurel and Hardy then?'

Elsa denied that she had envied Meret Oppenheim. Aragon only said that because he had drunk too much. Nobody by then was listening. They were relishing the 'patriotism is shit' insults Sadoul and Caupenne had spat at Keller, a Saint-Cyr officer, who took them to court.

'Caupenne's sordid apology put paid to his life as a Surrealist,' said Germaine.

'Sadoul never did serve his prison sentence,' said Carco.

Elsa laughed. 'No, Marie-Laure gave him the fare, and he fled to join us in Kharkov.'

Aragon sighed. 'Kiki's trial was more fun, of course; it was a theatrical farce.'

'It didn't matter what paedophilic fantasy Picasso was acting out with his latest Alice in Wonderland,' said Carco. 'Max Jacob was always present.' He went on to picture Max lying on an old mattress at the Bateau-Lavoir, sniffling as he tried to keep his feet warm; how he dealt the Hanged Man, Knave of Swords, the Cups from his greasy deck of tarot cards. 'The only time he paused was to kill a bedbug,' Carco said. 'I used to think it was that iron toilet that mesmerised him, but Pablo told me he was seeing Christ in a yellow silk robe trimmed with blue, gliding across the room.'

'Max was seeing him everywhere; even when he went to the cinema, Jesus would walk through a close-up of an oblivious Fernandel,' Aragon said with a laugh.

'It was our friend Doctor Louis Joullien who was the deus ex machina behind Pablo's Blue Period. He was in charge of the hospital in Saint-Lazare, and offered Picasso his patients to use as models. They had to wear their white caps that signified they had the clap, but they would cost Picasso nothing. I felt I should pay a visit, too, as a poet, and put on my best Zola suit.

'High windows shed a dim light on waxed floors; there was prayer, endless work. The public face was spotless, but not its inmates; there were no baths, showers or towels; I breathed through my mouth to avoid the stink of dirty flesh. My stomach turned over when I saw those gruesome tools in the infirmary, with its stink of ammonia and fleshly decay. Pablo was never a moraliser; his paintings had nothing to say about the real degradation and grief I saw, even though some of the women had infants at their breasts. I shudder when I think that such prisons must be rife in France now. In those days, I was glib. I dealt with the place as a metaphor for evil, scribbling notes for some future literary work. I used to tell myself that Baudelaire would have felt at home there.'

It was Elsa who asked Aragon about the funeral Chanel gave Radiguet. 'Some of the mourners were near fainting from the scent of the white flowers filling the church; everything was white except for the red roses on the coffin, like bloodstains in a fairy tale. Picasso was joking with Brancusi as he sketched the Negro jazz band playing the white hearse along, drawn by white horses in the rain.'

'Poets die otherwise now, against walls, on the edge of ditches that wait for them,' Elsa said.

The next day, Aragon learned that his mother was ill and dying at Cahors.

How to turn reality into fiction! Fiction enabled the writer to live the lives of other people, and to pass his hints along to a reader who was longing to enlarge his experience. Aragon's mother had lived the reality out of which he had forged his fictions, putting jigsaw facts together. Yet there were dark holes in his life that he would never understand now, for it was too late to question her. His mother was dying; and a boy was whistling a song about a girl who was sad because she had to sell herself; stifling guilt overcame Aragon, along with hatred for the shame he had felt since his youth. It hurt him because another winter was over, and his mother would not see the spring.

He sat by the bed, straining to hear the news on the B.B.C. The Germans were using their mechanical drone to jam the signal, rising and falling. It had been the smell of incense that made him feel sick when his father died; in his prime, the scourge of the Lyons Commune and, later, police chief of Paris. Why had Elsa wanted to come? Why had his father, an atheist, sent for a priest? It amused Aragon to imagine what the priest would have said if he had known that he was the anti-Christ who had written 'Front Rouge':

> When crowds came in from the suburbs
> And in the place de la République
> met in a black flood, closing like a fist
> the shops had shutters over their eyes
> so as not to see history go by
> I remember Mayday nineteen-seven
> when terror shook the gilt salons
> They forbade lessons for the children
> in western suburbs where rage was a far echo
> I remember the Ferrer demonstration
> when the black rose of infamy
> burst against the Spanish Embassy
> Paris it was not long ago
> that you witnessed the march for Jaurès
> and the cries for Sacco and Vanzetti
> Paris your crossroad nostrils still twitch . . .

His mother wanted to hear what was happening in the world. The news from the Far East was bad: the British Army was falling back in Burma; the Americans were losing the Philippines. The Japanese had won a string of victories, and were now bombing Port Darwin and threatening to invade Australia. There was nothing he could do except lie to ease her last moments; leaning over her, he whispered that the Russians were advancing along the whole front.

There were hierarchies of black wooden angels on the hearse, and the midges rose in a cluster above the canopy. An old horse was nervous between the shafts, jerking a crest of black plumes. The flowers that hung on each side gave off cruel scents as Aragon passed. Stars glinted on the panels of the hearse, and the black curtains had gilt fringes. They were burying some big-wig in the same graveyard as his mother, while a labourer in a blue smock wheeled her shrunken corpse on a cart that reminded Aragon of Lourdes.

His mother's neighbours had known each other since childhood. The men wore high collars and Sunday-best suits, stiff as totem-poles; the wives stood staid and tight-lipped beside the *curé*, who was down-at-heel in the Bernanos tradition. One family had their idiot child with them, having nobody at home to look after him.

They lined up to offer their respects, although most of them had never seen Aragon before. He felt alone until a youth took his arm to whisper that he had delivered his mother's food ration every week. She had confided to him that her son was a poet. Suddenly he began to murmur French poets' names: Villon, Gautier, Mallarmé, Rimbaud; they had all influenced his poetry, he said proudly.

After the funeral, Aragon heard that Sadoul was away in Toulouse. However, he was able to meet Lurçat, the writer André Wurmser and other Party members living in the area. He had not seen Lurçat for some time. The former Surrealist painter was now a Communist. He had quit Paris and taken a studio in Aubusson, where he painted his vision of the Dordogne countryside, its butterflies and flowers, for tapestries.

Aragon asked the writers for anti-Vichy pieces. As CNE members, he pledged them to combat Vichy anthologies and journals, to refuse to write for any paper or periodical that published collaborators. Lurçat said, 'Most anthologies are instruments of policy; they tend to be a last refuge for poets with national feeling, the fate that awaits born propagandists.'

When a *collabo* found a miniature coffin in the mail he knew that it meant he was a marked man. To endorse the threat, some coffins were real.

'It's not that *collabos* want to consort actively with the enemy; it's simply that they don't want an enemy,' Aragon said to Wurmser. 'A *collabo* wants the world to go on being the way it was before the war. Hitler has defeated us; the Germans boss us about on every level – yet the *collabo* shuts his eyes to this.'

* * *

158

Lydia reads Mallarmé's *Hérodiade* aloud to Matisse, then sighs. 'Sibyls saving their old nails for the Magi, a bleached dress kept in an ivory chest; how can you take this man seriously?'

'Hérodiade was a princess of Idumea; the Anglo-Saxons know her as Salome. Her stepfather was Herod Antipas, tetrarch of Galilee, who gave her the Baptist's head.'

Lydia sniffs, unmoved. 'He did not let his nurse say much. Her job seems to be to encourage Hérodiade to revel in the stink of old bones and the aroma of roses. His poetry reminds me of that useless table-rapping Indian-guide stuff my aunt's loony friends got up to on grey afternoons.'

'I have always felt that Mallarmé was a kindred spirit. How can you say you admire my work, if you detest his poems so much? My pictures are a timeless yet modern embodiment of everything he strove for.' Matisse picks up the book, reading, ' "For it is undeniably not from the elementary sonorities of brasses, strings, woodwinds, but from the intellectual word at its apogee that music results, plenteously and clearly, as the sum of the relationships existing among all things." I could be speaking my own mind! Mallarmé also points out that a short poem has a great deal of blank space around it. How the whiteness is like a silence around the work, which should dictate the shape on the page, in line with the demands of the idea or the meaning. Now that is exactly how I feel!'

Matisse smiles. 'Mallarmé died in the autumn, a sad season, the time in which Seurat painted his gas-lit band. Misia had gone with him to Verlaine's funeral, joining a cortège that left the boulevard Saint-Michel. Mallarmé spent the time reviling Rimbaud, that flea-bag, that provincial gutter-snipe who had treated his friend so cruelly. He did not notice how the procession was growing; there were thousands by the time the coffin reached the cemetery in the suburbs an hour later.' Matisse looks at his watch. 'Bonnard is late. Unless he comes soon, he will not get home again.'

'The poor man must be lonely now. Why doesn't he stay here?'

'Neither of us could make him feel at ease. He would soon miss his Spartan mode of life.'

Bonnard wears a mourning band when he arrives. 'Give me your hand,' Matisse urges. 'I can't tell you how much Marthe's death stunned us both.'

'I could not say much to anybody; to talk about it drained the life out of me. It shook me deeply. Forty-nine years we were together, and every hour was Marthe's; every woman was Marthe. I keep the door of her room locked now. You must know why. I spent too many happy hours painting her there. I find it hard to be stoic about it, as you advised when my brother died.'

Lydia says, 'We wanted to come to the funeral; but Monsieur Matisse is rarely well enough to go anywhere, these days.'

'Henri is lucky to have survived.'

Matisse jokes about the nuns calling him Lazarus reborn, then, catching Lydia's frown, tries to laugh the remark off.

'Everything I owned was in Marthe's name, you know. In order to hold on to my own things, I had to forge her signature on a will I drew up. I had nightmares. I cannot abide lawyers.'

Bonnard speaks of his present work, of the Saint Francis de Sales mural, pointing out how Vuillard resembled Francis de Sales. He is doing the work as a memorial to his old friend with its stained-glass blues, purples and mauves. 'On the other hand, I can't see myself ever finishing my white circus horse. I know where I have been, but it's not easy to see where I am going. You are one of my few remaining friends left alive. Sometimes I feel I am a Martian.'

Matisse grips Bonnard's shoulder in an attempt to lighten the mood, asking him whether he has seen the article in *L'Illustration* on the finding of the Lascaux caves. 'We are too old now to brave the climb, but I would like to see these paintings. We both know what a mess the reproduction of art can lead to. It is lines like these, with this vibrant kinetic energy, which I am aiming at in *Pasiphaé*.'

'An art gallery in the rocks is a charming idea,' Bonnard murmurs, with dreamy astonishment. 'Yes, to see such creatures by the light of an oil lamp would be quite dramatic. It would have the quality of a magic lantern show.'

'Or one of Moreau's canvases,' Matisse agrees. 'Primitive man was masterly in the use of ochre and soot. Prehistoric tribes knew a great deal about music and painting.'

'In the autumn of 1940 André went home to Chambourcy,' Bonnard says, when they discuss Derain's latest painting. 'His neighbours told him that the Germans were going to shoot him because he was a Jew who had made obscene drawings of the Führer. You know how a peasant can be. The *boches* let him use two of his rooms while they roistered and insulted him everywhere else in the house. He tried to work at his Rabelais wood-cuts but it was impossible under those conditions. He went to live in Paris until the Germans decided to leave.'

'You seem sure of what you say.'

'There are other versions, of course,' Bonnard says. 'Last year, he went with Van Dongen to Breker's Orangerie exhibition. Breker needed Maillol's presence so badly that he sent a Lieutenant Heller to escort him to the show.'

'I read Cocteau's 'Salut à Breker' in *Comœdia*.'

'The show was to raise cash for the Wehrmacht. Picasso wants Derain and Van Dongen shot, I hear. Though how he can say that when he entertains Ernst Jünger in his studio, I've no idea.'

'You know more than I do about what's going on.'

'Not so; Paris, for me, is on the dark side of the moon. Most of the friends I had there are dead.'

'I am often with Derain at Collioure; our shadows merge again on the quay as we face the *clocher*, spattering chrome yellows at our canvases,' Matisse says. 'Those days were blue and golden; they seduced us both with bright witchcraft as we hurled Nietzsche's thunderbolts at each other.'

'The Gestapo came round to ask him for proof that he was not a Jew,' Bonnard says. 'No? Then why did he accuse the German Army of vandalism and theft? He said he was not; there was no point, since he had no proof which unit had done it. As to being a Jew, it was not true. Then it came: several French artists had agreed to visit German art galleries. The Germans said he must go too.'

Matisse nods. 'An invitation arrived for me.'

Bonnard does not pick up on this remark. 'If Derain agreed, they would give him his house back. He argued that all he did was work, and never travelled. He heard nothing more until a model he used to paint turned up. Do you remember the Greek girl, Mimina? She had married Arno Breker, who was behind the visit. A few days later, the same officer arrived to collect Derain's luggage, and he was on a train to Berlin. He did try. He went off with a list of artists in prison camps, in the hope that he could help them. That must have given the Germans a laugh. No, his job was to smile for the cameras and pretend that the arts were flourishing in the Third Reich. When he got back, all he could do was to crack jokes about the colossal bollocks on Breker's nudes until the Germans warned him to stop. His name is mud now, of course.'

'When I first met him in Carrière's studio, he was a painting machine; he did a canvas twice as quickly as I could,' Matisse says.

Bonnard says he hates those Jews who use their profits in the casinos and speculate on the currency market, even in foodstuffs. Since they came, the price of everything had gone up. There were dozens of art dealers living now in Cannes. No longer was the Riviera the haunt of dud princes, retired appeal court judges who made a killing out of the Stavisky affair, or couturiers too old to face a visit to the fashion houses they had established. The bankers had gone, along with their clients: those aristocratic invalids, those mining engineers who had made their fortunes in South Africa. A tribe of exiles had taken their place: frightened Jews who hid cows in their garages so that they would have milk.

He takes out his wallet and hands Matisse postcards of Vermeer's *Street in Delft* and Seurat's *Les baigneurs*, explaining that he had stopped off to buy them on his way.

Matisse says, 'Both artists used the scientific ideas of their day. Yet they are such different paintings.' He lays the postcards on the bedside table.

Bonnard puts the postcards back in his pocket. 'Did I tell you that I refused a commission to paint Pétain's portrait?'

'They were not willing to pay enough?'

'That's not why I refused.'

'You mean you did not want to go to Vichy.'

'I could have used a photograph. No, only collaborators and school-children paint Pétain these days.'

Matisse has probably told Bonnard about his first flight in an aeroplane, but he decides that it will do no harm to tell it again. 'I felt foolish being weighed at the Victoria terminal before we piled aboard the charabanc for Croydon aerodrome. I don't recall whether I flew Air-France or Silver Wing, but I believe the aircraft was a Handley Page; although, again, I may be wrong. There was a pillar set with clocks showing the time at various Imperial Airways destinations. I could see the Lufthansa manager seeing off his Junkers with a Nazi salute. Aboard the plane, I sat in a chintz-covered armchair as though I were in an ordinary room – highly disconcerting and strange. The sort of thing Jules Verne used to dream up. The cabin lads wore page-boy uniforms with gilt buttons. At half-past twelve, a whistle blast came twice, a salute, and the mechanics pulled the chocks away, a green light was flashing in the window of the control tower. I could face a fine and six months in prison if I lit a cigarette, the cabin boy said. I remember how solid the clouds seemed; an illusion of not moving, yet we were soon flying over the beaches at Dieppe. It was almost over; there was the Eiffel Tower below, and no bigger than the model they sell. A few minutes later, we were landing at Le Bourget.'

'Sketching is the best way I know to arrive at the essence of a country,' Matisse says. 'Camoin became ill with diphtheria after he arrived in Morocco with Amélie. We thought he'd die. I sat with Amélie in the pharmacy, sketching of course, as we waited to collect his medicine. Outside, they were lighting the oil lamps in the bazaars; there was a smell of lamb grilling over blazing charcoal. Suddenly, there came the call to prayer from the mosque. It startled the newly arrived *colon*'s wife who, smiling nervously at Amélie, seemed about to say something before she changed her mind. Poor woman.'

'Suppositories?' I said, looking at the box.

'Those he will have to administer himself.'

* * *

As Aragon and Léon Nordmann walked along the Promenade des Anglais, the attorney was giving Aragon an eye-witness account of the executions at Châteaubriant.

'The German sentries took over from the Garde Mobile on the Monday evening,' said Nordmann. 'They fired some shots during the night, which made everybody jumpy. At nine o'clock on Tuesday evening the Germans came again, and the rumours became rife. Nobody doubted what was going to happen; the chief topic of talk that night was whether it would be death by guillotine or a firing squad. It was daylight before they slept. On the Wednesday, Lieutenant Moreau and Second Lieutenant Touya acted out a pantomime at the camp gate. They were arguing as to whether the trucks would have room enough to pass.'

The sea was a lucent kidney-bean green; the same green as in Aragon's poem, Nordmann mused. They embraced outside the Hôtel Negresco. Aragon warned him to take care, and waited until he could no longer see Nordmann in the silver-pink glare of the sunset. There were the same shifty black marketeers; the sea-front touts doing joyless deals and the whores drumming up custom. Walking home, Aragon passed many of the city's refugee tramps and down-at-heel trapeze artists; the tarts who lived on the promise of work at the Studios Victorine. None of them would lose any sleep that night because the Germans had tied twenty-seven hostages to stakes in a sand-pit.

After the Communist Youth Battalion shot Holtz in front of the cathedral at Nantes, the Châteaubriant sub-prefect's secretary went to Paris with the camp's records. There, the Interior Minister, Pierre Pucheu, chose twenty-seven names to atone for the crime. The Germans had already killed sixteen hostages at Nantes the day before.

Aragon stopped writing to stare at the horizon. It was hard to live with hostages who were about to die. The failing light was ashen over a slowly darkening swell. Two dogs nosed a ball by the sea's edge, one of them hurling itself at the waves every so often. Everything was as usual in Nice: street cleaners sweeping away the market rubbish, music on a radio below, Elsa writing in a kitchen made aromatic by the sawdust-burning stove.

All the hostages could bequeath their families were long nights of pain, and the grief that would start again on the morrow.

Barthélemy was writing to his wife. He saw the gendarmes snap to attention as Touya unlocked the gate to admit a German officer. After saluting, they came into the barracks and ordered each man to step forward when he heard his name. Barthélemy was one, Ploumarch another; fifteen men responded until they called the name: Delavaquerie. Delavaquerie was in another camp. The officer went on to call Guy Moquet's name. Moquet was seventeen years old.

The parish priest had arrived from Béré on his bicycle to hear the men's confessions. Madame Kérivel, a hostage's wife, had gone to kiss her husband good-bye. When she heard that Moquet would die, she ran to Lieutenant Moreau, and shouted that he was a criminal. 'Let the boy live! He is only seventeen. Let me die in his place with my husband.'

Moreau brushed her aside and sent her back to the women's barracks.

At three o'clock, when the German trucks arrived, the hostages began to sing the 'Marseillaise'. The gendarmes went through each prisoner's pockets before tying his hands. Then they stood, shoulder to shoulder, nine to each truck, still singing *Ils viennent jusque dans nos bras, égorger nos fils et nos compagnes*. The four hundred prisoners left in the barracks came out to sing, too, as the trucks drove out of the camp. They went on singing until the German sentry blew his whistle. Touya's shame and nervous disgust were clear to see in the awful silence that fell.

When, later, Elsa read what Aragon had written, she was to recall his face as he wrote, calm, even cold, without emotion. 'You need this; you look all in,' she said. She handed him a glass of brandy that she had been saving.

'It must be late,' Aragon said.

She asked him when he would finish the piece.

'I should complete it in an hour or so. How is your work coming along?'

'I don't know what I'm doing. Everything has become meaningless. Real events give the lie to everything. Writing about peacetime characters while living through this war is probably beyond my capability. I feel crazy.'

'Get some sleep,' Aragon ordered. 'When you work too long there's always a danger of despair creeping in.'

Madame Kérivel marched among the women's barracks that night, urging them not to give in to their grief; life must go on. She told them that the party they had planned for Sunday must go ahead. She kept this up for as long as she could, then sat down and began to sob. It was only possible to sustain heroism for so long, yet there were times in France now when everybody was ready to die for someone they did not know, so long as they were against the enemy. They were beautiful; their voices, their eyes, as they lived life like a love-song.

The next day, the gendarmes handed back to the men all that they had taken. They had changed; driven by shame and guilt they told the truth about the events in a sand-pit two kilometres north of Châteaubriant. They told how the people in the streets took off their hats as the hostages went by, still singing. They spoke of the farmer and his family who lived near the sand-pit, and had watched the Germans drive in the stakes. The sentries had driven these people at gun point into their kitchen, ordering them to bolt the doors and shutters. There was a machine-gun aimed at the farm during the executions. They heard the first volley of shots at 3.55; another volley came at 4.00, and the final volley at 4.20. The victims refused a bandage for their eyes, and had shouted *'Vive la France'* to the last man. Many of them roared slogans in support of Communism and Soviet Russia.

The Germans had packing cases ready for the bodies; these were all one size. One of the men was so big they used a crowbar to force him in. They left these crude cases stacked in the town hall overnight. Loudly vocal against their use, the mayor paid for coffins for his countrymen.

No martyrs, no memorial, said the German diktat. In the morning they sent the unmarked coffins in batches of three to several graveyards, so that no mourner should know their kin. Two of the dead were union men; Timbault was the Secretary of the Metal Workers, and Ploumarch organised the Chemical Workers.

Guy Moquet, whose father was a Communist, kept his courage until it was his turn; then he fainted. They tied him to a stake and shot him. His crime had been to distribute Gaullist tracts. His last letter was to his mother; in it he hoped that his death would serve some purpose. Moquet sent his love to her and to his brother, and said he regretted nothing. The Germans took down the stakes on the Sunday; as soon as they left, five thousand people brought flowers from all parts of the region.

One of the first questions the Radiodiffusion nationale interviewer put to Matisse was about the Prix de Rome scholarship, for which the students at the École des Beaux Arts competed annually. He said that it should die a beautiful death.

Elsa leaned forward, twisting her fingers in exasperation. 'I have heard it all before. Why do I listen to him? I can hear those damned birds in the background.'

Aragon nodded.

Matisse went on to say that Manet, Renoir, Degas, Cézanne – none of them had won, or needed to win, the Prix de Rome. Did any postcard-merchant sign up artists who got the prize? The cronies of the Beaux Arts were a mutual-aid society whose role was to rob artists of their instinct, their curiosity, and turn them into weak invalids at a time when their future hung in the balance.

'Some people drift to the right through inertia,' Elsa said. 'Matisse refuses to consider his position. He avoids any such quaint demands by painting as easily and disarmingly as a child.'

When they asked him how the state could help artists, Matisse said that it could finance free studios; it could offer travelling scholarships, so that artists could live or study in any country with nourishment for their talent.

Elsa shook her head. 'If he says his true love is France, why does he endorse Vichy? He is happy with the status quo. What he hates is the prospect of chaos.'

In Matisse's case, the myth would persist, and the world had to tinker with that, modify it, and wipe out any unsightly blemish.

'We know how he wants us to see him,' she said, 'how he presents himself.'

Elsa looked down from the balcony as the sun caught Tristan Tzara's monocle. He brandished his Charlie Chaplin stick; both were old props, and he swapped the monocle for spectacles as soon as Elsa came out to greet him. He was obviously showing off his maroon-coloured car with pale tan leather seating.

Elsa called back to Aragon who was coming down the stairs. 'Our impostor from Zurich is here!'

Dadaism was born in Hugo Ball's Café Voltaire in Munich. For the Rumanian, Tristan Tzara, Dadaism was a response to the dire carnage of the war. His Manifesto came out in *Dada 3*, the magazine which Breton and Aragon began to issue in France. It fired a blast against the romantic logic of psychoanalysis, and was for automatic writing and chance in poetry. Aragon read it when serving as a doctor at Courcelles, where the Germans buried him in an artillery barrage. There, he rescued wounded men under fire, and earned the Croix de Guerre for his bravery.

Tzara had not lost his schoolboy-trying-to-look-older face. Elsa always saw him in the Man Ray photograph, where he knelt to kiss Nancy Cunard's hand. She wore a top-hat, silver trouser suit and a mask. When Elsa reminded Tzara of this, he said:

'Man left at the start of the war. Breton is broadcasting for the Voice of America – poetic justice, I feel. He insists that the Yanks have only "rented" his larynx; his is no commitment. After his primal encounter with Freud, the "shabby Viennese G.P.", he claimed to have brought back the subconscious; I cannot imagine what marvel he will find in America.'

Aragon and Elsa knew what it must have cost Tzara to beg Breton to plead his case with the Emergency Committee, despite the fact that it had come to nothing. 'He was too busy hunting insects and butterflies to have much time for me,' Tzara said. 'I have spent a lifetime trying to escape being Sami Rosenstock, Moinesti's most famous son. These days, I have to run faster, that's all.'

Aragon filled their glasses with white wine. 'There was only one direction for the Surrealists, and we did not take it,' he said. 'Any slim link with life we had broke down when we refused to join the proletariat. By 1927 our posturing had no meaning any more. The only thing left was war.'

'There are too many old grievances; a hint of past betrayal stinks up the room. I could smell it at Air-Bel; rats scuttling off a sinking ship.'

Tzara told them that he lived at Sanary. 'When I reread *Anicet*, I asked around as to where you were and what you were doing. Sadoul gave me your address. I can see why the book has an eighteenth-century air about it. It holds up very well considering how long ago you wrote it. I liked the scene in the café where Anicet sees Rimbaud staring at the food the waiter has put before him, lost in the bliss of not eating it. You were right to call it a panorama. Picasso was Blue, of course, the spoilt genius bragging that his paintbrush is merely a tool to seduce women. You nailed Breton perfectly as Baptiste Ajamais. Yes, and Max as Chipre, a man who owns nothing and goes into exile. We are all exiles now; at the mercy of the four winds: Soupault works in Tunis; Artaud is in an asylum. He no longer writes to the Pope and the Dalai Lama; it is Hitler now. You had second sight to be so exact about Max's fate. I found it very moving to meet so many old friends and enemies again.'

'Have you heard any news of Max?'

'He stays buried at Benoît-sur-Loire: Mass every day, as he waits for the Gestapo to knock. They will come, of course; sooner rather than later.'

'You speak as though you have seen him,' Elsa said.

Tzara shook his head, then shrugged. 'We are all clinging to the same cliff-face. I overcame my fear and went to see what Paris was like. As I hurried to reach the hotel before the curfew, two men confronted me. What was more natural than that I should assume them to be Gestapo agents? Holding a gun to my head, they ordered me to keep my trap shut. I thought my life was over as they searched my pockets, but they were Mouffetard hoodlums, of course, and they knew that I was an easy target, a coward.

'Paris has gone to hell,' Tzara said. 'Wine, food, soap, toothpaste – everything in life is artificial now. I suppose we have only ourselves to blame: *gazogène* for petrol, acorns for coffee, and lies in place of truth. Servants want hush-money. They call it a wage-rise, but it's to buy their silence over some black-market ham hanging in the larder, or their *patron* listening to the B.B.C. The trenches in the avenue Kléber used to look temporary; now they have concrete parapets, and the machine-guns command those streets where the workers might march.'

'You must write, Tristan; the Resistance needs your voice.'

'I'm no Shéhérezade. I have no tales to tell that would keep them from chopping off my head. None of us can say much, or anything like those things that used to come so easily to us. What do you think I should write about?'

Sketches of Aragon

There are thirty sketches of Aragon pinned on the wall facing Matisse's bed; Aragon has counted them. Each one is a frame from a film sequence. The master must see his progress first thing every morning. They show that everything in Aragon's life has been fluid, shifting, even his desires. Both men and women have kissed his lips, and Matisse has made that clear in the curving charcoal shape of them. It is his mother's mouth, whom Matisse has never seen.

There is an armchair in front of a wall covered with variations on the same drawing. A large gilt mirror on wheels reflects some of these drawings.

'I was an illegitimate, born in Paris in 1897,' Aragon says. 'I came home as Louis Aragon, an adopted orphan, after spending thirteen months in Brittany. I learned to call my grandmother 'mother'; but it was my three sisters who looked after me. I felt closer to Marguerite who was my real mother, although I did not know it at the time. My case would have interested Freud, I dare say. Surrounded by women, I lived the happy lie, joyous, safe in the arms of my loving Marguerite. There were questions, but how was I to find answers? Why did my father go to Constantinople? If I look back, I learned to live with his absence in the old fairy-tale way, without anguish. I know now what it all meant. The way my mother had to live sickens me now; however, I understand better why she had to do it.'

After he lights a fresh cigarette, Matisse goes on drawing. 'Why did the Fauves feel they had to paint those places that the Impressionists put on the map?' Aragon asks.

'The Impressionists got rich painting such landscapes. Vollard was sure that the Fauves could do the same. His "Hollywood producer" instinct, Derain called it. It seemed divine intervention when we woke up one morning to find that we were Fauves. You are no different a person than you were the day before. Yet the label caught how we felt. Vauxcelles had a good day when he came up with that. Let's face it, the epithet put us on the map; it sold our paintings. There was safety in numbers; to have struggled alone – well, our success would have taken longer, if it came at all. Nevertheless, none of it was easy. When they voted me chairman of the Independents, I had to learn jury politics; I learned many tricks; some of which came in useful when I had to promote our paintings.'

Matisse pauses to reflect. 'I am a child running across a potato field, trying not to harm the crop: the earth covers my ankles, fills my shoes. If I look back, I can see Jean; his legs are shorter than mine, and he is stumbling in a haze of dust.'

Aragon smiles. 'I was six years old when I started my first novel. Each chapter had only a few lines. They were a rehash of things I had read in Zola. I kept on at it until I was nine. We had left the avenue de Vilars by then, and Marguerite was running a guest house in the avenue Carnot, near the Étoile. That drudgery ended when we moved to Neuilly, some time around 1904, and she could take me for walks in the park. I cannot say that I was in any way unusual; I was like any other pious French pupil except for my precocity. My tutor's name was Louis Andrieux. He was my godfather, they told me, which did not explain why he removed my father's photograph from its frame and substituted his own. I believed that my father was Fernand Toucas, who made his living as a gambler until Clemenceau closed all the casinos in Paris. I was eight at the time. I smashed my blue china cat and gave him all my savings.'

Matisse purses his lips amid the nicotine stains of his beard and goes on drawing. He has a few puffs of his cigarette, then lets it go out. He studies Aragon over the gold rims of his glasses. 'European sculpture is all about muscles and idealising forms, whereas African art is not,' he says.

'Where did you see tribal art first?' Aragon asks.

'At the World Fair, I think. It was the wrong *excursioniste Cook* ambience, all those crude Dahomey mud huts with straw roofs. There was a whiff of the real thing in a curio shop called "Le père sauvage". African art was in the air, or else how could the dealer hope to profit from those masks? In that sense, I can't claim to have made its presence felt in modern art. I bought some pieces and showed them to Picasso. I remember that one of the first things I pointed out to him was that nudes do not recline in African carvings.'

Suddenly, Aragon's Mercadier family reaches the Trocadéro on their visit to the World Fair. They stroll among Arab and English tourists in a world of frock coats, where soldiers wear red trousers. Aragon can hear the whine of Berber pipes and drums in the hot afternoon; then he watches the Mercadier family step into the cage to begin their Jules Verne trip to the bowels of the earth, starting in the sewers of Paris and going down to the catacombs. A guide's hoarse voice lectures on the iron and coal strata, the salt where miners swing picks in a fitful light.

Aragon smiles. It is a memory he can share with Matisse. Then he asks, 'How is it that you can square talking about art with your assertion that a painting must speak for itself?'

Matisse lifts his arm with a sharp theatrical flourish. 'What did Delacroix say? "Young artists, why do you wait for a subject? Everything is a subject, the subject is yourselves, your impressions, your emotions in front of nature. You must look inside yourself, not outwards." '

Aragon nods. 'How remote the world seems when Delacroix wrote that. He was urging artists to rid themselves of the church, patrons, ideologies, expectations.'

Matisse wakes early after a restless night. In his dream, he wore a Basque beret as three children pushed his wheel-chair along a forest trail. The children were invisible behind him, but he felt that they were his own. Suddenly, a German soldier with a rifle stepped out from the trees and ordered them to halt. Who are they, and what are they doing there? Marguerite (he recognised her voice) told the guard that they were not crossing the border, but searching for mushrooms.

Sighing, he opens the scrapbook into which he has pasted Ronsard's love lyrics. He wants Lydia to wake so that she can comfort him. Seeking solace, he draws Daphne turning into a tree, and a pen and ink study of Venus's Chariot for the Ronsard. There is always perfume and sex, sex and more sex.

Matisse takes up a violet crayon to work with. 'I want Frenchmen to read Charles of Orléans's ballades and rondels again. I have to shake the dust from those threadbare tapestries to reveal their jocund springtime colours. The same task awaits me with Ronsard's *Amours*.'

'You work so hard that I'm amazed that you don't collapse when you finish,' Aragon says.

'I am as strict about it as I was when I worked in the Louvre,' Matisse replies. 'I found myself envying Moreau, who sent me there, for his stern rigour and hard work. Twice a week from seven to eight, he would inspect our sketches; you could set your watch by him. Then from eight to ten he criticised our paintings in his studio. After lunch we all tramped back to the Louvre. There was a gruesome pecking order in his studio. If you were new you got the worst position; sometimes you couldn't see the model at all. He had twenty-five would-be painters, plus another twenty-five whose rich parents were financing them on some whim. It could be very jolly, too, with high-jinks, broken easels, and Three Musketeer tomfoolery.'

Matisse shows no emotion as he recalls their frolics. It is difficult for Aragon to believe that he took part, even when Matisse shows him a photograph of the candidates for the Prix de Rome, a gang escaped from a mental asylum. The amniotic fluids are not visible, but they surround the enchanter.

Aragon reads aloud:

> *Embrace me, Mistress! Kiss me, hold me.*
> *Hold me tight, breath to breath; warm my life;*
> *Give me a thousand and a thousand more kisses, I beg;*
> *Love needs, wants all without end; love allows no laws;*
> *Kiss me, and kiss me more, sweet lips.*

Lydia bustled round the apartment every so often, opening the doors; there is a burst of Charles Trenet singing 'Ta main dans la mienne'.

Matisse jabs towards the door with his pen. 'I suppose you must see him as a collaborator?'

Aragon does not respond.

'It is the devil's own job to adapt a woman to suit the image of our desire,' Matisse goes on. 'Ronsard's Cassandra had no love for her slave. Hélène de Surgères would not attend his Requiem Mass in Paris. People might read something into her gesture. She was deathly cold right to the end. She was an aloof muse.'

'I find it odd that all the girls he met were frigid.'

Matisse laughs. 'Queen Elizabeth sent him a diamond for love of his poetry; it can't have done much to assuage his bodily longings.'

'He said he read Aristotle and Euripides when the ladies gave him the cold shoulder. Is it possible, I wonder, that Freud studied Ronsard's case? All through his life he showed such a classic sublimation of the sexual urge.'

*   *   *

Literary France was applauding Aragon for *Le Crève-Cœur*. After finishing *Matisse-en-France*, he felt the urge to write fiction again. A visit by the publisher Robert Denoël interrupted him as soon as he went back to *Aurélien* again.

Elsa's face was pale; her eyes blazed. 'I am a Jew. I belong among those people you have made pariahs, a sub-species, in France. Yids, *yontres* – what do you call Jews, Robert? You made an early start, even before the Germans arrived. After that poison you brewed about the origin of the Jewish species, you had to publish your filthy primer on how to recognise a Jew.'

Elsa meant to attack Denoël, but he had smuggled a Jewish girl across the demarcation line.

'I know how you must feel, seeing me here; you must believe me when I say that I have given those ideas up. You can see that I am risking my neck for this woman.' Denoël glanced to where she lay sleeping. 'I get enough death threats from the Resistance. Believe me, I do. So how am I to behave? Should I sack my workers, who depend on me? I have gone too far; yes, I've gone too far, and there's no way back. I've sold shares to the Germans; I've taken their capital. Why did I do it? You cannot print books without paper, and you both know that the Germans control the supply. I would not be in a position to publish your novel if I had not done so. I would no longer have a business. I would be broke.'

The woman stirred. 'Calm down, or you'll wake her,' Elsa said.

Before he left, Denoël had read everything that Elsa had written of *Le Cheval Blanc*.

'Whatever you might think of me,' he said, 'I respect you as a writer, and I will publish the book when you finish it.'

'Will your German friends allow that?'

'I can see nothing that could trouble the censor.'

'You want me to keep my nose clean. Go talk to your friend Rebatet; he will tell you whether it is suitable for his New Europe. He knows what makes a bestseller. How many million copies of his book have you sold to date?'

At the end of May, Czech partisans killed the butcher Heydrich in Prague and Aragon and Elsa left Nice for Villeneuve-lès-Avignon.

* * *

Left alone with the girl, Matisse relishes each fondling as he arranges her thighs. He sets the scene; he deifies his bourgeois interior. With every prop he places, his pleasure grows as they come together; each change sparks an emotional charge that leads on to the next merging of tone and colour.

'Moreau's women were all monsters; they were Theda Baras, vampires and man-eaters. Whether he painted Delilah, Hérodias or Lady Macbeth, they were creatures of nightmare. I did not share his belief that the public wanted lurid scenes spiced with sex. No, the truth was that he liked to paint such pictures.'

'Mallarmé knew that to name a thing killed off a great deal of our delight in a poem,' Matisse says. 'You must use suggestion to evoke an object.

You have to keep the mystery of the symbol intact; it embodies a state of mind. I agree with that.'

The girl has no interest in what he is saying. She is not listening. She tells him her name is Lourdes; that she is telepathic. He does not ask whether she can sense how much he wants to feel her breasts again and run his hands under her buttocks. 'How do you use this ability?' Matisse asks.

She says she has lived with the smell of sulphur every day of her life. When she was a child, her father took her to various race-tracks. There, he would blindfold her and stand her on a box; she could hear him taking his hat among the crowd; then she would call out the names of winning horses.

'Sulphur – what do you mean by sulphur?'

'Some days I can see the Devil as clearly as I can see you.'

'Does my bedroom smell of sulphur?'

'No. I don't smell it now.'

'Is this Devil here now?'

Lourdes giggled. 'He's near enough to touch.'

Under fields of mint and khif, glorious veiled women stood on the rocks staring at the Atlantic, the wind thrumming their robes against their thighs and breasts; their children were scavenging for empties behind the French bars. Matisse found these women's carved wooden boxes of rouge and kohl charming; they could create art even when they used cheap Western powder compacts. Day after day, the light was unchanging; then, at nightfall, the bazaar merchants took down the goods they hung at first light over the doorways of their shops. There was the babble of trade, of crowds coming and going, for whom the storytellers never stopped working, in spite of open air cinemas. Matisse grips the girl's thigh. 'Djinns haunt the city, you understand, so that the women slam the doors they have daubed blue. They make sure their walls have shoals of luminous tiles, whose intricate mazes shield them from evil. Maybe you need blue paint, too; shall I paint you blue to ward off evil spirits?'

'You were so stern, a caliph in a fairy tale, until you touched me,' the girl says. 'I know you enjoyed touching me.' She is about to dress when she suddenly leans forward and kisses his mouth, gently flicking her tongue across his lips.

Matisse snorts. 'You are beautiful, my girl, and I am a sick old man whose mouth is sour with old age and nicotine. I'm afraid to ask how old you are.'

'How old would suit you?'

What a nerve! Matisse shakes his head; succumbing already to what she is doing, his eyes widen as he watches.

'Seventeen?'

She creeps gently under his guard. He sees her as Zorah, the archetype of all the girls he has ever painted. She is tenderly lewd, and touchingly performs those fleshy overtures he wanted from them all. She sits on the bed and unties his dressing-gown to open his pyjamas, asking quietly, 'Suppose Madame Lydia comes in?'

'She won't,' he urges now.

'She might.'

'Not when I'm working with a model.'

The girl is right; he is taking an insane risk. Suppose that Lydia did come in? His life as he knows it would be in jeopardy. Had he gone too far touching her? No, he had done nothing to initiate this. Yet, he tells himself that he cannot afford the luxury of regret. What was life for, anyway?

'I am a grandfather,' he protests.

She is a good girl; her father's good girl. Matisse suspects that he is not the first man she has tasted in this way. She forces him down until he lies against the pillow, murmuring, 'It's too big,' as she opens her mouth.

'You will kill me!' Matisse begs.

She looks up at him, her lips trembling in a smile.

In the tormenting thrill of orgasm, of searing pain towards his anus, the aberration of his surrender shakes him. She lies curled up against his thigh, pulses beating in her throat and breast. Her eyes stay closed, as a pearl of semen rolls glistening on her lip. She is a flushed nymphet from a *pompier* canvas; no longer an angel of mercy. Has she fulfilled a dare set by some school-friend? She cannot come there again. He hates what he has done; he has lost the certainty of being Matisse, of curbing his feelings to fuse them anew in colour and form. The girl has outsmarted his equilibrium, and he feels ashamed of his lapse.

Matisse closes his eyes again, telling himself that in Tahiti there were women in the clouds even. The sound of the birds awakens him, the sudden thrumming of their wings.

Lourdes has gone; the room is cooler and the light dimmer.

Matisse writes to Aragon to tell him that his attack of hepatitis has brought another pow-wow of doctors. Professor Wertheimer, who was in

Aix-les-Bains, has drafted in a Paris surgeon, a Professor Gutmann, from his retirement near Nîmes. They were there to allay Doctor Angier's fear that his patient might need another operation. Matisse says he knows now how the clerk feels who has been taking petty cash for years, and who now faces a fateful auditor.

Matisse winces as Wertheimer pressed his palm against his stomach. 'No man escapes from his Devil's Island.'

'Does it hurt when I do this?' Wertheimer prods Matisse's groin.

'There's a sharp pain. As to medicine, I am as ignorant as my forebears. It's the same with a great many things that happened during my life, and I couldn't understand: the Curies' experiments, the mechanics of Blériot's flight, the Theory of Relativity. Why learn anything about tungsten filaments until my light bulb fails?'

Matisse tries to calm his nerves as he waits for Wertheimer's verdict. 'It was so hot in the garden that the flowers had almost lost their scents. The only odour was the aromatic incense of the pines.

'I was studying *La conversation* when the gardener brought Clara MacChesney to my studio. She was nervous of the meeting, she said. It was as though climbing those four steps had somehow brought her into the cave of Borneo's fearful wild man.

'To put her at her ease, I told her I had three normal children and a happy marriage. I confessed I had most of the normal tastes of any man of my class living then.

'Flies hummed in from the garden, drawn by the smell of resin and paint.

'I told her I persevered to ensure that every canvas I offered the world was as perfect as I could make it.

'Then she said she knew that she was the last woman that I would ask to take off her clothes. She was not one of my exotic creatures. I put this nonsense down to her nerves. If I did not seek to mystify in my work, she said, what was I trying to say in *La conversation*? The man in blue-striped pyjamas was obviously me; but why did I stand like a statue? Was I sleep-walking when I met the Queen of the Night? The garden seemed tamed and strange, as ornamental as a Persian miniature.

'No, I told her, I had not been sleep-walking. The man and woman were in a state of suspense; they were about to speak, or had already spoken words that were irrevocable. It could even be possible that the man was about to sing an aria. The canvas spoke of illumination; it was latent with that strain, those emotional exertions that, when we stood back from them, continued to act as a force, twitching like Galvani's frog.

Could painting go anywhere? That was the question *La conversation* asked. It was a quest for the meaning of everyday life. I was at the mercy of mysteries, night and day.

'There, we were at the heart of things. If she turned, she would see that part of my studio where I found *L'atelier rouge*, and, if she faced left, she would see my *L'atelier rose*. What she did not say, but thought, no doubt, was that I was running a factory for mysticism there, where I turned out obscure canvases, one after the other.

'Was it all a dream? Did it really happen? In those days, we could share the feeling that there was no limit to time or what you could do with it; that we had no constraints and could find paradise any afternoon in our gardens.'

Wertheimer smiles as he goes to stand by the window. As his colleagues join him, Matisse studies the group, watching them over his spectacles.

When Wertheimer approaches again, still smiling, Matisse forestalls him with a wave of his hand. 'How can I feel well when some informer is denouncing Picasso and myself as Jews? The man finds secret messages inimical to the Third Reich in my paintings. He knows that I am a spy because I have been to America, Russia and Tahiti.'

* * *

All her life Elsa had seen Jews in a desperate plight, in Gogol's ghettos, in Warsaw's ghetto – now they suffered in Villeneuve. The authorities had thought of everything, even the two men who went into each house to turn off the gas and electricity. The order was to arrest one hundred and sixty Jews that night, whose names were on a filing system that had records of every French and foreign Jew in the city. A special police squad kept the key, a concierge told her, who had it from a reliable source that the Israelites were going to work camps in Silesia.

Elsa had noticed the concierge picking over the goods her son had helped her loot from a Jewish family's apartment. With the pittance Pardieu had paid the old Jew to do his abattoir accounts, it was unlikely they would find any treasure. The heap of chattels lay in the alley; nothing worth the bother of carrying downstairs. Numbed, Elsa stood listening until she felt she was safe. Then she ran home in spite of the trucks roaring by to the assembly point.

Aragon, alarmed that Elsa had not come home when she promised, went to look for her. On turning a corner, he found that he had become a witness to the round-up. He slowed his walk, trying not to draw attention to himself, until he was abreast of a motorcycle with a side-car. Not far away, an officer strode about, tapping his folded spectacles against the back of his hand. Breathing on the lenses, he polished them before putting them back on. Then he crossed the street to join his second in command. This man carried a briefcase under his arm and had lost his temper. He waved a sheaf of documents in front of two sheepish policemen before stuffing them away.

The young Doriot thug in the side-car turned to face Aragon. He looked nervous, fretful and intense. Aragon offered him a cigarette. A red-eyed spider was climbing in the old brickwork. Aragon could hear the creak of the driver's black leather coat. 'Those bastards are not keen enough. You have to turn over every stone when you're cleaning out this scum,' said the driver good-humouredly, blowing dust from the goggles that hung around his neck.

It was then that a man in the uniform of the militia chased four Jews into the street out of a side alley. He held two snarling Alsatian dogs on a leash. A nun followed, her coif fluttering as she remonstrated shrilly with the officer with the briefcase. Two of the Jews were men; the other was a woman who held a young boy by the hand. The child's happy idiot grin was macabre. It signified the start of a game he had never played before.

The driver poked Aragon's chest to demand a cigarette too. 'Probably sniffed the swine out of some cupboard. Those are Bazin's dogs, and they can smell Israelites six feet under. Marvellous creatures!'

One of the Jews fell down. His companion shrugged his shoulders in despair as the other man looked at him. The woman went down on one knee to lift the old man's head.

'Cardiac arrest is my diagnosis,' the driver said. 'The others seem to have shat their trousers.'

When Aragon felt it safe to return home, he learned that their Jewish neighbour, a doctor, had gone too. Then he watched similar scenes from their window. He saw patients leave the hospital in their night-clothes and climb aboard the trucks.

He heard the door slam in the courtyard. Elsa was standing under the fig tree, half hidden by the foliage. He caught her in his arms, and she told him what she had seen. He was angry. 'You were mad to speak to the concierge; she might have noticed your accent. As it is, we are not safe here any more. We should go back to Nice.'

'They were taking children and old people. They don't want the sick or old for labour. No, they are going to murder them in the Jewish reserve. How can we have any illusions about our fate?' Elsa shivered.

* * *

André Rouveyre had studied with Gustave Moreau, too. He calls on Matisse before going home to Vence. Sipping mint tea, he takes out the latest postcard he had from Matisse.

'I try to send more than a prose message with my letters and postcards,' Matisse says. 'Manet used to spice his letters with water-colours. I think that my correspondence belongs in the realm of the billet-doux; my postcards have the intent of an English Valentine card. They are the result of feeling playful.'

'I find it difficult to imagine Etta Cone writhing under Claribel's lingual assaults on her salty labia, but I suppose we have to assume something of that nature was going on,' Rouveyre says.

'I knew nobody who was better than Gertrude and Alice to take shopping,' Matisse says. 'In the last war they were in Majorca, where Gertrude spent her time reading administrators' reports, diaries and memoirs of Albion's empire builders and military defenders. She read Queen Victoria's letters aloud to Alice, who was knitting socks for *poilus*.'

'I can't see Alice Toklas knitting.'

'Oh yes, Amélie taught her.'

The sun is going down. 'You have to take into account that Rouault was born during the bloody massacres of the Commune – his mother was hiding in some filthy cellar in Belleville, as I recall,' Matisse says.

Rouveyre nods. 'The year Marcel Proust was born.'

'They decided Rouault's fate when they apprenticed him to a worker in stained glass. He told me once that he did not see any Italian or Dutch art until he was sixty-seven, but I took that with a pinch of salt. I don't know what would have happened if Moreau had not taken an interest in him.'

'I used to find Georges too crabby and peevish,' Rouveyre says.

They talk about the commission Rouault accepted to illustrate Jarry's *Ubu*, and how Vollard became a jailer again, with yet another tight-fisted contract.

'It was Renoir who advised Vollard to take on Cézanne; his own judgement was not a hundred per cent.' Matisse sits back, musing.

'Having Cézanne on his books would bankrupt him, he said. All part of the strategy of sympathetic modesty which he used to rob his artists. Vollard had a stubborn streak, laced with superstition, a quality he shared with Picasso. Luckily for Kahnweiler the *Demoiselles d'Avignon* was another of Vollard's blind-spots. He missed Picasso's Blue Period, too, convinced that the paintings were too gloomy to sell.'

'And you, of course, were one of his blind-spots, Henri,' Rouveyre says.

'I hear the Germans have built a military airfield at Villacoublay, where I used the windshield of my old Renault to frame the landscape. Ah, those lost pleasures of driving my automobile! One day, as I was sketching, I saw a flicker in my cracked rear-view mirror; a boy was creeping up behind the car. I could hear my skates on the pond; a booming, splintering rattle that echoed off the snowy banks as I crouched and ran. He had red hair; I felt that I was seeing an earlier incarnation of myself.'

*   *   *

Aragon and Elsa were high in the mountains near Comp, six miles above Dieulefit: the village God made. With them were two German Communists, Hermann Nuding and his wife, Jo, who had fled from a Gestapo death sentence in Germany.

Jo shaded her eyes to scan the rocks. 'Is that a chalet or a barn up there?'

They had stumbled across the ruin, which, later, Elsa named Le Ciel.

Aragon braked the car. 'It's hard to imagine how anybody could have lived here.' They started to climb the steep path.

'It will be godforsaken in winter,' Elsa predicted.

A lark was singing. At every footfall the cicadas went silent until they passed. Every step stirred hazes of aromatic perfume from the thyme.

Nuding went back to the car to bring the food, and they sprawled in the rock-strewn grass under the dry olive trees, drinking wine. Nuding stared up into the cloudless azure blue. 'Paul Durand-Ruel spent his life working for the triumph of Impressionism, quite as much as any of his painters,' he said. 'An old-fashioned crook, Alfred Edwards, saved him after the war of 1870, when his gallery nearly went broke. It was with the advent of Cubism that things changed; we found the void of modern life, its alienation; that was why Cubism needed a phalanx of critics and buyers with taste to sell it, and go on selling it. Like everything else, Art has to live with those conditions that create it. What we find in Picasso are past ghosts from feudalism, through Hellenism, to Christianity and the beginnings of monopoly capitalism. He's truthful enough to do this. Of course, this is not what the critics and dealers say when they salute the little bastard.'

'How does Gauguin strike you?' Elsa asked.

'Gauguin ate and slept with savages because he admired the way they lived and made art, yet there was no escape from his class. Even when he painted his Tahitians he would always make them as decorative as any Parisian woman.'

The sun was going down by the time they packed and set off down the mountain-side. Nuding was still talking. 'Stalin's pact was tactical; as a materialist, he had to be as cute as a shit-house rat,' he said.

* * *

Matisse sleeps fitfully. Is the history of thought, as Aragon says, a burden of domination? Do his paintings reflect nothing more than the status quo, for all his insistence on their visionary content? These ideas are so upsetting that he feigns illness the following day and orders Lydia to tell Aragon that he does not feel up to seeing him. When he changes his mind and calls her back, she has gone without hearing him. He feels bereft suddenly, listening to her footsteps along the hallway until she opens the door to greet Aragon.

The Black Door

Matisse does not deny that there is something unknowable at the heart of his paintings. The woman without a face wears a blazing tiger-stripe wrapper. She reposes in a yellow and red striped Louis XV easy chair. There are his usual arabesques of ironwork outside the window: sunlight on the parquet floor and flowers in a window box. Unlike other Matisse windows, this one does not open to another scene. There are solid white bars pasted to a blue sky, which may not be clouds at all, but some freak light on the window pane. The black door itself yields nothing. It is the sort of door that has often loomed in literature. Behind this door our lovers betray us; do not answer when Proust knocks; or it is that room of secrets, that Bluebeard's chamber, which must remain locked.

Drawings of Elsa

'What everybody wants to forget is that Rembrandt died a bankrupt,' Elsa says. 'He is still a bankrupt three hundred years after his death. None of those dealers who profit from his work ever thinks of arranging a discharge for him.'

'Are you working on a book, now?' Matisse asks.

'A novel I call *Le Cheval Blanc*. My hero, if he is one, is Michel Vigaud. It begins with his mother hauling him around various hotels where she spends most of her time taking opium; he goes to school, does his army service, travels in foreign countries, deals in drugs. What he wants most is to be the knight on the white horse who saves ladies in distress, hence the title. The only real success he has is as a singer. He marries a rich American, makes wildlife films in Africa, and dies fighting the Germans.'

'You've not left much out,' Matisse says. 'It should sell. I read your book on Tahiti before I paid my visit. While I was there, I couldn't help recalling some of the things you wrote about the island.'

'You're very kind.'

'I think I always wanted to see Tahiti. In 1899, I made a swap with Vollard: one of my paintings for Gauguin's *Tête d'un garçon*. What I had hoped for from the tropics was the light of another hemisphere, a light that was different from any in Europe. Of course, the real island was different, as you and I discovered. I did not find such a light. You found a maid who was a thief and a drunk.'

'She had her troubles,' Elsa remembers.

'I forget her name.' Matisse pencils in the delicate arch of Elsa's eyebrow.

'Vahine – what else? Her husband used to kick her about. She was ageing, too.'

'Demoralising. You say you tried watercolours?'

'Nothing I thought worth keeping.'

With eyes half closed, Matisse remembers Tahitian sunsets. They were all the local artists ever painted, after the fiery honey and blond skies faded to a calm blue, improbably soft and velvet. There was nothing to do except lie in the shade, weary with reverie. Everything Western was three months out-of-date, newspapers, reality; in the evenings he watched old newsreels, one of Amanoullah's reception by the King of England, then had cocktails at the Lafayette or the Lotus. He had kept a few bad souvenir snapshots; and those portraits taken by Murnau, the German film maker, whose work had deteriorated since *Nosferatu* and *The Last*

Laugh. In those days, Hollywood was busy maiming foreign competitors by buying their stars and their directors. Paramount had sent Murnau to find noble savages; he was shooting footage for *Tabu*. Matisse had told him he had spent three months being flabbergasted, as he put it, without an idea, a painting.

'What I was upset by in Papeete was the number of churches the missionaries had built,' Elsa says. 'Wiser now, I know that everything I hated so much came in the ships that brought the men of God. I saw what Gauguin saw: natives as colonial snobs, walking parodies aping Western customs, manners and vices. I saw those other things that had taken root: smallpox, syphilis and tuberculosis. It came as a shock to learn that the streets had electricity and drainage, to find Fords outside the shops and cinemas.'

'So I left Petrovitch Triolet and went to join my mother in London, where she was working for the Soviet Trade Commission. Things were not going well in Russia; the New Economic Policy was in force. I lived on the allowance I had from André and got a job working for an architect. I was hoping to save money.'

'You covered your desertion very well in your book.'

Elsa smiles. 'I learned a lot from listening to the monkey who used my powder-puff; he chattered incessantly as he ran amuck on my dressing-table. He said more than André did. He knew that to load a woman with trinkets and jewels did not mean a thing. It was hot. I'd lie on my bed dreamily masturbating while André plotted to make millions and studied horseflesh on the veranda. It was all very colonial. One lesson I learned was that Tahiti is not the place to teach your husband to speak Russian.'

'Why have I told you all this?'

Matisse shrugs. 'How did you and Aragon meet?'

'After reading *Le Paysan de Paris* I knew that we were going to meet. When I saw him in the Lilas, I used to think he was a homosexual; he was very physical with Pierre Drieu la Rochelle, very close to Breton. Yet he had tried to kill himself over Nancy Cunard. It was intriguing. He attracted me. Then at the Coupole one night, when I was with Mayakovsky and Ehrenburg, Vladimir introduced us.'

'Man Ray was Jewish, of course,' Matisse says.

'Did that worry you?'

'He had talent, and squandered it.' Matisse shakes his head. 'I don't think he knew what he wanted. His ideas have found far too many imitators. Breton said he was the prince of snapshots and the despair of the parrot. Of course he was ebullient, fecund, perceptive; and of course he made us laugh. I forget now whether I paid him for the photographs he took of Margot before her wedding.'

'I hear that he's in Hollywood now,' Elsa says; 'he'll thrive there. The only drawback will be the film stars. He'll miss the genius of the old Paris gang. Some of his things I used to admire are trite now: those violin sound holes that adorn Kiki's back, for instance.'

The light can change the colour of her eyes; sometimes they are blue or green, sometimes grey.

She was having difficulty remembering that useless life they lived light years ago in the Kurfürstendamm. 'Michel Vigaud was there in 1923,' she says; going on to admit that her life with Louis is not easy. 'I feel that I am a failure; that what I write is irrelevant. We shouldn't live together, now that we are working for the Resistance. It would be less dangerous to act apart from each other.'

'You run risks in the Occupied Zone. Don't you fear that the Germans will arrest you, or what they could do to you?'

'I carry this for comfort.'

Elsa shows him the cyanide capsule she has had since her release from the prison at Tours. Matisse shudders as she tells him how all English agents have them.

'Aragon has one too?'

'I don't know. I don't think he'd tell me if he had.'

'Surely he must know you carry yours?'

'Nobody does. Why did I tell you?'

'Because your secret is safe with me.'

'Life can be mysterious at times. When I was Elsa Kagan, I would not have dared to carry this poison around in case I used it. My days were darker then.'

Talking to Aragon afterwards, Elsa felt she had exposed too much of herself for the smudged charcoal drawing Matisse gave her. The trouble was that he was a challenge; a man she had to impress. In trying to do that, she had not seen how he had disarmed her; her guard had fallen. She had indulged in one of her worst vices: her past.

What she had not confided was her feeling that, deep down, Matisse's art was for men only; that he was monstrous up there with all his sacred belongings around him. He was above it all: the black market, the rationing; and even though he was ill, there was always a nurse at hand when he woke in pain. He could sport a biscuit-coloured suit, Manila hat, tea planter's pyjamas, or drift through the day in his dressing-gown. He had Lydia, his birds, and the great consolation of his art. He did not have to dirty his hands with any other business. He was beyond that. Her rancour was the same as that felt by women in the food queues who knew that the black market made some people rich enough to eat. Matisse was one of those fortunate people.

Charles of Orléans's Poems

'Charles's ballad lists everything: dropsy, migraines, colic, gout, and kidney stones,' Matisse says. 'I ache with him when he writes of palsy and old age. I am going to send André Rouveyre a few ballads that I have written out by hand.'

'The Hundred Years' War killed off the aristocracy,' Aragon says. 'The dukes and princes who survived fell back on fantasy and ordered their poets to embalm chivalry, honour, and heroism in epics of nostalgia like the *Chanson de Roland*. France had to be what it was before the English invasion. They forbade their poets any mention of Crécy, Poitiers or Agincourt, even the death of France's nobility by English arrows. The surviving nobles tried to fend off anarchy by losing themselves in games, pageants, rules and rituals.

'What they could not escape, of course, was the bubonic plague. It crept slowly from the Crimea. Paris had it by 1348; then it spread across Europe and England. They called it the Black Death because of the colour it left its victims, whose lymph nodes would burst in their groins and armpits. After one hundred years, a third of the population was dead.'

Later, Aragon spoke to Elsa of his visit. 'Many artists turn to history these days in search of a subject,' she said. 'You tell me that Matisse understands the Duke's period, but I see no evidence of that in his drawings.'

* * *

Matisse shows a sketch of Charles d'Orléans to Aragon. 'I based it on Fouquet's portrait of Charles VII. I felt there had to be a family likeness. The historian Thomas Rhymer attacked Orléans in the Rolls of Parliament, and it was the Duke of Gloucester who advised the King's

Council in 1440 that Orléans was England's enemy. Like Rhymer, Gloucester suspected Orléans of bribing English lords, of being too charming, and having a dangerous political insight. This was why the English moved him so often. Twenty-five years locked in different chambers, spied on day and night. I see the room, lit rarely by sunlight; sometimes dark because of the shutters. I know the room he talks about. It is my own. Please, read me the poem again.'

Aragon reads:

> *The flower of my past time of childhood,*
> *In youth became a fruit; then Folly, my mistress,*
> *Knocked it from the tree of Pleasure when*
> *It was still green and unripe. And for this,*
> *Reason, who repays all at her whim*
> *Without wrong or misprision, quite rightly*
> *In her great wisdom set me to ripen in prison straw.*
>
> *Here I have lain long without flight or freedom;*
> *I am content; it is no doubt for the best,*
> *Despite the way sloth wrinkles my skin as I grow old.*
> *The fires of fleshly desire no longer burn,*
> *Since they set me to ripen in my prison straw.*
>
> *Lord, grant the peace we desire!*
> *Let the waters of Delight refresh me!*
> *Let the hot sun of France burn away*
> *This crust of mouldy Sadness:*
> *Let the Good Time come again,*
> *God, cure my pain; for this*
> *The King put me to ripen in his dungeon straw.*
>
> *I am a green and winter fruit, less tender than*
> *The fruit of summer; so they must keep me close,*
> *Set to ripen in this dungeon straw.*

Matisse takes the book and selects another poem:

> *One day at Dover, looking to France,*
> *Every sweet delight I had known in that land*
> *Moved such a sigh from my heart, I longed*
> *Again for the country that I love.*
>
> *I knew that it was foolishness*
> *To nurture such sighs within my heart,*
> *When I see the start of good peace,*

186

That may give us all good.
For this, I turned my thought to comfort,
But nonetheless my heart did not weary
Of seeing France that my heart must love.

Then I loaded my desires aboard the Ship
Of Hope to go to France without delay.
And sent also all my fond remembrances!
Now, let God in His mercy grant peace
So that I see again the country that I love.

How can one praise that treasure, Peace, enough?
I hate war, and have no love of it at all;
It has impeded me a long time, rightly or wrongly,
From seeing France that my heart must love.

'The English allowed him to keep in touch with Blois, which he governed by proxy,' Matisse says. 'His secretaries had safe-conducts to come and go. Towards the end of his exile, news came of his wife Bonne d'Armagnac's death after an illness.'

Aragon puts the book back on the bedside table. 'I never understood why Charles did not include Joan of Arc when he wrote his celebration of French heroes. She freed Orléans's citadel from the English occupation, and that was the turning point of the war.'

Matisse points out that the valiant Maid was a peasant, acting on the say-so of voices; yes, because of that, and because of her sex and humble origins. He was of royal blood; there was no way he could exalt Joan in the same breath as Charlemagne. Besides, the English read every word he wrote, and Cardinal Beaufort of Winchester signed his safe-conduct permits, the man who sent Joan to the stake.

*　　*　　*

It was one of those run-down fairgrounds where lonely people go in hope of finding a lost childhood. Elsa pointed out the swarthy Nero on the top of the roundabout, his eyeballs rolling as he watched Rome blaze.

'It's either Rome, or the horror of Lisbon's earthquake,' said Aragon. 'All that's missing for me is the giant Armand's outsize chair, which they used to show beside the pygmy chair of the smallest man in the world.'

'There was a painting, too: that incident with the fiacre, where the scared cab man is jumping off his box as Armand tries to hire him.'

Elsa laid her head on Aragon's shoulder as they rode in the Roman chariot. The horses had lost their tails; she gestured towards these worn holes and asked, 'Where can I have seen such mutilated rumps?'

'In the Cartier-Bresson photograph of a derelict carousel in Cuba,' Aragon said.

There was no Roman chariot behind them; in its place stood two rusty bicycles. A gendarme swung his girl-friend onto one of them and bestrode the other. Farting loudly, he grinned amiably at Elsa and Aragon. He was a cog in the Vichy machine, whose duties would include reading a small part of the three million poison-pen letters denouncing Jews. Certainly his task would be to hunt people down who struck at the Security of the State; those Resistance fighters going out at night to fly-post walls, who handed out tracts and pamphlets to workers in the *métro*, who undermined church congregations and cinema audiences. However, this would-be Fernandel seemed a parody of all French gendarmes, who joke with bar owners to get free drinks and scheme endlessly to increase their fortnightly tobacco ration.

Elsa breathed a sigh of gratitude that the world turned in orbit.

*   *   *

Matisse learns that his son Jean has joined the Resistance and is hiding dynamite under his sculptures in the old studio at Issy. It is Lydia who tells Aragon about Jean's activities. The master will not discuss them directly. They arouse feelings that he cannot or will not confront. Aragon has to detect them during an impromptu discussion of *La leçon de piano*, whose central character was Jean.

There is no response from Matisse. 'Things never work out the way we would like. You can take it as three grey panels interrupted by a view of the lawn at Issy, a larger green echo of the grey metronome. Jean played the music. He was sixteen at the time, so I had to use a model to replace him. Behind him is my picture of Germaine Reynal, *La femme au tabaret*, which I painted two years previously. I thought she lent an air of an exacting teacher or angular muse. In the bottom left hand corner reclined my blue nude figure, another sculpture that seeks to hold art and nature in balance. I was happy with the pink I found for the piano lid; happy too with the arabesques of ironwork on the balcony.'

Aragon sighs. It was in moments such as this that Matisse healed his lost contact with his own childhood.

*   *   *

Some fool had opened a night-club behind Ruhl's casino. He was mad enough to think that the club had a future. A few steps below street level there was a poky semi-basement filled with small tables, dimly lit by green lampshades. The room was never quite as full as it seemed since the piano and performers took up space. Georges Ulmer sang there, whom Aragon and Elsa would see walking his dog every morning on the promenade.

They were there to wonder at a tall bizarre woman singer with dyed black hair who made her entrance every night to great applause from the club's staff. This applause seemed to shore up her illusion that she was a well-known international star, which the podgy announcer billed her as being. 'L'Étrange Farcy's' act was a gruesome instrument of torture. After her number, encore followed encore, until the master of ceremonies would overplay his hand to such an extent that she would scream that she had had enough of his insults. She would stand jerking at her false pearls in anger, she was through. The announcer would then urge the audience to beseech her to sing one more time; thus mollified, she would launch into a reprise.

'It is an awful way to earn a living,' Pierre Seghers said, who was in Nice on a brief visit.

'Very much of its time and place,' Aragon said. 'She is a crude metaphor for France under Vichy. It's why George Ulmer is a Mexican now, according to his passport.'

'Are we safe being here?' Seghers asked.

Elsa had shown him *Je Suis Partout*, which featured a report that the Communist Louis Aragon was living in Nice. They knew his address, those fascists 'who were everywhere'.

'One of Darnand's local scruffy ticks is trying to make a name by shooting me.'

'You are mad to take it so lightly,' Elsa said. 'The man was a Cagoulard before the war.'

Aragon laughed. 'Elsa thinks she has seen him following me. I tell her that her imagination is working overtime.'

'He knows that Darnand's men have guns!'

*　　*　　*

Matisse murmurs as he assembles his coloured cut-outs. 'Our Judaeo-Christian past marks us for life, and the stigmata do not fade with age. In spite of this, Jean Puy painted his *L'après-midi d'un faune*. Gauguin,

189

Derain, Bonnard – all of us were searching in different ways for a golden age; a Graeco-Roman earthly paradise rather than the Eden of the Jews.'

'It was the Greeks who gave the world the illusion of freedom,' Elsa says. 'Their philosophers could omit the mechanics of reality because they ran a slave economy.'

Matisse is not going with her down that road. 'How I used to love to hear Maillol recite from Virgil's *Eclogues*,' he muses. 'My *Paysage de Collioure* was a study for *Joie de vivre*, though I did not know it at the time. It became the local habitation for the sixteen nudes who people the landscape. My original title was *Bonheur de vivre* when I started it. It was only later that Albert Barnes suggested calling it *Joie de vivre*. Mallarmé's poems were my inspiration. I felt the presence of other artists as I painted – Watteau, Giorgione, Poussin, even Gauguin. I distorted classical form – the Arcadian girl playing Pan's pipes, for instance. I brooded for years on Poussin's nymphs. My nudes kept each other company; the foliage, the sinuous trunks and branches, echoed their forms.'

*   *   *

Aragon was thinking about his visit to Matisse as he queued to buy offal; horse meat, probably. It was usually a long wait, and there was often none left by the time he got to the counter, since it was not necessary to have a ration card to buy it.

He stared at the shining knives, axes and empty hooks; underfoot, the sawdust had no trace of blood. Two women ahead of him talked about their husbands. One of them had gone to work at the Volkswagen plant in Wolfsburg, believing that Laval's labour scheme would bring home French prisoners of war. An even greater incentive was the Third Reich's boast of higher wages, and the lure of cheap food and goods to send home. No food parcel had come so far, and she did not think any would. 'He told me in his letters that he lived in a hut that was no better than a kennel, and was slaving his guts out on piece-work twelve hours a day,' the woman says.

When the queue moved forward, he noticed their shoes: the down-at-heel, shabby, cracked leather; their clothes, too, like most people's, were all pre-war.

'I had my medical examination the other day,' her friend said. 'Everything was fine. I dread finding my call-up papers in the post now. They treat us like cattle.'

'God knows how we are going to get through the winter; things are bad enough with the price of food.'

Soon after he left the shop, he met with a crowd. He could hear the sound of marching men, engines, voices. Forcing a path through the people, he saw the glinting green and blue cocks' feathers fluttering on the Italian soldiers' hats. A man said they were from Ventimiglia, and that their pantomime plumage was no joke; they had fought in the desert, existing on seven ounces of bread a day.

As soon as they had secured the city, Aragon knew the Ovra agents would follow. He did his best to force a smile, then, waving his arms, he tried all his poor Italian to plead his way past the barrier to rejoin Elsa.

She had no idea that they had taken over the city.

'They will have lists of names,' he said. 'If we go now we can avoid showing our documents at the station.'

As usual, it was Lydia who answered the phone. She had heard the news. Aragon told her that his visit was off; that he and Elsa had to leave for Dieulefit. They hoped to catch a train to Digne. Elsa took the receiver and spoke in Russian while Aragon stared across the Flower Market into a narrow street where Italian shopkeepers and bar owners were already toasting each other and saluting the flags they had hung from their windows.

'Lydia will bring the *Themes and Variations* proofs with her when she takes us to the station,' Elsa said, handing back the phone.

Driving to the station they passed drunken bands of Mussolini's macaronis strutting along the promenade.

'Rommel's rout in North Africa left them no option but to surrender in droves; that's why they need this Roman circus,' Seghers said.

Only the hotel labels on people's luggage seemed festive. Not far away, a couple who had married that morning already looked unhappy in their finery. They were saying good-bye to the groom's parents. His mother shed tears as she clung to his arm. The son shook hands with his father, whose sulky peasant face gave nothing away as the train arrived at the platform.

Lydia kissed Elsa firmly, urging her to write or telephone as soon as it was possible. Aragon touched his lips to her cold cheek. They boarded the train to find a Jewish actor in the compartment, whom Aragon had met in Abraham's shop. His name was Samson Fainsilber.

* * *

'They left without mishap?' Matisse stares as Lydia takes off her hat.

'I did not like to see those frightened Jews jostling to get out.'

'Why do they see the Italians as such a threat?'

'I know you think that Mussolini is tolerant of Jews, but Italy is a fascist country. If the Jews thought France did not want them before the war, they are sure now. They don't need yellow stars. You recognise a Jew now because you can smell his terror. I feel ashamed when I see them.'

Lydia sighs. 'With the Italians here, puffed up and swaggering over us, what are we to do?'

Matisse fusses with the various objects that he uses in his paintings. It was a display set up for Aragon. He had owned many of them when Gustave Moreau was alive. Some had featured in his paintings before the First War. He uses them daily and finds they ring true; so he hoards them for their spiritual worth, for what they might yield again.

'A pity Louis did not see them,' he says.

'They were all here in the studio.'

'Not like this, the assembled cast. What did you say about Il Duce?' He laughs. 'Without Hitler's Ruhr and its coal, Mussolini is a circus turn in baggy trousers.'

* * *

More Italian troops were moving along the Alpine road on motorcycles, on foot, in trucks and armoured cars; they even rode mules. They met no resistance. Pétain's army was giving up its arms, losing its guns in rivers or burying them in fields and gardens. Few weapons would find their way to those *maquis* groups, soon to become active in the southern zone.

Samson Fainsilber smiled. Aragon used to see him, deep in arcane gossip outside the synagogue in the boulevard Dubouchage. His face was bloodless, chalk-white now, as he called his journey futile. 'Where can I run to?'

His fear was an indictment of France. Aragon said that he had made a wrong decision; with the Allied invasion of North Africa, the Germans would now extend their occupation to the Free Zone. Fainsilber's next train journey could take him to Silesia. He would be wiser to trust the Italian *carabinieri* than Pétain's gendarmes. So far as Aragon had heard, anti-Semitism was not one of Mussolini's chief concerns.

'Perhaps I can reach North Africa,' Fainsilber said hopefully.

Aragon and Elsa were going into the underground; to live in a world behind appearances, a world of risky meetings, rife with loaded questions, whose safe houses were dangerous.

The hotel at the foot of the Basses-Alpes was cold and dank; its clay walls had a smell of the grave. Elsa slept badly, knowing that the sheets were damp. By morning she was feverish; her sniffle had become a cold, but she forced herself onto a train to Villeneuve. There, Hélène Guenne-Cingria insisted that she went to bed, and nursed her while Aragon went on alone to Dieulefit.

After two days, she was well enough to travel. She went to meet Pierre Seghers in Valreas.

'Louis has gone to Dieulefit,' she told him, seeing his alarm.

There were two old women on the bus apart from Elsa and Seghers. It was easy to tell from their conversation that they were sisters, and their loud voices spoke of days spent in the open. The driver talked to them about the local market to which they had been. His cigarette smoke was adding to an amber stain left by generations of smokers on the once pale-green paint work. The women were so busy gossiping they gave no attention to Elsa and Seghers, or remarked where they left the bus.

Elsa looked back along the road, then up to the mountains. 'I hope I am right about this.'

Seghers nodded, hefting her suitcase onto his shoulder as they set off to climb to Le Ciel.

Seghers did not stay long. Aragon walked with him down the track to the bus, which was due to return in fifteen minutes.

'I can't see Elsa being happy here. Her health will suffer with the first snow.'

'Nuding's wife manages.'

'You know that Elsa is not as tough as Jo.'

'I know of no other hide-out safer than this.'

*   *   *

Matisse plays part of Ravel's Violin Sonata next door, thinking of the violin as a trilling lark ascending over the ruminations of the piano and cello. Lydia sits with her head resting on her folded arms, listening to news of Stalingrad on the kitchen radio. To shake off her gloom and terror, she calls to mind *La musique*, which Matisse said he painted as the antithesis of *La danse*. The two green hills soon became one. After that discovery, Matisse began his quest for a blue that was absolute. His sexless creatures crouched in foetal selfishness, yet they seemed dependent on each other for their unreal existence. Only the violinist stood upright. The others were cave dwellers who started life half turned away; but in the final version, Matisse had coaxed them to turn and face the onlooker. There was no togetherness among them, only calm as the music brought them together. This music, whatever it was, must seem almost tangible.

Matisse is carrying his violin when he enters the kitchen. 'Vlaminck's skill with a violin bow was greater than mine. At one time he was a racing cyclist, too, and even then he could still make a violin sing divinely. Not only that, he taught himself to paint. He would boast that he had never been in the Louvre, and never would. Despite all this, I'm sure I could always earn money with my violin if my paintings no longer sold.'

Lydia is not going to put up with any nonsense of this kind. The siege of Stalingrad, where the suffering defenders are holding out against the fury of Hitler's armies, is far too serious.

'You would not survive a day on the streets,' she says, holding a letter out for him to look at. 'This is from Varian Fry. He is now at 54 Irving Place, New York. He wants to know whether we know any French writers who cannot get into print for lack of paper or censorship reasons.'

'You mean he has become a publisher now?'

'It would seem so.'

The Conversation

The painting is yet another conversation, and another struggle to find unity and balance between the woman in yellow against the red who stands across from the woman in blue with a black background. The black is as heavy and intense as in any canvas by Goya or Manet; a mystery of light and dark, of shades and contrasts. Yet the women must not seem to live on separate planes, blonde and brunette.

All Oriental art is born of religious doctrine. As living creatures become decorative they lose any taint of humanist realism or idealism. Animal and plant forms must not appear as such to God. Matisse feels the same urge to be free of subject matter, serene and lost as he gilds reality. Yet it is often discord rather than harmony that lies behind his vibrant clash of colours, which creates instability in place of the calm he aims at. He cannot be other than a painter of his period, one who shares the malaise of the twentieth century. Is he putting too much of himself on show, or not enough? He has no way of knowing this except by intuition and feeling. There is always the same struggle, but that does not mean that there will be the same success.

The Idol

Matisse calls it *L'idole*, but it has nothing to do with that *L'idole* he painted during his Fauve years for which the Italian model Rosa Arpino posed. She had also appeared in his large canvas *Joie de vivre*, with ivy trailing from her hair. He saw her as a social outcast, too, as *La gitane*, a joyful mental defective, expressing her nakedness with furious lashings of pigment. He painted her left breast solid green, and her belly shone with a scrubbed luminosity. The intensity and violence of the canvas had always disturbed him. It did not resemble a Matisse; except for the exuberant way he had handled the pigment.

Again his model is his nurse, Monique Bourgeois, who ministers to him when he wakes in pain. He enjoys her washing and dressing him in the mornings. In that easy natural way he has of using women who are to hand, he has often given her shapes to cut out for use in *Jazz*. Her hair is raven black; her head tilts at an angle against a brick-red wall or screen with cross-hatching. Her left hand lies limply across the hand that grips the brown, carved, wooden arm of the chair she sits in. She wears a primrose-yellow necklace and golden bracelet; there are two jewelled clasps on the shoulder straps of her white dress. To her left, there is another grey-blue wall or screen, filled with darker diamonds. In front, standing on the corner of the black table, is a tall thin vase with flowers. Beside the vase is a squat lime-green jar; below this a peach reposes – or what Matisse remembers of a peach, since they are out of season.

It is not in any way a portrait, though it is clearly Dominique. It is as much a fetish as any tribal mask or, as Elsa Triolet might say: the girl is another Snow White. Nothing of what they talk about shows in her face, though Matisse says of the sitting that it is a tender flirtation. What is it that underlies their dialogue?

'Any dealings we have with eternity come through art, through music,' he tells her. 'The Church has always resented this truth. Yet, once upon a time, it employed artists to find images for the tales it had to tell. Artists no longer need stories.'

'You mean that Art has become a substitute for religion. Is God in all your canvases, perhaps?'

'I pray sometimes as I try to get to sleep. Prayer makes me feel peaceful. However, oranges are all we need to know of heaven on earth. When did you last see God in a painting?'

'The Renaissance?'

Matisse smiles. 'Do you see the Heavenly Father in Giotto's frescoes? I can think of no painter who was wealthier than Giotto. He made a fortune from land investment and used the law ruthlessly to defend his right of ownership. Usury was as natural to him as breathing, no matter how Dante frowned on it. The rents he charged for his looms were ruinous to weavers. His paintings of Saint Francis of Assisi make him look so vigorous you wonder how he became a saint or gained a reputation for poverty. We remember Giotto as a painter of religious subjects, but when he was alive his unlovely clients and cronies were all prelates and rich bankers.'

If Dominique's character is of no interest to him, why does he bother to paint her? It is a Nice picture in that she is no different from any Studios Victorine starlet. Is she on a film set, or about to attend a première? Maybe her white dress is vestal; maybe she is a woman, an idol, who is about to lose her equipoise, to cease being merely a part in a still life. All Matisse can see is the same *de luxe* mystery that invests all his paintings.

*　　*　　*

Aragon nursed his thumb around the tureen's chill cutting rim as he clawed more potatoes out of the soil. It was one of those mornings when the snot he sniffed into his throat was cold. The state of the barn worried him. There was still a great deal to do before the snow fell.

Nuding, like Crusoe, had worked hard to make the ruin habitable. The locals had accepted him as Jean, a man who could turn his hand to anything from hunting to butchery. He was a survivor with a survivor's skills; the first thing Aragon noticed when he arrived had been the rabbit skins nailed to dry on every door.

Jo had divided the barn into rooms using blankets hung on ropes. There was one lamp; they used candles when there was no oil. They slept on straw, wary of the rats. Jo had covered one wall with old newspapers, which Elsa tore down as soon as she arrived with Pierre Seghers. She did not want to find herself reading headlines that had led to both wars, she said.

'Our ability to adapt to events is not unusual,' Nuding said. 'Dialectical materialism is not some fanciful idea that Marx and Lenin chewed to death; it covers everything. Brecht is right: we must not throw this tool away when times are hard.'

Aragon shivered as the wind rattled leafless branches against the roof. There was ice to break before he could make coffee from the dandelion roots Nuding had dried in the sun during the summer. He had returned from a cold trip on Resistance business the day before, and, as he basked in the remembered blaze of Matisse's paintings, he scribbled a passage about his meetings with the painter.

There was the view from his bedroom in Tangier at the Hôtel France which Matisse had enshrined in the *Vue de la fenêtre*. Standing on the sill was an earthenware pot with a hot pink posy beside a pale blue vase with black and white flowers. Aragon tried to summon up the name of a black flower. There was a heart-stopping depth of blue outside the window; it edged a cream sand path where an Arab in a white djellaba rode a mule; then, higher, the English church with its green tiles. Something of this world at peace must live on somewhere; men knee-deep in the sea, casting nets, the colours of their women's dresses drying on the rooftops. Matisse had said how much he loved the smudged beauty of the newsprint sheets stacked to wrap meat in, which he pored over to the smell of couscous, fingering strings of garlic, sniffing goat's cheese on plaited palm fronds. Somewhere in the night the women would be ululating shrilly, hands over their mouths to hide the stiff sexual quivering of their tongues.

The stream was now in spate, and Nuding's hen was half-way across the surging brown flood, hopping across the snowy stones.

Nuding laughs as he hangs up his shotgun. 'No end in sight yet, my dear Eckerman?'

There were two letters for Elsa; one from Lydia, in Russian, and the other from Matisse, with some faded postcards of his Moroccan paintings:

'Do you recall the harem orgy in Bakst's Shéhérazade? It hit Paris like a bombshell. Everything had become possible with electricity. The city had never been short of sex, but it was you Russians who made it a spectacle, made the stage riot with brightly coloured lithe bodies. I knew the origin of this vision, of course – Delacroix, Moreau, Flaubert, I mean – but I found the ballet astonishing with its music by Rimsky-Korsakov. It was inevitable, not only that the Orient would escape the theatre and find a way into the fashion houses and salons of Paris, but that I should renew my own interests in it. I had *already been to Munich with Albert Marquet and Hans Purrmann to see the exhibition of Muslim art.*

Madame Davin owned the hotel we stayed in, she found me the studio where I met Zorah secretly. We had to avoid her brother; his instinct would be to kill her if he learned she posed for me. Only Jewesses and prostitutes could go without their veils.'

'You know the kind of busybody he means: a colonial procuress,' Nuding said.

'Despite her innocence and humility, Zorah would probably long in secret to be a motion picture star, too,' Aragon said.

'Zorah was a child, and as a child could pose no threat. However, that did not mean that Matisse put her in danger of her life,' Elsa said. 'He never gave that much thought. He may even have wanted her naked, like the rest of his women. Still, what he failed to do in Morocco, he re-created in Nice with Western models, where the veil is part of the illusion.'

'To put his visit into a historical context,' Nuding said. 'Those Morocco incidents that led to a stand-off between Paris and Berlin were over. By the time of Matisse's visit, Lyautey's troops were in Fez, and the great colonial venture looked all set to open up new markets. Casablanca could be a natural port for English coal. So, suddenly, everything was rosy as your friend set up his camp stool at the Casbah gate; the patrician Frenchman thinned down his oils and set about the sack of France's new possession. He says he was reading Charles Dickens during his first trip then, later, Arsène Lupin and Bergson. Why Dickens? Maybe he felt Dickens would anchor him to Europe; prevent him from falling under the spell of the exotic. Dickens was, of course, the Prometheus of a greater empire; his attitude to the times in which he lived was equivocal, confused; he hated what capitalism was doing to the world that gave birth to his characters. They do not talk to each other until the plot impels them to recognise their enmity or brotherhood.'

'Géricault is another painter I want to write about,' said Aragon.

'At least Géricault was progressive,' Nuding said. 'Matisse's art is a flight from reality; he fills me with a sense of loss. In his refusal to deal with reality, he deifies sensory deprivation in the end. Just think how enormous his task is after bourgeois physics has put out men's eyes, has written off the world as classical painters knew it, reducing it to cause and effect. It is his heroic task to redeem it, and serve big business at the same time.'

'Explain, please, how Matisse serves big business.'

'Most painters thrive on inspiration; they fail to see that capitalists deal in their fantasies as they deal with any other commodity. Matisse is as shrewd as Bizet. Most of his paintings, the ones I've seen, are a pretty refusal to see the facts of life by a genius who enables the transfer of money around the globe, and is still very much a going concern. Such artists train their sensibility to jump through hoops and are quite happy with the scraps the bosses toss them.'

'Capitalist bosses?'

'Every artist, French, German or English, has to interpret the market; must intuit when it is time to discover pubic hair, and when it is politic to focus on sunsets. Even you have to admit that there is something parochial about Matisse's attempt to make emotion an absolute.'

Aragon told Nuding to stop using textbook dialectics; he was being too crude, reductive.

Nuding laughed. 'I know how incapable my socialism is of producing art, with its unique priceless value.'

Nuding felt his role was to keep everybody alive physically and mentally. Left alone, they could fall into the depths of personal concerns. However, the atmospheric pressure seemed to get to him on certain days, making him easily upset by trivial things.

They were on edge waiting for Aragon to return. Nuding had spent the day reading Robert Louis Stevenson's *Dr Jekyll and Mr Hyde*. 'Hyde wears the uniform of the bourgeoisie when he acts out his fantasies in working-class districts, among prostitutes and the lower classes. It is significant that Jekyll and Hyde both wear evening-dress, capes and top-hats. Jekyll is a gentleman, while the brutal Hyde delights in beating the poor senseless with his walking-stick.'

Because Nuding would use both Stevenson's Christian names, Elsa thought of Aragon all the time. That and the smell of the ill-made candles would send waves of heartsick numbness over her, a fear that Louis would never return.

'Stevenson's story is a parable of good and evil; but he failed to depict evil and fell into melodrama's trap. Never mind; he had found the mythic mirror to reflect the Medusa that haunted his age.' Nuding paused. 'We have also to remember that he wrote the piece two years before Jack the Ripper began his stint. It was one of those time-bombs primed to explode later in the twentieth century. Freud had not yet given us the unconscious, the ego and id, but Stevenson was aware of them. He may not have had Zola's insight, but both men were writing about the same beast.'

'The same beast?'

'Class is the true dynamic of the tale: class and the class struggle.'

Elsa had gone to Pascal Pia's to bring back identity papers so that they could leave Dieulefit and move to Lyons. She found Camus there; he stood beside her at the window, worried about the darkening sky.

'These cards are based on the birth certificates of two stillborn children; our *mairie* comrades sift through hundreds of documents to bring the children back to life,' Pia said.

'The weather looks like being too bad,' said Camus.

Pia wanted to go back with her. It was out of the question, she said. If snow did fall, it would keep the Germans out of the hills.

It was Aragon who thought he saw her heading up towards Le Ciel. It was only a glimpse, and he would have to stand another ten to fifteen minutes before her reappearance. The wind was too bitter for this, so he went indoors to wait, shivering by the window. From there, the view of the hillside was different, so that whoever was coming would be clearly visible as they crossed the stream.

It seemed a long time before he saw her again, and when he did she fell. He ran towards the stream, blanket flapping, to find her lying with her knees under her chin. She was deaf to his entreaties. He picked her up and stumbled back towards the door, now banging in the wind. If it had not been for his first glimpse, she might have fallen and died.

The snow fell for days, drifting and burying the house. Aragon kept Elsa alive with broth that Nuding made from dried rabbit meat. As soon as it was possible to leave the mountain, Aragon went down through the sacred grove oak trees to Bourdeaux, where he telephoned Pierre Seghers.

'You were right, Pierre. Elsa will not survive the winter here. No, this call is simply to let you know what we are doing. You would be foolish to try to reach us in these conditions. We will come to you as soon as we can. We have papers. Yes, we shall head for Lyons when Elsa gets well.'

By the time Aragon reached the oaks again, the light was fading. The wind shook the bare branches. It was among those trees that the council of Huguenot elders, suffering in exile because of the Edict of Nantes, gathered their scattered flocks to pray for peace and transact affairs of state. It had been a long time before God heard their prayers.

1943

'PICASSO is on the line; he wants to speak to you.' Lydia shows surprise as she holds out the telephone.

Matisse takes off his spectacles. 'He's here, on the coast?'

'No, he's having a coffee in Le Catalan.'

'Old friend, it's me,' Picasso says. 'Are you there? I'm in Le Catalan. Do you know the place? Can you hear me? You don't say much.'

'That's because I can't think of anything,' Matisse says. 'Besides, you know I dislike this instrument. How did you manage to get through?'

Picasso laughs. 'I did not think that I would. I felt I had to talk to you, so I thought I might as well try. It is so cold in Paris that I slept in my clothes last night. Often bursts of gunfire wake me; so, to dodge my fear of firing squads, I shine a flashlight around the studio. I put a colour slide on the glass, and get some amazing effects. You should try it.'

'An amusing idea,' Matisse says. 'It doesn't strike me as being much else.'

'It's too cold for the *messieurs* to be out. The Master Race does not rise early. I know all about the pain of intimidation. I walked Kazbek by the river; he is too dumb to know anything, as the Americans say, but he can cheer me up with his antics. I thought about you while I stood looking at the Vert Galant. I feel I am Anubis, the jackal-headed god who bears the souls of the dead. Too many of my friends have gone. You can understand why I felt I had to talk to you.'

'Are you painting?' Matisse asks.

'If I paint Dora, she gets a fish or a fork on her hat; these days, I cannot stop thinking about food. Do you eat well? The Basque who runs Le Catalan buys stuff from the black-market boys, of course. Desnos eats here sometimes. Has anybody sent you his pamphlet about us yet? If not, I'll try to get one to you. I thought his piece on me was very good. You are there; so is Bonnard, who does not deserve to be, in my opinion.

'I shall go to the Flore soon, and sit by Boubal's stove. I hope Pascal has some good news from London when he brings me my coffee. You find everybody there still, even Vichy cronies and Hitler lovers. After the war, I must come and live near you; then we can talk as long as we want . . .'

Suddenly, the freak connection breaks off. Matisse stares at the telephone in disbelief. 'I had grown used to his voice; he might have been here with me. I feel lonely now.'

* * *

When Aragon and Elsa returned to Lyons, they had trouble finding a safe house. As usual on the first of the month, Elsa went to the *mairie* to apply for ration books, nervous until the clerk had finished with the forgeries Pia had given her. They were also short of hard cash. As Aragon said, people did not think about the cost of the offensive at El Alamein. Yet this mattered greatly when deciding the outcome of the war. What worried Aragon was how much British money was flowing into France. London's bankers were in command, and his fear was that they could go on dictating to opposed groups after the war.

They found René Tavernier's isolated house in Monchat, a suburb east of Lyons. It had many exits and stood on a hill, which made it ideal for secret meetings, Tavernier said, as he helped them drag their luggage up the long flight of steps. Camus was there already, he told them, and Mauriac would be at dinner later.

Elsa could not find words for what she felt about Camus as she watched him eat. He was his own myth; the stranger he had made his hero; a stranger who was elsewhere.

What could a novel like *L'Étranger* mean to Frenchmen now? As Aragon said later, Camus was an important writer, she was being too zealous.

'Is Meursault able to say anything to men and women who have to find the courage, daily, to face death, who go through hell for their beliefs?' Elsa regarded the novel as the vision of a wayward sensibility. It was no more authentic than those slivers of wood sold as the true Cross in the Dark Ages.

Camus had had the manuscript of *L'Étranger* with him during the exodus from Paris. Refugees hampered his progress, so that his engine overheated and he had to grab his novel before the car went up in flames. His first stop was Laval's printing press in Clermont-Ferrand, which his boss had rented. He said that the reason the Pétain government had not spent long in Clermont-Ferrand was its fear of the Michelin workers and what they might do when the end came. He went on to complain that he would be in Algiers now but for the American landings.

Despite his boyish look, Elsa noticed how the other guests deferred to him. They seemed to sense a depth in his ideas that she failed to see. His asides did not clarify so much as mystify, and his glib *pied noir* anarchism seemed to her to echo Bazarov. It soon became clear that he craved to be an instant classic; he talked too much about the Greeks. His lyrical evocation of playing in goal on the beach at Algiers did not interest her, and her interest waned further as he got to grips with Melville's *Moby-Dick*.

Had it been her imagination, or did Camus share the same fondness for his right ear lobe as Humphrey Bogart? She giggled when he turned up the collar of his beige trench-coat as he left.

Elsa and Aragon sat in the kitchen dissecting Camus's flashy metaphysics. This led them ineluctably to Céline. Elsa recalled the great effort she and Aragon made to translate *Voyage au bout de la nuit* into Russian, only to have Céline call him a 'magisterial cunt'. She shook her head. 'Sometimes, I despair of literature, and all its high priests. Do people still read Mauriac's novels, after what Sartre said about them?'

'Sartre's criticism will not deter people from reading him. You must hate Mauriac if you think that. You are being harsh.'

Elsa was unmoved. 'Look at it from Mauriac's theological point of view; with us, he must feel that he is supping with the Devil. He is now as far to the left as he will ever go, and he will repudiate it. When the war is over, he'll spurn any memory of his sojourn with the gypsies.'

After the first tender care of his mother, Mauriac fell into the clutches of devout nuns, devoted to Jansenism, their lips tasting of church and fog. They had left a husk of a man with a drooping eyelid, with an aromatic, ecclesiastical odour, certainly one of old suits and grim dresses stored in shuttered rooms: the clothes of the dead. He was a provincial who spoke to provincial men, knew their customs, their narrow pursuits; could guess to the last carat the weight, the burden, of their wedding rings.

Mauriac stood for everything that Elsa hated about France. What sort of freedom was he fighting for? He was a prisoner of his own obsessions, fated to walk those hot, dusty cinder paths through parched fields where his women failed to find the male body they desired.

Aragon reminded her that Mauriac had set up a centre for Austrian refugees after the Anschluss; many of these were Jewish. He had also spoken out against the armistice.

'Of course Mauriac hated the armistice, but in his heart he prefers Pétain to de Gaulle. He can quote Saint-Just until he is blue in the face; that will not stop Frenchmen killing each other.'

'De Gaulle is your idea of a hero on a white horse?' Aragon joked. 'You forget that he was a Pilsudski hero, who beat the Bolsheviks back from Warsaw in 1921.'

Another reason for Elsa to detest Mauriac was that he had not rejected Drieu la Rochelle. 'It seems to be man's fate to seek God until the end of time,' she said. 'The ignis fatuus of His presence, His absence, tempts you all deeper into the swamp. Mauriac's novels have God at their heart, while Camus's absurd fictions are the result of being bereft of Him. Mauriac is the more absurd of the two, of course; with his retreats at Solesmes and Lourdes, his yearning for beatitude before he cashes in his chips.'

After she undressed, he watched her wipe off her make-up. 'We are too close, and we know too much about each other,' she said. 'This war may have given us fresh subject matter, but we remain pre-war people, and we don't know how to treat it.'

Aragon said it had to be a problem that faced writers everywhere. In Waugh's *Vile Bodies*, in Huxley, the same characters frequented the same cafés and resorts, making love and throwing tantrums. The heroines in Drieu's books had their doppelgängers in Scott Fitzgerald and Hemingway. In sharing each other's blood, the avant-garde passed on the taint of vampirism in the same way as they gave each other venereal disease. Their infatuations were wild and reckless; they were in each other's hair like lice. Collaboration was merely an extension of normal literary practice, which was why Mauriac's idle gossip with a Gestapo agent had threatened the group he worked with.

Aragon had almost finished *Aurélien*, in which he was trying to come to terms with Drieu la Rochelle. What had he seen in Pierre? One of Drieu's abilities had been to analyse and portray social decay in Paris, Athens and Delphi.

Elsa laughed. 'Your sidekick was prone to the futility of seeking the absolute through sex with women; on top of that, he fell for women with hen-run appetites.'

Aragon shook his head. 'He left Doriot's gang before the war; why is he tempting fate by joining it again? Can't he see that organ-grinders' monkeys are now an endangered species?'

* * *

The six lemons glimmer in the early light of dawn. Matisse walks into his still life in some pain; he presses one hand against his iron girdle as he touches the edge of the dish with his finger. People are already awake in the old town; a fishing boat crosses the bay against the streak of pale lilac along the horizon. There are lights in the houses, and the sudden flashes, he realises, are the poor cycling in the narrow streets. Somewhere distant, there is the barking of a dog.

He feels alone, thinking of the men and women peopling Courbet's studio. The painting was a seminal work, an allegory for its times. Courbet's realism had been an affront to the prevailing taste of his day; but it was easy for him, too; the truth as he saw it was there in front of him. Even so, he could not dispense with literary allusion. His fellow artists were busy with naked goddesses, idylls latent with pornography that they sold to deck the villas of the new rich being built in the suburbs of Paris. What such artists were asking from nature was that it had order, a unity, which was visible nowhere else in their way of life. Such insouciance was no longer viable for Matisse.

The Lute

Piaf is singing for the children born in 1922, who are being forced into the *Service Obligatoire* to work in Germany, with Pétain's blessing.

'Moreau did not teach me to love the arabesque,' says Matisse, 'but he certainly confirmed my love for it. I spent three years in his studio; something had to rub off.' He is spending his afternoons working on *Le luth*. Dominique sits in a green chair to the left, wearing a Scarlett O'Hara-style ballroom dress; its black sash snakes from under the rim of a tawny lute she cradles. There are three patterned hangings in the background; they give a feeling of claustrophobia, which the richly charged red-patterned carpet intensifies. The table is as cluttered as the background design; there are three vases, a dish, and lemons.

Tabac Royal

In *Tabac Royal*, Dominique wears a white dress and sits again at the left of the painting. She clasps her hands under her chin, with her elbows propped on the arm of the chair. Behind her, there is a yellow door; on the table, set diagonally against a background of three varied wall hangings, there is a jar of blue lilac. This tobacco jar outshines the human figure and gives the picture its title. He has drawn it before, signing it with a flourish '*Je t'aime, Marie*'. On the other chair, at the bottom left-hand corner, which seems to advance out of the frame, the lute reappears with sheet-music.

'It was Romm who said that I peopled my earthly heaven with models with no sign of social or psychological associations. He criticised me for being too content with ready-made patterns, which I used without deviation. He said that I robbed my girls of their individuality; that I shifted their bodies onto a higher plane, idealising their expressions by making icons.'

'Are you doing that now?'

'I must have a living model. I have needed a model ever since those years I spent in the Louvre copying nudes. I want you here as a living presence, as someone around whom I can begin to chart this reality your body occupies.'

Lemons on a Fleur-de-Lis Background

The fleur-de-lis motif appears so often in the Orléans drawings that it is inevitable that it should recur in *Citrons sur fond fleur-de-lisé*. The painting shows the rose-coloured brick fireplace with a grey marble mantel, which he designed some years before. In reality, the wall covering is beige hessian, but he changes that. He opts to echo the red of the brickwork and paint the wall with fleur-de-lis. There are forget-me-nots in the green Chinese vase, next to which the half-dozen lemons shine, vividly solid, yet seeming to float on their greyish shadows on the mantel.

Another version that he plans of the same subject will include the portrait of Charles d'Orléans, based on the Fouquet painting.

Lydia looks at the finished work. 'Did you choose the forget-me-nots for some symbolic reason?'

Matisse pauses for a moment, then shrugs. 'My paintings are not that sort; you ought to know that by now.'

'So, the flower has no particular significance?'

'I confess I inclined towards symbolism when illustrating Orléans's poems. I suppose that a left-over of symbolism may have found its way into the painting.'

* * *

Aragon heard that there were demonstrations at Fiat's Mirafiori factory in Turin. On 12 March, the workers walked out in an attempt to force the government to keep its promise to indemnify those people who had been bombed out. They wanted bread, peace and liberty. The next day, the authorities offered three hundred lire to every workman willing to stay in line. It was the first time in fascist Europe that the workers had tried their strength against their bosses. When the Turin strike was over, trouble spread to the Pirelli and Breda works in Milan.

Aragon always had to have a theory and practice of dream as well as the material. It was why he had joined the Surrealists. Writing about Matisse, he had to defend luxury, which he saw as Matisse's chief gift to the world; his sense of a paradise regained, felt, ordained, given back to the workers in the present, who owned nothing except their value as labour. The masses had their dreams stolen every night, and could not attain them materially by day; capitalism used the machinery of their longing to sell them its jaded products. When the war was over, the people would find Matisse again, alive in those places they longed for, who had dealt with his pain by finding joy in sensuous creation.

As a painter, he was trying to tell the story of a happy man. Some critics refused to deal with this; they failed to grasp why artists should want things to be true that had no place in reality as they saw it. Matisse had to fight attacks of hepatitis to get down to the serious business of painting. He had to rise above the lethargy induced by morphine. It was a routine of fever, pain, night nursing and fitful sleep. If he did force himself out of bed for an hour or so, the pain soon felled him again.

Feeling blue, Elsa had drunk enough to feel hostile towards many people she had met in happier times. Gertrude Stein loomed large suddenly and became a target. 'Where is Gertrude? She didn't flee to America. Maybe she has found out that she is a concierge by nature, an arm of the state, a paid agent for undertakers, who knows all there is to know. Maybe Gertrude is doing her bit for the war effort.'

'What can you mean by that?' Aragon said.

'Oh, you know.'

'You can be very cruel, Elsa.'

'All I meant was that some official is taking care of her.'

'All honour to the man. What are you hinting she does in return?'

'Maybe she pays. Is that so bad? As a Jew, maybe she pays for her life to run smoothly. Others have to do that. Maybe she shares a cup of tea with this benefactor, some widower perhaps. I don't know his name. Doubtless he is a man who needs to confess the sins he commits on the other days of the week.'

'One of our groups could be watching over her, or her neighbours.'

Elsa laughed. 'The Resistance has no time for Jews. Was it ever vocal against the *Statuts?* The Resistance fighters attack Vichy and the Germans, but they choose their words with care when it comes to the Israelites.'

* * *

Matisse is insistent, brisk. 'What's the problem now, Lydia?'

'You mustn't scold me, please! This war is getting me down. You never deal with anything. I have to be vigilant in ways I can't believe; I watch the grocer's scales, in case I lose a gram.' She fires off a tirade against greedy shopkeepers and black-market peddlers. 'Do you know how women live, these days? You know nothing; you don't know what we have to pay for a sanitary towel, or how long women have to wait for them!'

Pasiphaé: Song of Minos

Matisse was to have illustrated Montherlant's poetry when *Pasiphaé* opened in the Thirties. Nothing came of the idea, until Montherlant arrived in Nice with an offer from his publisher. A portrait Matisse made of the writer appeared, badly reproduced, on the cover of one of his books. It was then that they had talked about *Pasiphaé*.

Matisse is lying fully clothed on the bed when he orders Lydia to lie beside him. 'Let me hold you. If I said I wasn't afraid, I would be lying. Please, kiss me, then! Kiss me!'

He senses a barb of accusation as she says that he is not being honest.

'I have always been honest with you.'

Lydia shakes her head. 'You know very well that the reason *Pasiphaé* will appear is that Fabiani knows every nook and cranny in Vichy's sewers.'

'If you mean what I think you mean, I have to say it was Vollard's suggestion that I should illustrate Montherlant's poetry.'

Before his illness, Matisse had no real experience of night. He finds now that he can work by propping a board on his knees using pillows. He fights the pain when it wakens him, and when it stops him from sleeping. He thinks that if he had not been ill he might never have begun the Pasiphaé project, nor if he had known how long it would take him. He feels as much anxiety as pain, so he is well able to share the Queen's fear of the beast. Yet she gave in, and was whirled among the stars for love of the white bull, Minos. Lost in his embrace, she knew that the Cretans would stone her for her shameless lust. Matisse understands this. He can almost feel the open ache of her sex, cutting its juicy fig into the lino.

Pasiphaé taunts him by being in the realm of all those pleasures of youth and early manhood. He feels them keenly still, but cannot act them out. 'And to lie down every evening in one's sadness as in a pigsty' is a line he speaks, cutting into the lino. Each white curve of her breasts, the lips of her cunt in the darkness, is agony. Her lips gape in the starlight; dumb as a fish seeking a hook she mouths the velvet head of Minos's pulsing erection.

Nézy, a Turkish princess, is the great-grand-daughter of Abdul Hamid. She posed for his *Jeune femme fatale au collier de perles* and his painting of the two friends. Matisse arranges her naked limbs until she is Pasiphaé, sprawled in the heavens awaiting her rutting beast. 'Linoleum gives an entirely different result from wood,' he says. 'I use the gouge with the same feeling as I use my violin bow; if you can understand that. Too much pressure can affect the line; in the same way as pressing hard on a string changes the sound.'

The sinister night he sees at the heart of Pasiphaé becomes too funereal as one black page follows another. It is then that he hits on the idea of using red initials. Although he changes these several times the book still has too much of an illuminated missal quality until he decides to align them with the austere typography by making them classical.

*   *   *

Aragon studied the crossword. Five across was clearly an anagram, but he could see only the jumbled clue, and there was nothing in the way of a solution. The clue to six down, read:

> *In Xanadu did Kubla Khan*
> *A stately pleasure dome decree:*
> *Where Alph, the sacred river, ran*
> *Through caverns measureless to man*
> *Down to a sunless sea . . .*

A question mark followed these lines. As Aragon pencilled in

Coleridge's name, he realised with a pleasant shock that he was able to remember what came next:

> *So twice five miles of fertile ground*
> *With walls and towers were girdled round:*
> *And there were gardens bright with sinuous rills,*
> *Where blossomed many an incense-bearing tree;*
> *And there were forests ancient as the hills,*
> *Enfolding sunny spots of greenery.*

When Sadoul arrived to report on the activities of the Étoilles cells they had set up in Lyons, Aragon told him how much he used to admire Valéry Larbaud's translation of *The Rime of the Ancient Mariner*. Then, with fresh excitement, he broached a new idea.

'We have to talk to any judge who is humane enough to refuse to enforce Vichy's deportation decrees by sending workers to Germany. We must enlist them into a National Committee of Jurists, along with lawyers and other court officials. I want us to seize on any legal unease that's going on in Vichy courts. We must take the initiative; and, by doing so, isolate the Germans and their henchmen.'

Sadoul was unsure. 'You really think you can recruit the justices?'

'We won't know unless we try. We did it with writers, editors and journalists; some doctors have come over to us. We can't stop them shooting our people, but they must not use the machinery of the law to sanction the killings.'

Sadoul envied Aragon's grasp of detail, his insight into what was going on. 'I don't know anybody who can extract more from reading a newspaper than you do.'

'It is a habit anyone can acquire,' Aragon said. 'I did not train to be an engineer, but it was easy to spot a major defect in our tanks during the First War. The army contractors were saving money by not providing escape hatches for the crews, who roasted to death when a shell hit their machines. I designed a key that made the War Office happy. Think how much it cost to train and replace those crews. Sadly, this ability does not help me in real life; it is of no use when it comes to Elsa.'

'I don't understand what you mean.'

Aragon paused before replying. 'My fear is that she is going to leave me.'

'You're crazy! The love you have for each other is a legend.'

'I know something is wrong; but I have no time to delve into it, even if I dared. I know that she is not happy about my current book. I am dealing with my life with Nancy, and she hates me for doing that; nor can she forget her jealousy of Drieu.'

Sitting by the window, Elsa looked distant as Sadoul kissed her cheek. He talked about Aragon without touching directly on their conversation. It was Elsa who turned to him, laughing. 'We are like Sacco and Vanzetti, or Laura and Petrarch. I'm not afraid of being shot – my fear is that we won't face the same firing squad. Even greater, though, is my fear of what will become of us if we survive; our slow decline into old-age bickering and forgetfulness. People will forget the poems he wrote for me; they will seem high-flown and affected, after I'm dead.'

How could Sadoul understand? He listened to her woes as though the substance of them had truth and was not the work of her capricious imagination.

'Sometimes I feel that I have never been me; that I have been living in a limbo, waiting to become a real person. I hoped that marriage would license me to find my true identity. Sometimes I still feel that way; but I find it quite natural to live in hiding, under a false name. It intensifies these feelings I have. I suppose being a Jew has something to do with it.'

'You're ill-suited for this life,' Sadoul said. 'You are under a great strain; it's bound to tell, after working so many months in the organisation. Often I find myself holding my breath as a German examines my identity papers. I want to get it over with; to spit in his face and run. I can see myself running for an eternity, then his bullet hits my spine.'

*   *   *

Lydia fills the electric kettle and plugs it in. Shaking the cloth, she charges the sunlight with a haze of dust, so that Matisse has to take off his glasses and clean them. He pinches the bridge of his nose, before hooking them on again to examine the photograph of Derain's painting *Les deux hangars*. He purses his lips critically, saying, 'My chief fear is that this is a horse that could, at the crack of a whip, launch into an aria from *Lohengrin*. What have they done to poor André? He has become soft since outraging the Louvre guards with his copy of Ghirlandaio's *Christ Carrying the Cross*. They crowned him France's greatest painter during the First War. His Charing Cross Bridge canvas showed us the Thames blazing cadmium-yellow, under cobalt-blue girders. His stay in London was more fruitful than mine. It was as though Van Gogh, our father, had risen again to start laying about him with orange and purple, colouring

213

the Houses of Parliament green. When I asked him where its history had gone, he told me that Vollard had not paid him to paint history but views of the Thames. I can still remember where he lived: Blenheim Crescent, Notting Hill Gate.'

The air-raid warning is a shock. Matisse has to use the stairs to reach the shelter because a power cut has disabled the lift. The concierge shows them the way; then, as the first bombs hit Cimiez, Matisse finds that the book he thrust into his pocket is Bergson's *Creative Evolution*. He has not looked at it since he tried to read it in Morocco, but can remember Georges Duthuit discussing Bergson's ideas. The philosopher's view of the world chimes with his own; they share the same feeling about time and space. Even as he reads, his paintings flame again in his memory to define what Bergson says about certain events looming in the flux of time.

Matisse is an inveterate idealist in a material age. He conceals his idealism in the material itself: the red of his studio, which disappears, turns the furniture into ghosts. Such a view of the world is not much avail when a bomb could fall on him at any moment.

'Do not stay, Monsieur Matisse,' warns the concierge. 'Cimiez will suffer more raids. The Americans will land here. There are rumours that they are going to evacuate all citizens of your age anyway. You would do better to live somewhere up in the hills. Another night or two like this and your health will fail again. You tell him, Madame Delectorskaya; you know he has to go.'

*　　*　　*

Elsa was to meet an agent called Rodet arriving on the last train at 7.30 in the evening. She sat on the platform of the country station. She nodded to the station master as he went by. She watched as he hung his cap and jacket on the fence before kneeling to work in his small garden.

A couple came along the track, the old man pushing a bicycle; they spoke briefly to the station master as they passed. In the afterglow, the scent of crushed lavender grew stronger, the bird song sweeter, so that Elsa drifted into a reverie. The clinging presence of the pre-war perfume held her in suspense; and, as the light faded, the scent intensified until she felt virginal again: the girl called Wild Strawberries.

Rodet was the only passenger to alight. Elsa knew his face at once. His real name was Altgelt, and he had been a good friend to Modigliani and Chaim Soutine when they used his café between the wars.

'Chaim is dead,' he told her.

'The Germans?'

'Indirectly.' Altgelt began to sob. Brusquely, Elsa took the handkerchief out of his top pocket and handed it to him. Altgelt blew his nose. 'Chaim and Marie-Berthe were living with a cabinet-maker near Tours. Chaim fell ill. Marie-Berthe put him in a hearse and drove back to Paris. The surgeon diagnosed perforated ulcers and internal bleeding and operated at once. It was too late. Picasso and Cocteau turned up for the funeral at Marie's family plot in Montparnasse. I did not join them at the graveside. Cocteau has known for some time that I am with the Resistance. Why tempt fate?'

Elsa saw Soutine's blacks and blues setting off a red cavern of meat in his *Carcass of Beef*. There was also his *Woman Wading*, after Rembrandt's *Hendrikye bathing in a Stream*, admiring her reflected cunt under the white bell of her raised dress.

Altgelt shifted his body from side to side. He blew his nose again. 'Chaim used to say that death always stood next to him. He nearly bled to death in a graveyard after his father beat him. Another time he spent the night hiding in a chicken coop, avoiding the rabbi's son, who had kicked him around. It was the rabbi's atonement for his son's crime, the bribe, you could say, that enabled Soutine to study art. Speaking of these "deaths", he said they derived from his failure to escape being a Jew.'

Altgelt had met him when Soutine lived in the passage de Dantzig near the Vaugirard hospital. He had just turned twenty then and was working as a railway porter or digging ditches. 'Anything's better than the *shtetl*,' he would say. 'He told me his parents were beggars. They used to whip him if he refused to beg. I knew the truth; his father used to mend clothes.'

Altgelt sighed. 'He never wanted to talk about Smilovitch. It was as though he had murdered his family and buried them in shallow graves. He found a job with a photographer in Minsk.'

'I used to see him at parties, but I never got more than a few grunts out of him,' Elsa said.

'*Meshugge*, without a doubt *meshugge*,' said Altgelt with a laugh. 'Believe it or not, he thought his hair was falling out! That lovely thick bush! I had Jean Bilite's photograph in my restaurant: the one in which Epstein, Krémègne, Soutine and Yoshi all sit like down-and-outs. Chaim never lost the common touch; he was a man of the people. As a Litvok, you will understand that,' said Altgelt.

215

Elsa flinched in the dark. It was a long time since anybody had called her a Lithuanian Jew.

They were counting the money Altgelt had brought. Elsa told Aragon that Soutine was dead. 'Drieu used to admire his work,' he said.

'I tell you that Soutine is dead, and all you have to say is that Drieu la Rochelle admired his work: a man who wants to wipe all Jews from the face of the earth.'

'Drieu is not somebody who wants the Jews slaughtered.'

'He's not a killer; no, merely a patriotic Frenchman who detests the Israelites. Perhaps he hates them because he married one and lived off her money. No, he doesn't hate them; any more than the Lithuanians hated them, who could not wait for the Germans to march in but murdered the Vilnius Jews themselves.'

As they walked to the church, Aragon said to René, 'Whenever I try to understand Atget's photographs, I feel that I am a latecomer at a crime scene. He was at the murder scene before me; he left Brassaï and Cartier-Bresson the language of photography in his will. I can hear the silence in which his shop-window dummies stand, and feel the presence of death in the emptiness of their clothes. We go to question his basket-sellers, his furniture, cooking pans, corsets, toupees, the emporiums and the Mouffetard second-hand shops, but we have lost the truth in faded sunlight. He put the corpse of the past under lock and key in his old trunks.'

René crossed the road briefly to talk to an old man. They parted with a nod; then René came walking backwards, marking each word by jabbing his finger upwards, before turning to Aragon to inform him, 'The Gestapo has moved to the avenue Berthelot. They have taken over the École de Santé Militaire. Doubtless they feel safer there than the Hôtel Terminus. The building has thick-walled rooms and cellars to muffle the screams.'

'What did this Fichet do?' Aragon asked.

'We suspect that the Germans broke him. They used to chauffeur him around the streets to identify our people. We found his body lying under sheets of newspaper in a churchyard. There was no sign of a wound, so we had a doctor look at him. He hadn't died of natural causes. He may have found the guts to drown himself in one of their bath tubs.'

'Did he work for you?'

René nods. 'At one time, before they captured him. I will bury him as one of my own; despite what I feel. Can any of us know how long we would hold out?'

It starts to rain, and René turns up the collar of his jacket.

The silent couple did not raise their heads as they stood beside their son's body in the open coffin. The mother hunched her shoulders in her wet raincoat, a puddle spreading on the flags around the ferrule of her umbrella. René was about to offer his respects when Aragon heard the trucks arrive, then the thud of boots as German troops leapt out and ran shouting to the church door. The priest waved for Aragon and René to escape by way of the vestry. After fighting his way through a curtained door, muffled and dusty, Aragon found he was alone in the yard. He ran across to the stone angel and, in desperation, used her arm to swing his legs over the wall.

In the outbuilding, he could hear the girls singing at their sewing-machines above. The rasp of his breath in the sudden chill was louder as he halted to listen. He had collided with a side of beef hanging from the ceiling; a prop from a Buñuel film, or the Soutine painting Elsa had talked about. It was an illicit slaughterhouse under the workshop. Forcing the carcass aside, he opened the door, startling scrawny chickens perching on a rail outside. They flew everywhere as he flailed through them. The women were crowding at the window by now, laughing as he picked up his hat and slammed the yard door.

After such a scare, Aragon felt that his role in the Resistance required the same agility and insight into mechanics that was second nature to riders on a fairground Wall of Death. He knew that the image of such a dare-devil rider stemmed from a passage in *Le Cheval Blanc*, when Michel Vigaud took fright at the idea of becoming one. It seemed a harking back to his Surrealist time of life. Surrealism, however, had not answered since the late Twenties. There was nothing in it for him now, when he had to use cold logic to stay alive in the labyrinths of secret operations. His aliases were no longer affectations. François la Colère, Arnaud de Saint-Romain – they were names out of France's glorious past, but they served to introduce him to comrades with whom he kept faith. The odd thing, almost calm-inducing, was that he felt no qualms about risking his life for others. A man of ideas throughout his life, it was his ideas that had led him to feel. He had never lost touch with reality in his old pursuit of the arbitrary image; the strident, half-hearted attempt to flush out the supernatural.

Simone in the Striped Armchair

Matisse studies his picture of Simone sitting in the striped armchair. Venus in a shell, or a Louis XV armchair, where was the difference? She would like to pursue this topic, but he says he would prefer her to tell him the stories she heard from her hairdresser.

Sometimes in the dimness with the curtains drawn, Matisse imagined noon. He feels the motion of the boat, sees the sun's molten shimmer on a lake, but does not know whether it is a memory or not. What is real is the brightness. Then he swims off Collioure, treading water above twirling shadows on the sandy bottom, staring at the inlets where the wind rattled his sketchbook when he was drawing Amélie and Margot.

He remembers this again when Lydia ushers in Tériade with Angèle Lamotte. She is tiny and chic, with a sweet, melodious voice; a frail creature from a Perrault fairy tale; yet, with the help of her sister Marguerite, she is tough enough to run *Verve*.

Tériade tells him that his missing *Atelier rouge* has turned up in a London night-club, the Gargoyle. 'It survived the blitz, and was blazing unseen in the dark above the bar.'

'It was such a big canvas; how come it wasn't noticed?' Angèle cannot believe the story.

'No night-club I was ever in was frequented by people in need of art,' Matisse says. He has not seen the painting since 1912, yet he feels an old surge of recognition, the blinding shock of red.

His Issy studio had white walls, so the walls in his canvas were blue-grey to begin with. He did not know how the Venetian red came about, but the initial blue-grey ground gave the final red a vivid, deep saturation. There was no perspective in the classical sense, yet he created depth out of the flatness; it emerged from the overall vibrancy.

The changes came fast, day by day; the chest of drawers that began life an ochre-yellow took on the same spindly ghost of an outline as the grandfather clock; since the clock lacked hands, and had nothing to do with real time, it seemed a confirmation of the illusion of time's banishment from the painting.

Matisse charms Angèle with the cut-outs he shows them. 'I am calling the book *Cirque*; the cut-outs celebrate the Cirque Médrano: that ammoniac smell of urine, the ponies, the elephants lumbering to Oriental music, the jugglers and clowns. There will be nothing of gravity in *Cirque*; the performers defy it. There will be an elephant levitating above a ball; there will be a clown, an acrobat, and a knife-thrower.'

'I know better than to ask when you expect to finish the book,' Tériade says.

Angèle talks about the material problems of reproduction. 'Are these printable, with such colours? My vision blurs even as I look at them.'

Matisse nods. 'I don't know much about the molecular behaviour of my colours. Of course, I sense that there is one, that colours have different wavelengths. Did any Intransigeant fail to read Chevreul's book on the theory of colour? All the ones I talked to knew of it. I did, too. Picasso used to say that the vibrations I set up, when using a mauve and green, created a third colour. The Orientals knew how to give colours a maximum intensity by setting them near their complimentary neighbour. There is never any absence of colour; contrary to what some painters would have us believe; shadows are not black; they are full of colour.'

* * *

The American landings in Sicily seem to confirm the concierge's fear that Nice would become a war zone, although there have been no more raids. Le Rêve is the name of the villa that Lydia found in Vence. Matisse has settled in his new home; his friend, the poet André Rouveyre, is a neighbour. Matisse describes the view towards Saint-Jeannet for Aragon, a village that reminds him of Baudelaire's Giantess . . .

> . . . sometimes, when the summer's sick suns
> Had sprawled her body across the countryside,
> To sink in listless sleep in the shadow of her breast,
> As a peaceful hamlet drowses at the mountain's foot.

After doing a tiny drawing to back up his description, Matisse goes on to describe the solid stone walls, glazed doors and high windows of the villa itself. Its design is a Gallic stab at the Anglo–Saxon colonial style, of which the retired British admiral who built it had been proud; it could suit him very well. There is a balustrade along the terrace, hung with ivy; geraniums glow there, and he glories in the palm fronds tossing outside his window in the morning. He feels Tahiti everywhere. When he steps outside the garden, sees the girls and villagers on their way to market, there is a smell of wood burning that remind him of the islands. He feels he is in command of his fate now, and that he can use the energy from the past to convert into fresh vitality, a vitality that will allow him to complete the work he has still to do.

Aragon must tell Madame Triolet that he is reading *Le Cheval Blanc* with great pleasure, Matisse ends.

* * *

Aragon had not been able to broach the war or the Resistance with Matisse except through Charles d'Orléans. He spoke of *Pasiphaé* when telling Matisse that he was living a tragic sense of his times: 'they make that myth seem like a cry echoing the thing that we never talked about.' What they could not discuss was Montherlant's paean to the Wehrmacht – 'France shall kneel to her proud conqueror, let Paris be the first to be raped by the army from the East.' The union of Vulcan and Ceres, the Ruhr and rural France, would be ideal.

Matisse had told him once, 'In the end, political discussion poisons everything.'

An idolater, a guest, Aragon said nothing in reply.

There were no lights in the bus. Hunched in a corner, Elsa hugged her knees, shivering as the driver hit low tree branches and skidded on the wet grass beside the road. She could smell wine from the driver, chicken cages; the mud left by earlier passengers going to some village market.

At last, the driver braked and opened the window.

Elsa craned forward. 'Is something wrong?'

'This is as far as I go.' The driver lit a cigarette.

Elsa could see nothing. 'Where are we? You can't mean to leave me here, miles from anywhere?'

'Léon will be here shortly.'

Elsa had moved forward until she was standing beside the driver, who seemed to be listening.

'There he is now. He will take you to his parents' farm. You have to walk a mile or so. Good luck, madame.'

Elsa felt the cold barrel of the shotgun slung on the man's shoulder as he lifted her down from the step. He gripped her arm and led her into the narrow lane, telling her that Aragon was not at the farm; that he would not get there until tomorrow. Oddly, his voice reminded Elsa of Thirion. She could hear his laughter again as Aragon read out a passage from Apollinaire's *Les onze mille verges.* In it, Prince Vibescu went to the Russo-Japanese front to satisfy his lust at The Joyful Samurai, a brothel in Port Arthur.

Elsa woke to the screaming of pigs. Did they know they were about to die at the hands of the three men in shirtsleeves who drove them towards the barn for the illicit slaughter? Dressing quickly, Elsa closed the window and went down to the kitchen.

The women fell silent as Elsa entered. The farmer's wife was there, who had helped her upstairs after she fell asleep at the table. In the yard, three children were over their fear now, and were running round with the bladders. Elsa knew why the farmer's wife had advised her not to go outside. Sauckel had taken two of her sons to labour for the Todt Organisation. If one believed Vichy, out there were Pétain's archetypes of the New Moral Order, whose forebears gave birth to Joan of Arc: in reality mean, die-hard *collabos* – vintners as gnarled and twisted as their olive trees. If she believed the Marshal, they would send any woman witch enough to abort a French foetus to the guillotine. Their women kept to their kitchens, said their prayers, and gave their lives to their children. No, Elsa shook her head; she was being alarmist, letting her nerves sour her judgement.

The butcher left the barn, wiping his hands on his stained apron. His assistants came after him, past the woodpile, carrying tubs of steaming pink flesh. She could hear the humming of bees, which had begun to swarm in a nearby tree. More people were arriving; then, suddenly, the rain came, huge pelting drops that shook the heliotropes.

After the rain, the people began to leave the farm and the outbuildings; a priest came riding a bicycle, holding an open umbrella. He propped the bike against the wall and made a futile attempt to brush the mud from his soutane.

By the time the two gendarmes arrived, everybody had gone; the older man took the parcel of pork from the farmer's wife, touching a finger to the peak of his cap. He joined his companion, who was inspecting the wasps; then, after looking at his watch, they walked together to the gate.

Elsa felt relief at seeing Aragon; he wore a jaunty, far from clandestine straw hat and dark blue neck tie with red spots. He strode briskly across the muddy yard talking earnestly to René. They were to return to Lyons at once.

* * *

Lydia and Monique use Linel paints to soak sheets of paper with strident and subtle colours. They hang these sheets to dry: green, gamboge, orange, ardent red, profound blue, and chrome-yellow.

As Matisse cuts out the various shapes, he tells the women how he feels. 'It is the action of the blades, the marriage ring comfort as I work the handle with my thumb, which gives me the greatest satisfaction. There is the sound, too; a world away from the one my brush makes on a canvas.'

*　　*　　*

Whenever Aragon and Elsa went to Lyons, they left the train before reaching the Gare Perrache or the Gare de Vaise. They would get off at some stop where they could board a tram into town. They were always wary in case they were trailed to meetings by some agent. The streets and alleys of the city became hourly more dangerous. If the Gestapo had your face in their files, it was foolish to walk anywhere. There were plainclothes police at the railway stations and on all the city's bridges. Since many clandestine meetings took place between the place Carnot and the place de la Comédie, this was an area that the French and German police kept under close observation. There, Resistance men hatched their plots that Dumas would have thought far-fetched, which they passed on in the form of urgent messages. It was there they wrestled with the enemy as at the bottom of a murky lake; there they worked out codes and whispered the addresses of safe houses. It was there that agents went on transmitting until radio-locator vans found them and the police kicked in their doors. There, the Germans threw their captives downstairs in the grey light of dawn, their faces as white as their shirts. Few would have found a role in a spy film; they were colourless men in business suits with glasses; scholars; plain women as down to earth as their underwear.

The place Bellecour was hot as Aragon strode across it, passing the Charité and turning into the rue des Marronniers. He was on his way to meet Elsa at the Trois Tonneaux restaurant.

The air was cool in the large room; the marble-topped table chill to his arm. He sat down with a glass of wine and read his newspaper. The Allies were ashore in Sicily, but Radio-Vichy had nothing to say about their progress. A waitress was chalking up the menu for the evening meal; an older woman was filling carafes from a barrel, so that the air was sharp with a sour, vinegary smell. The breeze shifted a beaded curtain now and then to dim the brilliance of a white shirt hung on the line in the sunlit yard.

Aragon glanced at himself in the mirror, musing for a moment where that tall, dark, blue-eyed poet had gone who drank in the Café Cyrano with the Surrealists. Perhaps it was the slant of the sun, the colour of the awning, that lent the place the air of the café near Schiaparelli's *maison* in the place Vendôme, where he used to wait for Elsa while she went to show her trinkets. At any moment, she would join him, talking of meeting Giacometti, who was also designing fashion jewellery for the salons; and how miffed Schiaparelli had been that Elsa had not offered her the jewellery before she took it to other houses. Schiap knew she had come to her as a last resort, and she must not demand anything foolish in the way of price. Her spies had told her that Elsa had been to that waif, Coco Chanel. Elsa imitated Schiaparelli's laugh. 'You must know that Coco is afraid to trust anybody. As a Red, you must have known she would show you the door.'

Elsa used rings rather than the glass beads then in fashion, using string instead of thread. Each necklace was unique, made in secrecy for fear of imitation. It was arduous toil that needed patience, a flair for intuiting what might attract bored women who spent their lives shuttling around the rag trade circuit. Elsa's book *Cocciers* chronicled her deals with bulk traders in the slum *arrondissements* of Paris, in the rue des Rosiers, or Blancs-Manteaux, where she found her suppliers. In Le Sentier and the Pletzl, Jewish baker and kosher butcher sold their wares; there, on the Sabbath, bearded men with ringlets met other bearded men in black suits at the synagogue: Zionists, pressers, tailors and street-traders. Amid the smell of matzos baking, they read the Yiddish daily paper, while hotly discussing the latest news.

Elsa had to beg the dealers to sell her enough materials for her needs. Some were refugees who had escaped from the Tsar's Polish ghettos; others were recent arrivals, worried by the way events were shaping. In her own lonely poverty, Elsa saw the daily bread behind the glamour; saw the daily grind of the women and girls, scrimping and scraping, who put in every stitch that went to make up the fantasy clothes in the fashion houses. She knew the system, the political order present in every pleat and button, of those new styles that sold each season as revolutionary.

'You must abide by Jean-Paul's decision. It is too risky for you to go on working in Lyons,' said René. 'As for returning to Dieulefit, Jean-Paul does not see that as wise either, for the same reasons. His orders are that you go to Saint-Donat, where the safe house is near enough for you to attend our monthly meetings.'

Aragon and Elsa left Lyons in secret. Only Sadoul knew where they had gone. As soon as they settled in Saint-Donat, Elsa began to write *La Vie privée ou Alex Slavisky, artiste peintre*, whose hero was a painter called Alex Slavisky, based on Matisse.

'Slavisky? Why a name that has a ring of Stavisky, a Jewish swindler?'

'I don't know. It's as good as any other. Why should I have to explain everything I do?' Elsa said coldly.

Elsa pulls a face. 'I hated the childish charade they play, calling each other Madame Lydia and Monsieur Matisse, employer and employee.'

'Matisse is old enough to be her father.'

'I don't think that would deter him if he felt well enough.'

'You mean you think he is still sexually active?'

'If not active, then something very close.'

'Close – what do you mean by that?'

When the *maquis* men came back, they were smoking their first cigarettes since the ambush and talking about the sixteen men they had lost. Some wore bloodstained German combat jackets, which they had looted from the dead. The grenades that hung from their belts thudded against their thighs as they jumped down from the truck. One of the two wounded men did not move; they crouched around the other to ask him how he felt. Well enough to take the lighted cigarette they held to his mouth. His friend walked up and down the track, kicking at the dust, glancing at the truck from time to time. Then the other wounded man died; four men rolled him in a sheet and stumbled with his body to the edge of the field where they had dug a shallow grave. Two men helped the last man from the truck and set him up on a crude crutch. They moved quickly, for the German tanks were not far away. Two women had come from the village. They wore traditional dresses and black head-scarves; their split clogs clicked on the rocks, and their black stockings clung to their skinny legs. They were doling wine from wicker-covered flasks as each man passed. Another thunderstorm was breaking in the mountains towards which they were heading.

When they reached the barn, a mist came down; the lightning forked as the thunder rattled in the mountain passes. The men's expressions had not changed; they spoke in the same laconic phrases they had used since leaving the truck, their faces set in disbelief. Soon the air in the barn was blue with cigarette smoke; they fell in the hay and went to sleep as quickly as tired children. They had done it. They had survived. There was nothing to discuss.

A mother had lost her son, and her tears were useless against the hard future. She would mourn him when they told her where his body lay.

* * *

Matisse wakes with a dry throat; he stares about him as though he does not know where he is. Lydia pours a glass of water from the bedside carafe.

'In my dream, my head is spinning; I am at Issy, working on *La conversation* or *La famille du peintre*. I call for Amélie to put on her hat, and we set off, our shadows merging sometimes at our feet. We pass gardens where unseen women sing and handymen are at work with shears. Then we are trudging in the country – a dour worn-out pedlar and his wife. There is a church bell tolling, and I look up and see the smoke as the train waits at Saint-Germain-en-Laye. It is dark when we reach the Gare Montparnasse; then, we are in the boulevard passing the Dôme and the Rotonde, lit by gaslight as they used to be. I hear laughter; people hail me. Rodin is there, drunk, his arm around Gauguin's shoulder, urging me to join him for a drink. Then Apollinaire looms up, his uniform smelling of mushrooms. He wears that war bandage pinned around his head, and he calls me *maître*. He is with Victorine Meurent, Manet's Olympia. I shake my head, and we hurry along the rue Delambre to our hotel.

'From my window, I see a crowd of dead revellers in the street. I walk up and down, agitated, looking out every so often where they stand singing under the window, raising their glasses as they wave for me to come down. Amélie opens Chateaubriand's *Mémoires d'outre-tombe* and begins to read; I sit down; I am sweating; my collar is choking me. There is a knock at the door and Gertrude Stein's sister, Sarah, comes in. Her torn dress reveals her left breast, which she tries to cover with the flap of material. She apologises that it is so late, but she is leaving for San Francisco in the morning with her husband, Michael. They want to see what the earthquake has done to the city. She wants to take some of my paintings with her. It worries me that she might want the painting I am working on and which is giving me so much trouble.'

* * *

The six men wore ragged uniforms and were haggard and unshaven. Only two of them knew any French. When Elsa spoke to them in Russian they surrounded her, their faces lighting up, touching her to make sure she was real, smiling, laughing, as innocent as schoolboys. The Germans had been using them to defend their garrison against *maquis* attacks. Two of them had been in Brittany building the Atlantic Wall. At the first chance they had fled into the mountains, where they had lived rough until the *maquis* found them. What the Resistance had to know now was whether they had any useful information and whether they would join them to fight the Germans.

The boy who could quote *The Brothers Karamazov* said he had no influence with his comrades. They distrusted him because he had been a commissar. The Germans captured him when his unit tried to save a herd of cattle, which the enemy was driving towards Minsk. The snow during the night had hidden the rustlers' tracks well enough for them to stage an ambush. As soon as the shooting started, they drove the cattle into the trap, firing blindly so that the animals died along with the Russians. When he came to, he found himself under a bloodstained snowdrift amongst the dying cows, his arm broken by a bullet. His comrades were all dead, as were the farmer and his wife. For a long time there was only the pain of the cattle; then he heard trucks coming. They had arrived to load the meat. The German who fell over him wore a butcher's apron tied round his greatcoat. He was a thin *Feldwebel* with a haggard face who seemed relieved that it was not some partisan booby trap he had fallen into. He took pity on him and ordered the two corporals to throw him in the truck with the rest of the meat. It began to snow again as he looked back. It would soon hide the bodies of his comrades.

He began to cry. Tears were running off his thin white nose by the time Elsa found a handkerchief to offer him. He looked like Soutine's *Pastry Cook with a Blue Hat*.

'If they don't want to freeze this winter, tell them they should throw in their lot with us,' Yves said. 'They don't know the terrain as we do; they don't have our communication system. If they don't join with us, they will be at the mercy of the Germans, who will hunt them down and destroy them.'

On the way back in the truck, Elsa scribbled a paragraph towards *Les Amants d'Avignon*. They were lines that made her heartsick and numb for pre-war days. She did not like to think what women were doing in Paris. Some of them were having fun, as usual. Not as much fun as women had before the war, though, because the champagne was now in enemy hands.

She had to shake off her mood, try to see things in proportion. She knew there were other women: radio operators with charmed lives, others who could face a firing squad if the Germans put a bogus English pilot into the line.

*　　*　　*

André Rouveyre says he is there to remind Matisse of their mutual friend Mecislas Golberg, a Pole, a poet, dramatist and art critic. 'We knew the police threatened to hold Golberg's residence permit, so that he had to give up his political work. When he began to interest himself in art and aesthetics, he found the time and energy to help you clarify your ideas for your *Notes d'un peintre*, even though he was suffering from tuberculosis.'

Matisse shakes his head. 'You mean that I should have acknowledged my debt. Why do you bring this up now?'

'What Mecislas suffered was only a beginning,' Rouveyre says. 'It is obscene what we are doing now to the Israelites in the flats at Drancy.'

'You mean that drab apartment block the Communists used to boast about.'

'They keep Jews there now, fifty in one room, without running water or toilets! Our gendarmes have been arresting them since 1941. This in a Paris suburb! There are so many now; they are starving. Until recently, it was the French police who manned the guard towers. French police, not Germans! Other *flics* earned overtime rates escorting Jews to cattle trucks at Bobigny – headed, they say, for labour camps in the East. We have to speak out, Henri.'

'Will you speak out, André?'

'We owe it to Mecislas.'

'You mean, I owe it to Mecislas.'

'Mecislas would be in Drancy now, if he were still alive. You remember his sympathy for outcasts, our lepers and victims. He was active fighting the squalor, poverty and injustice of our industrial society, while we dallied with the morality and social standards informing it.'

'Picasso has not said a word. I don't see how I can make any difference to what happens to these poor people.'

To dispel the tension, Rouveyre tells Matisse that Mickey Mouse, Donald Duck and Popeye have joined the American armed forces. 'Donald Duck pilots a Flying Fortress to bomb civilians.'

Matisse sighs. 'The cinema used to be such a wonderful distraction,' he says. 'These vile wars change the world so quickly. Although few of us see death and brutality at first hand, we all suffer in the shadow of them.

Yes, let me think it over; let me think whether I can do anything about Drancy.'

When Rouveyre goes, Lydia asks, 'Why say that? You know you will do nothing of the sort.'

'André seems to think that I have magical powers to change the world. My function is to paint; not to bear witness.'

* * *

Everywhere notices are warning France of a plague of Colorado beetles; a pest only slightly less greedy than the Germans, Aragon told Elsa. As soon as he arrived home, he leafed through his notebook seeking an image: Goya's nightmares; a tragic stage of lost actors; agonies of Olympics; an odour of brimstone in the air, from the mines of Silesia . . .
Then he wrote:

> *I write in this land where flensing butchers*
> *Lay bare our bones, nerves and entrails;*
> *Where forests are burnt torches,*
> *And fleeing the blazing cornfield, birds in the air . . .*

It was the panorama of the siege of Port Arthur during the Russo-Japanese War that upset Aragon as a child in Le Musée Grévin. Alfred Grévin set up his hall of fame when Daumier was in prison for *Gargantua*, and Diderot was having to use allegory to attack his enemies. Aragon was shaping other waxwork figures by the light of flickering newsreels: Hitler, Pétain and Laval, all busy as sacristy fleas.

How could he strip Pétain of his Verdun glory and decorations and put him in the pillory? He saw Pétain's aide, Captain Bonhomme, a symbol of France, faithful as a dog, who would, if needful, hold a chamber pot for the hero of Verdun to piss in.

Aragon had kept a cartoon by the Englishman, Low, of Signor Mussolini, spouting poison on the balcony of the Palazzo Venezia, which he had torn out of a paper he found on the dockside at Plymouth. Julius Caesar could have told Il Duce that ice-cream sellers, notaries and gondoliers do not conquer empires; and that to be a circus Stromboli was no sort of apprenticeship for an emperor. It would not have stopped the Duce craving a cheap fiefdom. It was easy to gas and gun down tribes of fuzzy-wuzzies in Abyssinia; not many Italians had died doing that. The victory left Mussolini unsatisfied with his first slice of empire. It had been too much of a triumphal slaughter for his legionaries, a ceremonial victory.

Aragon wrote:

> *A ruthless gang infests our land rustling*
> *Our herds, whipping pigs from our sties;*
> *As werewolf and vampire they rend our flesh*
> *With claw and fang under merciless skies.*

Laval was an altar boy before he drove a village bus; then, after studying law, he began a swift ascent to earn the fur coat Stalin gave him when he signed the alliance treaty. Aragon gave him pride of place in his Grévin museum for his ceaseless pre-war grubbing for wealth and power: buying up country newspapers for a song. Laval now used his presses to make more millions printing inter-zonal passes.

The first cartoon showed him marrying Dr Claussat's buxom daughter and taking her to the Fauburg Saint-Martin, where a pawnbroker, a notary, a midwife and a cheap dentist were their neighbours. Laval had to put up with a grimy cobbler's shop next door, his poky office stinking of the tripe that steamed all day in a shop below. These people were no help if you were trying to impress trade union leaders.

Aragon tried again:

> *As I write now, among men who lie in filth and dirt,*
> *Hungry and voiceless . . . here, where mothers mourn*
> *Their sons' quartering by Herod's order,*
> *Who fears Laval seeks his crown . . .*

In June, in a speech to veterans, Pétain had tried to sell them the idea that he and Laval were as one, just as he was with them. Laval did the thinking for the outfit and he had Pétain's full confidence and trust. He could offer no explanation why his Premier gave Hitler Belgium's gold reserves, nor why Laval saw fit to surrender every share in Bohr's Yugoslavian copper mines; nor could Pétain say much about Laval handing over colonies and air bases to the Japanese. That was no way to keep an empire intact.

> *Ghosts, ghosts, ghosts*
> *Generals with no armies, Admirals with no fleet*
> *Well-paid to rise late, sleep early*
> *Forgers, gravediggers, crooks, slave-traders*
> *Pens that suck at every ink-well*

That Vichy steak-house, auctioning
France's flesh, roasted or raw . . .

Dancer and Armchair, Black Background

Matisse has already sketched his Venetian chair, but now decides to feature it in *Danseuse et fauteuil, fond noir*. He works in bed with his canvas propped against the lid of his work-box. Nézy is to his right, lazing in an armchair. He has already painted the background black and dark grey; colours found nowhere in the actual room. Nézy has lost her face and hair, as well as her chic head-dress. Her head is an angular pink shape against the crooked geometry of a yellow chair. Only her thighs have gained splendidly in transit to the canvas. Matisse has lost the white tiles of the floor in a blackness that sets off the ellipse, circle and sinuous arms of the rococo chair to the left. It is the baroque Venetian piece, whose back and seat are two ornamental clam shells, varnished silver, which join in an odd polyp-like hinge. He told Aragon he had been searching for such a chair ever since Ciboure. It bowled him over when he saw it in an antique shop.

The clatter upsets Matisse as Lydia tosses her car keys on the table as she enters the room with a bouquet of flowers.

Nice was stifling. It was too hot to drag around the shops, and she was miserable.

Matisse tries to soothe her. 'Why are you sad?'

Lydia groans. 'I said that the Italian armistice would finish Angelo Donati's plan to send the Jews to Italy and North Africa. The Germans are now busy flushing them out of hiding. All men have to drop their pants at barricades to show their foreskins!'

Matisse shakes his head. 'You witnessed this?'

'The hotel basements are hell-holes. The old doorman at the Hôtel Excelsior told me the Germans are using it as an interrogation centre. Even the Atlantique, their command post, is full of women and children. They are going to deport every Jew in Nice.'

*　　*　　*

Sadoul brought Matisse's letter to Aragon. They talked about *Le Musée Grévin*, which Aragon had almost finished; then they discussed the trip to Paris that Aragon and Elsa were about to make.

Pierre Seghers had held on to the letter for some time. It was a reply to the letters Aragon had sent Matisse in July and August, and told how he had been cutting more plates for *Pasiphaé*.

The National Writers' Committee was meeting to decide a course of action in the event of an uprising. The organisation had come a long way to feel such optimism, and it cheered Aragon enough to forget how miserable his last trip had made him. The meeting would also select the books the Committee was going to publish, so that Elsa's bag would be heavy. It held the finished manuscripts of *Les Amants d'Avignon* as well as the piece on Gabriel Péri. Later in the day, before Sadoul left for Toulouse, they had news of Laurent Casanova. He had escaped from Germany to Paris, and gone into hiding in Michel Leiris's apartment, where he was busy persuading Picasso to join the Party. Danièle and Maïe Politzer had both died in the camp at Auschwitz.

To avoid the station concourse at Lyons, Aragon and Elsa went to the platform by way of the marshalling yards, guided by a railway worker. It was raining, and the light was fading fast; the boy who had begged his father to take him held a hurricane lamp to light their way through the several wagons. His father, César, sent him scuttling on ahead to scout the tracks, a task that pleased and excited the lad.

The driver and his fireman nodded down to César as they came abreast of the engine. None of the passengers on the platform paid any attention to their sudden appearance as they shook hands with César and the boy and entered a compartment.

Elsa sat by the window, rubbing at the fogged glass as she watched César and his son talk to the driver. She saw the old man take out his watch and hold it up to the light; then he nodded to the driver and he and the boy returned the way they had come.

They were travelling this time on papers in the name of Aragon's father. Elsa must remember that she was Blanche Andrieux. It was a role calling for her to wear her pre-war fur coat, which gave off a nasty smell as it dried out in the airless carriage. 'It is useless trying to get a fur cleaned in such times of shortage and austerity,' she told Aragon. 'The cleaners told me that the chemicals are unobtainable now.'

The weather brightened as they left Lyons. It became light enough for Aragon to add a stanza to *Le Musée Grévin* to mourn the death of his friends before night fell:

> *I salute you Maries of France with a hundred faces –*
> *When you return, for you must return*

There will be flowers to assuage your longing,
There will be flowers the colour of the future,
There will be flowers when you return.

And:

Alas, their sowings glisten
With blood in this endless summer
That drags on too long . . . Listen,
They took Danièle and Maïe . . .
Will they pluck all our petals, one by one,
Ravish them all from our sweet France?

The plainclothes Gestapo men and a squad of armed green-uniformed
Feldpolitzei boarded the train at first light. There was nowhere to run as
the Germans searched the train. Every passenger had to wait, trapped,
trying not to show fear.

When the fat *Feldwebel* waddled into the compartment and demanded
their papers, Elsa told herself that God had fed this chosen pig well,
whose belt buckle's *Gott mit Uns* glinted boldly on his belly.

Aragon had used up all the German he could muster that had any
bearing on the situation. He fell silent as a second soldier began to rifle
the passengers' luggage. Then, when it was Elsa's turn, he tried to
explain that she was his secretary, who was carrying documents on behalf
of the Vichy administration. The soldier was about to open the bag when
both he and the *Feldwebel* clicked their heels to an order shouted in the
corridor, and left.

Elsa coughed into her handkerchief as people lit cigarettes to calm their
nerves. When the train moved on, it left behind a lone family under
guard. Their faces where white in the greyness. Then the headlights of a
truck swung under the box-girder bridge the train was crossing, and Elsa
had a last glimpse of these forlorn people being thrust down the
embankment as the smoke from the engine hid them.

When Breton published his pamphlet *La Misère de Poésie*, he taxed
Aragon with having written 'Front Rouge' in Moscow. It was, in his
opinion, a 'poem of circumstance' with no future in art as such. It did not
blaze a fresh trail for poetry and, by giving in to proletcult urges, Aragon
had debased himself with lines like:

The dogs the dogs the dogs conspire
and as the pallid treponema eludes the microscope

so Poincaré flatters himself he is a filter virus
The race of dancers and daggers of tsarist pimps...
the mannequin grand dukes of the casinos
Informers paid twenty-francs a letter
all white dry rot of the emigration
slowly finding shape in France's bidet
The Polish snot and Rumanian drool
the vomit of the globe
spawns to blacken Soviet horizons....

Breton had not wanted Aragon to go to prison, but equally he had no time for his agit-prop; it was too much of a public act of treachery to have any place in the Surrealists' dreams of revolution. Not long after Breton published his pamphlet, Éluard set out his feelings, saying that Aragon's incoherence had become calculation, his skill was now base cunning; he was a different man, one whom Éluard had banished from his mind.

Later still, Éluard lent his name to a manifesto issued by *Counter-Attack*: 'We are for a united world, one that has no truck with the present police coalition against a Public Enemy Number One; we prefer the anti-diplomatic brutality of Hitler as being less of a threat to peace than the frenetic drivel of politicians, though we are not fooled by him. We are members of the human community, who have been betrayed just as much by Sarrault as by Hitler, just as much by Thorez as by La Rocque!'

In his youth, Paul Éluard was Paul-Eugène Grindel, who worked in his father's real estate firm, naming streets after Jarry and Lautréamont. Aragon and he had not spoken since the piece in *Counter-Attack*. Now, in the Gare de Lyon, Éluard looked strained in the eerie light filtering through the blue paint masking the glass roof. He seemed older and wiser than that voyager who, when Gala left him for Max Ernst, began a world cruise, dreaming in his cabin, eating at the Captain's table. Existence was indeed elsewhere.

There were bright yellow Stars of David everywhere. Women wore them on their coats; men on their suits. They were barbarism's latest fashion accessory: an emblem of hatred.

'Yes, the stars are mortifying,' Éluard said. 'Every Jew has three of them, for all occasions, and they come off his clothing card. Barbet-Massin, Popelin makes the cloth; the Germans got it cheap, twenty-one francs the metre. People say that Alibert had the Rothschilds in mind when drawing up the *Statut de juifs*. It was because they had meddled in an election he lost. We know how xenophobic we are. They devised the

Statut as a tool for the *boches* to loot the Rothschilds. The *Statut* is the key that unlocks the Baron's stables, to enable the Germans to export the old man's stallions for vital war work: screwing German mares. Of course, what the decree means is that no hotel can admit Jews; they have to sleep in the open like tramps, prey to the gendarmes. The last carriage in the *métro* is theirs; they cannot go to cinemas, theatres, or use any telephone box. No Jewish child can play in the parks. To break these rules means a large fine or being sent to Drancy, which leads to deportation.'

'Now that the Jews are naked in the glaring light of public interest, Paris can accuse them of every sin: building the Maginot Line, losing the war, making fortunes in black-market food,' Nusch said. 'The Jews are to blame for everything, even the weather. I am afraid of what might happen next.'

There was a thin wafer of moon above Éluard's apartment in the rue Marx-Domoy. They were near La Chapelle's desolate marshalling yards and the slag and coal heaps along the Canal Saint-Martin. At dinner they talked about Max Ernst waking in a sweat after dreaming of buggering a fully clothed man sitting on his knee. This led Éluard to find Man Ray's group photographs at Le Paradis, the cabaret on the boulevard de Clichy, when friendship was a more light-hearted affair.

Elsa did not like the look of Nusch, a pitifully thin skeleton. She was no longer that beautiful nude heroine of Man Ray's *Facile* studies, the curves of her erotic breasts and belly dark against the light; her bracelets hinting at bondage, manacles, as she held her ankles.

She was angrier, too. 'A *boche* commissioner fixes the rations, yet the government levies the tax price. Then the Germans and the local Prefecture of Police must inspect every vegetable bound for Paris, so that a cabbage is half dead by the time I buy it. Even if he has a truck and fuel, a retailer is breaking the law by dealing directly with the grower. I can't believe the waste! The government adds to the mess by putting a ceiling so low on the price of fruit and vegetables that it's not worth the trouble to pick them. Then they set a tax on beans and peas, so heavy that they vanish overnight while crops of them rot in the fields. If there weren't a black market Paris would be famished.'

Elsa looked up to where Picasso's portrait of Nusch hung on the wall. It was an object from another world, a cruel reminder of other times, when life had circuses and harlequins. As a child, Nusch beat the drum for her father, an acrobat, who in turn beat it for her. Éluard had been with René Char when they saw her, a girl doing her circus routine on the street – or were her acrobatics to exhibit her lithe body's aptitude for other tricks, Char suggested. When she posed for Picasso, he saw her as a throw-back to those wistful women of his Blue Period. In other portraits, such as the one Elsa could see in the dimness behind the table, he punished her for her beauty, using nightmare distortions.

'Some mornings, after the curfew forced us to stay the night at Christian Zervos's flat, we would waken to see Pablo's *Night-fishing at Antibes*,' Nusch said.

'It may have been at the back of my mind when I wrote "Liberté",' said Éluard. 'I can hear Pablo saying that a poem should be an act of war. Not that his night-fishing is that.'

'Even to talk about it makes me feel homesick,' Aragon said.

*   *   *

I think of this, André, Matisse writes to Rouveyre, *because Lydia found herself recently passing a counterfeit bank note she came across in her purse. How? Was it the work of a Resistance group trying to undermine the currency, or some gang of common criminals? When I studied the thing, I could see that it was a work of art; I know the physical pressures of engraving, the pains that go to create such delicate forms – one slip, you ruin a plate. Such skill is a danger to one's eyesight, too; then, in the end, to have created something false, worthless, which will not pass muster. Ah, there is a darkness quite as impenetrable as my own . . .*

*   *   *

When Aragon arrived with the news that the militia had taken over Castel-Novel for use as a prison and torture chamber, it clouded Elsa's day. She had been happy because *Les Amants d'Avignon* had appeared.

They used art to forget their depression. 'I used to read those newspapers that Picasso cut up for his brasserie collages,' Aragon said. 'He chose lurid tales: in one a woman poisoned her lover; in another a tramp confessed to the murder of a chauffeur's wife. In the end, it turned out that the chauffeur had killed her. The lightning flashes of Pablo's ideas were always hard to nail down. What he said one day he would deny the next. The *Boîte de Suze* has facts and figures about the spread of cholera in the Balkans, during a war that was then a distant calamity in a backward country. I had no great sympathy for its people until their conflict led Europe two years later to Sarajevo. Picasso, though, was taking the dying man's pulse.'

* * *

The American general, Patton, made a speech in Ajaccio praising the first Free French landings. Leclerc's men had gone ashore in late September, escorted by the two cruisers *Jeanne d'Arc* and *Montcalm*, and the destroyers *La Fantasque* and *La Terrible*. The Resistance fighters had already captured the port.

While Patton gave the world his thoughts on Napoleon Bonaparte, Matisse remembered the island he had painted, his Turneresque sunrise, and the crackling heat. It was in Corsica that he made his surrender to the Mediterranean; it was there that he found the roots of his own freedom.

* * *

It was cold that winter. The room Aragon rented had no proper heating. They queued for food, which petty shopkeepers doled out in grams; they had more power than they knew what to do with, unless they were dealing with an attractive woman.

Rain came on an icy wind rattling the window panes. The wind shook the ragged curtain where Elsa shivered in bed, fighting her fear that the Germans had arrested Aragon by reading Agatha Christie's *The Mysterious Affair at Styles*. She had finished Freeman Will Crofts' *The Loss of the Jane Vosper* and found the Christie a deft exercise in class nostalgia; her only comfort was to know that the class had gone into hiding until the war ended. Christie's husks were their old disguises. It was the frozen tics of their characters that always led to murders. It had to be murder, of course, which brought them on-stage to stall and lie to Poirot, the master detective, whose keen intellect never penetrated deep enough to reveal the identity of the real killer.

Laying the book down, she thought how much harder it was now for men or women to commit a crime of passion, when executions had become the norm. Before the war, she and Aragon had sympathised with such killers. Yet, surely it had to be true that jealous lovers still slept fitfully in a dream of ending somebody's life. Did they find it easier to kill their husbands or wives with mass murderers in authority everywhere?

Aragon's clothes were sodden when he got back at first light. Some drunken German marines had delayed him, blundering out of a brothel with their flashlights' horseplay probing every shadow. They passed so near to the doorway he hid in he could smell the spirits on their breath. He shivered, a scared water rat, watching them prop each other up, as they smoked a last maudlin cigarette, the rain thudding on their borrowed umbrellas.

His clothes dried out during the next day; but the stove had baked his shoes, making them grey and hard to put on. They left for the station, tired and irritable. It rained all the way, and when they arrived the train was late. Since Germany had looted most of the S.N.C.F.'s rolling stock, the French suffered in unheated trains whose carriages often had broken windows. As soon as they were clear of the station, the rain blew in, until Aragon stuffed the hole with a newspaper. None of the other passengers seemed to care one way or the other.

Aragon looked at his watch, tapping it glumly to indicate to Elsa what she knew already: that they would be late and that, unless they caught the bus at Saint-Vallier, they faced a ten-mile walk.

It was eleven o'clock when they arrived in Saint-Vallier. Any hope that they could reach Saint-Donat had gone. The hotel restaurant would serve no food until the next day. When Elsa unlocked the room she said that she could still smell the previous occupant: a German. Aragon scolded her, shutting the door of the sombre wardrobe. He struck a match as she threw back the plum-coloured quilt to find that the maid had not changed the sheets. A brief glimpse of greasy patches on the walnut-leaf wallpaper turned Elsa's misery into rage. She went to confront the manager, who was still drinking with his cronies. He resented her talking to him in that way, he shouted; if she didn't like the room she needn't sleep in it.

'Believe me when I say, madame, stop going on or you'll find yourself in the street again!'

'I am staying here!'

'No more crap, then!'

At the station, Elsa learned that a post van left early on its round in the morning. She went back and ordered the manager to ask the maid to wake them at 5.30 a.m.

Aragon was already asleep. She lay down next to him without taking off her clothes.

She felt as though she had only slept an hour or so before the knocking woke her. It was 4.30. When she asked why she had come so early, the maid explained that the commercial traveller had to be up at 5.00, the

237

farmer from Roussillon at 6.00, with her weak heart she was not going to run up and down every half-hour. 4.30 would have to suit all the guests in the hotel.

Aragon sat up, nursing his swollen foot; then, sucking in his breath, he pulled the nail off his big toe.

The way to Saint-Donat was arduous. It took six hours in all for the postman to deliver and gossip his way round the villages, as well as eat his lunch and air his opinions on the state of the world. Not that he cared much, he said; nature meant more to him than politics. That was why he was a postman; it enabled him to spend his life in the open air. It explained, too, why he could answer any question they cared to ask about the animals and flowers of the district. Elsa did not press him; she brooded on the brutish hotel manager.

In the almost empty cinema, Elsa could see that the man was looking at her every so often. Something in the way he sprawled his legs in the aisle-seat sent a spasm of sensual response along her thighs. She sensed that his fly was open and that he was handling himself. He hid nothing; his posture was an open invitation.

The Surrealists did not have time for women, but Elsa shared their language of desire, and was as much a slave to the idea of carnal desire as they were. Unlike the Surrealists, though, for her it could be a weakness. She had to flee her dreams rather than succumb to them; they were a maze of dark corridors hiding forbidden fruit.

This stranger made her feel weak at the knees, as open to manipulation as a Hans Bellmer *Doll*; created to be played with, used. She knew when he gave a signal that she would go.

As she leaned forward, listening at his mouth, he handled her breasts roughly; then he tore her dress open and wrenched her nipples, forcing her to kneel. She had an image of herself as that dutiful handmaiden in Zichy's drawing that Triolet kept in his wallet. Her lips had seemed to Elsa too dainty to do more than kiss the cock her dream lover urged her to suck as he leaned against the round table. It filled her tiny hand, while her other toyed gently with his balls, as Elsa now found herself doing to the stranger.

His pubic hair smelled of urine as she tried every nicety of fellatio that used to bring soft moans from Aragon, but they had no charm for this brute, who fucked her mouth so hard she felt each gag would make her vomit, before relieving himself with a gush of sperm. This she had to swallow when he tightened his grip. Then he shoved her away;

nauseated, she got up and ran, shaken by the realisation that he could have been a German, a soldier suffering from syphilis or gonorrhoea.

She blamed the war. The war forced people to do vile things; it forced men and women to betray each other and lie to save their skins. Hers was only one more betrayal. There were worse acts of treachery, those that sent a friend or lover to the firing squad. It was asking a lot to expect any other sort of behaviour. People were mortal; they were weak; they lived without confronting reality, babied by the everyday. How could they know their weakness? It was the war, she told herself again; but she was lying.

As she halted on the bridge, staring down at the winter Saône, she felt she had tarred and feathered herself too by dressing up the dirty commonplace in literary images, using Bellmer's *Doll* and the Zichy girl. They had their real existence, of course, but she had used them to dignify what men paid prostitutes to do as part of their act. Other people managed to live without the need for such deceptions, such language.

Lovers hate the passage of time as they wait for each other. Men and women during those years shared this feeling, and as the hours dragged, their sense of unquiet grew. After the fear, with its burden of guilt, there were childish quarrels of a cruel nature. These were so intense, so freakish, that it was impossible to keep them up.

Elsa switched on the bedside lamp. 'Where have you been?'

Aragon unbuttoned his overcoat shivering. 'I couldn't get back any sooner.'

'You said you'd be home before dark; it's almost daylight now. Where do you go when you are not here? I know that there are things you won't tell me.'

'The more you know, the greater the risk. You can't tell what you don't know, so it's better that you learn only what is necessary. That is enough.'

'There is enough uncertainty, without a breakdown of trust in each other. Have you anything on your mind?'

'I don't want to waste time in guessing games; I'm very weary.'

Elsa said nothing.

'Why don't you accuse me of getting into bed with some man! It's what you think I've been doing! I can't believe I am saying this.'

'I've seen how they shake hands with you.'

Aragon began to undress. 'You are being a scold, Elsa. Please don't say any more.'

Elsa heard her voice become shrill. 'I know that it's true. You are going with men! You are more discreet these days, that's all, so as not to hurt my feelings. Do you want to bugger me: would that make you happy?'

'That's a sordid thing to say, Elsa! You are with me always, wherever I am; you rule all that I do, the way I think, every gesture I make.'

'I cannot imagine what you will get up to when I am dead. You will probably paint your raddled chops, like Baron Charlus. I know everything; I know your secrets. I'm ageing; is that why you no longer want me? Is that it? The war drags on; I am the Dorian Gray portrait you hide at home; no longer your Ziegfeld Follies girl.'

'We are both growing older.'

*　　*　　*

Matisse's new glasses have large Zeiss lenses; he tells Lydia that they make him look like an owl. His oculist explains how harsh colours rob the retinas of their pigment, which is why his eyes tire easily. It is not a question of enforced total darkness; rather he should listen more to the radio and rest them from time to time, then they would be fine.

He tells the oculist, 'When I started *La desserte rouge* in 1908, I found the work taxing but satisfying. At first I let green dominate the painting, but by the time Shchukin took possession of it, it had become blue. I suppose Émile Druet's photograph must still exist somewhere. Not that it would tell you much, being black and white. I was not happy, though, and asked Shchukin if I could work on it again.

'In its final metamorphosis, only the antler patterns on wall and table-cloth were blue. A tone, rather than a line, stopped the wall's hungry red from taking over the table-cloth; that, and the pattern of yellows, the carafe of white wine and fruit. The window frame revealed a countryside similar to that which Gauguin painted in Brittany. My otherworldly luminous trees showed the presence of a moon somewhere. There was nothing of my early obsession with the light on glass stoppers. I was striving to create the illusion that things are never going to change in the room; that the serving girl – I must call her Caroline – would always hold the fruit-stand cradled that way.'

1944

BONNARD sat near a small table in the corner, with Poncette on a chair beside him. A pale winter sun lit the chill room. It was painful for Cartier-Bresson to see the old master scarfed against the cold, surrounded by so many radiant canvases.

Bonnard pulled out a handkerchief and polished his glasses. 'I brood every night now over the Kodak snaps I took of Marthe. We all had a Kodak in those days. God, it seems centuries ago! She sat on a chair in the garden, a bright nude in a patch of sunlight, holding her breast. Everything about those snaps is alive with my love for her; such a beautiful forest nymph!' He raked his brow with his thumbnail and sighed. 'I try to forget such memories.'

'All the Muses are women,' Cartier-Bresson said. He framed the room that Bonnard had shown in so many ways in various paintings. It had the feel of a monastic cell, except for the wine-coloured table-cloth. A peasant neighbour in a faded blue jacket crouched on the hillside, pruning his vines. Four rust-red chickens moved around a goat tethered to a brass bed-head serving as a gate, as though waiting for Bonnard to fix them in a landscape.

'You and Matisse have been fortunate living under Vichy rule,' Cartier-Bresson said.

'You think so?' Bonnard said. 'I'm too old to care one way or the other. I hate war, that's true. I have a vivid picture of the widows of 1917 in their black dresses. Matisse and I often reminisce about women's gowns in those days.'

Cartier-Bresson stops what he is doing. 'Yes, they were the black-gloved women of my childhood,' he said. 'Manet's lovelies who shook the sultry summer air with their fans; those dainty bunches of violets; those hats, those perfumes; the air of secrecy, and sudden glimpses of their naked flesh.'

Bonnard called a halt to the session by offering Cartier-Bresson a treat; a relation had sent him a tin of tea. 'Do you like tea?'

Cartier-Bresson nodded, going over to inspect Bonnard's postcards: Vermeer, Renoir, a Cézanne, and a Seurat.

'I buy them at Aimé Maeght's gallery in Cannes.'

'Do you visit Matisse at all?'

'The petrol shortage makes buses infrequent, but I go sometimes. I see him more than in the old days.'

Bonnard showed Cartier-Bresson a photograph of Toulouse-Lautrec. 'He had just come back from London, where he had been sketching Oscar Wilde at his trial.'

Cartier-Bresson shook his head, finding it hard to take in that Lautrec had been Bonnard's contemporary and friend; that they had shown their work together.

Bonnard said there were times when he did not believe it either. 'Later, with Matisse in his pomp, Signac told his wife, Berthe, that he thought he had gone to the dogs when he saw *Joie de vivre*. It was a golden age of art, of murder, too; doctors used to treat eczema with arsenic.'

'How is the war affecting Matisse?'

'No. We share the same inability to deal with the world we have to live in. We don't discuss things like that.'

'Aragon said that his illustration for the blinding of Polyphemus in Joyce's *Ulysses* was the only true image of pain in his work,' Cartier-Bresson mused.

'Yes, cruelty held no attraction for us, even my illustrations for *Père Ubu*. Henri told me he swapped a canvas for one of those cruel portraits Picasso made of Dora Maar. I don't know which of them felt he had the best of the exchange. Picasso hates my work, of course. I used to think that it was the serenity of my life with Marthe that got up his nose.'

They shook hands by the gate; Cartier-Bresson paused in the road to call over his shoulder, 'I'll give Matisse your regards.'

'You are going to see him?' Bonnard called.

'I hope to, soon.'

* * *

'Now that Henriot is minister for propaganda, we shall have to work harder,' said Aragon, reading the paper. 'Rommel is inspecting the Atlantic Wall, which can only mean that the Allies intend to invade soon.' He paused, smiling. 'De Gaulle is striving to become the great white father to Algeria; he has "freed" his children at the palaver of National Liberation in Brazzaville, applauded by Governor Éboué. The key word is "desirability"; it is "desirable" that our native subjects win seats in the metropolitan parliament, that we give them French citizenship, and that they obey French laws. Pleven seems to think that we have no peoples in colonial France to enfranchise, or any racism to abolish. There is no hint of any notion of self-government. Do they think that our colonial subjects have not yet heard of the Atlantic Charter?'

Girl in a Green Dress with Oranges

Matisse's nurse Monique, who has washed and dressed him daily for many years, is entering the Dominican Convent of the Rosary at Monteils. It is a move that has been coming for some time. She says she intends to devote the rest of her life to the way of perfection, and thinks of her surrender as the first step. Matisse says he knows the feeling well, and that he can understand what failing to live in a state of grace is like.

'You know that I am going to miss you.'

'I will come to visit you when I can.'

'You must, even though it will not be the same.'

'You will find other models.'

'Of course, but I shall be sad when you go.'

'*Lux in tenebris lucet,*' Monique says.

'My light always shines in the darkness,' Matisse agrees. 'I'm afraid I can only see the Church as the mother of dark obscurantism; mine is the garden of Allah rather than Eden, a garden of earthly delights. You know that instinct has been, and still is, my religion. I have my music, my interiors, which are profane, pre-Christian and hedonist. You must not expect me to succumb to Christ's conjuring tricks, any more than Valéry did. It is because the universe we live in now is so relative that I feel I must try in my art to show the lineaments of the absolute.'

'I shall not stop pestering you, you know,' Monique says. 'I shall find a way to coax you into the Church.'

Jazz

By March, Matisse has given up using the title *Cirque*, and begins to call the book *Jazz*.

Rouveyre smiles. 'You call it *Jazz* because the Americans are ashore in Sicily now?'

'No. It was Tériade who began to call it *Jazz*, and the idea grew on me.'

Lydia looks closely at a blue silhouette. 'Who is this?'

'Monsieur Loyal, Joseph-Léopold Loyal, ringmaster of the Cirque de l'Impératrice and Cirque Napoléon during the Second Empire,' Matisse says. 'Seurat drew him once, with one of his clowns.'

Lydia laughs. 'People will think he is de Gaulle, with that huge beak.'

Matisse shares her laughter. 'I intend to do a Little Red Riding Hood wolf, too. My colours in *Jazz* will be cyclamen, blue, green, yellow. Do you know what Van Gogh told Cézanne when he called him mad? He refused to believe that his curves were demented; I'm using that statement in *Jazz*.'

Bonnard writes:

Did you hear that three thugs tailed Misia, Bébé Bérard and her secretary in the métro? As soon as they reached the apartment, one of the men knocked her down, clamped her mouth, and tore off her earrings. Bérard put up a fight, got to the door and rang the bell, then the men ran off. She found her earrings the next morning where the thieves had dropped them. The story is that they were coming home from the Opéra, but I think it's far more likely that they had been to some dive to buy opium.

* * *

'Pierre Pucheu's trial is an indictment of Vichy,' Aragon said. 'They will find him guilty, a verdict that will send a signal to all Pétain's toads.'

Pucheu was facing an army tribunal in Algiers. After the Germans occupied the Free Zone, he left the Vichy cabinet and fled to North Africa.

Elsa nipped a handkerchief between her lips to remove any surplus lipstick. 'Is the timing right? Surely, it will allow Pucheu's lawyers to argue for a delay?'

'Where will they find any credible witness to speak in his defence?' Aragon was sure the court would turn down his request. Guilty could be the only verdict. There was no doubt that Pucheu chose all the Châteaubriant victims.

When Pucheu went to the wall, he shook hands with every man in the firing squad, then shouted the order to shoot.

Annélies, Tulips and Anemones

The dress that Annélies is wearing is bright orange; she sits on a green chair, reading a book. On the blue-black table are anemones and white tulips, the tulips fill the vase to her left, the anemones to her right. Like all Matisse's pictures the work aspires to the ideal. He paints the girl into his harem of idle women who have nothing to do except pamper themselves all day. The role does not suit Annélies.

'You ask me which of my paintings I like best: I would say *Le tapis rouge*, if I had to decide.'

246

'Delacroix said the public had no understanding of artists; that what it did was to accept them grudgingly, sooner or later,' Annélies says.

Matisse nods agreement. 'Working in the Louvre, I lost all awareness of living in my own time. What was I doing looking at old masters? What had they to say to me? Linaret died in the Louvre. He had a heart attack while copying Cimabue. When we turned out to bury him in Montmartre Cemetery, somebody said that all the Louvre guards were Linaret's friends, but who would remember him in the future? It was before Marquet moved in with me. He was living on the quai de la Tournelle, painting the view of the Seine from his window, while I painted the river from the quai Saint-Michel. We used to meet in the early morning to wait for the La Villette–Saint-Sulpice bus to take us to the Buttes-Chaumont, to Jambon's workshops. Jambon had a contract to decorate the coaches of the Trans-Siberian express. He paid us one franc, twenty-five centimes an hour for garlands and shields – all one-and-a-half metres high. I did not stay long; Jambon gave me the sack.'

Listening to Verdi's Requiem on *Radio Roma*, Matisse is sure that Arturo Toscanini is conducting, with his usual sublime frenzy. Yet, how could this be so? Not only had Arturo condemned Hitler, but he had refused to perform in Italy after Mussolini came to power. Can it be an act of defiance by some partisan, or are the Italians trying to redeem the vain matinée idol? No, it is more probable that freak weather conditions are interfering with the radio waves.

Later, when Lydia tells him that Amélie and Margot are under arrest for being Resistance agents, Matisse feels a sense of sharp reproof that Toscanini was conducting the Requiem. The maestro had spoken out early against fascism, whereas Matisse has never come face to face with anything except nudes and still lifes. All the news he has feared to hear about the arrest of other men's children bursts into his mind. He learns swiftly what some fathers have lived with for years, and it has no place in his scheme of things. Unlike any other pain and bitterness he has felt, it surges in his body again and again, stinging and cold.

Amélie is a prisoner in Fresnes, charged with belonging to the same group as Margot. A letter speaks of the prison's landings, cells, chapels, kitchens and corridors in such a way that Matisse pictures it falsely, as a Piranesi engraving. All he has to go on otherwise is what Apollinaire told him about his five days in the Santé, accused of stealing the *Mona Lisa*. Matisse has the photograph he clipped from the front page of the *Journal de Paris* showing Apollinaire handcuffed to the police inspector. He told Matisse how the night was light enough to see the ivy on the walls around the courtyard he passed through into the second room. There, they asked more questions before giving him a rough shirt, a towel, sheets and a blanket. Then they marched him along a maze of corridors to Cell 15, where he stripped under an electric bulb left on night and day.

'Apollinaire consoled himself by writing six poems in the Santé.' Recalling all this is more upsetting for Matisse than the Piranesi engravings.

On looking back, he did know Fresnes prison. He had glimpsed its grey utilitarian walls when driving his Renault beyond the Porte d'Italie, where he used to visit the flea market in the Kremlin-Bicêtre. It was easy to imagine Amélie's misery on hearing the sound of trains heading for Paris on the ligne de Sceaux.

Is Amélie in danger? Yes, she must be in danger, and it worries him. He knows that there are interrogations in such places; although Amélie would never reveal anything to anyone. This new, alien woman has aspects of his wife, but he cannot fathom her latest portrait. Even stranger, his daughter is yet another unknown to him. Why did they choose this moment to act? The Allied forces were there to do the fighting; that is why they had come. It was their job to liberate the country; to bring normality to France again.

It is no time for heroics. Amélie is too old to sleep on a bed with rusted iron slats.

It is awful; he cannot envisage her cell, or that smell of menstruating women she lives with, the low life of Paris. He flushes with shame, knowing how stubborn she is, and nods gravely to salute to her powers of endurance, her depth of sacrifice. Sudden flashes from their lives together hurt him, make his heart ache. Why are his eyes full of tears? He does not want to touch his pencils or brushes; he prefers those photographs he had taken of Amélie at Collioure.

Lydia sighs. 'You haven't touched your food.'

'I'm not hungry.'

'You will make yourself ill. Then I shall have to nurse you. I can put up with your selfishness most of the time, but if you fall ill again it will be too much.'

Every morning now he wakes with a feeling of loss, and it is hard to renew his sense of life, of colour. Margot is mad, too. There is no other word; no other word can define what she has been about, out there in the real world that he has avoided for so long. He had lost her a long time ago. When? How had it come about? He shivers, waking after dreaming of his daughter, her Ophelia corpse drifting among yellow reeds; her skin flayed to reveal her muscles and veins in the coarse reds and blues of an anatomy chart. Now her name is the concern of enemy machines; the Gestapo have filed it in their archives. They have torn it from him, from its rich place in his interiors; they have taken her body into limbo.

* * *

The sirens wailed at ten in the morning as the American bombers came over the city, scattering thousands of incendiaries. Aragon and Elsa watched the rain of high explosives from Tavernier's terrace, where they used to wait for the sunset.

'I think the Allies' message is the end is coming soon,' Aragon said.

Tavernier smiled as he lifted up his son, Bertrand, who squirmed in fear and excitement. 'This will delay Sadoul.'

'I'm glad we were not caught in it,' Aragon said.

Aragon and Elsa walked the streets after the second raid on the following day. The Perrache station was out of action and oil tanks were still blazing on the outskirts of the city. The odd thing was that the École de Santé was a ruin and that Fritz Hollert, who had served briefly as the chief of the *Einsatzgruppe*, was among the half-dozen S.D. men killed.

A sudden aroma of rich coffee and perfume came through the acrid smoke as they passed firemen trying to save a blazing warehouse. 'Probably a black-market cache,' Aragon said. Two women went by aimlessly, their arms full of bedding, ahead of a rescue party with dogs. Then there were volunteers digging at the rubble, their picks sending bricks into a flooded crater. One of them called out for help, and his mates scrambled towards him. He had found a grey ghost crawling from under charred timbers with a woman in his arms.

Aragon shook his head as a gendarme blew a whistle. The stretcher bearers were running with their bloodstained burdens towards a green florist's van.

A woman wiped away her tears with her apron. She was one of a group exchanging stories of premonition and escape. They turned, holding out their arms as though to beseech two trucks that sped past laden with packing crates that served as coffins.

The newspapers listed the names of the seven hundred people killed; most because they went out to watch the bombs falling. Aragon learned that the Germans were combing the prisons for a work force to repair the runway at Bron. With the railway station hit, the airfield was their only escape route.

* * *

The Major's French diction was as correct as his manner. 'I do not share the Führer's view that your father's art is degenerate. I admire his paintings. You were his model several times. In *La famille du peintre* you stand at the right of the picture, wearing a black dress and holding a tiny yellow book; somehow alone, I always felt, Frau Matisse.'

Marguerite did not want to be the daughter of Matisse. She loathed the way he tried to exploit the fact that he was her father. 'I prefer that you call me Madame Duthuit,' she said. 'Treat me the same as you treat your other victims. Did they give you this job because you love art?'

'Does your father hate Germans too?'

'Why don't you ask him? He is seventy-four years old, and a sick man. His only interest in life is his work.'

The Major said that her father knew of her arrest. Sadly, he had made no enquiries as to her whereabouts.

'You are lying.'

The Major seized her hair, then punched her with his fist.

'You and your mother are Franc-tireur Partisans. I want the names of others in your group.'

Marguerite repeated that her mother had nothing to do with it. There was blood in her mouth.

'Your mother was making more copies of the papers we found on you. What I must know is how you came by such detailed information on our western defences.'

The first things she saw when she regained consciousness were his shiny jackboots. She was naked; she felt sick and her body hurt; there was blood on her hands.

'Get up, Madame Duthuit,' he ordered.

Marguerite stood up, pressing her spine against the glazed brick wall. Glancing down at her body, the number of bruises amazed her.

'It's the hours you keep,' Marguerite told him.

'I don't understand you.'

'The horror is that all this is nine to five; now, and tomorrow and the day after,' she said, sighing.

'My duties call for longer hours than nine to five. You don't know what having to do this does to a man.'

'You do kill people.'

'Often, madame,' he assured her.

'It doesn't worry you?'

'I obey orders.'

'Are you going to kill me?' Her calmness unnerved her.

'Not if you tell me everything I want to know.'

'Stop going on about your guilt feelings and your aesthetic insights. Let's keep to the business at hand.'

He lit a cigarette. 'Can you not see that your ability to endure pain is pointless? In the end, you will talk.'

His subordinates used other tricks. They would feign seeing her for the first time despite the fact that she had stood in front of them for hours, hardly able to keep her eyes open. They tried everything to humiliate her, to degrade.

The Flowers of Evil

Matisse's pain does not allow him much respite. He listens to the B.B.C. to learn of victories that will free his daughter. Lydia taunts him for his failure to deal with Baudelaire. 'Where is Cézanne's top-hatted dandy; the poet poking a corpse with his cane? Where are Baudelaire's flowers of evil? I see no evil.'

'Gallimard gave Rodin a few francs to illustrate *Les Fleurs du Mal* in that vein. I am not trying to outdo Cézanne or Rodin. As I pointed out to Aragon, nothing would be easier than to decorate the poems with a troupe of sexual acrobats, all thrashing their legs in torments of lust. That is not my intention.'

'I always see Baudelaire in a winter dawn, being woken out of a warm dream to find three bailiffs dragging him out of bed so that they can strip the sheets to sell.' Annélies sighs. 'Amazing that he had the strength of character to play the scene.'

Matisse uses Lydia, Annélies Nelk, and Carmen, the girl from Haiti, as models for his illustrations to *Les Fleurs du Mal*. As Annélies poses for *L'invitation au voyage*, Matisse tells her, 'It was General Aupick who left his step-son with Captain Saliz of the Paquebot des Mers Sud. The other passengers were army officers and traders, a rag-tag army of crooks whose desire for travel had its origin in empire and profit. It would soon be too hot to stay on deck, and too hellish to lie in his narrow cabin, thirsting for cold water that wasn't brackish after weeks in wooden barrels. He had to wait some time before the albatross fell from the rigging. It happened near the Equator, and the idle crew had nothing better to do than torment the bird. Later, in a storm off the Cape, Baudelaire found he had the coolness and nerve to help save the ship. Courage is not something we associate with Baudelaire, but he had courage that day.'

As he starts to draw Carmen, she asks, 'If her real name was Jeanne Duval, why did she use the name Jeanne Prosper?'

'Jeanne Duval was a Creole, born in Nantes. Like any aspiring actress she spun a tale about her birth in exotic San Domingo. She had been a prostitute more often than a leading lady. She was forty-five or fifty years old and half paralysed when Manet painted her in 1862. Her white, violet-striped gown, black fan, and the lace curtain behind her were probably of as much interest to him as her swarthy baby-doll face.'

Matisse talks as he draws: 'The tropics bored Baudelaire. Mauritius bored him too; he said his sole thrill came through seeing a Negress flogged in the market place. My own voyage was to the Galapagos islands. I went to find out whether a tribe of cannibals had eaten some German explorers. It was a tale I heard from a baroness. Don't ask me why I felt I should do this. I was alone in Tahiti, unable to find anybody who would go with me. I suppose I was homesick. I could appreciate how Baudelaire felt, alone with the stench of dead sharks rotting in the tropic sun. For him, it was a choice between sylphs or syphilis. He began the voyage home, up the west coast of Africa, aboard the *Alcide*. After my own adventure, I boarded a sinister English steamer, white with scarlet funnels. We sailed under a sky as blue as the wing of a Morpho butterfly; as blue as the blue brooch I bought for Amélie.'

'All we know about Jeanne is what we can infer from his poems, where Baudelaire's chief concern is himself,' Matisse says. 'She was a Muse, a woman on whom to work off his lust and spleen. He celebrates her thick blue-black hair (and how thick it was), yet her black skin evokes for him a *flic*'s uniform or Beelzebub's cloak.'

* * *

Along the landings, past women scouring the stone staircase, Marguerite stumbled into the courtyard, half-hearing the whispered messages, before the guards marched her back to her cell. There, she lay on the soiled mattress, huddled under a blanket smelling of other people, to wait for the soup trolley. On her wedding day, her father had sent her to Man Ray so that he would have a likeness of her, despite having painted her portrait so many times; in those days, freedom was not a crime against the state.

Everything had to be in order; yet there was no order in her chaotic memories. Oddly, the person she longed to see most had died at forty: her old teacher, Juan Gris, always calm at the heart of storms. She hummed a tango they used to dance to. She knew she must not think about Georges or Claude, yet she did. Her capacity for invention had never been great, but to say nothing led to the beatings, and she could not bear those. A *Feldwebel* came with a portable typewriter to take down her confession. She found the sound of the machine pleasurable; as though its clattering keys could lend credence to her falsehoods. She lied about meeting a woman at the railway station near Brest. She hoped that her description, based on Estelle Abeille, a teacher she had known, did not mean some innocent being accused. She could not deny having the documents, but she must not confess how the Resistance had gained the information through a chain of laundries it had set up in French coastal towns. These laundries offered special low prices to German soldiers, so that the Francs-tireurs were able to deduce the location and strength of their regiments through their shoulder flashes.

Her cell was as dank as an outhouse and in the same sort of repair. Its walls had names, dates of birth, dates of arrest, also crude desperate scribbles, old graffiti with a list of sexual needs. There was nowhere for her to go except into the past. She could see herself in her father's picture, *Intérieur à Collioure*, standing on the balcony with her back to the window. Her father was painting her mother sleeping in a green dress in the room facing the sea, her straw hat lying on the green chair where she left it. The bed was pink, moving into the rainbow-hued space of the walls, a blend of blue, green and pink; the salt smell of noon was intense.

If she could wake there again, the girl in a hot orange-red dress, staring into the past, whose voice would she hear? Would it be her father's voice as he painted Amélie?

How could she have been so uninteresting for so long? Her father lived her life more vividly than she did. He gave her life in colour; yet, when she saw herself in his pictures, she was still missing. Alone now, all her attempts to renew her life by bringing to mind his paintings failed. In her despair it seemed that, along with the furniture, she had been one more object for him to master.

She thought of herself as a Free French woman; it was a calming way of coming to terms with what had happened to her. Would she betray her comrades in the end, her mother even? Nothing in the way she had lived had prepared her for her present situation. The guards were smoking, talking about an accident. The driver of an army supply truck had lost control on a hill and crushed some children against a wall. One of them said that there were angry women in the streets screaming for the driver to be shot.

The Germans served *ersatz* coffee made from acorns at 6.30 every morning; the sour black bread came later, and the soup at noon, ladled into her mess tin by way of the door hatch. The hardest thing to bear was the prying eyes. She hated the guards using the peep-hole during the night. When she was a child she used to change the goldfish water in her father's laboratory jar, and she had worried then that the fish had nowhere to hide; no strand of submarine weed, no gravel, marred the purity of the element in which they floated.

She had nothing to do except wait to suffer more pain. How long could she endure? They were torturing other women too; she heard their names whispered in the yard. Did they cover their ears, as she did, when she heard their screams? Was her name on others' lips? Prisoners came and went, yet nothing changed. In the courtyard, one of the women began a shuffling grieving dance, her hand over her eyes as she moaned. Soon, this was too tiring for her. She began to rock her body, holding her arms stiffly against her sides.

A prisoner whispered, 'What are you in here for?'

The sign on Marguerite's cell door, in which she took pride, read: *Espion*. She had nothing to say about this. She did not want any talk of that nature. A prisoner had told her that there were microphones hidden in the cells. It was hard to decide who was asking the questions and why they wanted to know.

'Why do you ask?'

'You are not here for listening to the B.B.C.,' the woman said.

'Ravensbrück means bridge of the ravens,' said the S.S. officer. It was a pleasant three-mile walk from the station, through the woods beside the lake. Then she would come to the black door of the camp, where she would learn just how bad things could be. There was nothing soft about life in Ravensbrück. With luck, she might escape becoming a victim of one of the surgical experiments, but the road gang would be her fate if she evaded the short life of a guinea pig. Every morning her first task would be to help shift the corpses of the women who had given up and died during the night.

'Let me save you from this,' he urged. 'I can only do so if you tell me the truth.'

'I've told you all I know.'

'You have lied to me, Madame Duthuit. I respect you, but you have lied to me. The matter is no longer in my hands. You leave for Ravensbrück on the next available train. I hope that the Allies arrive in time to save you.'

*　　*　　*

Sitting outside the café, Elsa watched a family leave the hospital, pushing a pale child in a wheel-chair under a black umbrella. They said nothing; perhaps the doctor had given them bad news. The girl seemed normal until she bared her teeth in a lop-sided grin, and thrust her tongue around her gums, grinding her jaw from side to side. Her pale, rickety legs hung limply, one black stocking round her ankle. She was one of the many victims of conditions in France.

Three army trucks braked across the road, and the soldiers jumped out and lit cigarettes to wait for the Soldatenkino to open: a military cinema off-limits to civilians. What irked Elsa was that the scene was so casual, so everyday, in spite of the Normandy landings. She had felt the same disgust after the Dieppe raid, when the Germans were promising to free the sons of those brave French housewives who helped to save blazing buildings.

She saw the woman she had come to meet, Yvonne Devignes, who put her life at risk by binding Éditions de Minuit books in her kitchen. 'It's a routine now, part of my daily domestic chores; one of those neat practices that go to make up my life; something to keep me from going mad.'

Yvonne glanced at her reflection in her powder compact. 'In *Huis Clos*, Sartre told us that Hades has Second Empire furnishings,' she said. 'A valet introduced us to Inéz, Garcin, and Estelle who began to rehearse and act out their misery. I did not stay to the end. We are going to see a lot of plays that are cheap to stage, but which fail to confront the issues in the post-war situation.

'Brasillach was at the Vieux-Colombier when it opened,' she went on. 'I was talking to Camus's wife, who pointed out that the *collabos* had the best seats, while our men on the run filled the others. The Occupation has blurred and falsified every human relationship. A comrade present had dined on S.S. boss Kurt Lischka's salt herrings, followed by a polite interrogation without water; and, two rows away, lolled the traitor Brasillach. Ten days later, the Allies came ashore in Normandy. It was mad. A stranger came up to Sartre, who had been watching in the wings, and told him that the Germans were about to arrest him. Prior to the lights going out, there was more drama in the stalls than on-stage in Sartre's ghost play. Perhaps I'm not giving him his due; the play did have a certain resonance, given the circumstances. He was telling us that Hell is trivial and boring, which is true enough. We all while away the hours deciphering trivial messages from the hell of our daily lives.'

'The truth, as I see it, is that it is unlikely that posterity will read my books,' Elsa said. 'However, I work hard to write readable prose, and keep my narratives up to date. I don't write very well about women; I don't understand them.' She went on to tell Yvonne how she would have gone home to Russia if she had not met Aragon. 'I was living at the Istria, in the rue Campagne-Première, along with Mayakovsky, Léger, Man Ray and Kiki. So I was not far from Aragon, who shared an apartment at the time with Sadoul and Thirion. He had his partial insights; I had mine. He used to run off to that Austrian cow, Léna Amsell, whenever we had a row. Nowadays, I want to be faithful to him, yet I find that a constraint. It is an obligation that should free me, but it doesn't; it is galling. Although I long to escape from him, I know the future belongs to him politically, and that I do too.'

'I want a future in which we can accept things as they are, not as symbols or signs of something else,' Yvonne said. 'I want to feel that I can live in the present. Do you know that the Egyptians used honey to preserve their dead? During the endless nights, the dead came and stood at my shoulder; and I used to think I could smell those old embalmers at work.'

*   *   *

'Was *Le Penseur* pondering the ravages of frost and pigeon shit on the other sculptures in Rodin's garden, as his creator did? Even Rodin

256

changed his mind at various times about what was on his Thinker's mind. Maybe, as Satie said, with critics' advice being so dear to Rodin, one of them had posed for the statue. Again, the Thinker could have been considering the violent social changes around him; the strikes that gave Baudelaire the heart to roar, "Kill, kill General Aupick!"

'An astute manufacturer of fountain pens divined at once that the statue was brooding on his product not long after *Le Penseur* became public. Later, there was a move to install him across from the Bourse to worry about stocks and shares. The plan amused Rodin; but art lovers were up in arms.'

Annélies would like to scratch her itchy left nipple, but has to be content with a stifled yawn. The sweat trickling under her tuft of ginger pubic hair makes her feel nervous.

The military might of America's factories is being landed on the beaches of Normandy. Waves of bombers attack the town of Saint-Lô, and kill eight hundred civilians in a single raid. Matisse listens to the D-Day broadcast by General Eisenhower. The Allies want prompt obedience to their orders; there would be time, after Hitler's defeat, for a free France to elect its own representatives and government.

Tuning in to Radio-Vichy, Matisse hears Marshal Pétain say that he is the head of the rightful government; that Frenchmen must obey the Germans or they would face the prospect of special measures in the combat areas. He begs his countrymen to remain calm and follow orders.

'All very confusing,' Lydia says.

Three doves perch on the wire cage in bright sunlight slanting through the window. Matisse sits sketching the bird he holds. He wears a dressing-gown and woolly cap with a white brim, almost a turban; he could be an Armenian rug seller. It is a private moment on which Cartier-Bresson chooses to eavesdrop, to click the shutter of his Leica.

'The hardest part about being a prisoner of war was trying to work as slowly as I could and make a mess of every job they set me,' he says. 'I did try to escape.'

'Why waste time taking photographs if you say you want to paint?' Matisse asks.

'At first, I had no interest in photography as an art form. I saw it as a tool to make an instant drawing. Now I spend every waking hour being vigilant, waiting to press the button. The good photograph comes about through coincidence; it is not a question of coincidence when it comes to drawing. Kertesz has the supreme gift of being present at the right moment, which I don't have. People do not understand how anguished one feels, taking photographs. Did I capture what I saw? Did I choose the right moment? Anguish is always there; you feel it, because you can erase nothing.'

In the afternoon, Matisse agrees to another session in the garden, where they discuss Bonnard. 'He will have to find someone to move in with him,' Matisse says.

'As soon as the war is over I will go to Kashmir, to Egypt,' says Cartier-Bresson. 'We all need another dimension after what Europe has gone through. Nowadays we must produce a card before we can buy film, paper, or chemicals. Doisneau takes snaps of a police inspector's card and bleaches the print to give a stranger a new identity.'

Matisse has never been camera-shy. Over the years he has grown ever more benign, at ease with himself. He shows Cartier-Bresson a photograph taken on his wedding day, saying, 'I don't think you can imagine how I felt about my top-hat. I saw myself as a perfect dandy. I mean, just look at that expression! I painted my pride and joy in *Intérieur au chapeau haut de forme*. Black was the colour of the Reformation, of Protestantism, as worn by my upright forbears. How grim Baudelaire looks wearing our deadly uniform; yet how different we are, and how raffish he is in the Étienne Carjat portrait, which I studied when I drew him.' He sighs. 'It was many years before I disowned my top-hat, and shed the soul for this white light.'

* * *

Aragon had been to Oradour-sur-Glâne once; it was no different from any other small town in France. 'We don't know why the swine chose the place,' said Jules. 'They wanted the massacre kept secret. This is not their usual practice, if they carried out the action as a reprisal for the kidnapping of two of their officers.

'After the early rain, the sun shone. Then a hundred and twenty troops of the Panzer Division *Das Reich* arrived in eight trucks, two half-tracks, a motorcycle, and a Citroën. There were two militia men to do the translating. They told the townspeople, after herding them into the main square, that the Germans were searching their houses for arms and prohibited goods – whatever that meant.'

'What sort of weapons did the Germans find?' Elsa asked.

Jules shook his head. 'Oradour had no link with the Resistance. We know that the Division came from the Eastern Front, where it laid waste to Russian villages to deter the partisans. They were troops who were grateful to get out of Russia with their lives. The Germans had to recruit men from Alsace to swell their ranks, which is why it is harder to understand or forgive the massacre.

'They marched four hundred and fifty women and children to the church. There, they split the men into groups, locking them into a coach house, a garage and two barns. At 3.30, somebody fired the first shot to signal the massacre. Then an officer named Dickmann went in to finish them off; only seven escaped by crawling through a hole into another barn, where three of them died. Meanwhile, the Germans were machine-gunning the women and children in the church, which the S.S. then set on fire, tossing in grenades. Only one woman escaped by jumping from the window.

'Cartridge cases and broken bicycles littered the street; they burned the schools; they burned the post office and the hotel. The only houses they left standing were those they had used as a command post or places to bed down. Everywhere there were heaps of ashes in human shapes, bodies of babies in their prams.

'The afternoon tram from Limoges arrived. The Germans removed everybody who lived in Oradour, then they told the driver to take the others to Limoges.' Jules paused, shaking his head. 'If they could let the passengers go, why shoot the militia men? There was something very odd about the whole operation.

'The Germans stayed until Sunday morning, then tied their looted ducks and chickens to their trucks and left. We have sent all this information to Marcel Duhamel. He is writing a piece for *Les Lettres Françaises*. We had to suspend all acts of sabotage in the area until *Das Reich* left for Normandy.'

In June, Philippe Henriot was in Germany to inspect the bomb damage to Leipzig and Frankfurt. In Berlin he met Goebbels and talked to Sauckel about increasing food rations before making a speech to French workers. On his return to Paris, he sent his son to Germany to swell the labour force. He then took his wife to the cinema in the Champs-Élysées, where a *fifi* man saw them and tailed them back to the rue de Solferino. At dawn the next day, three cars braked outside the ministry and Henriot's executioners, posing as militia men, fooled the concierge into opening the door. Henriot died serving France, while his wife screamed in their bedroom.

The Nazis gave him a state funeral. The Cardinal Archbishop of Paris was there, and 400,000 Parisians filed by the coffin outside the Hôtel de Ville.

'That's too many,' Elsa said.

She listened for the B.B.C.'s sequence of hollow drum taps that heralded nightly messages to the *maquis* groups. Since they had no meaning for her, she surrendered to their poetry. The lines were a litany from Surrealist poems: *The hippo is not carnivorous; the moon is full of green elephants.* What did they signify? Why should Madame Ducdame resemble the Dauphin or the tortoises torment the turtledove with a screwdriver? One message struck her: 'Le premier accroc coûte deux cents francs' – a warning found on café billiard tables.

Soon, the fear would be over: the fear of meetings, and failures to meet. Soon, there would be no more need to wait for agents who failed yet again to appear; then, later, more empty quarrels over an agenda, tactics, strategy – their inability to make decisions on the workers' behalf.

Aragon was waiting in a football ground. A rusty tin roof sheltered two rows of torn cinema seats, shedding their veneer on the weeds that grew there. He shaded his eyes against the sunset. It blazed above the garden on the far side of the pitch. Beans were in flower, and a woman in a straw hat reached up to twist them round a trellis. The bird that Aragon had failed to name was still singing in the poplar grove. He had dawdled along the dusty path, listening to its song, killing time in the belief that he was too early for the appointment.

The old woman had no teeth in her open mouth. She wore sun-glasses; her shoes were too big for her, so that the heels clacked as she shuffled along on her walking-stick. Surely she could not be his contact, and yet she came forward to the bench where he sat.

After her divorce, she told him, the war came and her husband had nowhere to go. His parents lived with them, too, until they died, sleeping in a single bed yet bickering every day. His old man was an alcoholic, who died believing that he had the power to walk through walls. When a tractor ran his mother over and killed her, her husband joined the Resistance, for want of something to do. She did not mind, she said, it kept him from under her feet. She had come because he was too ill to meet Aragon, who was to give the papers to her. She told him the date the British would make the parachute drop.

As she left, she met an older woman with a shopping bag near the poplars and they locked arms to walk on, their bodies leaning at the same angle.

'I have too much to do to lose sleep waiting half the night for a plane that might never make it,' Aragon said. 'Besides, I have no right to break my own rules by taking foolish risks.'

The idea of the parachute drop excited Elsa. 'We must go; they have invited us.'

On the night of the drop, they joined the mission leader in an old *gasogène* truck and set off for the landing area, passing men huddled on farm carts who nodded silent greetings. They were all heading for the same destination, the plateau above Saint-Donat. Eight armed men were already in charge of the landing area. The mission leader spoke briefly to one of them, then they set off to pace the triangle, one hundred yards on each side.

'They should have crossed the Loire by now,' a man called out, who stood not far away.

The boy laughed. 'The R.A.F. is always late!'

'You have been before, then?' Elsa asked.

'Yes, I come every time. They give me cigarettes, and I can get chocolate for Grandma.'

'Aren't you afraid?'

'Not of the Germans,' he boasted. 'The plane will be a Halifax or maybe a Hudson. You must watch for the parachutes. The canisters can kill you if they miss the triangle.'

Two Englishmen landed first on the far side of the hill; the boy told her they were members of S.O.E. Above, the plane circled back, then the canisters drifted down. They were six feet long, made of grey-black steel and lined with rubber. After the *maquis* hauled the chute in and cut the harness, there was the sound of laughter as they hammered one of the clasps that had twisted on impact. They unloaded the three inner containers and bundled the parachute inside before carrying the canister away to bury. They loaded the sten-guns immediately, then gangs of men hauled the containers to the trucks and carts. One of them handed her half a chocolate bar, a taste from another world; he was smoking an English cigarette. In the cart, they shared out the Colt pistols, fuses, detonators; then they stored the boxes of ammunition away. There were also Thermit bombs, they told her; plastic explosives, Nobel 808, which gave you a headache unless you wore gloves to handle them.

By now, Aragon and Elsa were both tired, and none of the others had anything left to say as the carts set off in different directions under the waning moon.

They had been asleep for an hour when German fighters woke them, roaring low to strafe the village. As they fumbled their clothes on, a neighbour rushed into the kitchen shouting that three armoured columns were heading for Saint-Donat.

Crouching, they ran up the vineyard slope. Sick with disgust, Elsa heard herself squeak as the bullets chopped a hail of twigs down. It was no help to cover her ears as she thrust her body against the earth, yet it was what she did. Somewhere, other women wailed as tiles flew off the roofs and shattered in the street. There was a smell of smoke; a terrified horse ran by as Aragon helped her up the hill towards the stone wall. There, she opened her eyes. Under fire, Louis was a stranger; she envied his control. Her own surges of fear were becoming a purgatory.

They climbed higher. Elsa now felt suddenly icy cold as the hot sun dazzled her eyes. André and another armed man had joined them; he carried a pair of binoculars. The sun was high, and the cicadas were loud against the distant roar of tank engines as the Germans reached the village.

'I don't want to think what's going on,' André said.

'There's nothing you can do,' Aragon told him.

They had not been in Saint-Donat long enough to get to know its people. Elsa had not seen the man with André before. When he took off his shirt, a thick green and yellow serpent tattooed on his shoulder jolted Elsa out of her reverie. It filled her with such bodily unease, coiling under a slick of sweat, that she wished the others were not there. The sun was high; the odour of the pines so intense that they might burst into flames at any moment.

The Germans had made a day of it before retreating to their fortified garrison. They had raped fifty-seven girls and women, aged thirteen to fifty-eight years. Those who had put up a fight sat in a daze, bruised and bleeding. The Germans had looted every shop. A motorcycle and side-car were burning in the square, set on fire by a shot from a drunken corporal.

The Germans had pillaged their house along with the others. They had not found Elsa's manuscripts, which she kept hidden under the floor of the garage across the road. Her skin itched with shame over her lapse on the hillside while it was all going on. She felt sick cleaning up the mess in a smell of German piss. Aragon chose to feature the smell in the tract he wrote to refute Vichy propaganda that such raids were reprisals for *maquis* activity in the area. He said that the enemy looted and raped to terrorise the people, and that the only response left was to rise up and fight.

Lemons and Mimosa on a Black Background

The lemons float in clusters like elliptical fishes against the blackness, which Matisse scores with leaf shapes. He scratches in more leaves around the pot of mimosa.

After the rain, the sun shines and the garden steams. Matisse closes the umbrella to find that the changed light charges the scarlet and pink of the geraniums; they are vibrant in the haze. He unties the string of his portfolio as the birds begin to sing. Gardens delighted Renoir and Monet; but this one has too much atmosphere for Matisse to cope with.

'Ageing has changed Van Gogh's *Sunflowers*,' he tells the girl. 'I think, I don't know, of course, but I think that you would modify your idea of the painting had you seen Vincent's palette on the day. Another thing that haunts me is that Gauguin was a few feet away, painting Vincent painting the sunflowers. Years earlier, of course, Manet tackled Monet's wife and son in their garden while Monet painted him. Enter Renoir; he borrows canvas, paints and brushes to attempt his version of Monet's family. You see the same friendly and loving art-as-play quality flow gently on in his son's early films.'

Annélies busies herself with a study of some poppies. The rain has filled each cup, and the petals shine with drops. She lives locally; had arrived one day without preamble to show him her drawings. Were they good or bad? As soon as he said he liked them, she asked what price they would fetch. After selling some at the gallery as he suggested, she came back and began to insinuate herself as a model. She said she was happy to pose for him, and would be grateful for any advice he could give her.

'Zinc white was discovered in 1840,' Matisse explains, 'Cremnitz white is colder; it doesn't cover a canvas nearly so well. Vermilion derives from the worm, of course.' He pauses, looking round him. 'Sometimes, I see them here painting away – Rembrandt, Delacroix, Gauguin and Van Gogh. No, it's not my imagination; I couldn't tell you who will be present on any given day. It is they who arbitrate the questions inherent in my work; they who decide how I place my objects in the world. They are as real to me as any living painter. They are my friends, family almost.'

Matisse tells how Skira's mother got Picasso to illustrate Ovid's *Metamorphoses*; and how Pablo, when he finished a sheet, would blow his bugle to summon Skira. He laughs. 'Picasso knows nothing about music. The only tune I heard him whistle was from *Petrouchka*, and that was shocking enough.'

Matisse can hear his voice rambling on about how he can smell the sea in oil of turpentine. 'I suppose I smell the sea because I know the oil derives from the resin of our maritime pines.' His voice cracks suddenly. 'My work could be no more than a jaded parody of past ideas; the slapdash shorthand of an old man trying to immobilise his serenity.'

'My friend Chantal was on the sea front when the American plane crashed in the bay,' the girl tells him.

'The concierge's brother told me that it was a Lightning.'

'Chantal said that she saw no sign of a parachute, so the pilot must have died.'

Matisse waves any more discussion away. 'In pre-war days, I loved women's shops, where I would smear every shade of lipstick on my hand. It gave me great pleasure to see how my ginger hairs impeded the greasy flow.'

* * *

Time stood still when a woman sat in front of a mirror to comb her hair. She was that Elsa Aragon first saw writing letters to Lili and Osip on the terrace at the Lilas, smiling over her glass of Russian tea. She was the girl whose French he corrected, who came with Mayakovsky to the Coupole. She was that Elsa who defended the Bulgarian, Dmitrov, accused of firing the Reichstag. She was that vital Elsa, eager to dance, whose body trembled in his arms as Lili told her of Mayakovsky's suicide over the telephone. She was that gentle Elsa who comforted Robert Capa at the funeral of Gerda in the Père Lachaise cemetery.

She was Ella Kagan before she became Elsa. When she was Ella, she wore tight-laced boots that she longed for somebody other than her mother to undo. Thrusting his arms under her armpits, Aragon picked up her lipstick and began to shape her/his lips awkwardly while his other hand fondled her/his breasts: a vaudeville double act he had seen once. He shared Petrarch's envy of Laura's mirror; he saw Elsa as an object, an adornment, as he surrendered to the thrill of transvestism.

The room was dark behind them; they seemed to be moving towards the light. 'I am your creation,' he said. 'I would not have become the man I am, if I had not met you.'

By breaking the Germans at Montélimar, the Americans had freed all the country between the Isère and the Rhône valley. They were fighting now to take Lyons. Two of them had come to the mountains to find Aragon.

Nobody they met knew where he was. Some said that he was not far away. His orders to the various newspaper editors in the region had been to take over the printing plants and defend them when the Germans retreated. One editor they talked to was awaiting the text for the latest *La Drôme en Armes* to start a print run. The Americans should go to Dieulefit; the villagers there would be sure to know.

Their mission was to escort Aragon to join André Rousseaux, the literary critic of *Figaro*, who was now in charge of Radio-Grenoble. He was seeking writers to help him run the station.

As they left Dieulefit, the thunderstorm broke, flooding the street with sudden rain. It was cold in the jeep as it rattled along rutted tracks, through swift streams; the rain had turned to hail and sleet. With the wind gusting, the canvas fluttered and thudded, and the cold pierced their combat jackets; then the rain cleared as abruptly as it had started. To the west, the storm cloud lifted to show the red blaze of sunset. They had reached Romans and began to climb the road that led to Saint-Donat.

Aragon and Elsa were working on *La Drôme en Armes*. Elsa was upstairs when the jeep arrived. Aragon was afraid that a German patrol might be about to commandeer the house for the night; he found his pistol and went to the window. He saw the Americans climb stiffly out of their vehicle and walk slowly towards the house, as though it were a dream. As he ran out to greet them, he called up to Elsa to leave working on the paper. The Americans had come!

'You would be wise to hide the jeep in the barn,' Aragon said. 'You may think this area is free, but the Germans were here not so long ago after they dealt with an Allied parachute drop. We had been out on our paper round and when we reached Romans we had to take cover from machine-gun fire. The Germans shot a child in Saint-Donat because they saw a tricolour hanging from a window.'

The talk went on for hours as they drank the hot *marc* that Aragon served to celebrate the event. 'When we made this *marc* in the autumn,' he said, 'we joked about being liberated when we opened the first bottle. You find us cold, without coal or wood; but this will warm us.'

They talked about what they hoped to achieve using radio. One of the Americans laughed. 'What we want is a stampede, a stampede to cap the one that Orson Welles sparked off when he told New Yorkers that the Martians were coming.'

Aragon explained how there was often an air about a certain street that they didn't like, where a man loitered suspiciously at the corner.

The danger with secrecy, he went on, was that a two-man cell with a mimeograph machine would create an illusion of reality that was no more than a pious hope or a swindle. Often you began to believe your dreams. He tried to describe the state of mind of the French, warning the Americans that they must try to understand what the years of occupation and German propaganda had done. People everywhere had soaked up the presence, if not the ideas, of the Germans. They would fall at the first hurdle if they did not grasp this. His unspoken fear was that there was more to learn than he knew already. Never mind what he celebrated in his poetry. Jean Cassou's sonnets were one thing; the Vél d'Hiv and the workers' flats at Drancy were another. His thoughts came in a rush; he had been trying to shape his ideas for a long time, but they were not in order yet. Self-interest, he said, became the norm when the Germans took over; there was no charity, no civil conscience. Pétain had called for family values, and that was what he got. The family had closed up tight; feeding its own mouths, and shunning neighbours for fear of betrayal. It was the vision of Hobbes, each man as alone as Crusoe in a state of nature. There was a sense of fear and malice wherever you went, a struggle to survive. People hung on to anything they had for their own needs; there was no room for others. Women were worse than men, greedier, more eager for gain and pleasure. A meal would cost four or five thousand francs, yet restaurants were full. At the same time commodities – soap, alcohol and sugar, oil, tea, coffee, tobacco – were gold, and traded at awesome prices.

'Our sufferings were certainly those of the flesh,' he said; 'but we suffered in the spirit, too. It has been hard getting through each day, afraid of how it might end.'

When Aragon caught a whiff of Elsa's perfume, he remarked on it; for the Americans, it was not unusual. 'I have hoarded and rationed my Guerlain since the war started,' she said. 'The last time I used it was at Nontron, when you failed to notice it.'

Aragon laughed, saying that he was sure now that France was alive again.

* * *

'History?' Matisse shakes his head. 'Who has any use for history? I was writing my *Notes d'un Peintre*, and busy painting *Harmonie rouge*, when Captain Scott left for the Antarctic. You see; I have enough decisions to make, enough problems to paint a canvas, without having to worry about mundane matters such as my health or everyday trifles. I follow the path Cézanne trod, who shied away from social events and disliked intimate conversations. His great hero, of course, was Balzac's fictional painter, Frenhofer. We were all admirers of Frenhofer, quite as much as Delacroix or Gauguin. Cézanne said that a picture needed "enough bluishness to make the air felt". It was Cézanne who taught us to express perspective using colour. We owe our freedom to him.'

Matisse rolls over onto his side. 'When models changed positions in those days, you had fifteen minutes of Chopin or Beethoven. Our masters were very thoughtful and uplifting.'

The bedside lamp light reveals how thin his hair is as he sips a glass of Vichy water. He gestures towards the window and smiles. 'Those olive trees in the garden are hundreds of years old; that is history.'

* * *

Her killer had shot into the woman's left eye; her body lay askew; her fall had rucked up her low-cut dress with blue polka dots to reveal her garter-belt and torn nylons. Her bag had come undone, strewing lipstick, identity card, some coins and letters. She had a glove in one hand. Elsa could smell expensive perfume, which was suspicious in itself in those days of *ersatz*. Her knickers had gone, which hinted at rape, but there was no other sign of it. There were two men sitting in a car nearby; the driver, a young man, smoked a cigarette. His tie was bright yellow. He had a thin Hollywood moustache to strengthen his small weak mouth. His face looked thirty years out of date, and she felt that he used mascara on his eyelashes. In the passenger seat was an older man, a fat butcher, whose ambition and drive lurked behind a prim caution.

The only thing that Elsa could do was to pick up the woman's handbag, in the hope that she would find an address. Then she might be able to notify her family of her death.

Her name was Charlotte Loisy, and there was a piece of paper with a Grenoble number inside her identity card. Her purse held two studio portraits, one of her alone, the other with a naval officer. The snaps dated from the same period or day, since she wore the same dress, and had the same hairstyle. Some letters signed Pierre showed the postmark Dijon; others had come from the naval base at Toulon, and looked more recent. A German voice answered when Elsa telephoned the Grenoble number. Elsa left the phone box quickly, her curiosity at an end. If Charlotte Loisy were her real name, the Resistance had killed her for being a spy or collaborator.

*   *   *

In Paris the workers close the *métro*; the engineers are idle, so are the textile workers, and the staff in Paris stores shut down their shops.

'Things have come to a sad pass!' Matisse rattles the newspaper. 'Now we carry sugar in our bank vans instead of gold!'

None of this comes as a surprise to Lydia. She knows about black marketeers hiding beef and salt pork in coffins. 'It's a good investment; two pounds of sugar fetches a hundred and fifty francs. Meat costs three hundred to four hundred francs, and for butter I have to pay six to eight hundred francs. This load was probably on its way to one of our tempting restaurants, where we play our part in the black market every time we pay the bill.'

*   *   *

Twenty women stood outside the Palace of Justice in Montélimar. All had their heads shaved. The men guarding them had no stomach for the job; they had to shield them from the fury of a mob that whistled and jeered, waiting for the prison trucks to arrive. The only woman not hanging her head in shame had sore red heels and was wearing white sling-back sandals. Her face was haggard, grey, empty of any feeling. The others were tarts whose crime was to have slept with the enemy and charged for it. Inside the stifling, noisy court, people ate and smoked with an air that was reminiscent of the Terror. The accused sat on a bench; one of them dabbed blood from a broken nose. The guard, who wore a red, white and blue armband with the Cross of Lorraine, told Elsa with a grin that they would all shit themselves under interrogation. The three judges who entered to loud cheers also wore the same armbands. In spite of her resolve that she would sit through the whole business, Elsa's disgust became too much and she left the court feeling sick.

The people's rage was easy to understand: the *milice*, the real collaborators, had torn out women's eyes and cut off their breasts before strangling them; they had made obscene jokes in blacksmiths' forges as they celebrated a blood wedding and heated irons to burn their captives. In the name of France, Frenchmen had outdone the Germans in their foul treatment of their own people.

Elsa could remember one of the girls in the prison at Tours asking her, 'Am I a collaborator because I enjoy whipping a *boche* NCO's arse to shreds?'

Two men who stood by the wall with their hands tied behind their backs said nothing as they waited for the firing squad. They were guilty of serving in the *milice*. Somebody had given them a last cigarette. Since they could not take them from their lips, the man with the lank black strands of hair brushing his bristled cheek had his left eye screwed up against the smoke, reminding Elsa of Camus suddenly. There was no shortage of volunteers for the firing squad. Twenty men stood in line, willing to shoot. They wore armbands crudely inked with crosses of Lorraine; a symbol chalked on walls everywhere.

A man stepped up, removed their cigarettes and trod them under his boot as he offered to bandage their eyes. They looked at each other for the first time, then shook their heads. The officer strode back to the firing squad; there was nervous laughter and a jeering cheer from the crowd as he raised his arm. One of the men, the one whose blue pin-stripe trousers had mud stains, leaned back against the two bright metal sheets advertising Pernod and Dubonnet on the wall as though to brace himself.

When the order came, Elsa looked away; the squad fired. Some bullets ricocheted off the metal, as she had known they would. Both men had fallen; the one with his ankles neatly crossed stared blindly. The other lay arching his body, until the man in charge ran forward and shot him through the head.

One of the Force Française de l'Intérieur men pressed the light switch in the hallway. The suspect's name was Raymond Ducasse they told Elsa as they climbed the narrow stairway to the room he had lived in at the top of the house. The concierge took a bunch of keys from her apron pocket and unlocked the door. The only light came through a window in the roof, crusted with bird lime. As the two men set about ransacking the room, the dust rose. Then suddenly a dog began to bark, scaring two cats out of the kitchen. As there was nobody now to look after them, Elsa opened the door to the landing so that they could escape when a lodger left the house. It might give them a chance. The men were searching for documents that might name other traitors. There was nothing much to find: an empty wardrobe, a chest of drawers, a bedside cupboard with books on it. The sheets had semen stains. Elsa's guess was that they were the result of pathetic masturbation. Ducasse's room was the epitome of solitude; it was not the haunt of a gymnast, it smelled of stale dreams and those murderous hopes that led him to join the *milice*. Yet there was nothing to connect him with his crimes, nor any evidence of his brutality, only a photograph torn from a newspaper that showed Doriot wearing his Iron Cross. His Himmler spectacles were the emblem of a renegade; this was Doriot, champagne swiller and orgiast, who made sure he had fuel for his gangster cars and newsprint for his rag.

A pair of broken glasses lying on the books had obviously helped Raymond make out the dense print of Victor Hugo's *The Hunchback of Notre-Dame*, whereas Gide's *The Counterfeiters* was easier on the eyes.

Aragon brought the latest edition of *L'Humanité* with him. It was urging Parisians to rise up and fight. The headline called for death for Germans and traitors.

'I can't take any more provincial revenge,' Elsa said. 'I want to go home.'

'We have plenty here to keep us busy. Nevertheless, if you have set your heart on Paris, we'll go.'

'I know I don't live up to the ideal of what a Comrade should be. People suspect the way I dress, poor as we are. They know that I will slip back into a life style they despise; yes, because I am different. Besides, I'm sick of not having a home.'

'Then we shall try, no matter what the risks.'

*　　*　　*

Matisse tells Lydia that she was right, de Gaulle does look like Monsieur Loyal. The General strides along the Champs-Élysées, arms swinging like a toy soldier as he drives home a flat response to the people applauding.

'He seems bored and irritated,' Lydia says.

Rouveyre has seen the newsreel before, and prepares them for what will happen next. 'You will hear shots soon as the militia fires at him. People die in the next scene, and there is more shooting in Notre-Dame.'

Matisse reads the banner. It proclaims that General de Gaulle has saved France. 'Is this liberation a coup d'état in disguise? I have yet to vote for de Gaulle. The General is a stranger; he is a voice on the air waves; the creature of the B.B.C.'

* * *

In Lyons, the Germans had blown up the bridges over the two rivers when they fell back. Since there was no gas in the city centre, no telephone system, every government office moved across the Rhône in order to keep in touch with what was going on. Aragon was busy setting up the first public meetings of the Writers' Committee and creating a new Ministry of Information for the area. He was also grieving for those comrades whom Klaus Barbie had tortured to death in the Hôtel Terminus. Everywhere he witnessed sickening acts of revenge; there were bodies scrawled with bloody messages every morning on every street corner. His work and grief kept him from poetry or the novel about the Resistance he planned to write. He was also fending off demands to act as a commissioner for the Marseilles area. When he refused, they begged him to take on the job at Toulouse. As he pointed out, Jean Cassou would be a better candidate, as a local man. He told them he was busy writing *La Diane française*.

There was tension and chaos everywhere, with theft and looting by bogus *maquis* men wearing armbands of the Force Française de l'Intérieur that led to gang wars between the authorities, lynch mobs and Resistance units. More horror came to light at Bron airfield, where they dug out a hundred corpses, mostly Jewish prisoners, from the bomb craters they had worked to fill.

In Paris, Aragon and Elsa returned to their old apartment in the rue de la Sourdière, which their concierge told them the Germans had requisitioned twice. 'What could I do to stop the swine? Not so much as a piece of paper to pretend it was legal. I did hide some of your books in my lodge, but I saw them taking others away.'

The Germans had let cigarettes burn scars along the edge of the large white table. The gramophone worked still, but records were in poor condition. 'Blind Lemon' Jefferson growled his song in the night as Elsa lay in bed with Aragon, her eyes closed, knowing that they were home safe at last.

At the cocktail party at *Les Lettres Françaises*, Elsa kissed Simone de Beauvoir's prim cheek to clinch the Liberation. De Beauvoir told her that she had kept her looks, and that her recent novels had impressed her.

'If the coming winter is as bad as recent ones, I shall go mad,' said de Beauvoir.

'My clothes are threadbare; my shoes will never stand up to the weather if it's another winter like the last. I felt sick and tired all the time. I nearly died at Dieulefit. You had a narrow squeak, too, I hear.'

'There was a sheer drop where I fell off my bike coming down the mountain.' De Beauvoir bared her teeth briefly to show the gap.

No, Elsa had not met Genet yet, nor read anything by him. All she had heard was that he was a homosexual petty criminal.

A genius? That was true?

A sense of future betrayal underlay the meeting, a sense that they were sharing a last supper together. Elsa felt the same unease during de Beauvoir's account of the first night of Picasso's play when, she said, they had begun to feel that the future was theirs again.

A portent came when Aragon and Elsa learned that Robert Denoël was in hiding. They were waiting for a taxi in the rue de Courcelles when Jeanne Loviton, once Valéry's Platonic lover, told Elsa, swearing her to secrecy.

Early the next day, Aragon and Elsa went to the address in Montmartre which Jeanne had given them. The publisher had not shaved; he looked miserable, ill and scared.

Aragon shook his head. 'What will you do? You can't hide here forever.'

'I will stay put until the people exhaust their rage. My life isn't worth much right now. I doubt that they would listen to anything I said. I don't want to face being lynched. When things calm down and I see what sort of justice they mete out to others, then I might give myself up. I want a trial, you know. I have to stay here. I don't know where to go. Will you speak up for me when I find the guts to turn myself in?'

Paris knew it as the Hôtel des Ducs de Savoie in the seventeenth century; it was where Balzac set his story *Le Chef-d'œuvre inconnu*. Picasso told everybody that it was once part of the Spanish Embassy. Jean-Louis Barrault had used the two large rooms at the top of its spiral staircase to rehearse in, which Picasso made into studios. The building was on the rue des Grands-Augustins, and had many Bluebeard chambers and passages where the Minotaur could lick his wounds and temper his cruelties, hiding his misery during the war years. Now that the

Liberation had come, Aragon and Elsa found Picasso in the courtyard, waving a welcome. They climbed the stone spiral staircase to reach the dark door with the iron ring.

Sabartès was waiting by the half open door, which he flung wide to admit them. He wore his usual rusty black suit and beret; even the frames of his glasses were black. Elsa saw him as being sinister and had never liked him; a feeling that was mutual.

Aragon, Elsa, Paul Éluard and Nusch, Picasso, Roland Penrose and Lee Miller posed for the photograph. They sat on or grouped around an iron-bound trunk, the window behind them. Aragon stood to the right, with Elsa sitting awkwardly in front, holding her knee. Next to her were Éluard and Nusch, while Picasso hunched forward on the end of the group. Behind them stood Roland Penrose, the Englishman, with Lee Miller; both were wearing army uniforms. In Man Ray's *Indestructible Object*, it is a snapshot of one of her eyes on the metronome, and her calm lips float across the sunset in his *Observatory Time – The Lovers*. She was the beauty from Poughkeepsie who lived with Ray, then went on to make a career for herself as a photographer. The U.S. Army had recently freed her from house arrest for refusing to leave a war zone in Brittany. She took her photograph *Bombs exploding on the fortress of Saint-Malo* through a hotel window, under a shell-torn fringe of curtain: a black cloud rising on a fortified hillside over the rooftops and chimneys of Saint-Malo. She was now in Paris on an assignment for *Vogue* magazine to record the liberation of haute couture.

'At least it doesn't stink like Saint-Malo,' she told Elsa.

She had ceased long ago to work as a model for *Vogue*. She had left Surrealism behind to photograph the London blitz, then talked herself into uniform as a U.S. war correspondent. After the Normandy landings, she hung around field hospital tents to record the surgeons operating.

Picasso wore a suit and spotted tie for the occasion; no safety pins to hold his pockets together, no shoelace to hitch his watch to his buttonhole. He had given up the ambiguous Basque beret he wore during the war. He stood puffing a cigarette beside his dud Flemish stove, that loomed like some prop from *Metropolis*, primed to fire lightning bolts at any time.

'Elsa Triolet was always a cow,' he informed Lee Miller. 'She will be intolerable now that she's a Resistance heroine and a successful writer. It will put muscle in her arm when she sticks her *bandilleras* in my neck.'

Aragon was glancing through the script of Picasso's *Le Désir attrapé par la queue*. Camus played the Chorus when he directed the play's first performance: a reading in Louise and Michel Leiris's apartment. All the women – The Tart, Thin-Anxiety and Fat-Anxiety – are in love with Big-Foot, Picasso's version of himself.

'Being ringed by the forces of evil infected me,' Picasso said. 'I did an awful thing. I let my indecisiveness – cowardice, more likely – decide when Cocteau came to ask me to speak up for poor Max Jacob. I told him that Max was a devil, a born survivor. Then Max died. You know that he died at Drancy? I did bury him, though, which took a lot out of me.'

Aragon nodded understanding. He knew how Picasso lived in terror of authority and was afraid of death.

'Matisse came through all right,' Picasso said, with a show of relief. 'They tell me that you are writing a book about him. Was he okay when you last saw him?'

'Painting radiantly, but with some difficulty.'

'There never was a time when he didn't do both.'

'He spends his time cutting shapes out of coloured paper, which he assembles into patterns.'

Picasso taps his script. 'The cast included Dora, Sartre, the Beaver, Queneau and others. They did very well, all things considered: Éluard can tell you. My protector, the *flic* André Dubois, was here. Maria Casarès came, so did Braque; and there was a rich Argentinian couple who wanted me to paint their bathroom door. I hear Matisse took on the job and is being plagued by the wife.'

'The Anchorenas?'

'That's right.'

Aragon was reading the scene in the bathtub where Big-Foot, Onion and Round End make up to the Tart and her cousin.

The Cousin:	If you don't stop going on, I'm getting out.
The Tart:	Where is my soap? My soap! My soap!
Big-Foot:	The hussy!
The Onion:	Yes, hussy!
The Tart:	This soap is good. It smells good.
Round End:	I'll give you soap that smells good!
Big-Foot:	Sweet infant, let me rub you down!
Round End:	What a bitch!

'I was with Marie-Thérèse when the shooting started in the rue Henri IV,' Picasso said. 'I was shitting myself, so much so that I made a sketch of Maya to calm us both. I met a historian coming home. He told me that the barricades were blocking the same streets as they did during the Commune. He said he had seen Cartier-Bresson risking his life to photograph the sniping battles. Lee got here first; so my liberator, as so often, turned out to be a woman. Then Hemingway came, but I was out. He left me a case of grenades as a present, which put the wind up my concierge. A far deadlier gift than that old Browning of Jarry's that Apollinaire gave me. They might come in handy, Hemingway said, to throw at critics who were stupid enough to interrogate me about aesthetics.'

Éluard and Nusch were talking to Penrose, the English Surrealist painter. 'It is the winter that worries us,' he said. 'The Germans harvested every crop before they left. They said the food was for Paris. The grain, which wasn't even ripe, went back to Germany with them. Now, with the Seine bridges destroyed, how will food from Normandy reach Paris – assuming that some herds have survived?'

Éluard was telling Penrose that Picasso had joined the Communist Party.

Elsa laughed when Aragon told her the news. 'Let's hope they don't ask you to make Pablo toe the line.'

Picasso's eyes glittered with rage. 'Jockeys weighed in at Longchamps, as usual; scrap-iron merchants became nabobs; crooks grew rich making playing cards and cooking pots. Don't ask me how, or why.'

'Did the Germans give you much trouble?' Elsa asked.

'I was Lipchitz, they insisted, and where was my yellow star? All I craved was food; I could only paint food, and my play is full of it, too. Any colour sense I had I lost entirely. I was living among monsters. None of my paintings was any good during those years. My sole success was to make sure that Arno Breker did not steal all the bronze in Paris. The Resistance boys took my plaster models to Valsuani's foundry. They loaded my bronzes onto a stolen enemy truck to bring them back here.'

'Camus had no consideration for Leiris's neighbours,' Picasso told Elsa. 'He began every scene change by thudding his cane down, then reading the stage directions. Michel Leiris played me; he made a good job of Big-Foot. The Beaver did well with the Cousin; Sartre was Round End, and Zanie de Campan did the Tart, Bost played Silence, while Queneau made a powerful Onion. I never found out what Maria Casarès thought of the performances. Do you want to see the photograph that Brassaï took?'

'That charlatan, Sert, had fifty guests in his apartment to see de Gaulle's royal progress to the Arc de Triomphe. Chanel was one, and that bitch Lifar, too, Hitler's crony, who ran the Paris Opera Ballet and went on dancing for the swine. Then the shooting started! As the windows went, glass crashing into the room, they all fell on their faces and scuttled under Sert's tortoise-shell table – you know that shitty ecclesiastical bric-à-brac he lives with – screeching like banshees as bullets hit the wall – all except Sert, that is. The Franco lover had balls, I'll say that for him; he stood out on the balcony.' Picasso grimaces at Elsa. 'Again, Coco showed she had bigger balls than mine. The *fifis* set her free after a few hours – a telephone call to one of her friends in high places, I've no doubt. They would help.' Picasso shrugged his shoulders. 'We are all free now, and I celebrate with thirty blasts on my French Army bugle every morning.'

'You seem very full of yourself.'

'Yes, my liberation is just that – one long, juicy fuck; schoolgirls are queuing up for my body,' he boasted with relish.

Aragon paced to and fro; he was unable to relax. Seeing Elsa with Picasso, he joined them.

'When I did see Hemingway he showed me an S.S. insignia, which he said he tore from the uniform of an officer he shot,' Picasso said. 'Do you believe a word he says? I don't. Then again, we are all phoneys. Our enemies pay us to reassure them that art is alive and well, and we kowtow to the illusion of fame this brings. We have the same problem as Greta Garbo or Gary Cooper: how to detect and avoid the bad script – although I don't know why we should bother to try. As I see it, things can only get worse in this respect.'

* * *

Lydia reads the obituary of Aristide Maillol to Matisse, who nods sadly. His death is for the best. When his son Lucien went to face a purge committee about his father, they jailed him for serving in the *milice*. Matisse sighs, shaking his head. 'Aristide had trouble during the last war. The Germans had a plan to use his studio as a gun site to shell Paris, no less! Clemenceau had secured him the Légion d'honneur, yet he had to intervene to save him from a tribunal that accused him of collaborating and sending coded messages.'

'It was simply gossip – without evidence or proof?'

'People said that he was pro-German. If that were true, it was because the Germans respected his work more than the French. You know what Aristide was like, how easy it was to flatter him. Anybody could do it, women better than men. If he liked the look of them, the fact that they were German would not matter. He would sign his name for anybody who brought him some food.'

'No wonder the villagers threw stones at his house.'

'You agree with them.'

'I didn't say that.'

Maillol had gone to Perpignan to plead his son's case with the justice officials. Having failed to move them, his friend Dr Nicolau was driving him back to Dufy's studio when there was a rain shower outside Prades and the car skidded off the road and overturned. Maillol was unconscious, his jaw broken and teeth missing. Nicolau got him to the clinic in Perpignan, where he died of uraemia twelve days later.

The last time Matisse spoke of him was when Maillol's girl-friend, Dina Vierny, brought a letter and they talked as she sat for her portrait. It had been a joyful visit. She had posed for Bonnard, too. Matisse had told her she looked like Manet's Olympia. Lydia had kept from him the fact that the Germans had arrested her for helping refugees to reach Spain, using a footpath Maillol told her about; or that it was Arno Breker who interceded with the Gestapo to save her from Auschwitz.

'Aristide was very dear to me. It's like having part of my body torn away.'

* * *

Six weeks after the Liberation, Aragon and Elsa were among those who went to the opening of the exhibition of Art and Resistance paintings by Picasso and others. Their friend and comrade Laurent Casanova, who was now a government minister, opened the show. To Picasso's disgust, the paintings came under fire by the students of the École des Beaux Arts, who tried to rip them from the walls. He was angry. 'I say students; but many of them murdered Frenchmen not so long ago. I have not changed. I am the same man who sent *Guernica* to New York to raise money for Spanish refugees, where it makes a political statement daily in the heart of New York, a statement that is not welcome in Paris, it seems, in spite of the Liberation. The world has come through these awful years; even my character Love went looking for a job as a suburban bus conductor. All this while Dora lost her mind, wandering the streets, telling the police that men had attacked her. If they hadn't stolen her dog, it was her bicycle! What do people want to see now in an art gallery? Some daubs by dead Impressionists, no doubt!'

The Théâtre Française held a gala evening in honour of the Resistance poets – Aragon, Éluard, Superveille and others intoned their poems in front of tricolour drapes. Jean-Louis Barrault read a poem by Claudel.

Cocteau was with Éluard and Aragon in their box. The Resistance had not forgotten his 'Salut à Breker', but his presence at the gala meant that a pardon was on the cards. Waving wasted hands, as bony as those of any camp victim, he revelled in tart tittle-tattle that began with the government leaving Paris. By then, Dominique Leca and Gilbert Levaux, Reynaud's cabinet secretaries, had reached the Spanish border, where the Civil Guards opened their trunks and found 18,000,000 francs' worth of gold and de Portes's jewels. 'Your hero Arellano Marín had already made off with thousands of Spanish workers' money in his suitcase to start a new life in the Far East. Settled in Vichy, the deputies would saunter into the Petit Casino while our venerable senators lounged in the Salles des Sociétés Medicales. I went on having boys, but not as many as before the war. None of my lovers could take the place of my Raymond. I am an old python, whose skin is flaking away. My doctor, my masseur, can do nothing. I buried Soutine; I heard Karajan conduct the Berlin Opera – *Tristan und Isolde* for Wagner's anniversary. Like Paris, I tried my best to appear indomitable. After his tour of our old brothel, his little dance, Hitler flew back to Berlin. He could think of no nicer way to win over his rape victim for the loss of her virginity than to send her the ashes of Napoleon's son. The sarcophagus arrived in a macabre torchlight parade at Les Invalides. The fates had already sent Otto Abetz to try me. Then I met Ernst Jünger, who felt it was his duty, discreetly of course, to let everybody know how much he hated the Führer. All this, while some doltish impresario is staging *Mignon* in the Tuileries gardens.

'Now France heaves with dirty money,' Cocteau railed on. 'There is no cash to rebuild anything, but if you have a dud project, you have no trouble finding a backer.' He smiled. 'You know this, of course; how could you not since your party is part of the system. You do own the Banque du Nord? You certainly own the shipping line, France Navigation; and during the Spanish Civil War, you were buying gold bullion from the Republicans.'

Éluard scanned the audience with opera glasses and said, 'The light is poor, but, yes, it is Valéry with de Gaulle.'

Aragon watched Cocteau greet Louis Jouvet, who had recently returned from exile in America. 'Why should I feel guilty?' Aragon said. 'I do, though. It was the same the night we phoned his mother and told her that he had killed himself.'

'The little prick has always known more than was good for him,' Éluard said.

On his return, Cocteau began again. 'Don't you think that Jouvet looks even more like a Sioux chief, after his American sojourn? I have just been telling him, not a day passed but *Je suis partout* called for the Germans to shoot me. It was the same after the fracas in the Champs-Élysées; the headline read, "Monsieur Cocteau Salutes only the Jewish Flag." I assume that my refusal to recognise the rag of the Anti-Bolsheviks is why I'm being whitewashed, if that's the word. Strait is the gate. Maybe I should have gone to America too; I would have had less grief. All of Paris knows that Colette wrote for *collabo* papers. I suppose keeping Goudeket out of the gas chamber has been her saving grace. Coco, of course, kept her German lover at the Ritz. Ah, fashion! We know that it has a bloom again because of the foreign currency it brings in. Schiaparelli and Christian Dior need have no fear of the purge; it will not last long. We are all hungry; if we didn't have Jean-Pierre's food parcels from California, I don't know what we would do.'

Cocteau had heard that Brasillach gave himself up because the *fifis* arrested his mother on failing to find him. 'Is that true? I would never survive four months in some squalid attic.'

When Éluard asked about the death of Max Jacob, Cocteau replied, 'Max wrote to me on his way to Drancy. He gave the letter to a scared station guard, who brought it to me. I sent an appeal to von Rose at the German Embassy. You must be aware that Picasso refused to sign. By the time the Gestapo told von Rose of Max's reprieve, their infernal machine had done its work. When I went to the memorial service, Pablo was lurking outside the church – nervous of being noticed. I knew he would not be part of the congregation. I thought I would dash off a poem to shock your adoring Party girls; a couplet or two to draw their attention to Pablo's clay feet.'

A daily column had begun to appear in the papers headed 'Arrests and Purges'; it came after the births, marriages and deaths, listing collaborators' names, and the sentences passed on those whose trials were over. Elsa had no doubt that life in the prisons must be worse now than when the Germans ran them.

'Duhamel told me that de Gaulle had nothing to say in regard to Pétain's trial,' said Aragon. "So, the General favours silence, then!" I said, when I heard that. Of course Pétain is not going to atone for his crimes. De

Gaulle and Pétain are part of the same toy soldier set. De Gaulle's craving for power springs from the same roots; they both identify their aims with those of France. Such men are only worth having around on Bastille Day, or when somebody has to say something lofty at Clemenceau's grave. I resigned, of course, and handed my note to Mauriac.'

'Who tore it up, I hope. Did he?'

'No, you are right, I couldn't walk out. Nevertheless, our duty is to hold firm among this plague of toads creeping out from under stones everywhere.'

'You will have to be less defensive, Louis; show more force and aggression. These people have no intention of including us in their scheme of things.'

The cinemas opened after the theatres; electricity was in short supply because the Germans had sabotaged the hydro-electric plant that served Paris. Elsa saw Fredric March's Doctor Jekyll become Mr Hyde, and felt she could smell the old clover and dusty alfalfa in the barn again.

* * *

Writing to Marquet in Algeria, Matisse explains that the invasion had caused him no great upset, apart from three shells falling in his garden at midnight and tearing down tree branches.

Lydia brings him a piece of shrapnel when she goes to assess the damage, and says:

'Cheer up, Henri. Things might have been worse.'

'That's very true. I cut out my Icarus as a result of those shells.' Matisse laughs. 'Did I start with the idea, or did I end up with a rocket burst and a figure who looked like the Greek flier when I finished snipping away?'

'You seem to be in a good humour.'

'Too many wars have torn too many holes in this century,' Matisse says. 'The last war killed my friends – perhaps my mother, too. Renoir was right: war always kills the wrong people. I rejoice that Rome has fallen to the Allies, and that they are here in France. They will save my little girl; I know that she will be alive when they find her.'

Aimé Maeght pointed out that Nice had not changed much. All the council would have to do would be to scrape off the camouflage paint the Italians had daubed on the sea-front buildings. There were the same fishing boats in the bay, and the fair was flourishing.

'Every vacant room in some apartments is full of potatoes and wood for the stove,' Lydia says. 'If you visit our Anglo–American library, you will see empty shelves; the Germans stole seven thousand books when they left. They took every work in English from the shops. Did they haul them off to Berlin? No, they burned them somewhere.'

Matisse sighs. 'All I can see are old snapshots whenever I visit the sea front: the ones I glimpsed from my various windows.'

Maeght questions Matisse about his childhood. 'My father traded in grain he bought, first from Vilmorin in Paris then, later, from the Corn Exchange,' he replies. 'He supplied the people around Bohain, and had an interest in everything from cattle-cake to manure. Men say: honour thy father. I remember he had keys for everything. I never knew what my father felt about the defeat at Waterloo. Did he feel the same about the Franco–Prussian war? You see how little I know about him. Every family has secrets. Those things I never heard him say; thought I had missed; that simply were not there. I suppose France's retreat from Mexico cost us dear at home; to add to the difficulties my father was having as the country's grain trade came to terms with the growth of the international market. I cannot blame him for that. I don't know. That time has gone, long ago. He left me his peasant thrift and realism. I remember when he came to visit me at Issy, he walked round the garden shaking his head, saying he could not believe I had so much land lying fallow. I can't say how much I inherited from my mother. She sold paint, which she knew enough about to grind and mix – well, we were very alike, you know.'

The light is fading. 'You are lucky to have electricity; my supply is very erratic,' Bonnard says. 'I don't know what things are coming to in Cannes. Not only have Pétain and his crew stolen the food from my table, they have affected my feelings about the colours of my interiors. I shall be glad when the war is over. First Vuillard dies, then Marthe.'

Matisse nods in agreement. 'It is easy to feel used-up and ill-done-by, now; age and illness, I suppose.'

After they leave, Matisse listens to the Suisse Romande orchestra challenge the night across Europe with Beethoven's Pastoral Symphony.

*   *   *

The Haute Comité de la Résistance de Paris invited Maurice Chevalier to join the march to Père Lachaise and the Mur des Fédérés. Aragon, Elsa, Picasso, Éluard were there, too, as the crowds shouted Chevalier's name, which had been under a cloud during the war. Unlike Piaf, the fairy godmother of Stalag III, who smuggled prisoners out in the guise of musicians in her orchestra, Chevalier had apparently sung for the enemy without demur. Aragon, who knew better, wrote that Maurice had aided his group, the Étoilles. Defending him in *Ce Soir*, he said that certain people wanted Parisians to believe that the Germans had the singer in their pay.

The heat was not the same but, at the gate, Elsa recalled the afternoon Koltsov drove her and Aragon to Gorky's estate, where the guards refused to admit them. Doctor Levin's arrival had ended the argument, and they stood there in the blazing sun unsure whether to return to Moscow. Then Koltsov saw Levin coming and went over to him; when he rejoined them, he was weeping. Gorky was dead.

'For such a foul-mouthed, down-to-earth man, I have to say that de Gaulle has the gift of solemnity,' a marcher said, with a laugh.

Aragon half turned to Elsa, with a smile. 'France's prodigal son has agents in every nook and cranny to laud him,' he said, 'even though his tribe will prove more fickle than the one Moses led out of Egypt.'

* * *

Matisse winds the gramophone, adjusts the horn, and puts on a record of the Busch Quartet playing Beethoven. 'What would I do if I no longer had music at my command? Beethoven always soothes my nerves. Unlike his symphonies, his chamber music reverberates with private feelings. I am sure that he would have responded to my interiors, just as I respond to his.' He lights a cigarette. 'They play this sonata with the same *brio* as Goya painted; his canvases dried in one skin, thus preserving every cut and slash of his brush. You can see how he dashed in that artful black mantilla, those witches and ogres of the supernatural that hover in the dark! He used a palette knife, or one of those bamboo spatulas he cut, his fingers too. Manet learned a lot from Goya: a masterly use of black, flaky grey and white. Music can make up for so much.'

'Even when it sells soap powder as fresh as flowers,' Lydia says, with a laugh.

* * *

Elsa felt that it was an eerie image from a dream as she picked up the still from *Das Kabinett von Doktor Caligari* that lay outside the synagogue in the rue de la Victoire. It showed Conrad Veidt as Cesare, his face chalk-white, stalking the painted set in a ballet of fits and starts to signify that he was sleep-walking to commit murder. It had the look of going behind appearances; a novelist's commonplace trick. For a moment she felt she was the insane narrator and, just outside the frame, she glimpsed the mad presence of Werner Krauss as Doctor Caligari.

The old bearded Jew had grey ringlets of hair hanging under his *streimel*, a flat hat trimmed with fur that Elsa knew from her childhood. His white, bloodless hands gripped a faded prayer shawl around his shoulders. She would have liked to ask how he came to be in Paris. Had he survived the round-ups by hiding in an attic room under roofs like those in Caligari's cabinet? He was a relic from Soutine's world; he was one of those Hassidic Jews who danced with the Torah. He had been part of that world where calves tottered into abattoirs, and strangled roosters raised the spectre of the dead albatross.

Elsa felt unreal seeking her origin; having to admit to that which she had kept hidden during the war. She was a Jew; yet she felt she had nothing in common with Jews or their grief. Altgelt, killed during the Liberation, had known that the German Jews buried the Sefar Torah and the scrolls of law in their cemeteries in Berlin.

The drab woman told Elsa that she had been a prisoner at Drancy. She could still hear the children's fearful whispers in the night about going to Pitchipol before they wept with their mothers in the morning. The only toilets were outdoor latrines; part of the martyrdom, she said, wryly. It was the Israelites who ran things, she said; working-class immigrants had less chance of survival, being doomed by the sense of their true identity; they did all the real work, the kitchen chores, the hard labour. In October they began to starve; it was October again, and she was still hungry.

It was Yom Kippur. After the calamity, the rabbis were dead. A cantor intoned the prayers. It was the hour of truth; voices speaking from a burning bush; the prayer of Kaddish. The survivors went on imploring forgiveness of their sins, praying for God to restore Zion when he came to reign over the world.

1945

'LISTENING to Schoenberg, it occurs to me that he was also a painter,' Matisse says. 'I should like to see his canvases some time. Music has to become structure or else it would not exist; it has to change, in the same way that painting changes. That doesn't mean that I can accept Schoenberg. I do not care for his music; but it speaks of our times, our ruins. Vienna was such a banal city; with its ghastly rococo statuary, its burlesque cupids.'

'Warnings resound in the music of this century, don't you think?' Lydia says.

Matisse sighs. 'I miss playing chamber music with a cellist, a pianist.'

Lydia has heard this before. 'If you are serious you should put an advertisement in the paper and find some musicians.'

'Derain and Puy would talk about art as soon as they stopped playing. Besides, people no longer live music as they used to. I find my own ability woeful as I listen to Kubelik on the wireless or the gramophone. Music haunted my work far more in the old days; the house was full of music – Pierre practising on our Pleyel. Did you know that Liszt wrote testimonials for Pleyel, who sent him free pianos and re-strung any that he broke at concerts? No, playing as part of a group is out of the question now.'

Matisse asks Lydia to turn off the radio. 'Such discords bring to mind Max Jacob. Why? I suppose because Schoenberg is a Jew too, from Bratislava. I find it hard to come to terms with Max's death. He must have been seventy years old. I remember him when he first arrived from Quimper. Picasso will miss him. He worshipped Pablo. His religious fervour did not stop him making sexual advances to the hearse driver at Eva's funeral. We were both in love with the *sardane*. I read his poem about the dance years ago in his volume *Le Laboratoire central*. I liked Max. It was typical of him to adopt Indian dress so as to avoid wearing his yellow star.'

*　　*　　*

The day Roger Stéphane arrived to interview André Malraux, the sunlight was thin and bright in the snowy mountain air. Malraux was at Altkirch, near Strasbourg. Under the name of Berger, his alter ego in *Les Noyers de l'Altenburg*, he had captained the Dordogne *maquis* until joining de Lattre de Tassigny's Fifth Army. It was all too easy to see only the

287

Lawrence of Arabia aura, Malraux the adventurer who had acted out his own legend in the dream narratives of his novels.

Malraux said how deeply shocked he had been to hear of the murder of Stéphane's father by Darnand's militia men the year before.

'They will pay,' Stéphane said.

'Charles Maurras is too wily to serve his life sentence of solitary confinement – a judgement that he had the gall to call "Dreyfus's revenge". Your father's killers read that deaf viper's article in order to find your father,' said Malraux. 'We both know that the *milice* H.Q. in Lyons was in the same building as Action Française?'

'They will atone for their crime,' said Stéphane grimly, lighting a cigarette. 'I can live with my loss until they do. You must feel worse than I do; I read of Josette's death.'

Malraux turns away curtly. 'You didn't drive all this way to talk about Josette,' he said brusquely. He offered his guest a glass of *prunelle*, the local wine, as he took off his beret. His elegant, tailored tunic still set him apart, a denizen of some pre-war night club. 'I hear that you were with Cocteau. He told me once how, visiting Picasso in the rue la Boétie, he found a name for his angel, Heurtebise. Otis Pifre's name was on the brass plate in the lift, and Jean misread it as Heurtebise; thus are angels born. These days, he is in need of more than an angel or two.'

Stéphane said he had paid a visit to Aragon in Nice, who had been writing about Matisse. 'I suspect he plans more volumes.'

'And Elsa, the divine muse?'

'Older, of course; getting peevish, I thought.'

'I hear that Sartre is in New York; that he met Breton on Broadway, fed up with Jacqueline and all his pals in exile. When he spoke of being homesick for Paris, Jean-Paul gave him the shits with the spectre of our new Robespierre – Aragon, of course – purging any writer who cannot show he is a true Jacobin.'

'The last time I saw Sartre was at Saint-Jean-Cap-Ferrat; he came with the Beaver on bikes for a camping holiday. Under the circumstances – it was 1941 – I thought it was the ideal thing to do.'

'Early in the war, when I came to urge you to join de Gaulle, you said you could not see yourself as a royal lick-spittle in exile; that you would sooner sign up with the Red Army,' says Stéphane. 'Do you still feel that?'

'I did not carry out my threat then; I see no reason to change my mind now.'

Malraux spoke of his leg wounds before his capture in 1940. 'The Germans imprisoned us in Chartres cathedral.'

'You mean Sens, surely?'

'Of course I do. Yes, it was Sens. I wrote of it as Chartres.'

Chartres cathedral burned down in 1194, Malraux reminisced; the people of the city toiled half a century to rebuild it: glaziers and enamellers piecing together the three great rose windows and the forty-seven lancets. Then there were all the other craftsmen. 'Some of them had come from as far away as Canterbury. What an undertaking, given the technology of the time! As agnostics, we can have only the vaguest idea of what Chartres meant to its builders and the pilgrims who journeyed there. Each colour, fused into each shape of glass, meant the use of gold, copper, manganese and other minerals from far-off mines; brought to the city at huge cost.

'So, yes, I would wake in Sens and imagine that I could see the Holy Virgin burning at the heart of the Rose of France. There were the blues, too, the emeralds and rubies that went to make up Joseph and Mary's flight into Egypt. Below, peasants bore sheaves of celestial corn, with bright gangs of butchers, bakers, blacksmiths and other artisans seeking glory.

'How could the city sustain such an effort for so long?'

Stéphane no longer chimed in to amend Malraux's version of events. He let the writer make sense of the fall of France. 'Thomas à Becket found safety in Sens cathedral,' reminded Malraux, 'where I shivered on the tombs, loathing the thud of German jackboots as the guards went by, humming banal lyrics.

'It was a windy day when we got to the camp; we saw the letters the *boches* had allowed us to write flying everywhere. They had not mailed them.'

'How did you escape?'

'The Germans were using a builder's yard as a prison. I found some carpenter's overalls, got a plank, and walked out with it over my shoulder. When I saw myself, I burst into laughter. There was lamp-black in the pocket, and I had rubbed it on my face inadvertently. I looked like a nigger minstrel.

'After a short rest at Roquebrune, I became Colonel Berger of the *maquisards*, hitting German garrisons and rail lines. We blew up an ammunition train near Toulouse.'

Behind Malraux, Stéphane could see a snapshot of the hero lying in a foxhole in the snow with a German light machine gun. Myths were not true, yet they were not false; they were bids to find meaning. You must omit nothing in the quest for self. It was easy, natural even, for autobiography to become fiction.

Stéphane did not know the opera Malraux put on the gramophone.

'Hindemith's *Mathis der Maler*,' Malraux said. 'I found this Tele-funken recording in Colmar. Hindemith upset Hitler in more ways than one before he went into exile in America. The Führer could not abide his naked soprano singing in her bath in *Neues vom Tage*. After this prelude, "Engelkonzert", Mathis is at work on a fresco in the courtyard of the monastery of Saint Anthony, singing of the coming of spring. Schwalb arrives with his daughter Regina. He is the leader of the peasants and has been wounded. Hindemith was already asking how the artist should act during a war.'

'I had seen the face of Grünewald's Christ everywhere during the war: in the prison camp at Sens, among my men in the Dordogne. I saw it in the faces of the bearded Fritzes we beat here at Altkirch. Our men had come across the altarpiece in the Haut-Koenigsburg caves. I was looking at the finest work of art in Northern Europe, Grünewald's last masterpiece. He painted it for the monastery of Saint Anthony at Isenheim. Amazing how it came through the Peasant War; then later, escaped the purge the Revolution made of religious artefacts. The closed wings showed the darkness of the Crucifixion: Christ's battlefield body, blue bloodless lips and green belly shrunk back on pelvic bone. His body hung on a rough and ready cross that sagged under his weight. His crown of thorns was more a rook's nest of barbed agony. Was he suffering from a skin disease, or were his wounds the result of a scourging? For me his flesh mirrored the torments of his worshippers, suffering in a hospital for the care of skin diseases. Maybe one of their corpses served Grünewald as a model? There was no inscription in gold; just printer's ink on a scrap of parchment nailed to the beam.

'Grünewald was as much a master of night as Goya,' Malraux said. 'He could feel that day of total eclipse, that darkness over the face of the earth.'

Stéphane said nothing. In Malraux's narration things fell into place with the magisterial certainty of a Theban play. He had kept himself clean-shaven during the war, coldly aloof with his snake eyes; but his troops had to be medieval saints for him to rub along with them. In the end, he outdid himself by bringing the altarpiece to Strasbourg, standing to attention for de Lattre de Tassigny to pin the Légion d'honneur over his heart.

Elsa, Nusch and Lee Miller were drinking together at the Hôtel Scribe. It was now the headquarters of the American press corps. American sergeants smoking fat cigars ran the reception desk, but the hotel's

French waiters served in the restaurant. There were steaks for dinner; omelettes, with toast, jam and cream coffee for breakfast. When he was not boasting over cocktails at the Ritz, Hemingway used the place. Lee had a room on the first floor, hoarding her precious petrol on the snowy balcony, along with her champagne.

The white helmets of the American MPs on duty outside the grey Opéra *métro* echoed the snow in the streets, acid-yellow and streaked with soot.

Laughing, Capa stepped out onto the landing as he threw a joke over his shoulder at Martha Gellhorn. He saw Elsa and gave her a bear hug, scraping her cheek with his bearded chin. He stank of whisky.

'How are things with you and Louis?' he asked.

Elsa smiled and shrugged. 'You are busy as ever,' she said. 'Your photographs fill all the best magazines.'

'I have to pick up a camera now and then, or the booze would kill me.'

'You are too modest; you know that you have been "the world's greatest war photographer" since 1938,' Elsa said.

Along the landing, Hemingway roared for Capa to get his ass back for the poker game.

Elsa stood listening at another open door. A greasy journalist in a lurid South Sea shirt paced to and fro with a beer in his hand. His cigar dimmed the room with a blue haze as he spoke of a trip to Havana, courtesy of Pan-American airways. Another American, out of sight, said, 'Of course the Russkies are crazy, you're not saying anything new. Eisenstein is a Jew; so what else could you expect? I can see why Stalin made such a song and dance about Lend-Lease, when Sergei was being lavish with his roubles in Alma Ata. Alma Ata? It's some shit-hole Shangri-La in Kazakhstan. How do I know all this? Lillian Hellman was in Moscow. Bernie Fellows had a letter from her, about how she was taking tea with Eisenstein in his apartment at Potylika, when he was cutting *Ivan the Terrible*. He couldn't stop talking about Mexico, and was crazy to see *Bambi*. His own movie has to be God awful, from the sound of it.'

Unable to resist, Elsa edged the door open so that she could see more of the room. The speaker sat sprawled in an armchair, pants around his ankles; a naked girl knelt between his legs with his cock in her mouth; after war, the arts of peace.

'Some of us gave our lives fighting fascism, in the hope that peace would bring change.' Aragon capped his fountain pen and tapped the desk with it. 'The Germans have bequeathed us their stool-pigeons and thieves.

They infest the country; bored, they hide the holes in their rancid socks, practising their skill at "Find the Lady", happy to let anybody bugger them for a smoke. France, the Eternal! They did the *boches'* dirty business; they have done it all; yet they keep going, in love with their tattoos and body odours. It has all come round again: a new regime that retains brutality to maintain order. There is another gang of fairground barkers, dumb now and washed-up; pimps and thieves; jockeys who have fallen off their horses. They dream up things they would like to do to nuns, to schoolmasters, the arresting officer, the judge. All night long there is an acrid smell of archives burning. Is the party over? Is it just about to start? They close their eyes to savour the stench of their farts.'

Aragon had come to Salabert's chill, cramped office to attest to the death of a man who had died in his arms, both eyes blown out by a bomb blast.

Salabert drew his scarf tight and cleared his throat with a cough. 'There's nothing I would like more than to put the war behind me, but, sadly, there are mornings such as this. Was I dreaming when I used to laugh at Arizona Jim drawing his six-guns against the Cagoulards in that pre-war Last Chance saloon? Henri Bergson would pass my office often, on his way to the *métro*. He had become a Catholic, of course, but he chose to go to the *préfecture* to register with the rest of the Israelites: Academic. Philosopher. Nobel Prize winner, and a Jew. If we have any Jews left in Paris, they are mainly working-class; that was a terrible business, Monsieur Aragon.'

'If there's nothing more you need, Monsieur Salabert, I'll go now,' Aragon said.

'Everything is in order.' Salabert slips the document into a folder. 'I can't tell you how relieved I felt that his widow decided not to join us. One of the trials we lawyers have to bear.'

Aragon picked up his gloves. Salabert rubbed the misted window and said, 'More snow coming, I fear.' He took a watch from his fob. 'I saw Mistinguette, you know, speed past on her bicycle to cheer Leclerc's tanks into the city. What a day! Everybody knows that she made a fortune singing for Radio-Paris and speculating in the black market. However, a purge committee's scolding was the best solution. No more Bismarcks, von Hindenburgs, Hitlers; no more wars, Monsieur Aragon.'

'Did you know that Bismarck saw the Serbo-Croats as a gang of sheep-stealers?' Aragon said.

Laurent Casanova was about to climb the narrow staircase. He halted when he saw Aragon come out onto the landing and shake hands with

Salabert. The son of a railway worker, he had been Thorez's secretary before the war. 'I'm sorry I'm late,' he called; 'you've finished, then?'

'Everything's fine,' Aragon said, coming down.

They walked briskly to join Elsa at the Rotonde. 'Pétain is a sick old man; they are all sick old men, a parade of mummies,' Casanova said bitterly. 'Louise Renault had kidney disease and senile dementia, but his wife tried hard to blame some Red prison warder for murdering her Baron Samedi. She must have known her X-ray would reveal a prostate the size of an apple.'

'A sadistic Prussian with his boot on her neck was always more desirable than rule by the workers,' Aragon said.

'There is no Moscow blueprint; nothing except the line Thorez preaches,' Casanova said.

Home from the Soviet Union since November, Thorez was telling France that the Communists were not going to make any demands of a social nature. They wanted to defeat Hitler with the help of the French people: workers, bosses, intellectuals and peasants.

'He has bodyguards and drives around in an official armoured limousine. His guards live at Choisy; serve at table, and take their meals in the kitchen,' Casanova said, moving among the tables in the café.

Elsa rose from her chair to peck Aragon's cheek in greeting. 'Very Communist, I dare say.'

'The worst thing I could think of happening to me would be to find that people ignored everything I said,' Aragon says.

Casanova shrugs. 'Your error, comrade, was to moon over so many bourgeois heroes; and you failed to question the spirits Matisse called up from the grave: Charles d'Orléans, Montherlant, or the classical verities of Ronsard, at a time when the cult of Pétain kept Vichy France together.'

'Lies were all that made life bearable,' Aragon says.

* * *

Marguerite looks at the photographs for a long time: her grandmother Héloïse and her father in front of a shaky studio seascape. Apart from her need for the albums, she talks feverishly about the Soviets taking Berlin.

It is not long, however, before her euphoria fades.

Matisse is sketching her, amazed by her calmness. He is sad to see how her trials have worn her face. It upsets him more to hear that Lydia has shown her his *Pasiphaé* drawings. Marguerite says, 'It was a virile hero out of Montherlant who beat me. He was cool and urbane; when he was not hurting me, he admired his fingernails the way the gangsters do in films. After the interrogation, I was sick into the bucket I had to use for everything else. My mouth was open like Pasiphaé's as I cried in the night. Did you hear my screams, father? I tried so hard to stifle them.'

Matisse leans forward to touch her hand; he can say nothing. 'Jean was angry that I chose Montherlant's poetry; now you are making me feel I betrayed you. I don't want to feel that I failed you.' It hurts to say this.

'It makes no difference now, although there were other poets you might have chosen,' says Margot. 'Don't worry; people will soon forget the war. They will soon forget the filthy prison cells, the dead; they will see the Third Reich as an aberration; they will want the light of your paintings.'

Matisse finds solace painting the woman in a yellow dress, which he had been working on when Marguerite arrived. It is not easy to renew those feelings he had when he started. André Rouveyre has nettled him, too, with his use of the word 'indifference' when talking to Lydia about his cut-outs for *Jazz*. Everything is suddenly chaotic again, and made gloomier by Tériade ringing with the news that Angèle is dead. Tériade is close to tears. 'How can I go on living? Tell me what I can do. Her body was too frail for cancer to eat to the bone. She died bravely. She was always brave.'

'She suffered so much,' Matisse says. 'She has given in; said to herself: I have had enough. Angèle was all grace, and a courageous woman.'

Marguerite tells Lydia about her ordeal. 'The Germans handcuffed us together for the bus journey to the Ravensbrück train. The officer in charge said that if we attempted to escape or signal to anybody his men would shoot.

'I tried to keep up with my friend's moves, but my wrist soon became sore. A Vichy judge had given her the death penalty for knifing her Nazi lover in a jealous fit; then, a believer in mercy, sent her to a death camp to save her life. She used to wipe her nose on her sleeve, suffering from a bad cold. I couldn't fathom where she found the emotion to kill anybody. She was drab, absent; lost in constantly telling a rosary, resigned to anything that might happen.

'On the train, I couldn't think about time. If I thought about time, I would reach my destination. My only hope was that an accident would break the chain of events, events that ran to a schedule. What I did marvel at as we neared Belfort was the damage the R.A.F. bombs had caused. Every factory ruin meant an end to the war; that the suffering would be over soon. After dark, the searchlights were blazing again on the other side of the border.

'We spent dreary hours moving at walking speed, in fits and starts, until we ran into an air raid. It was a job to get Arlette to join the escape. I had to push her out onto the track and drag her into the tunnel. Her breath smelled quite awful as she ran beside me. She began to laugh when we came across one of the sentries urinating. As I tried to pull her into the tunnel, he followed, warning us to stop or he'd shoot. He knew Paris well, he said, and he would go back there after the war. He had been drinking. His maudlin reminiscences were comic given the situation. He took us to a hospital where we found the others. They were lying in wards without light, filthy with vermin and dirt, listening to stories from other prisoners reprieved by the Allied bombing.

'I was not alone, so I had to stay sane. I was lucky. I saw a face I knew, a man who helped me escape; the others died without names, only those pale blue numbers tattooed on their arms.'

'You were angry when I showed you *Pasiphaé*; do you feel the same way now?'

'Montherlant will not be tried for his beliefs,' Marguerite says; 'in time, they will elect him to the French Academy. I find that hard to stomach. France has many upright murderers – we know some of their names. Some will hang or be shot, but many will not pay for their crimes. What happened to us had an awful logic. To be sent to a death camp was lawful, you know; until last year, French law sanctioned murder. The law is such a useful tool.'

Paris is under snow; the lawyer, Jacques Isorni, is trying to defend Robert Brasillach, editor of *Je suis partout*.

Matisse shakes his head. 'It cannot be right to put Georges Simenon under house arrest because the Germans filmed his books.'

'He is not a Frenchman, besides he is the least of our problems,' Marguerite says.

Matisse's letter found Aragon in the Basses-Pyrénées, where he was ill with low blood pressure. Matisse touched on Margot's sufferings and said how painful her time in prison had been for him; even Dostoevsky would find such events hard to write about.

Despite his mother's petition and an appeal for clemency by Mauriac, who begged for pity for a young man's wild oats, they shot Robert Brasillach at Fort Montrouge. His mother refused to let her son lie in a common grave. She implored de Gaulle to let her bury him in the Père Lachaise cemetery.

Seghers wrote too, to say that he was printing 'Ce n'était qu'un passage de ligne', the story Elsa had written about their border crossing and their spell in prison.

* * *

Taking the road to Saint-Jeannet, Bonnard climbs uphill to the left, until he faces the ochre-yellow villa under the grey rampart of rock. The garden is not what it could be; there are some palms and olive trees, but not much in the way of flowers. It does not seem likely that there will be any, except for stray seeds.

Matisse wears a Manila straw hat, slacks, a cardigan over a pale blue shirt. 'We owe a great deal of our sense of ourselves to other people,' he muses. 'Reverdy taught me about clothes; I think of him whenever I put on a suit. He used to say that one must not give in to anecdote, yet Max Jacob boasted that he made him a convert by acting out the Stations of the Cross in a café.'

He puffs at a small cigar. 'Nothing gives more pain than to see a friend change out of all recognition. I remember I was going to visit Renoir at Cagnes and ran across Sergei Shchukin on the tram. I was dumbstruck as he lumbered by, making his way into the Second Class section. He had taken his cotton profits out of Russia after 1905, but the Soviets got his art collection. He stuttered something about being with the people. It shocked me so much that I forgot to ask where he was going. When we met, he was a vegetarian and an Old Believer, and I took him to the Bateau-Lavoir. There were worse shacks in Russia, he said, but he had never thought to find one in Montmartre. Where was the Seine? It had the air of a boathouse.

'Picasso told me it started life as a fire-trap piano factory; then, later, a blacksmith bought it and installed a forge. When it became a lodging house, the rents were low enough to attract the anarchists, who went there at the end of the century.

'I can see Picasso's caricature *Monsieur Stschoukim, Moscou*; he gave Sergei a snout and pig's ears. It was all of a part with the place: icy cold in winter; a sauna in summer that smelled of drains, dogs and varnishes, where a sex-mad Van Dongen pounded his women into a frenzy. Egypt fascinated Shchukin, you know. He was in love with the museum we built in Cairo, which is sadly in decline now. Later, the poor fellow lost my respect by saying that, if he was still a collector, he would buy Dufy's work. How is one to explain this aberration?' Matisse shakes his head gravely. 'I painted the portraits of Zorah and the Riffian for Shchukin; the landscapes I did for Morosov and his wife.'

Bonnard becomes aware of the shutters at Le Rêve. 'Light bothers me these days. I fear it, yet it is everything; without it, I would have no life. Surely you, of all people, can understand that.' Matisse laughs. 'My doctor wants me to wear dark glasses when I work on my cut-outs. In Africa, the ideal time was after sunset, the colours in the afterglow.'

Tapestries from the Congo, panther skins and rugs, hang on the walls, along with more recent paintings. Everything needful for his work is near his bed, where there is a revolving stand with dictionaries and volumes of the classics. Next to the telephone there are pencils, erasers and a stack of paper. Nothing here of the dry-biscuit, frugal life Gauguin and Van Gogh lived. Suddenly, Bonnard felt the urge to be with the old Nabis gang trooping into Volpini's to argue about Gauguin's paintings.

'Are we going?' Lydia puts on her hat.

A taxi is waiting to take them to the restaurant.

Matisse says that he had dined there once with the Jolases. 'He was from Alsace. He published my attack on Gertrude Stein in his magazine. He was fluent in English, French and German. I did six drawings for *Ulysses*: the blinding of Polyphemus, and the road to Penelope's palace in Ithaca, which I based on the garden at Issy. I have not met Nausicaa, Aeolus or Circe, as Ulysses did, but I have come a long way.'

Bonnard shows no time for Ithaca. 'I do understand Ulysses' homesickness. Often, I feel like a domestic; but I don't mind how useless all my scouring and polishing are. I am free if I see painting as being no more than any household chore. I can stick my nose in apple cupboards whenever I wish, and spend hours staring at the beauties. I have lived with an artist's vocabulary throughout my life. I don't use it much now because I find it no longer applies. I look back on those days when Louise Hervieu used to give Marthe painting lessons. First the shadow of her enormous hat in the hallway, then the glimmer of those big white sheets of paper she spread out on the floor for Marthe to copy twigs over and over. I asked her to give me lessons. She knew how to cope with Marthe's bad dreams; she knew what would entertain children under a summer chestnut trees – magic, and slices of cherry tart.'

'Vuillard and I came late,' Bonnard says. 'We had spent the day in the country. Maxime Dethomas – you remember big Maxime – was with Lautrec behind the bar. Henri had shaved his head for his role, and wore a waistcoat cut from the Stars and Stripes to tempt the guests to taste his American cocktails. I found Mallarmé sipping one of Henri's demonic creations. Over his head, there was an English sign: "Don't speak to the man at the wheel". I felt tired and hungry; I fell down after two drinks, and they carried me off to his sick-bay. Misia's hang-over cures were in great demand the next morning.' He pauses. 'Marthe used to envy Misia her chic, her imperious gamine quality. The play Thadée wrote disgusted her. She could not forgive him for his portrayal of her as a perverted vamp.'

Bonnard leaves abruptly soon after they return to Le Rêve. Matisse says, 'I think Pierre protests too much. He was never one to resist a fling with other women. When Marthe found out, he used to send the poor girls packing. Cézanne had his share of troubles with women, too, and I had mine. Manet wounded his models when he rejected the heroic stances which other painters had taught them. He got up Dubosc's nose by calling him an old plaster cast. Pierre is trying to live down his past, his delight in the flesh of girls and the stormy scenes that led to.'

*　　*　　*

The offer of a Spanish visa did not stop Drieu la Rochelle trying to kill himself once more. When the bells of Notre-Dame and every other church rang out to celebrate Leclerc's victory, he failed again. There was a warrant out for his arrest, and he lay low in the avenue de Breteuil, writing his last testament before swallowing more sleeping pills and turning on the gas to make sure.

'I told you De Laretelle's accusation of cowardice in *Le Figaro* would be too much for him,' Elsa said. 'He probably chose the middle of the night; there is less demand for gas then.'

Aragon grimaced, and shook his head. 'In his last note he wrote, "This time you must let me sleep, Gabrielle." '

'Why that break in your voice? You are grieving for the swine! They would have shot him, you know; the same way his friends shot ours. You are in danger of forgetting Gabriel, Georges Politzer, Maïe and Danielle.'

'I can't excuse what Drieu did; but I won't bury my memories with him in his grave. One must respect a man who has the courage to kill himself. Don't let him start another feud between us, Elsa.'

'You hope he died with your name on his lips, eh? No, he asked for Malraux to be his literary executor.'

'He would be too busy with the Dirk Raspe novel he was writing, his Van Gogh character.'

'That comes as no surprise.'

'Why?'

'It was on the cards that he might end up wrestling with God in the Low Countries. After all, he rooted around long enough in the entrails of fascism trying to descry the spiritual. Sadly, he was born with a sweet tooth in circles where consumption was conspicuous. So, yes, it doesn't surprise me that Van Gogh would appeal to him: a saint mired in the Borinage in the rain; in debt and racked with guilt because he couldn't make his mind up whether he was a painter or a clergyman.' Elsa laughs.

Aragon said that Matisse would appreciate knowing how Paul Éluard had done his bit during the uprising, writing leaflets and making phone calls at the rue du Dragon Art School, with *Joie de vivre* above his desk. 'What time could he have had to gaze at *Joie de vivre*?' Elsa said. 'His chief worry, he told me, was that the concierge could be spying for the Germans.'

In Milan, the partisans were hanging the corpses of Mussolini and his mistress on lamp–posts, but Hitler's vaunted new weapons still fell on London.

After her adventures with the Rainbow Company of the 45th Division, Lee Miller returned to Paris. She met Elsa and Nusch to show her photographs. 'These two Buchenwald guards fell to their knees as soon as anybody came into their cell. You can see how they beat them, their bloody faces; but how could the prisoners find the strength to kill fifty of them? This horror is afraid he might go the same way; you see how his eyes bulge in his head. Some guards wore civilian clothes that had a flea-market look; they had come from the storage dumps we found in the huts: bales of human hair, eyeglasses, children's toys and dolls. By then, the camps had no fuel to burn the corpses; there were heaps of bodies beside the ovens. I could not distinguish the women from the men except for their vaginas, their bony pelvises. There's not much to choose between their awful shanks.' She riffles through the photographs. 'I found this German officer's corpse at Dachau. The inmates probably held him under until he drowned. I found these two stiffs hanging out of a railway wagon. This is another Buchenwald guard; he hanged himself; his fat blue tongue stuck out of his mouth like an egg.'

Lee Miller passed more pictures across the table. 'This is me in Hitler's tub, in the Prinzenregenplatz, Munich. Maybe I was drunk. I was drinking a lot. I was filthy, of course. I had to have a bath, no matter what. I lived in his apartment, awake all night because of U.S. Army trucks roaring up to the front. I don't believe it either. Maybe by then I was a little crazy. Maybe that's why I stayed there. How was I ever going to be clean?'

She lit another Lucky Strike. 'After I did my fashion assignment for *Vogue*, I went back to London and quarrelled with Roland; so I came here. Where am I going? To photograph the Salzburg opera festival, if I don't crack up. Tell me where anybody is going. Why is it that I cannot feel this war is over? I can't stop hating them. What have I done to myself? I don't see how we can begin to live a normal life again.'

It had been dark when she reached Dachau. At first light, she found some prisoners feeding the camp's Angora rabbits. They had used the fur to knit scarves and mittens for the S.S. They told her how eating the rabbit food had kept them alive.

Europe listened to Admiral Doenitz report the death of Adolf Hitler and vow that Germany would continue hostilities. The war was all but over; camp victims already filled the Gare de l'Est. Red Cross women led these human skeletons towards the exits, where buses were waiting to take them to the Hôtel Lutétia.

No longer Abwehr headquarters, the government had taken the hotel over as a registration centre. The walls of the foyer were full of identity cards and snapshots of missing children. Elsa watched Madame Zlatin, who ran the hotel with Frenay, console grieving relatives and friends. When the mothers could not find the names of their children or loved ones, they would haunt the foyer to show their snapshots to new arrivals.

Elsa slept late after celebrating the surrender. The roar of American bombers woke her, flying low over the city, and distant thuds told of the artillery's role in the celebrations. She opened the window as the sirens wailed a last all-clear over the church bells. When, finally, she heard the phone ringing, it was Aragon.

'Come out now; meet me, and we'll join the people in the streets,' he said.

'Are you at the office?'

They pushed their way through the crowds in the place de l'Étoile. Large tricolours hung from the Arc de Triomphe, lit by floodlights; to stroll along the Champs-Élysées was impossible. They turned back towards the place de la Concorde, also full of joyful people.

As they forced their way through towards the Opéra's red, white and blue lights, a squadron of the Garde Républicaine came along the rue Royale. Every dragoon had a gay Sabine shop girl behind him, shrieking as she clung to his armour.

'All we're lacking is the Chorus from *Rigoletto*,' Aragon said.

Robert Desnos was dead. He had joined the Resistance and ran the usual risks until friends alerted him that the Gestapo men were on their way. He did not react fast enough. The Germans put him on a train. His wife Yuki trailed hopelessly from one official to another trying to save him. The last she heard was that a Czech student had seen him with some typhus patients in a truck from Buchenwald. He was still babbling about Surrealism when he died at Theresienstadt.

'I feel awful now; I should have spoken to him when I saw him in Montparnasse that time,' Aragon said.

*　*　*

'How much longer will these purges go on?' Matisse demands. 'I thought we had done with firing squads after Lyons and Annecy, those Molière trials in village squares; men pouring mercurochrome on women's shaven heads, maltreating waitresses, pinning charges on any porter or prostitute who made the enemy feel at home.' He pauses. 'Simone is coming at three?'

'Did she say so?' Lydia examines her nails. 'Then I suppose she will. She is usually on time.'

'How is her brother?' Matisse asks.

'Improving. Life in Germany was very hard. On top of that, of course, he finds that his wife has been unfaithful.'

'She slept with a German?'

Matisse goes to the window and looks out on Montparnasse. 'Juárez brought the war in Mexico to an end with a firing squad. Manet looked long and hard at Goya's *Tres de Mayo, 1808* before attempting his *L'Exécution de Maximilien*. He studied photographs and illustrations as they came out. In those days, the upper crust did not take either politics or swimming seriously. Life was a concert, high tide, sunset, then the evening ball. Death by firing squad took place off-stage and had its own rules: the blindfold and gentlemanly conduct. Manet chose to paint four big canvases, which shows that he took the business seriously despite his contempt for the genre. In Manet's second attempt, the Emperor is in uniform and wears a sombrero; the sombrero had become as bright as Christ's halo. Napoleon has washed his hands of his puppet. The firing squad is to the right of the canvas, where Goya put his. Manet got into trouble when he dressed the squad in our uniforms. Juárez's men shot Maximilian. Why should they wear French uniforms? What was he trying to say?'

'The Emperor was reactionary, a Habsburg,' Lydia says.

Matisse accepts this verdict with a wave of the hand. 'Dear, oh dear, poor Manet! After he died, his work fell into the hands of his mercenary and stupid family. Vollard's chief mistake was to assume that Léon Leenhoff was Madame Manet's brother, not his son. Leenhoff was a failed banker, who had gone into breeding rabbits, chickens, even worms to go with the fishing tackle he sold. He kept one of his Maximilians in his outhouse, rolled up under a wardrobe. Vollard told the story better than I can, how Leenhoff had already hacked off a sergeant loading his rifle to sell as a portrait figure. The cracked remnant he was offering Vollard was one that Madame Manet loathed. Édouard had lavished so much time on it, when he ought to have been painting something more tasteful! Vollard shook hands on the deal and sent the canvas to the restorer, who told him that Degas had left the missing sergeant with him a short time before. When Vollard showed Degas his canvas, the painter began to rail against the family. Vollard must sell him his firing squad at once, and insist that Madame Manet find the sergeant's missing legs. Leenhoff's retort was that the sergeant looked far better without legs. Vollard sold Degas the piece he had bought, and Degas glued the sergeant back, leaving the canvas bare where there were any gaps.'

Matisse sighs. 'I used to envy Manet his brushwork, his friendship with Baudelaire, and the fact that Mallarmé came to see him after teaching all day at the Lycée Fontanes.'

* * *

Listen to the wail of the Syrians killed with darts
by the bombers of the Third Republic
Listen to the groans of the dead Moroccans.

Aragon recited his lines sadly. 'Our gendarmes are looting shops and burning cars in Damascus. In Algeria, it has become an act of treason to read a newspaper. We are punishing Sérif and Guelma using weaponry from the arsenals of the Western democracies. Who in the bourgeois world will object to waging a war to defend democracy? It has taken us just three days to kill 45,000 men, women and children. Is this victory? Is this peace?

'We stole the natives' farms, but had no work for the families except to serve in our army; we built roads, administered, planting those crops we knew about growing: grapes. We had oceans of wine for which there was no local demand because Islam forbade drink. So, we upset our vintners from Burgundy to Roussillon by shipping the stuff home. The British knew more about building empires; they knew why they built them. Our empire may have lost any use it had, but we go on murdering our inferiors.'

Camus lit another cigarette as soon as Aragon left. It was a warm evening. Malraux had showed up at the offices of *Combat* in the autumn, where Pia had tried to comfort him. 'André has an odd idea of the medical profession; he seems to believe that doctors are like priests or artists; that they are the sum of tested routines that lend them a shaman's magic power to conquer disease.'

'I hear that you started a book at Chambon,' Elsa says.

Camus nodded. 'My plague novel, *La Peste*: a metaphor, of course. It's set in Oran because I ached to be back again among those sunburnt bodies on the beach. Every summer morning on the sands felt like the first morning of the world. Why was I at war, in hiding? Our plague: a young priest loses his faith at the sight of the black pus flowing out of the wounds. The phone company announces: "Two hundred victims today. A charge of two francs will be added to your telephone account." The tram company has 760 workers instead of 2,130. A man is in love with a woman, and as soon as he sees the first sign of the plague on her face, feels he has failed to love her enough; yet he also feels disgusted.'

'How do you end this allegory?'

Camus smiled. 'Doctor Rieux listens to the jubilation in the town at the news that the plague is over. He knows what the happy crowds do not know, but could have learned from medical books: that the plague bacillus never dies or vanishes; that it can hide for years in furniture and linen chests; that it waits in bedrooms, cellars, trunks and bookshelves. He knows that a day will come when, for the affliction and enlightenment of men, the rats will run forth again to kill in the happy city.'

'If it is awful to suffer for an idea, it is far worse to suffer without one, which is how most men die,' Elsa said. 'Why does Art attract us so? We gravitate to it like moths to a flame. When Allied planes blasted Goethe's oak in the camp at Buchenwald, the prisoners fought over the splinters, convinced still that they were quick with the spirit of German enlightenment.'

Camus lit a cigarette and told Elsa how he was going to attend Pétain's trial to hear what Paul Reynaud had to say. 'His ephedrine shots are all that keeps the Marshal going now. He is deaf to the voices; he has forgotten his past; history means nothing to him now.'

A gang of *zazous* on bicycles rode by, ringing their bells. The boys wore zoot suits, which had crossed the Atlantic as swiftly as any other uniform. The girls had mops of hair over their brows under large floppy hats. Their *ersatz* plaid skirts were short, and they wore clumsy cork-soled platform shoes. Each of them sported the umbrella that was essential to a *zazou* girl.

'You are as naive as those *zazous* if you think his trial will bring an insight into evil. Evil is not glamorous; not as Olivier plays Richard Crookback.' Elsa drank her coffee. 'Brasillach faced the music, but Maître Isorni feels he can add an inch or two to his stature by saving the Marshal's skin. Is there any defence he can plead, apart from Pétain's senility? In an everyday murder trial, the weapon has a label; of course, there can't be one in Pétain's case. Pétain's *flics* were not acting on their own initiative when they herded the Jews into cattle trucks. The Marshal's trial will not purge the guilt of France.'

* * *

Paul Valéry is dead at the age of seventy-four. There is to be a state funeral. The coffin will proceed with muffled drums through the city. The golden catafalque will lie near the Trocadéro, lit by torches.

> *Refuge, refuge, O, my refuge, O Whirlwind!*
> *I was in, thee, O movement – outside all things . . .*

Matisse speaks the dancer's lines from the end of Valéry's 'Dance and the Soul'. 'If I say that Goya's sleepwalkers had wings,' he continues, 'then I know I am awake. We have an electricity supply this morning. The lift is working again. Who uses the thing so early? It isn't light yet.'

Matisse sits up in bed, sighing relief to find the bedside lamp working. 'It's no good; I can't sleep now. I shall draw myself.'

He makes a crayon sketch first, then pen and ink.

'Tiring as this is, I must put my back into it; as you find out when you learn to row.' He hums to himself. 'Debussy wrote of Stravinsky's *Sacre du Printemps* as primitive, with every modern convenience. Like Stravinsky, I must recycle everything, renew everything, purge one form to create another by oblique cropping that offers revelation. The antics of an acrobat! When it came to artists, Gautier said that he valued acrobats more. Manet, you know, tried to paint like Titian; Van Gogh copied Delacroix. I have seen Picasso sign a canvas with Manet's name.'

'Picasso has been a joker all his life,' Lydia says.

* * *

'Why are we doing this?' Aragon asked.

'We have an invitation from de Lattre, and I want to see first-hand what Hitler has done to Europe,' said Elsa.

Lake Constance, as seen from General de Lattre de Tassigny's speedboat, was a series of picture postcards in the changing light. Aragon and Elsa were at French Army Headquarters at Lindau, where she found de Lattre witty at times, although his vanity was flabbergasting. He wore his medals with the bombast of Othello, and was as boastful about his trade, his seven wounds, his citations. At one time, de Lattre had visited Clemenceau every morning to listen to him abuse Field-Marshal Smuts as the swine who sabotaged the Treaty of Versailles.

Aragon asked de Lattre what had been his role during France's defeat.

'I found myself accused of treachery towards Giraud when I tried to bar the German thrust into the unoccupied zone,' said the General. 'They arrested me and sent me off to the *préfecture*. There, the Mayor embraced me and wept as he locked me up. My men had surrendered, but only after they were cut off and told that I was dead. My sole comfort was to hear that my wife and son had reached Gibraltar. When I escaped from Riom, Pétain had the gall to send his congratulations. I wrote back and told him that the only way he could atone for his treason would be to die as soon as possible.' De Lattre smiled. 'Pétain will not confess his sins. The Marshal explains General Catroux's tit-for-tat dealings with the Japanese. We find that Japan did not invade Indo-China because Catroux banned the transport of American fuel and war supplies across Tonkin. We learn how, with a nod from our ambassador to Tokyo, he sent food and medicine to the Japs in Kwangsi.

'Am I seeing myself in the role of Beau Geste? Do you know that Foreign Legion adventure, written by an Englishman called Wren, whose hero has to redeem his honour after being unjustly accused of stealing a jewel?'

'I see no resemblance to Gary Cooper,' said Elsa.

De Lattre laughed. 'I came across 100,000 F.F.I. men last September;

they signed up for the duration of the war. They were a gang of *clochards* until I got some uniforms from the Yanks. You know, of course, that André Malraux also joined me then? I used his Alsace-Lorraine brigade to take Altkirch. It was a very bloody action. On top of that, he got the telegram telling of Josette's accident. How awful that a pair of *ersatz* shoes should trip her up like that, throwing her under a train, just as the war is about to end. André took it very badly.'

Aragon's army life had taught him when to speak and when to stay silent in the face of a superior officer's boasts. To Elsa, it seemed that he had too much respect for uniforms. She had no such ability or training and relied on her feminine guile to deal with de Lattre. Often there were Americans at the dining-table, too, with whom she could find no rapport. 'Who wants Glenn Miller's orchestra playing among our ruins?' Elsa said. 'Those sickening saxophones are so pompous, so smug! Are they the true voice of America?'

After her first encounters with those strange gods, dirty and unshaven U.S. troops, whose uniforms and shoulder-patches spoke of another universe, the novelty was over. She had eaten and enjoyed the earthly manna of their K-rations – ham and eggs with tin-opener, biscuits, a packet of cereal, powdered coffee, lemonade crystals, cigarettes, chewing gum, and chocolate bars. Those simple pleasures had gone. The Americans were crass and vulgar; they had no culture – not only that, but they barred her and Aragon from entering their zone.

De Lattre said he did not care much for Lake Constance or Switzerland. Every bit of turf they could see had come from Austria by truck. Elsa would have found more to amuse her at his villa outside Algiers; teams of bronzed young men in shorts chasing basketballs. 'De Gaulle was a regular visitor. You would not think that he had spent the war in London, living like a poor relation, such was his mood of expansionism. I did not believe it when he ordered me to take Stuttgart, where he hoped that the Allies would allow him to set up a seat of military government. I agreed with him: France has to recapture her former glory, but Eisenhower was not happy. Devers warned me that he would cut my supplies if I took the city.' De Lattre dismissed this threat with a cheerful smile. 'Forgive me for boring you with my logistical problems.'

'In May, de Gaulle sent me to Berlin. My orders were to insist on the same status as Montgomery when ratifying the surrender document. After a slanging match with the Americans about the aircraft they put at my disposal, I landed to find that nobody expected me. I soon grasped that Marshal Zhukov was humouring de Gaulle by allowing France to sign anything; nor was there a tricolour among the flags of the Allies. I had to send my aides to scavenge for material. They came back with a blue serge rag they'd torn from a mechanic's overalls, a white cloth, and a red piece from a swastika. Some meaty Red Army girls agreed to stitch these together. What they made in the end was a Dutch flag. They had sewn the strips of cloth horizontally. I found this out just before we hoisted the flag.'

* * *

Waving, Lydia drives off along the avenue Secrétan, leaving Marguerite and Matisse at the gateway to the Parc des Buttes-Chaumont.

'We both need a day out, some time together, but don't overdo it,' Matisse warns, as his daughter pushes his wheel-chair. 'You must tell me when you want to rest.'

On his lap is the faded copy of the *Revue Européenne* that includes Aragon's 'A Feeling for Nature at the Buttes-Chaumont'. 'It was Breton who said on impulse that he, Aragon and Marcel Noll should go for a night walk in the park,' he informs Marguerite, pointing to the bridge they are coming to. 'Aragon called it the Mecca of suicides. You can see the rusted iron grille they had to put up to deter people from jumping off.'

They encounter the family sitting around a rough shelter made of branches. A girl is scouring an iron pot by a campfire. Nearby, her brother is splitting willow wands to make pegs. The grandparents sit smoking pipes. Their son is working on a rusty motorcycle and side-car, with a pair of binoculars hung from his neck.

'Who are they?' Matisse asks.

'Gypsies? People with nowhere to live. Displaced persons they call them now; they are survivors.'

'Gauguin's ghost is here.'

'Why do you say that?'

'I don't know; the swarthy creature fixing the bike may perhaps have something to do with it; but what? There are so many stories about Gauguin. Gide was tramping the coast of Brittany, in a bid to dispel his uncertainty about becoming a writer, when he came across Gauguin at Pouldu. Intrigued, Gide took a room for the night at the auberge; but, too timid to intrude, tried to overhear what Gauguin was saying, unaware of who he was. Gauguin always signed on raffish crews: a hunchback, a painter whose costume left no doubt that he could walk on Galilee, and a slut with a monkey. Did you know that he dug part of the Panama Canal?'

A heady scent of cyclamens alerts Matisse to a sudden vision of palms, breadfruit trees, and ferns taller than a man.

'Mango trees, banana trees, and island deities,' he says.

'Your mother was domestic, one could even say menial,' Matisse tells his daughter.

'She did not, like Ibsen's Nora, slam the kitchen door because domesticity and art would not mix.'

'I could not see your mother other than she was. Amélie was an aspiring woman, always at odds with her nature. Did she ever care for my fauve portraits of her, my sense of theatre? No, she put up with my foibles. What would Gauguin have done without Mother Gloanec at Pont-Aven, what would any of us do without such women? Pissarro's wife was a shrew; she hated painters; while Mette Gad was foolish, cold, and self-pitying. She could never come to terms with having married the wrong man. Gauguin's sin in her eyes was to abandon the Bourse. Pissarro couldn't see why Gauguin went to Tahiti. He said it was a stunt. He told me that Gauguin had gone there to cook up a few colourful dishes to satisfy the public's craving for old gods; for the spiritual, which materialism was killing in their lives.'

*   *   *

Elsa soon began to use the phrase that de Lattre's men used to describe him: 'Général Théâtre de Marigny'. What she did not know was that the General was a Parti Communiste Français supporter. She did not learn this until he provided them with a Mercedes and driver to take them on to Germany. After jabs for tetanus, smallpox and yellow fever, they set off to inspect the ruins in the East.

In August, America dropped the first A-bomb and destroyed four square miles of Hiroshima. They visited the same horror on Nagasaki three days later. Elsa began to sleep badly and have nightmares. She was a passenger in a horse-drawn carriage on her way to Prague to meet Hitler. She was shaking so much that the gladioli she was taking to him were quivering. Stopping in a park, the driver gave her his hand to alight, and pointed to a restaurant beside a lake. She set off along a scented tunnel formed by lime trees.

The Führer's uniform was grimy. He was playing chess, one among several old men, silently intent on their own moves. He looked ill and in need of a shave; his eyes were bloodshot. The gladioli were now in a tricolour paper; Hitler took the bouquet like a blind man, handing it to a nurse who stepped smartly out of the shrubbery. She was a stern, grey-haired woman who took off his tunic briskly. 'I will be as gentle as I can, mein Führer', she said; then, slipping off his braces, so that his britches fell round his ankles, she swabbed his rump with antiseptic cotton-wool and took a syringe from a kidney dish on the table. His intake of breath as she injected him made the players look up from their games, shaking their heads and touching their forefingers to their lips.

The odd part came later that same day when Aragon showed her a piece in a newspaper. It said that the Führer was alive. He was living in a small town in Bohemia. This Hitler turned out to be Frantisek Kysparek, a Czech tram conductor.

Aragon laughed. 'Apparently, the German troops had known Kysparek well; they paid him to pose with them for snapshots. When the Gestapo found out, they forced Kysparek to shave his moustache and comb his hair another way; then they jailed him.' Aragon laughed. 'There is a happy ending, though. It seems that Hollywood's talent scouts have put him under contract.'

'I find this story macabre,' Elsa said. 'I feel that the world is going mad. No wonder I have nightmares.'

By four o'clock on 15 August, the verdict on Pétain came; the sentence was death, with a plea for mercy. Two days later, de Gaulle commuted the sentence to life, and the old Marshal left the prison at Portalet for the Île d'Yeu.

*　　*　　*

'I did not know that Proust based his Saint-Loup on Cocteau,' Lydia says.

'Bébé' Bérard, the son of an undertaker and pupil of Vuillard's, had found fame as a stage designer. He is in the news with his costumes for Cocteau's film *La Belle et la Bête*, which Jean Marais is trying on. 'Look at his lacy gloves and fangs.' Lydia hands the magazine to Matisse. 'Can you believe that he spends five hours being made up as the Beast? There are electricity cuts everywhere; they affect Cocteau's schedule, and his cameras are failing suddenly because of their age.'

'Quite heroic, given the state of the country now, don't you think?' Matisse says.

'Do we need a fairy tale with costumes made from old curtains and rags?' Lydia asks.

'Rouveyre says that Jean's eczema is so bad he has to wear a paper mask pinned to his hat. Where does he find the time and energy to rehearse a play and direct a film?'

* * *

There were fewer 'Mines cleared to hedge' signs where the three U.S. Negro soldiers swung their detectors beside the road. Aragon and Elsa passed road gangs filling bomb craters and clearing rubble; there were prisoners spread out across fields, jittery harvesters locating mines. In another field, a woman hauled a plough harnessed beside a bony cow, which a child guided. The military signs that cluttered the telegraph poles showed that they were not far from Berlin. The autumn leaves were falling by the time they reached the city.

After glancing at the headlines in the morning paper, Aragon and Elsa left the Am Zoo Hotel to inspect the ruins of Berlin. The British had allowed the Russians to set up a memorial where one million of their men had died. There were greetings and messages in Russian and English, obscene drawings by men from Bognor Regis, the Urals and Stalingrad who had fought for two years, and survived to scribble their names around the fireplace where Hitler had warmed his arse.

Aragon pointed out Breker's statues in the inner courtyard of the Chancellery; Allied bullets and shrapnel had hit them too.

There were petrol cans in the trench in the Chancellery garden.

'Surely these can't be the same cans they used to douse the bodies,' Elsa said. 'It all seems so unreal.'

Aragon shrugged. 'This is the spot the Russians saw Hitler's corpse.'

'I find it hard to imagine the scene.'

Passing under the Brandenburger Tor they came to the Russian sector. There was a portrait of Stalin in the Ünter den Linden, across from the shell of the Adlon Hotel. In the basement a lone waiter had survived, whose menu now offered high-quality black-market food, which he served up wearing his pre-war black tails. He sent an assistant who wore a blue-spotted bow-tie, a pre-war coat with a fur collar and mittens to barter for him in the Tiergarten, which was in the British zone; a man with a vulpine face, whose grubby shirt often had no collar. It was where Aragon and Elsa met him haggling.

There, GIs traded their Mickey Mouse watches for Russian vodka, since most Ivans were eager to own that emblem of imperialism. Such watches cost the Americans $4, and could fetch $500. It was a barter economy. The German mark was valueless and people dealt in cigarettes, tobacco, chocolate and consumer goods. There was no choice other than to use the black market, to join in the endless hunt for bargains, tripping over the tree stumps left by the battle for the Reich Chancellery.

The Femina Club had a telephone on every table to enable lonely strangers to strike up an acquaintance. When the phone on Elsa's table rang, she heard the voice of the red-haired, two-stripe NCO she would see if she looked to the right of the stage. He had a stammer, but the war had given him the brash assurance that any woman was available if a man had nylons, Camels or Lucky Strikes. He came over to join her, carrying a copy of *Stars and Stripes*, the paper the U.S. Army printed for its troops.

It was raining. To escape the drab ruins of the city for a couple of hours, they went to see Laurence Olivier's *Henry V*. As they gave their tickets to the girl at the door, she craned forward to see a squad of German soldiers march by with their hands clasped on their heads. A pink-faced Russian boy with a tommy-gun escorted them; he waved when he saw her.

There were foul ponds everywhere, the outflow from broken sewers. The air stank of gas leaks, or so they thought until an ageing journalist from *Good Housekeeping* told Aragon that the smell came from rotting corpses, which the rubble women dug up every so often.

Elsa grimaced. 'I don't see how those scarves they tie around their mouths help much.'

The Russians were stockpiling coffins, ready for an increase in the winter death rate. Thousands of those refugees who had walked hundreds of miles to bring their lice from the East, pushing what they had salvaged in their prams and barrows, would die.

Aragon was suspicious of German traffic police. However, there were few of those; the traffic was largely military and policed by Negroes.

* * *

Picasso muses on General MacArthur as the lift takes him up to Matisse's Montparnasse apartment. The General has accepted Japan's surrender aboard the warship *Missouri* in Tokyo Bay, thus wiping out the stigma of

Pearl Harbor and setting the seal on the U.S. victories at Midway and Leyte; America's navy is dominant again in the Pacific.

'So, you are in Paris at last,' Picasso says, as Matisse pours a glass of wine for him. 'De Gaulle is like all our military saviours,' Picasso continues; 'there are more portraits of him than there were of Pétain. All generals are chips off the Boulanger block; they are all murderous prima donnas.' He sips his Calvados with relish. 'Yes, the GIs have chased the Germans away, but they are the sons of those racists who murdered and tortured Cubans when they invaded the island. We can only hope that they persist in growing more ridiculous by the hour, as they are doing. The Americans treated me fine when I was a decadent bourgeois, but I don't sell half what I used to in New York. I am a Communist. Every time I open a cable from a dealer, I know that it will cost me. Of course, you and Braque must be doing all right.'

'Why did you embrace Communism, Pablo?' Matisse asks.

'I said it all in the article in *L'Humanité*. All my friends are Communists. Besides, I was always an agitator. Breton called me a Surrealist in 1925. Two years later, the Surrealists aligned with the Reds. Some things you can't solve by writing them backwards, as in magic. I think it all depends on the weather.' Picasso laughs. 'The Americans don't trust me. They have sent a baby intelligence officer to me. He denies being one, of course. He assures me he is my guardian angel, but I am sure he is an American spy.'

Picasso goes on to recall the self-portrait he did of himself as a new arrival in Paris. 'I wore stout boots; I had my easel under my arm. I had a leather hat – just the thing for Paris! You and I have both lost hair worrying where we were going in our Art. In my old age, I am as famous as the Eiffel Tower now, and my nearness to other Paris landmarks leads every Tom, Dick and Harry to my door. All last year, after the Liberation, they never stopped knocking. Most of them were boys, dumbfounded when I turned out to be the great Picasso their old art teacher had told them about. I was not at all what they expected. I was a dwarf, for a start.'

'You soon got used to it,' Matisse says; 'and, of course, you put them at their ease quickly.'

Picasso laughs. 'I thought that Hitler's vile beliefs would die with him; but no, they chalk my name on walls against which they would like to shoot me. Every day, Vlaminck abuses me for being a degenerate Jew.'

'I never had much time for Vlaminck. I understood why Vollard would not speak to him for six years.'

Picasso nods. 'Did you hear aboout the show Jean Cassou arranged? The École des Beaux Arts students tried to terrorise me; a scum of left-over fascists demonstrated against the paintings. The poison's still there; I had to defend my portraits of Marie-Thérèse and Dora, the painting of my cat killing a bird, my tomato plant.'

'Yes, I read something about it.'

Picasso grins. 'I did my first cut-outs when I was seven years old,' he says; 'you have found the scissors late in life. Let me say that I don't doubt that Amélie and Margot were brave; but I can imagine what it did to you – my God, I'd have pissed down my leg waiting for some Master Race thug to knock on the door. That's no way for a painter to live. I mean, not knowing where the Germans had taken them. You would worry, of course. Margot could always twist you round her little finger.'

'This Neupert had sold my *Harmonie bleue* to a French Jew named Aktuaryus.' Matisse shakes his head. 'Is that a name? Apart from my brush with death, the arrest of Amélie and Marguerite, my war was uneventful; although the Germans did export my *Baigneuses à la tortue* without a licence.' Matisse refills Picasso's glass. 'Degand was here the other day. He tried to discuss spontaneity. I told him that I no longer sought spontaneity. I toiled hard to paint *Le rêve*.' Matisse shows Picasso Lydia's photographs. 'And this *Nature morte rouge au magnolia* took six months to finish.'

Picasso laughs as Matisse shows photographs of the Leda panel. 'Are you sure about this? I can see you are not, since you are having a hard time finishing it. Why do we paint for such people? Only the shits of this world can afford our work.'

During the war, Picasso said, he had tried to see himself as a sailor chasing a red butterfly, or he painted the Seine. Failing that, he might as well have done with it and sketched Marie-Thérèse when she came round for her bag of coal, or Sabartès cutting himself while shaving.

'Some people tell me that truth hides in enigma, but anyone who thinks he can plumb our private lives by brooding on our paintings is a fool. Our canvases are not tarot cards, or tea leaves. We have to cultivate our enigma; we are creators; the enigma is the best shield against calumny and impudence.'

Picasso smiles. 'Has anybody told you about my play? The last act ends

313

with a big golden ball smashing the window and blinding everybody while Big Foot cries, "Light all the lamps! Summon every ounce of strength to hurl flights of doves against the bullets; lock up and bar all the bombed houses!"'

Margot. Litho Essai Septembre 1945

Matisse transfers a portrait of Marguerite to the stone. The Franc-tireur Partisans will sell the lithographs to raise money for the widows of men killed fighting the Germans.

There is also to be an exhibition of those paintings he did during the war years. When Brassaï arrives to photograph him during the *vernissage* at the Grand Palais Salon d'Automne, Matisse invites him to Montparnasse for coffee.

'Take off your coat,' Matisse urges.

Brassaï's hooded eyes are black as sloes, his feline face Semitic. Lydia is curious, but does not ask how he came through the war unscathed. He brings with him a whiff of perfume and opium pipes; his delicate lips are too red to be masculine, Lydia decides.

Matisse laughs. 'You know what the Bal des Quat'z Arts used to be like. I wore my bed sheet as a burnoose. I tied a red cord around my head, and used burnt cork to outline my eyes. I thought I could pass for an Egyptian scribe, whereas I must have looked rather comical. Our Silly-Symphony antics began in the art school courtyard; then we ran pell-mell along the rue Bonaparte. Our maenads were more erotic than the girls of the Folies Bergère. They wore more paint than clothes and could run as fast as any Amazon or Atalante. All our costumes were nominal; some of us had home-made swords, spears and cardboard shields. From the Left Bank we crossed to the place de la Concorde, drunk, howling war cries. Our object was to molest as many willing, or unwilling, girls as we could; to brandish our arms and insult any stuffed-shirt we met.'

*   *   *

Madame Dubois had scant interest in Matisse's paintings, but as the wife of the police official who shielded Picasso during the Occupation, she felt that a visit to the Grand Palais was necessary.

'Whenever I try to relate art to life,' Dubois said, 'I remember Simenon's investigation into the Stavisky affair. He thrilled Paris by listing every suspect and providing evidence for their guilt, yet we did not make one arrest. He had an artist's licence, you see. The artist has a freedom not given to lesser mortals. I think the illusion of freedom is more necessary than ever in the light of Auschwitz and Dachau. These canvases show the life we cannot live; they go against the grain of reality as we know it. We don't want to hear the truth any more. People want to forget the Occupation; they don't want to see their faces in fly-blown mirrors; they want to smell of something sweeter than cabbage soup.'

Dubois smiled. 'We have to forget our everyday world; we have to embrace Matisse's vision. His images devalue by the hour, and they reflect the same ageing process as their creator; but we do not visualise them as being subject to time, especially as we stand in front of them. They have to be eternal; that is their value for us; Picasso, on the other hand, sees Art as a war, an affair of violent skirmishes and feints.'

'Pablo never struck me as much of a family man,' Madame Dubois replied.

For Célimène, the Grand Palais was somewhere to meet her new lover, who was whirling her round Paris for the holiday she deserved. It was her old school-friend, Athalie Tardieu, who had wanted to see the Matisse exhibition.

Athalie and Célimène had time to look at the paintings after an abortive shopping expedition. Célimène said, 'I had a lodger once who could never stop talking about Matisse.'

When her boyfriend Édouard came, she was happy to stay longer, her head nestling on his shoulder as they strolled. Then she saw the actress Maria Casarès, and whispered fiercely:

'You saw her? She looked more beautiful than she did as Nathalie in *Les Enfants du Paradis* that day we went to the Victorine Studios.'

'You've forgotten that you accused me of ogling Arletty's charms too much that day. You hated me saying that she didn't have much in the way of tits for her German flyer to fondle,' said Édouard, laughing.

'My God, just look at that tiny waist! You can see by the way she dotes on him that they are in love. Who is he?'

'Some famished *colon*, evidently, with a skin like that.'

Maria Casarès was with Camus, and what she saw in Matisse's paintings was an eternal echo of the love she felt for Camus.

Lydia went to the Grand Palais alone, wearing a head-scarf and dark glasses. As the mistress with the keys, who advised, arranged, protected, she had done her best to keep the war from Matisse. She had indulged his whims and soothed away his irritation. She was the woman ready with her camera and benzene to rub out one reality so that he could substitute another.

It was difficult for her to imagine Russia's plight, those hordes of fatherless children. The destruction was worse than that left by the Thirty Years' War. Across vast tracts nothing stood upright except the broken chimneys where a village had been. The Germans had cut down every telegraph pole, along with any wood that might shelter partisans. The Red Army, led by Zhukov, Timoshenko and Tulbukhin, had driven out the invader. Lydia was proud that her countrymen had defended Henri Matisse's paintings with their blood. Lydia was about to leave when she caught a glimpse of the art critic, Jean Cassou. He had not recognised her and seemed lost in thought.

Matisse's paintings were reminding him of his time in prison. In Toulouse, as Jean Noir, he had dreamed the death of dreams in his *Sonnets written in Solitary Confinement*. Matisse had left the war out of his canvases; and Cassou never used the word 'prison' in his sonnets. He had even made a translation of Hofmannsthal's 'Die Beide'. There were no lice, dirt or bedbugs, and no hunger. Cassou escaped his dark solitary confinement by creating poems in his head, or longing for the food parcels his wife would bring.

* * *

Franco did not want Laval, so the Ju-88 flew to Linz, where he surrendered to the Americans. They drove him to Innsbruck to hand him over to the French Army, which flew him to Paris and thence to Fresnes.

Like Amélie Matisse, Madame Laval found herself in the women's section, grieving that it was the first time she did not have Pierre with her. She had always been afraid that her husband would go too far and ruin her and Josette. 'He had more regard for stud horses and bulls' semen than international affairs,' she said bitterly.

At Pétain's trial, Sadoul told Aragon, one *flic* after another quizzed his pass before he got into the Courts of Justice. The Marshal feigned sleep, deaf to what Laval was saying to defend him. Perhaps the treachery of the crowd who stoned his train at Pontarlier had shocked him into silence. His Cagoulard bodyguards could no longer shield him – yet his jeopardy did not seem to have sunk in. The empty rhetoric he had made use of since Verdun, all through the Vichy years, had gone. There was no way to excuse his part in genocide; with senility had come silence. Only his one-time junior officer, de Gaulle, could save his skin.

'Laval stood with his hand in his pocket as he addressed the court on Pétain's behalf. A cheap Forum touch that made the photographers jostle each other to get close-ups. The women kept up with every word on their machines; as soon as he had done, he left the court as though the guard with the sten-gun had no business at his side.'

'When Laval ran the railways, he made sure that there was a bottle of La Sergental on every table in the dining-cars,' Sadoul said.

'Some of the Surrealists swore by it; they said a glass of it would make your prick stand all night,' Aragon said. 'We never did get a public inquiry when pollution affected the springs.'

'A trifle, in the light of what he did later for France,' Sadoul said with a laugh.

Sadoul said that Bonnat's florid ceiling painting brought to mind Marie Antoinette's trial.

Aragon told him how Degas and Bonnat met on the *impériale* at the turn of the century. They talked about artists whose work they admired, and realised that they shared the same tastes. Degas could not fathom why, given Bonnat's style.

Sadoul laughed. 'I did understand why you were so keen on the *impériale* as a metaphor, but the bus belongs to the past. It started life at the Exhibition.'

The White Elephant's Nightmare

Simone asks Matisse to lean his head back, leaning over with drops to treat his eyes. 'Open wide, Your Excellency,' she orders. 'There, that will soon make you feel better.'

'A blessed relief,' he admits, blinking.

He sees her as a blurred shape. As his vision clears, he looks round the room. 'Every artist comes to terms with perspective, or he rejects it. I make an effort to think of the sum of particles in the universe, then see my paintings as a crude translation of some of them. I can't see nature often in this way; it is hard to visualise the universe as Einstein did. I cannot change my practices. There is no escape from representation, with all its fictive demands; even though I might end up with a pink or red studio in the end, using subtle hues to define the spatial element.'

'Do you suppose Simone gives a fig for your metaphysics?' Lydia asks.

'Quite often, it is the quest for a fruitful error that leads to the truth. Satie knew that. I saw him as the master of volcanoes, he never used water when he washed; he scrubbed himself with a pumice stone. For

Socrate, Satie culled the account of Socrates' suicide from the *Phaedrus* and the *Phaedo*.'

The girl grins, pretending not to know who Socrates was.

Matisse wags a reproving finger. 'Satie's ballet *Parade* was the first to make use of real sights and sounds. The score called for sirens, typewriters, a dynamo, an express train, an aeroplane, Morse code and a lottery-wheel. The dancers mimed everyday occupations. It opened at a Sunday fair; a Chinese conjuror, an American girl and two acrobats were romping outside a tent in an attempt to lure an audience inside. The managers of these acts failed to convince the crowd that they are not the real show.'

'Everything was a fairy tale in those days, on stage and off,' Simone says. 'You are very old, Monsieur Matisse; you don't realise that things have changed.'

'You mean I'm out of date.'

'I didn't say that.'

Matisse can hear the Pentecostal bells of Notre-Dame. Below, a Sunday painter dabs at a canvas near the Pont Neuf, his suit as natty as any Landru wore. He tilts his bowler hat and steps back to view his efforts. 'What is a Sunday painter?' Matisse says aloud. 'When we start, we are all Sunday painters: Gauguin was one, Douanier Rousseau another – certainly the best known. My father is dead, and I have just come home from Seville, where I froze my brain.' He purses his lips. 'I share the fears that pharaohs had; I dream the same dreams that pharaohs had; never forget, young woman, that elephants have nightmares too.'

* * *

The charge against Laval was that of plotting against state security and having intelligence with the enemy. He had also failed to create a government in exile in North Africa. His attorneys refused to conduct a defence, on the grounds that the state wanted a swift verdict. The president of the court, Mongibeaux, had no control; he failed to censure the jury when some of them abused Laval, and he found fault with everything Laval said. When Laval shouted for a swift verdict of guilty, Mongibeaux ordered the guards to remove him. Somebody in the audience began to applaud Laval, which caused an uproar. 'Arrest him!' one juryman cried; 'give him twelve bullets!' howled another.

By the next day, Laval realised that the court had no time for his plea of the double game strategy, a defence strategy he had dreamed up in exile to pass the time at Sigmaringen Castle. He told the president that, since every question already had an answer, it would be as well for the serene majesty of the law to leave it at that. Mongibeaux was angry. Did that mean the accused thought he had impunity? No, Laval did not think he had impunity, but there was a truth and justice above, and which Mongibeaux ought to embody. Such insolence made a juryman roar that Laval would have justice.

Mongibeaux said that the high court would have the last word. Laval told him to keep it. To Mongibeaux, this meant a refusal by Laval to answer any more questions. Laval said he would not, in view of the court's aggressive attitude and Mongibeaux's mode of questioning. Mongibeaux adjourned the hearing, ordering Laval removed, as the same angry juryman screeched, 'It's you, Laval, you are the cause of all the trouble! Swine! Give him twelve bullets! He hasn't changed!'

Laval did not flinch; shaking his head, he said he would never change. Mongibeaux was on his feet, waving his arms. 'Please! This is not some public meeting!'

Laval smiled. 'The jury – before a verdict – it's fantastic!' This so incensed a juryman that he blurted out that France had already judged Laval.

Sadoul said that the Laval trial was beginning to trouble him. 'A guilty verdict is going to rebound on us.'

'You think the Party can halt this farce,' Aragon said. 'Go and upbraid Mongibeaux about it!'

'The Party could question the dubious legality of the business.'

'Any form of words I found to defend Laval would choke me before I uttered them,' Aragon said.

Mongibeaux declared Laval unworthy, ordered the seizure of his goods and condemned him to national odium. He summed up his crimes and added, 'For these reasons, and in view of articles 87 and 75 of the penal code and the ordinance of November 1944, this court sentences you to death.'

Sadoul shook his head. 'Is everybody going mad? I hear that Malraux is to write propaganda for de Gaulle.' He laughed. 'Do you think he will be more a man of the people than Giraudoux?'

'Is that important? We're not fighting a war. Under his Nemo mask, he has always been de Gaulle's man; a crook who is a sucker for old values and loyalty. André will deplore the need to act in our present climate, but I feel sure his scruples will not prevent him from carrying out his duties rigorously. Anyway, we are all de Gaulle's creatures now.'

Why, Elsa wrote to Aragon, had Mauriac chosen the day that Pierre Laval came to trial to resign from the Front in protest at the purges? She reminded him of her prescience in Tavernier's kitchen.

Elsa's book of short stories, *Le premier accroc coûte deux cents francs*, had won the Prix Goncourt. The title story was about the night she and Aragon attended the parachute drop. She had re-read the piece, and found the event so remote that it might have happened to someone else.

Every night, she voyaged back to Tahiti, as Anne-Marie in *Les Fantômes armés*.

* * *

Picasso made a quick sketch of a flamenco dancer on his napkin and handed it to the waiter. 'You are going to question me, Dubois; or do you think I will confess?'

'Your politics are not my concern,' said Dubois. 'You know as well as I do how people will not see eye to eye now. They are free.'

Picasso grinned. 'Is our century heading somewhere at last? That's the only worthwhile question. I am joyful now. I feel as I did when my father took me to see my first bullfight: those humbling rites, that need to watch my mouth in case I ruined the matador's luck. We spent the morning with the breeder talking about what his bulls could do in the afternoon. I watched the awesome ceremony of the matadors donning their suits of light. Soon, they would drag the carcass out of the arena. Listen! Don't you hear the nightingales singing? Don't you know what the guitar is saying?'

Dubois smiled. 'I don't see what this bullfight mumbo–jumbo has to do with you joining the Communist Party.'

'Manet did not know the first thing about bullfights, either,' Picasso said. 'That did not stop him painting them. If you want to find a jewel or a gold nugget, you have to dig out tons of earth. Even then, more often than not, what you will have found is fool's gold, or the false dawn of a fake revolution.'

Dubois lit a cigar. 'Madame Valland bluffed her way into the Einsatzab Rosenberg,' he told Picasso. 'She sent crates everywhere except Berlin. She had files on all the art works and every Einsatzab employee. In the closing stages, she helped the railmen thwart the Germans' attempt to get art treasures out of France.'

'I hope Dominguez's name was on her list. Oscar dined out at my expense all through the war by copying my paintings and selling them to the *boches*. He had the gall to tell me that forgery was his contribution to the war effort.'

Dubois brought their coats, and helped Picasso into his. 'My boss, Luizet, went to Fresnes, along with the judges, and other officials who were there to make it look good. He told me that Laval's lawyers got there in time to find that their client had taken cyanide. Apparently his wife stitched the stuff into his coat early in the war. It failed to kill him; either he hadn't shaken the phial, or it had been there too long. After two hours with a stomach pump, the doctor revived him enough to face the firing squad. Laval was with Naud and Baraduc when they came out. The warders had tied him to a chair to carry him; he had no shoes, a raging thirst, and vomited everything he drank. The firing party tied his hands, despite his plea to die with dignity. They had all been primed with rum. As the order came to fire, Laval tried to stand, a comic stage-turn whose arse has stuck to a chair, shouting "*Vive la France*". The prison was in an uproar. It's always the same, no matter who is being executed.'

*　　*　　*

The tyre of Denoël's Peugeot had punctured, making him stop on the corner of the boulevard des Invalides and the rue de Grenelle. Jeanne Loviton went to use the telephone at the *préfecture*; when she came back, she found Denoël dead, shot in the back.

The police stood with their thumbs in their belts, not even searching the street for a cartridge case. The officer Aragon spoke to about the business said it was either a crime of passion, or if the *fifis* had done it, they had taken their time.

Aragon wondered whether he should tell Elsa about the murder. He took her letter from his pocket, and picked up the thread again

. . . As you know, geraniums grow everywhere as though nothing else happened, and bridge parties still meet in the hotels. Gold is still abundant in some churches, and there are intact fortresses, steep crags, waterfalls, sombre pine forests, and those deep, blue, motionless lakes. I meet Germans who have never seen an Allied bomber – but yes, they say, they heard them go over at night.

There are people living near the railheads and camps whose domestic power supply would ebb when the crematoria started up each morning. The ashes from the camp ovens fell white on their front lawns. Yet they insist they didn't know what was going on, and they tell you with pride that they were acting

Shakespeare, even during the Allied air raids. No doubt Schiller's translation made them feel that Shakespeare was German.

The train arrives at Nuremberg, and there is nothing left of the platform except a slab of paving. It is cold; the sky is leaden blue; snow is on the way again. I shiver with the fat man who told me he worked for British Movietone News as we travelled together. He blows his red nose, and informs me that one of the last 1000-plane bomber raids of the war had done for the city.

The reporters, newsreel crews and Reuters men, have their headquarters in Schloss Stein, a big castle outside Nuremberg. They have their food free, but they pay for the booze that the Americans supply. It is the home of Baron Faber, the pencil manufacturer, whose factory is unscathed.

Nuremberg has gone; everything is rubble, apart from the Palast Hotel Fürstenhof and the Opera House, which is a cinema now for Allied troops. Even the Hotel Fürstenhof has a crater at its centre, so that you have to cross a plank to go from one wing to another, past a tarpaulin that hides holes in the walls. The purified drinking water comes in bags, which hang in the corridors.

The Palace of Justice on the Fürtherstrasse, which used to be the regional appellate court, is another building left standing. A bomb hit it, but the Americans fixed the damage very quickly. The British judges arrive there in bullet-proof cars. They have an escort of a military police jeep and two armed motorcyclists. Sometimes a Sherman tank is guarding the building; more often, there is an armoured car, with guards checking all credentials.

When you enter the courtroom, the thoughtful Americans hand you a seating plan and an outline of the career of each of the defendants. The court is full: there are numerous lawyers, interpreters, the press, and throngs of visitors. Only the Russian judges wear uniforms; the British and Americans are in civilian dress. The dock is large. The lift, which brings two guards and one defendant, reaches the small door at the back. The prisoners come up in order of precedence – Goering first; then, after he takes his seat, comes Hess's monkish bald patch, with its scurf. After due process, you know that many of these men will die.

The Germans have kept records of everything they did. The prosecution lawyers have stacks of these documents, which they read out to prove what the Nazi state machine was doing. The defendants remain impassive. Some listen more than others, some will show a small spasm of anger occasionally, but for the most part they look as bored as the guards, who, because they lack earphones, understand nothing.

I sit to the right of the dock – perhaps seven yards – from the accused. Sometimes, when I take off my earphones, I hear blasts of jazz whenever the courtroom door opens. They are from the radios of the American guards. When

I am not masquerading as a reporter, I sit at the far end of the courtroom and overlook the dock. There are about 150 seats. I put on the earphones, and tune in to a French or Russian translation of proceedings. If I want Goering in German, I turn the dial to Speaker and hear his voice coming over the earphones. The eight judges all have their own sets.

It is this simultaneous interpretation that makes everything drag so; even the cross-examinations are boring. The Allies deem translating to be so stressful that interpreters do not do it more than a few hours. There is a system of lights: a yellow one that sets a slower pace, and a red one that brings the hearing to a temporary halt. It is easy to tell when an interpreter is about to fail; he begins to slow down, then to stammer and make errors, so I wait for Lord Justice Lawrence's red light to come on. It means the trial will stop to allow the back-up team of interpreters to take over.

They call the American case the 'common plan'. Its focus is the history of Hitler's regime. Britain is in charge of Hitler's aggression and the Third Reich's treaty violations. The Russians cope with crimes against humanity in the U.S.S.R. and Eastern Europe, while the French are prosecuting war crimes in the West. It seems that the lawyers had problems to start with; those who came from the civil law countries, France and Russia, had trouble with lawyers who came from the common law countries, Britain and the United States. Under the civil law a person cannot take the oath and testify on his own behalf, but he has that right under the common law. He can make an unsworn statement at the end of his trial under the civil law, and say whatever he wants. To iron out these anomalies, they will allow the accused to do both: they can testify under oath, and will be able to make an unsworn statement when the trial ends.

The house where Albrecht Dürer was born is a ruin. Not far away, a British plane hangs in the rafters of a church; the pilot's body is still in the cockpit. It will stay there until they can clear more rubble and bring it down for burial.

Eating in the Hotel Fürstenhof, I see people pass by outside with their carts, searching for wood to burn. Hundreds of women with small children cook every day on open fires in the ruins. Such a spectacle makes it hard for me to swallow food.

Then, later, at the long bar adjoining the Marble Room, officers joke about Julius Streicher's sexual tastes. One of these men, who has access to Streicher's pornographic collection, passes around postcards he has pilfered. There are various rumours, myths and gossip about all the prisoners. Next door, a German band plays jazz. The waiters grovel and ingratiate. I prefer the old woman who hawks out-of-date maps by the door of the dining room; she has a friendly greeting for everybody. There is also a ghastly cabaret I cannot bear.

Germans clowning and fawning to earn enough to feed themselves; the acts are more awful than our Farcy woman. However, there is nowhere else to go at night to find electricity.

Goering is a lord of the jungle still; everything centres on him. He keeps his fellow war criminals in line by bullying. He is no longer the big fat man; his gabardine, pearl-grey uniform, shorn of his old insignia and medals, hangs off him. He looks soft and venal, hermaphroditic even, yet his order to Heydrich set in motion the extermination of the Jews. I have to keep reminding myself that he is a thief who stole treasures from every art gallery in Europe.

Hess is a madman. A psychiatrist studies him every day, making notes about his behaviour. Keitel and Jodl sit upright, very Prussian in army uniforms, ready to defend their honour to the death, while Doenitz and Raeder are in civilian dress.

Goering pretends that he does not speak English. I suppose it's a ploy to give him time to weigh his replies. You see him smile long before the interpreter finishes. Even behind his dark glasses, I know when he is looking at me. When the Reichsmarschall looks at a woman, she knows he has only one thing in mind; his gaze is openly lecherous, as he grins and nudges his cronies.

Hess clenches his fists, grimacing in pain; his eyes blaze in dark sockets under bushy brows that jut from his chalky brow. He is suffering with stomach cramps. After a whispered word to his defence counsel, he leaves with a guard. An hour later he comes back to cross his arms and doze; or open a book he carries with him. If you can believe this, he pores over Edgar Wallace, when he is not reading Grimm's Fairy Tales.

Leni Riefenstahl has her special camera in the courtroom to film the gods' twilight. My Movietone friend is very envious of this machine, he tells me that the reels are thousands of feet long, so intent is she on capturing every scene and word of the tribunal.

Somebody described Alfred Rosenberg's The Myth of the Twentieth Century as the Nazis' bible. I find that trite. It is the wild farrago of an asylum crank, nothing but a tome full of raving platitudes. He believes that it is women's nature to delight in the spinning-wheel and loom. The son of the Estonian shoemaker sits where he belongs, next to Frick and Frank, both loathsome men.

Speer and Schacht are alert. They have their wits about them. Every so often, they scribble some pedantic note and pass it along the line to the interpreters. You can tell that Doctor Hjalmar Horace Greeley Schacht, ex-President of the Reichsbank, feels that he should not be in the dock with a man like Kaltenbrunner, who hung men on meat hooks. After all, Schacht survived the camp at Dachau, sent there for his part in the bomb plot against Hitler.

After I glimpse the families of the defendants on their way to visit them, I become fascinated by the wives. I find myself imagining how easy it would be for Frau Goering to help her husband commit suicide. All she need do when visiting him would be to pass a cyanide capsule into his mouth as they kissed. I feel the comfort of the capsule, like a sweet. In the same way, one evening I found myself trailing Frau Louise Jodl through the snow to the ruin where she lives, wanting to question her about her devotion. Nothing came of this ridiculous urge.

I lie in bed shivering now, as I try to write some lines towards Les Fantômes armés. *There is a summary of the day's events in court on my Philco radio, which the Americans broadcast nightly, as a lesson for the German people.*

Aragon was with Yvonne Devignes, listening to two crippled children with accordions fill the narrow street with a bravura tune. 'Anybody who thinks he can find the soul of France these days will have a hard job,' Aragon said. '*Collabos* everywhere are busy with false narratives that hide their past; they will emerge as heroes, not the thieves and liars of the Occupation. Just as the *flics* from the guard towers at Drancy flaunt medals for bravery, having joined the rising at the last gasp. Small beer, you say; yes, we have no notion yet how vicious monopoly capitalism is going to be, now that it has the power of the universe at its disposal; although the destruction of Dresden, Hiroshima and Nagasaki should give us an idea.'

'The Communists have the largest party in the Assembly,' Yvonne said. 'You have a million members, and your newspaper has the biggest circulation in Paris; you should be ecstatic.'

'I hate Péret, living in Mexico throughout the war, for calling my poems "dishonourable". He is a long way from Catalonia.'

'Not having read his pamphlet, I guess that he misses Surrealism, and is up against a blank wall.'

'You're right; Péret isn't the cause of my grief. On the face of it, history would seem to be on the side of Communism. It's a personal flaw. I hate to admit to it, but I'm weary; these days I'm feeling high and dry, even though, in my dreams, I hear Dante and Petrarch's voices. I am dumb. Don't all of us become the man we hated when we were growing up?' He sighed. 'I have wasted my life tinkering: patching here, tacking there, having to make do with the sham. I hate these purges that we know will not purge. Wrathful Françoise is no longer in hiding. My secret war is over; no more the import and export of contraband poetry. Other perverts thrash the Montmartre girls that Herr Dannecker used to whip.

Other politicians are dolling themselves up for the Musée Grévin. They concoct Christmas messages to deliver in Pétain's stead. One war is over, but others are in the making. Yet I stay as upright as a diver in my orange suit, bubbling in a fish-tank. What can I do? Gossip says I was born a prince, with an odour of religion, a smell of denial; but that I have foolishly tampered with that side of myself. I have forfeited my inheritance to shine Stalin's boots, and live with the threat of a good kick up the arse now and then.'

Yvonne said, 'I don't know what it is that you hope for from Stalin. He will never call for a second French Revolution.'

'Not after killing off the Comintern. Every night now, I dream that when day dawns there will have been a right-wing coup.'

'We don't live in Ruritania.'

Aragon stood up, glancing at his watch before leaving. 'It took radical thinking to reveal the law of gravity, yet it was obvious whenever an apple fell off a tree. Now we can only grasp the theory of relativity by discarding old norms. Dialectical materialism ruled my life before I knew, or could accept, that it did. I was an acolyte for a long time before I learned to write:

> '*My comrades gave me back my eyes and my memory*
> *I had forgotten what every child knew:*
> *That my blood was red and my heart was French*
> *I knew only that the night was black*
> *My Party gave me back my eyes and my memory.*'

Pierrot's Funeral

Matisse picks up the telephone, expecting to hear Lydia's voice, but it is an American woman who asks whether she can visit him before she leaves Nice. 'My name is Phaedra Clergue. Before the war I worked in the New York art market, which was how I met your son Pierre. I got your Cimiez address from him before shipping out for Europe. When I phoned the Régina, they gave me your number in Vence.'

Matisse shakes his head, reflected in the mirror. 'This is not a good time. I do not feel up to seeing anybody. Tomorrow, perhaps.'

'Tomorrow will be too late, I fly to America.'

Despite feeling suddenly lost without Lydia, Matisse finds himself agreeing to her visit.

The Negro stops the olive-green car by the gate and helps a woman with a walking-stick up the path to the house. She wears dark glasses, and an expensive fur hides a lieutenant's uniform. Half-way up the steps, she waves her driver away with a token salute.

Matisse reaches the door as she is about to knock.

She takes his hand. 'I felt I'd never meet you, unless I saw you today. My first idea was flowers, which seemed the wrong thing to give an invalid. I know you are a cigarette smoker, but I hope these will please you.' She hands him a box of cigars. 'They are okay?'

Matisse shakes his head, not knowing what to say. 'They are fine, except you have been extravagant.'

'I charmed a four-star general who works for the Art Looting Investigation Unit of the U.S. Office of Strategic Services.'

'That sounds very grand.'

'Sure, but it's nothing I can talk about.'

Matisse snips the Havana, and leans forward to meet her offer of a light. 'If people smoked Virginia tobacco or drank Indian tea during the war, you could guess that they were friends of friends who met R.A.F. planes in country fields.'

'Call me Phaedra,' she insists. 'It was my birthday yesterday. I almost told you that when I phoned, but I decided you might think I was trying to twist your arm.' Ill-at-ease, she tears a scrap of paper into smaller and smaller pieces, staring at herself in the mirror. Tossing the scraps into an ashtray, she stubs out her cigarette. 'Now that I am here, I don't know what to say; I don't know what tone of voice to use.'

'You must speak as you feel,' Matisse urges.

Phaedra was in Nice to rest after medical treatment. A Messerschmitt had strafed her car. It was not a serious wound, but it had become infected after an operation. She hoped that the limp was not permanent. She moves to the window, standing with her hands in her jacket pockets to watch the wind lash the palm fronds. 'James Joyce said that history was a nightmare. You feel that strongly when you land in Europe. There have been too many assembly-line murders here.'

Trying to shake off her mood, she says she has a camera with her and would Matisse mind if she took some photographs. After a few attempts, she gives up, saying, 'I'm doing this badly,' and runs her fingers through her hair distractedly. 'I'm just an all-American girl, but I am ageing.' She sighs. 'Ah, the bitter-sweet taste of what it was like to be young, and young sexually. An age of ruins and firing squads is all that youth can look forward to now. Van Gogh used to fret about finding the heat to melt the gold. He said that he painted to make his life bearable. Is that true also of your work? How do I find a way back into the world you paint? Help me to come home. Tell me about your sleight-of-hand with eternal truths. I came here to trace art treasures looted by the Germans. What I learned was that art has no relevance now. We live in a crazy world that gets crazier by the hour – with slaughterhouses everywhere; jitterbugs and zoot suits, and the mass graves of children. We have neon; we have rivers; we have graveyards. What am I to do? Study medicine? Is medicine better than charming snakes in the art market?'

'The United States is going to bring Coca-Cola to Europe in a big way. America will make you rich, Monsieur Matisse. Art dealing in Paris was always a cottage industry, with the Steins arbitrating taste, making and breaking reputations. That bohemian idyll is dead. When New York becomes the art capital of the world, things will be more business-like; your son knows that. Like any other market commodity, art will sell.'

For someone with her background, it irks him that she shows so little interest in his recent paintings. Each time she speaks, he foresees a daunting future. He has a sense of being on trial, quite as much as any Vichy collaborator, and feels that she equates him with France. It is not something he can put his finger on, but everything she says suggests that he is living out a life-time of error.

Is he going to be ill? It is hard to know why this woman has such an effect on him. Is this how Marat felt when Charlotte Corday surprised him in his bath?

As he dips his pen into the ink, he sees it as an act of self-defence; he begins to sketch her.

It is five o'clock. The sky is darkening.

Phaedra is using the bathroom when the telephone rings. It is Lydia. 'You sound so far away,' he says. 'I need you here.'

Lydia feels his disquiet. 'What is wrong? Are you feeling bad?'

He gives way to the conviction that he is a prisoner, and says, 'Come as quickly as you can,' putting down the receiver as Phaedra returns.

'Harlequins, saltimbanques, street performers – they were dying out long before Picasso began to paint them,' Matisse says, nodding for her to light his fresh cigar.

Phaedra smiles. 'While you were selling the myth, even after the carnage of World War I, that there were golden-age men and women who lay around in the nude eating acorns and berries, reigned over by the good housewife Ceres – isn't that right?'

Matisse demurs, making a tacit wave of the hand. 'The artist finds his own road through the intensity of his quest, after he tears out the eyes of other painters from his head. There are years of darkness, then he sees the light again.'

What is Lydia doing? Why is she so late?

'I have always known the gift of ownership, and I want to share my treasures with the world.'

'Don't you think the fact that we would all like to be part of something private is one of the chief attractions of your paintings?' Phaedra adds that a friend had taken her to see *La danse* at Merion.

'You did not get a letter of refusal from Barnes's dog, Fidèle, then?' Laughing, Matisse goes on to speak with regret of his mural. 'Catalan fishermen danced the *sardane* on the beach at Collioure. My painting was as public as their dance, yet Doctor Barnes was jealous of his Ali Baba cave. I had the magic Sesame, but the armed guards used to depress me. There were no armed men in Moscow at Shchukin's Trubetskoy Palace, which was open every Sunday.'

'Armed guards have been watching over art ever since the public outcry over Manet's *Olympia*.'

Matisse agrees. 'Barnes's collection was homely in a jigsaw fashion. You could see African and Oceanic art, medieval treasures, next to some superb Renaissance paintings and Modiglianis.' He sniffs.

'Citizen Kane's Xanadu.'

'Oh yes, I see what you mean.' Matisse laughs. 'As soon as I saw the lunettes, I knew I was in trouble. My first reaction was that the colour of the sky and garden would serve to balance the chromatic scale of my mural. I went to Padua to see Giotto's frescoes again, then to Milan for Leonardo's *Last Supper*. *La danse* was the biggest thing I had tried. I taught myself to use a long bamboo rod, with charcoal tied to the tip. It was like the rod with which servants lit the candles on chandeliers. I hired Goyo, a house painter, to cover large sheets of paper with Linel colours. Leaving him to paint, and Lydia to pin the shapes on the sketch, I used to stroll with my dog in the rue Désiré-Niel. Not far away, there was an arcade with a shooting gallery, where I would unwind. I was working on the illustrations to Mallarmé, so I needed Lydia Delectorskaya. What would my life be without Lydia's labours on behalf of my art?

'I packed the three canvases to take to America. The dollar was falling, so I cabled Barnes to send the last payment in francs. I got to New York in mid-May. Pierre gave me a lift to Merion the next day, where I had a row with Barnes over the stretching and placing of the canvases. I suppose I had a heart attack; but it was not serious. I was unhappy, tired, worried that Barnes would not like the work. After a whisky, I rested for an hour or so; but there was still an atmosphere. You say you have never met the Doctor? He grew rich from selling Argyrol; a silver compound used as an antiseptic in the treatment of the eye and the nasal passages. The story is that he found it when seeking a cure for his gonorrhoea. It became widely used to prevent blindness in new-born children. I don't know whether it was Barnes or his German partner, Hermann Hille, who made the discovery. Barnes went to law to prove it was his, then sold it with fervour. In later life, he could wallow in his philanthropy and bad temper; an amateur painter, he went on to become an art collector. He was clumsy, bossy and used to ghost-write abuse. As I say, he used his dog as his secretary. All his friends came under fire, sooner or later. He had lofty notions about saving the American Negro. People said that the reason why he got on with dogs and Blacks was that he could not see them as equals. Sometimes he donned overalls and scrubbed floors so as to hear what visitors said about his collection; if they were not enthusiastic, he would throw them out.'

'Mauclair said that my odalisque paintings had the "decor of shabby Turkish baths, stupid faces and inaccurate anatomy". During the years of my *Mille et une nuits*, my model, and my mistress, was Henriette Darricarriere.' Matisse knows that he is boasting now.

'Some people think of that period as an endless Shéhérazade filibuster to postpone death,' Phaedra says.

'Henriette was nineteen when we met. She was a dancer. We were happy until my wife chose to return to live in Nice. I left for Tahiti. As soon as I came home again, I found Clariette, another dancer. Amélie suffered from a spinal disorder. I was in a process of unlearning, after which I learned to live with my repetitions. I imagine that my dancers were a subconscious prelude to *La danse*.'

Despite his vision of future art as a collective activity (he hoped that his murals for Barnes showed that), Matisse has never sought to be a popular artist; that it had happened in some ways did not escape him, and things only ever worsened.

'Your dancers are alone in the abyss. None of them shows any signs of being with the others. You know we are alone; despite what we may try to imagine to the contrary.'

'Who are you?' Matisse asks. 'I could deal with you, if you were here to interview me.'

'I am not your Queen of the Night; but a near relation, I guess. I am a fan of Charlie Parker and Billie Holiday, so you can guess I need the sublime in my life; not a quality many people want, these days.' She shows Matisse a snapshot of her mother in a white straw hat, holding a bouquet of wild flowers; of herself when she ran the High School paper. 'For years, I could not defend my roots. I was busy trying to escape a life I saw as a prison. I taught myself everything I know.'

Merion was the fate of art when it became the prey of private collectors. Matisse had been at the mercy of collectors from the start. On the other hand, Phaedra could see Matisse's colours, his arabesques, reds and blacks, yellows and purples, being used in fabrics, curtains and wall coverings. American production methods were going to kill off his precious art; America would tame his art for mass consumption. 'Everything is going to become a copy of a copy; your singularity will cease; your patrician authority will become a thing of the past.' In part, she based her augury on Duchamp's theories. Matisse's only solace would be that he would not be alone; the same thing would happen to his friends.

Toulouse-Lautrec had not limited his colours to those found in nature; but she thought his great achievement had been to introduce art into the realm of mechanical reproduction. Lautrec could paint, he could draw, he had ability in abundance; yet it was the popular art form of the Japanese wood-block print that drew him into advertising tobacco and cabaret.

'More people see reproductions of my work than the originals,' Matisse says. 'I do not know how it could be otherwise.'

'Why did you come?' Matisse stares at Phaedra. 'I am too old to allow your message to upset me. What did you think I could say to you?'

'You want me to go? Pity. I should have liked to have stayed longer. I think we have more to discuss.' She smiles. 'Picasso told me that there is only one Matisse. That's not true. There are many facets to Matisse, and few people know them all.'

Matisse smiles. 'Picasso's hat always hid a rabbit, a red ribbon or a lightning sketch. His nickname for Braque was "My dear Wilbur". Why? Wilbur Wright's machine flew because he made it with canvas and piano wire. Picasso said that he and Braque were clowns in the same circus; both he and Braque used canvas and were intrepid aerial performers.'

Matisse finds the hypodermic syringe Phaedra used in his bathroom; he drops it into the waste basket, wiping the fog from the mirror. He is unhappy that she had to inject herself in his house, the ante-room to paradise. It could have been that she was in pain, but he suspects that her need for drugs has nothing to do with her war wound. He can remember his own morphine-induced lethargy, the easing of pain.

'Nuremberg is a banal ritual of erasure; a factual accounting that fails to explain anything,' Phaedra says. 'We are not seeking an answer to the war; we would rather buy the lie of the unspeakable evil of the Germans. It is easier than facing our own guilt. Our avenging angels ought to bring pictures of their Nagasaki atrocities to court: those thermal heat prints that were all that remained of women and children after the blast, those shadows in the dust. The survivors – men, women and children – had black, flayed skins that hung in bloody tatters from their flesh.'

Matisse shakes his head. He can think of nothing to say, other than that he has to struggle to find the strength to take up his brush each morning and start again, painting the same objects in the room.

'Friday is always a bad day. I feel fragile. I had to use your bathroom, you know; I can't get by otherwise.' Phaedra looks at her watch. 'That's my driver back.'

The jeep's headlights shine in the road below.

A shutter bangs in the wind. The moon appears briefly and fades again behind racing clouds, over the lights of Saint-Paul. Her syringe means nothing; she steps out into the dark, hesitates as though she has lost something, as the wind wafts her perfume.

'The essence of my art is pleasure; and that is the only future I can envisage for myself and for the world,' Matisse says. 'I did not disembark at Aden, even in my dreams; I felt no urge to travel to Harare via Djibouti. My journeys into Africa took me only as far as I wanted to go. I never had a shipwreck, faced no catastrophe – there were only some strange windows opening on unfamiliar landscapes. I changed little – maybe I should have changed more, called perhaps for a dish of figs and a green spear. I loved to listen to the native musicians, the rattle of dry seeds in a gourd, envying their ability to coax a droning yet complex music from one or two strings. Maybe, my life – my art – has been the result of a similar dexterity.

'All I long for now is a fairy-tale ending; nothing more; a happy ending.'